ON DANGEROUS GROUND

ON DANGEROUS

GROUND

STORIES OF WESTERN NOIR

Edited by
Ed Gorman, Dave Zeltserman,
& Martin H. Greenberg

CEMETERY DANCE PUBLICATIONS

Baltimore
❖ **2011** ❖

Cemetery Dance Publications
132-B Industry Lane, Unit #7
Forest Hill, MD 21050
http://www.cemeterydance.com

The characters and events in this book are fictitious.
Any similarity to real persons, living or dead,
is coincidental and not intended by the author.

First Limited Edition Printing

ISBN-10:   1-58767-192-1
ISBN-13: 978-1-58767-192-0

Cover Artwork © 2011 by Stacy Drum
Interior Design by Kathryn Freeman

TABLE OF CONTENTS

INTRODUCTION

JAMES SALLIS

Inside us all, as Americans, is a cowboy struggling to get out. Our native novel claims hegemony, not with the European novel of the individual finding his or her place in society, in fact, not with the novel at all, but with the romance: with tales of the individual pitted against society. James Fenimore Cooper's mountain and plainsmen became cowboys riding into town to set things right, private investigators walking mean streets, repo men with codes, courageous, outriding cops or politicians, and gangstas—became, ultimately, us. We are a strange people, eager at one and the same time to be left alone and to repair the world about us, Thoreau and Clint Eastwood riding double, notions of manifest destiny, freedom and all those other big words that make us so unhappy coursing and clotting in our veins.

Though perhaps finally we were not so much formed by those characters and by our nascent national literature as adumbrated by them. As it reaches beyond the borders of formula to seize more and more of the world in its grasp, popular fiction at its best—in Black Mask stories, in Fifties science fiction films, in original paperback novels—can become the secret biography of

INTRODUCTION

a people, recording in double vision the culture's official vision of itself and the evidential one. Nowadays nothing tells us more about our society, about the disparities of appearance and reality, about what we have wrought in building our imaginary cities and filling them with real people, than crime fiction. Hammett and Chandler recollect our attention not only for their precedence and brilliance, but as much because their tales occur at America's edge, with the frontier used up, at almost the very moment that our society was shifting from rural to urban.

And perhaps nothing tells us more about the American psyche than the image of our West. It is burned into our brain, engraved on our heart, trapped like dirt and blood beneath our fingernails.

Because—and this is one measure of its enduring power—the image is duple, one side heroic, the other horrific. It never allows us to forget that this nation was wrested from its inhabitants and from nature itself by violence, that violence built this nation tall and wide and immensely rich. It reminds us again and again what complicated, contradictory beings we humans are.

Our Western myth, then. It energizes us still, as it has always energized us. Such myths and self-images are tools for living, adaptive mechanisms as essential as skin and organs. But as with any adaptive mechanism, once those images are used up, once they no longer work for us, they all too easily can turn on us. Our only defense is to remain aware, and to question.

Here are twenty-one stories that revisit our frontier, that place of blinding sunlight and dark shadows that so greatly resembles our own hearts. Listen to the plink of banjos, the shush of tumbleweed as it rolls, the bucketing run of water off flat roofs, the restless motion of corralled horses and unbridled men. Listen still more closely and you may hear, behind all that, the sound of a nation speaking its secret name.

James Sallis
Phoenix, Arizona

HELL

BENTLEY LITTLE

The Arizona sun rose early and hard, unfiltered by clouds, stronger than it had been in New Mexico, more unforgiving than it was in Texas, and Perris looked to the west, wondering how much farther he had to go, thinking not for the first time that he should turn back and call it clean.

But no. This wasn't regular prey. This was another Ranger. And when one of your own went bad, you didn't quit until it was quitting time. It wasn't good enough simply to make the effort. You had to get your man. Honor demanded no less.

He threw the dregs of his coffee at a too-brazen crow, then saddled up, packed his gear and pissed out the campfire. His ass hurt. A week without wiping would do that, and once again he climbed carefully onto the roan and ambled off at a pace that wouldn't cause him to bounce around unnecessarily.

He reached Tubac by late afternoon, the white-painted fort gleaming at him from across the desert like a beacon. This was godforsaken land, and if it was his to decide, he'd let the Mexicans have it, but he had to admit that it was nice to see buildings again, and people, and after stopping at the river to water his mount, he headed up the slope to the fort.

He could tell that it had been a while since they'd had visitors. Nearly all of the residents turned out to greet him, and the ecstatic faces of the two women told him all he needed to know about the social life of the community. The general in charge, a man named Starr, practically begged him to stay on as their guest for the next two months, warning him that travel in any direction would be nigh impossible until the advent of the August rains, letting him know that the skeleton of more than one traveler lay bleaching in the burning sands out there. "This is it," the general said melodramatically. "Last stop before Hell."

Though Perris didn't worry about his ability to survive in the wilderness—he was a Ranger after all—he did graciously decide to stay at the fort for the next week and take advantage of Starr's hospitality, enjoying regular meals, regular baths, a comfortable bed.

And letting his ass heal.

He'd been after Tim Curtis on and off for six years and on this particular sojourn for the past two months. An extra week wasn't going to make a difference in the outcome—and it might just rejuvenate him enough that his wits and reflexes would be sharpened for the inevitable confrontation. Lord knows such an edge would be vital. He wasn't dealing with a novice here. He needed all the advantages he could get.

Starr's wife Josephine was one of the women who'd greeted him when he'd come up from the river. A broad florid woman with coquettish eyes in a lined parchment face, she made it her business to show him around the compound and introduce him to the owners of the outlying houses. The other, younger woman was a widow whose husband had been murdered by Apaches last fall. She, too, was eager to spend time with him and seemed full of questions about what was going on in the towns and cities of the civilized world, although he was not really the man to ask about those sorts of subjects.

A few of the army men stationed at the fort also had wives, but they were squaws or Mexicans and stayed hidden most of the time.

The rhythm of life at the fort was different than on the trail, and Perris had a hard time getting used to it. He was awake at night later than everyone else, up in the morning before anyone, and he spent the daylight hours walking restlessly around, waiting either for something to happen or for the mess bell to ring. He shot a coyote on his third morning there after seeing the scavenger approach the fence, and was promptly dressed down by the general, who told him that it was the buzzards and coyotes that cleared the fort's refuse and kept the surrounding perimeter clean. The general pronounced coyote "ky-o-tay" like the Mexicans did, and not "ky-oat" like they did in Texas, and Perris had never felt farther from home.

After supper that evening, while he was smoking by the fence and staring up at the stars, thinking it was time to press on, Mrs. Starr emerged from the kitchen and stood next to him. She stood *too* close, but he didn't try to pull away because it might have been an accident that their arms were touching, and he didn't want to offend her. The two of them remained there for a moment, not talking, not acknowledging each other.

The general's wife broke the silence. "You never said. Are you after someone? That why you're out here?"

"Yeah."

"You hunting an outlaw?"

Perris nodded grimly.

"What did he do?"

"Something too vile for your ears to hear."

She shuddered and he felt her body inch closer.

"I aim to bring him back to Texas so he can face punishment. Failing that, I will execute the punishment myself as a duly sworn officer of the law."

"Execute?" she said.

He nodded.

Silence greeted that. He sensed her pulling away from him, and was not entirely displeased. They remained like that for a while longer, him smoking and staring up at the sky, she looking out across the desert, and finally she left, saying she was needed back in the kitchen.

He didn't watch her go. He felt cramped even with her gone, even looking up at the endless expanse of stars. The closeness of life in a fort was not for him, and while he longed for the comforts and companionship to be found in town, the trail, lonesome as it was, was vastly preferable to being cooped up here. He found himself actually missing those uncomfortable nights on the hard rocky ground, those days of seeing not another living soul.

Behind him, one of the officers started playing a fiddle, a screechy scratchy sound that grated on his nerves. Others started whooping and hollering, and he could tell from the echoing thump that soon began to overpower the voices and song that people were dancing.

Perris crushed out his cigarette on the side of the fence, put the butt in his pocket for tomorrow and walked back to the barracks and his bed.

In the morning he awoke early and packed his gear. Several of the men saw him but none said a word, which was just as well. He didn't feel like explaining. His hope was to get away before the general found out, but the smell of frying bacon made his stomach grumble, and he thought it was probably a good idea to wait until the horses had been fed and watered. It would save time later.

Taking the cigarette nub out of his pocket, he lit it and headed toward the gate. He let himself out and was halfway down the sloping trail when he heard the sound of a woman humming somewhere up ahead. The river was near silent and sound carried, so she didn't have to be close or humming loud for him to hear, and he found himself wondering if one of the squaw wives had come down here to wash clothes or bathe. Indian women liked river water and never did seem to get used to bathing indoors.

He had not meant to spy, had only come down to clear his head and get away from the buildings and the fences while he waited for breakfast to be cooked, but Perris crept forward slowly, careful not to snap a twig, crush a leaf or do anything that would alert the woman to his presence. There was movement up ahead and to the right, a flash of white by the water's edge, and he crouched low so as to see through the curtain of leaves.

It was the widow, Mrs. James, and she wasn't doing anything, wasn't washing or bathing or picking berries, was just standing there, looking at the river. He figured she wanted to be alone, like him, and had come out here to get away from the confinement of the fort. He intended to turn back and give her privacy, but when a man jumped out of the bushes and attacked her, when, as she attempted to cry out, he put his hand over her mouth to silence her, Perris ran forward, knife drawn.

The man was dead before he knew anyone was there. Perris stabbed him with a strong side thrust, slicing upward instead of pulling out. In one smooth motion, he swung Mrs. James away from the spurting blood. She was crying, shaken but not hysterical, and she managed to compose herself in a matter of moments. He shouldn't have been surprised. She'd seen her husband's body after the Apaches had been at him, Perris remembered, so she was constitutionally strong.

She looked down at her attacker's body. Perris recognized him from the fort but didn't know his name. "Is he dead?"

Perris nodded.

"Good," she said fiercely. "Good." She kicked dirt on the dead man's face. Looking up at Perris, she threw her arms around him and kissed him full on the mouth in a manner that made her intentions clear. He did not even pretend to resist. Even as the body lay behind them, she reached down for him, felt him, and he pushed her to the ground and took her hard and fast, like an animal, not knowing if that was how she liked it, not caring, thinking of Annie all the while, guilt and arousal mixed up inside him like mud on the banks of the river.

He left her there afterward and strode quickly up the slope to the fort, where he got his gear, grabbed his horse and rode away, heading west. He didn't want to stay and face an inquest and answer a whole bunch of useless questions, so while he really wanted breakfast and regretted not letting the roan finish eating, he knew it was important to get away from Tubac quickly. Mrs. James could deal with the aftermath. He had the feeling she would have no problem answering any and all questions to Starr's satisfaction.

Still, he kept one eye behind him for the next two days in case someone had been sent to bring him in.

The desert was hot and empty, but it was good to be alone in the wilderness after the restrictions of the fort, and the land was not nearly as inhospitable as Starr had made it out to be.

Besides, Curtis had made it through here.

HELL

The truth was that he did not really know where he was going. The west was big. And open. While it was true that strangers tended to be noticed because there were so few people out here and anyone new obviously stood out, it was equally true that there were places a fugitive could hide where no one would ever see him. The last concrete information Perris had was of a sighting in Santa Fe perhaps a year or so back and a conversation where Curtis talked about moving west to ranch sheep. That could have meant anywhere, but careful attention to the recent migration of settlers led him to believe that his quarry was somewhere in Arizona.

He had some unexpected luck in Prescott. At a cowboy bar on the row, he heard tell of a nearby valley where several sheep ranchers had been putting down stakes over the past few years. Curtis wasn't there, but one of the hands knew where he was. Perris had to beat the information out of him—being a Ranger didn't carry much weight in these parts, not with these people—but the man finally admitted that he'd worked with Curtis back in Santa Fe and had helped him buy the sheep for his new place up on the Mogollon Rim.

Perris cursed and spat. The Mogollon was east toward New Mexico, at least two days' ride from here. Not long, really, in the scheme of things, but any backtracking felt to him like a waste of time and only rubbed in the fact that he had missed his man the first time through.

Only, he consoled himself, that wasn't exactly the case. He'd come into Arizona from the south. The Mogollon was a good two hundred miles north of that, and it wasn't reasonable to have expected him to canvas the whole eastern border of the territory. Still, he couldn't help second guessing himself and thinking that if he'd just headed west from Santa Fe instead of taking that Tucson trail, this whole ordeal would be over with by now.

How would it be over, though? He'd imagined all the different outcomes many times in his head, had played out the scenarios so often that he knew them by heart, yet he still didn't know how it was going to end. Not really. He knew how he *wanted* it to end, but that was so at odds with his duty as a Ranger that it tied his stomach up in knots just thinking about it.

For two days, he followed a trail that turned out not to be a trail, which faded away into nothing on a grassy ridge crest above a deep rocky canyon. He was sure that he'd been steered wrong by the ranch hand on purpose—and had half a mind to go back there and beat the man within an inch of his life—but Perris could see the Mogollon from here and knew he could reach it by tomorrow, and as long as *that* information turned out straight, he could forgive such a trespass.

He slept that night on a flat rock in a forest of pines, using his saddlebag as a pillow. Smoking, staring up at the sky, he thought about all of the men he'd brought in, all of the outlaws he'd captured. He felt good about what he'd done and was proud of his work. Once the Curtis problem was solved, he'd feel even better. No one else seemed to give a damn anymore, but he considered it a black mark on his record, and he wouldn't rest easy until the man was brought to justice.

An owl hooted, flew above his head. He watched it tree in a ponderosa. He remembered the very first manhunt he'd been on, searching the bottom lands for a coward who'd killed a little girl to shut her up after the unspeakable things he'd done to her. There'd been a team of Rangers looking for the man, but it was Perris who'd found him huddled at the base of a cottonwood, cradled in the tree's massive exposed roots like a baby. He'd wanted nothing more than to shoot the killer where he lay, but he'd restrained himself and taken him to jail instead.

Would he make the same decision now?

He didn't know.

He thought not.

In the morning, he awoke with the animals, before the sun. Supplies were running low, so he had some hard biscuit softened with water and a few *pinyones* he'd gathered the night before. He had the makings for coffee, but he was alert enough as it was and didn't want to waste time. Today was the day, and he was anxious to be off. *By tonight it will be over,* he thought, and the realization sent an unfamiliar tingle down his spine.

It took him most of the morning to cross the series of small hills that led up to the base of the Rim, but from the last one, the tallest one, he spotted a telltale plume of chimney smoke a short ways up ahead. *It could be campfire smoke,* he told himself. *Or it could be someone else.*

But he knew that wasn't the case.

HELL

It was Curtis.

Now that his prey was finally in his sights, Perris approached slowly, carefully, not taking a straight tack through the trees but riding south, then east, then north. A man like Curtis was dangerous when cornered. And he was a Ranger, too, so he knew all the tricks of the trade. Perris would have to be at his best in order to maintain the element of surprise that would be his best weapon. It had been a long time, and if he was lucky the man would be unprepared, but in his experience a fugitive was never completely relaxed and even while sleeping kept one eye open. It would be hard to get to the man without him knowing.

Perris had hoped to find Curtis living in a cabin in a clearing, but of course as a sheep rancher he needed more room than that. So Perris was disappointed but not surprised to find that the forest ended and a long plain stretched east along the base of the Mogollon. In the center stood a house, a barn, a corral.

There was nothing for it. He would have to approach head-on, and he drew his pistol as he spurred the horse to a gallop.

The sound carried, bounced off the rock walls of the Rim, and it brought out two figures: a man and a woman. Perris's heart thudded in his chest as the hooves of his horse thundered over the hardpacked earth. He expected to see the man raise a shotgun he'd been hiding or dash for the house or barn to get one, but instead he remained standing, watching, protectively putting his arm around the woman as Perris drew closer.

A look of recognition and contempt crossed the man's features when he finally saw who it was.

Perris pulled on the reins, brought the horse to a dancing stop. He was still holding the pistol, and he dismounted, leveling it at his quarry. "Tim Curtis," he said with all the gravity of the Rangers behind him.

Curtis shook his head. "Frank," he said. It was almost an admonition.

He motioned with the gun. "Move away from her."

"No."

"Now."

Annie glared at him, and Perris tried to ignore her. "You know what you've done. Don't make it worse."

"We're *married*," Curtis said. "Why won't you leave us alone? We've been married five years now. We have children. We have a life."

"Father and mother gave their blessings," Annie spat out. "The whole family came to the wedding except you. Now you tracked us down all the way to the wilds of Arizona? You're...you're crazy!"

Something hardened within him at those words. Not only had Curtis stolen his sister, but he'd turned her against him, her own brother. "A Ranger..." he began.

"I'm not a Ranger," Curtis said. "I quit that life. I'm a rancher now. I raise sheep."

"You can't quit being—"

"Leave us alone!" Annie screamed. Her face turned red with the effort, the muscles in her neck bulging, veins visible in her forehead. *She* looked crazy, he thought.

Perris kept the gun level. "He has to pay for what he's done," he told his sister. "He has to be brought to justice."

"What has he done? Huh? Tell me what he's done!"

"Tell me, too," Curtis said. "Then we'll all know."

Perris moved closer, keeping his eyes on his sister. Anger had distorted her features. It reminded him of how she had looked in the throes of passion, when he had come upon them back in Laredo and Curtis had been on top of her. In his mind, he saw her face, sweating, contorted, her eyes rolled upward, her mouth open and screaming but not with pain. As at the time, he was filled with rage, a red hot anger that caused him to quiver all over and filled him with the desire to kill.

"I know what you really want!" Annie shouted. "You think I don't? You think we all don't? Even father told me you..."

He slapped her then, just to shut her up, and it felt good. Her cheek was warm against his hand, and he could see an imprint of his palm on her soft white skin.

He heard crying off to his left and turned to see two young girls huddled in the open doorway of the house. They looked so much like Annie when she was a child that he thought his heart might break.

"Go inside, girls," Curtis said firmly. "Play with your dolls. Don't come out or even look out here until I tell you you can."

"Daddy?" one of them said.

"Go inside, filly."

Perris backed up.

Annie was scowling at him, but Curtis held out his hands, trying to appeal to his better nature. "Look, Frank. We don't want no trouble. Why don't you stay with us a few days, we'll all have a nice time, and then you can go back to Texas…"

"He's crazy!" Annie shouted.

He shot them both. Him first, two slugs in the chest that spun him around until he fell backward where he stood, then her, straight through the stomach, red blossoming on the white linen like a rose.

The girls screamed from the doorway of the house, twin cries of hopeless anguish that pierced the air and seemed to grow out of the last fading echoes of gunshot. He'd been through this often enough that he knew what to expect, but no fists came to beat on his back, no one threw themselves on the bodies. The two stayed inside like their daddy had told them.

Good girls, he thought.

Perris holstered his pistol, turned toward the house. In the doorway, a face backed into blackness rabbit-fast. He almost ordered them out, but they'd been through a lot today, and he took pity on them. He walked into the small log structure and found them huddled in the far corner. They both flinched when he approached, but he crouched down next to them and gave them his warmest smile. "I'm your uncle Frank," he said. "I'll be taking care of you now."

Both of them burst into tears.

They looked just like Annie, he thought again.

Something stirred within him.

He picked up the crying girls and hugged them tight. "Come on," he said. "Let's go home."

ALL GOOD MEN

TERRY TANNER

Largo Loco, bad Spanish for the tall madman, wasn't the tallest convict in Yuma Penitentiary, or the most insane. There was a Swede with two inches more height, and several men just as crazy, but the name stuck to the gaunt Mexican because Lazaro Lujan was hard for the gringos to remember. He'd counted on being hanged after chopping up his wife and four kids with an ax in a drunken rage, and had been crying about the injustice of a life sentence since the day he got there.

"I'll get you a rope, if it'll stop your whining," I used to tell him.

"*Veneno*," he'd say, hissing the word and flicking his tongue, like a serpent speaking. He'd told everyone in the joint about the twenty-dollar gold piece he swallowed the day he was arrested, and had re-swallowed regularly to keep from being killed for it. Nobody ever saw the money.

"Out of circulation," was the way he put it. "You get for me the *veneno*, and I'll get for you the gold."

I came here chained to Jasper Sipes and his brother, Martin, and haven't spoken to either man since the day we left the courtroom. Jasper was sure I planned to kill him, which was true. To wear on his nerves, I used to stare at him when no one was looking. He took my squint as some kind of evil-eye, and it spooked him so bad that he took a swing at my neck with a shovel, and got himself thrown into solitary.

Seeing things others miss is the way I get by, taking notice and thinking things through. When they put me to work tending the chickens, I wondered why we were feeding them clean, unbroken wheat from gunnysacks stacked in a shed beside the henhouse, and where the dead rats came from that the hens would be pecking at some mornings. Playing dumb, like I didn't really care, I learned that the territorial legislature had decided three years back to put the convicts at Yuma to work raising wheat to help feed themselves. Like a lot of half-assed ideas, it didn't work out, but the prison was left with two tons of poisoned seed-grain. Chickens don't die from eating strychnine, and that's why the warden fed it to them, not to us prisoners, or any of the other livestock.

I began rinsing the grain every morning before throwing it to the chickens, and dumping the water in an old crock to evaporate. It was five months before I could scrape two teaspoons of white residue off the pot.

The captain switched me from chicken duty to kitchen cleanup before Largo Loco came into the place, so I had what I had and no chance to get any more. I didn't want to give Jasper too big a dose, and have him taste it, and I sure didn't want to give him too little. I told Largo Loco I'd take his twenty bucks. If half of my *veneno* worked on him, I'd know I had a lethal dose for Jasper. We set a date for the deal, allowing him a couple of days to get his fingers on the coin.

The stash had been in my cell, wrapped in waxed paper, and I put it in a tobacco sack and carried it to the kitchen, where I stuck half of it in a hole in the mortar behind the kitchen stove, and used a dab of mud to hide it. Then I wandered through the main yard, and slipped Largo Loco his half. The gold piece looked clean as the day it was minted, but I spit on both sides and rubbed it on my pants, before swallowing it myself. With Largo gone, everybody would be looking for it, and the turnkeys would be shaking down the cells for more poison.

My client took a long time dying; it wasn't over until late the next morning. If he told anybody where he got the stuff, the accusation was lost in the gasping Spanish maledictions he spewed at everyone he knew, dead and alive. After that I slept better, knowing I had enough left for Jasper. I'd decided to do Martin in the yard, in bright daylight.

I had the run of the kitchen, since I'd started fixing for the warden and his occasional guests those little niceties beyond Josefina's bread-and-beans imagination. That common little Mexican woman trudged up the hill from Yuma every morning at dawn and supervised the preparation of a daily fare as common as she. I could see from his rounded belly and the way he prowled the kitchen that Warden Seth Pike yearned for something better. While mopping up one afternoon, I overheard him bragging to one of his captains about how well they used to eat in New Orleans, when he was stationed there with the Army. Next day, I let it be known around the yard that I'd once cooked at a famous whorehouse and restaurant in the Crescent City. It was a lie, of course. I'd never been east of San Antonio, and the only cooking I'd ever done was on a chuck wagon in New Mexico, when I broke my ankle and couldn't ride. But illusion serves as truth to a hungry man; that's common jailhouse wisdom.

When a long, hot fire was needed for baking, local cooks preferred to use ironwood. The *iron* in the name may be optimistic, but it doesn't behave quite like wood, either, being much heavier and harder than mesquite, or oak. It took a week of watching the firewood box before I found just the right piece, a splinter, really, flat and narrow, less than ten inches long. Shaping the stake against the stones of my cell became something of a nighttime hobby for me, and when the balance felt right, I polished the sides until they were smooth as a maiden's thigh, and sharpened the tapered edges by working them against the steel bars. When walking the yard, I'd carry it in the crotch of my pants, to have it ready when my chance came. It came on a Sunday, when the guards atop the wooden tower were eating watermelon and tossing the rinds out into the desert, popping at them with rifles and revolvers. Gunfire from the tower wasn't unusual; it gave the guards a chance to strut and was supposed to have a sobering effect on the residents. All eyes were watching them that afternoon, frisky as colts, blasting away at the rinds and taunting each other between shots.

ALL GOOD MEN

Martin Sipes stood in the shade at the corner of the yard, spinning a bullshit story. I edged closer, pretending to listen, and when I heard gunshots clustered together like popping corn, I brushed carelessly against his back and drove the splinter deep, angling it high. Steadying him for a moment by his quivering arm, I shoved the blunt end again, with the heel of my hand, until it disappeared inside him. I walked slowly away while he leaned in the corner with his mouth moving and no sound coming out. Everybody else walked away, too.

Nobody remembered seeing me anywhere near him; as far as the others could recall, he was alone when it happened. Naturally, Pike had to slap me around a little and lock me up, but everybody knew that with zero evidence there would be no trial. I heard later that he joked privately about the mysterious Apache who'd snuck up from over the wall and put that fat little arrow into Martin Sipes. I'd done Martin first because he was the younger of the two brothers, and by far the less wary. Jasper did the thinking for them both.

We'd been riding together a couple of weeks, when we got the idea to stop the stage on the Prescott road. We were lucky, as it turned out; there was a rich couple on board, and we took the shotgun by surprise. Jasper went into the brush with the woman, and left her there. Nobody got killed, and we divvied up the money and took off, with me heading for Camp Verde, where I knew some riders I could bunk with. The Sipes brothers made a beeline for Wickenburg, and got caught before dawn. By the time they rounded me up, they'd had plenty of time to convince the sheriff I'd planned the robbery and done the rape, and they just happened to be riding with me. The judge gave them each five years to serve, and their testimony got me life without parole. From their point of view, I could understand why Jasper would lie to save himself, and Martin would lie to save his brother. On the other hand, I don't forgive a thing just because I understand it.

Warden Pike wasn't a cruel man. After the initial beating—which everyone agreed was proper—he paid me no mind, except to order that I always had water, and something to eat now and then. He even sent Padre Nilos by to visit me. It's a jailer's oldest trick, keeping a man alone until he's thinking in circles, and running a priest in to lead him from the wilderness when his mind is judged soft enough. I ignored the papist for a couple of months. Late in July, I came down with the chills and fever rising from that tangle of marsh between the high ground of the prison and the cool waters of the Colorado River. I was pretty sure I was dying, and not that sorry for it, so weary was I of the isolation, and of the heat: an extreme I'd never seen before, making me feel I was slow-roasting in a stone oven.

My only disappointment was not to be dying clean, and I don't mean that state-of-grace horseshit that Padre Nilos talked about to his flock of black sheep. Closing books is what I mean, and balancing scales. Even the warden had to know that killing Sipes wasn't a matter of choice, but one of obligation. In the craw of Yuma Penitentiary, we were all seeds or rocks, and the soft were soon rendered pulp. I'm as gravelly as the next man, and with Martin gone and the means at hand to get Jasper, I was making a place for myself at Yuma. My mistake was in underestimating Warden Pike. Lacking any evidence, I thought he'd keep me in isolation for a few months, and then let me work my way back to the kitchen. Instead, he seemed determined to keep me in that little stone niche if it meant eating Josefina's cooking forever.

If I talked to the padre when the fever was on me, I can't say. A fevered man is likely to talk to anyone who visits him, whether his own mother as a ghost, or some forlorn figure sweeping the hall, appearing in his dreams as Gunga Din.

When my mind cleared after the fever, I could see the genuine passion Padre Nilos felt for my soul when he thought I was dying. I understood the agony he must have endured when Largo Loco slipped away, victim of his own hand, unrepentant and unredeemed. I suddenly recognized, in this tortured man, a reliable tool.

Nilos was hard at his mumblings that morning, eyes first open and imploring, cast toward the little window high on the wall, closed when his head bent to the stony floor in sobbing remorse. Up again to the window, down once more to the floor. With a moan, I threw myself on the floor beside him and forced a choking sob from my throat. He prayed and fumbled with his beads and

I sobbed, until we were praying and sobbing together, kneeling in that shaft of window light. God, we must have been a sight to make a bishop proud!

He returned that night with a chunk of cheese and a heel of light bread, my first variation from cornbread and water in four months. When I tried to thank him, he protested that Josefina, that saint of a woman, had prepared it for me. I knew he was lying; Josefina held a convict's view of the place, resigned to serving her time like everybody else, and returning at night to her family. It was Padre Nilos who fed the outcasts.

Warden Pike didn't send for me, just stopped by one evening and talked to me through the little barred window in my cell door.

"I'm expecting some company," he said, "and was thinking on what I might feed them."

Secrets keep in jail about as long as they do at a quilting party, and I'd heard the governor was getting off the train next week, on his way to Los Angeles. He'd be traveling with the attorney general, and was prepared to discuss a new outfit the politicians were cooking up, to be called the Arizona Rangers. Pike wanted in, and the fact that the governor was stopping to see him, gave him hope.

"There's no better quail shooting in the territory than that mesquite thicket east of here," I said.

"No doubt they'd enjoy a quail shoot," he said. He stood quiet for a moment, resting his fingertips on his pink cheek. "You can understand the problems of an old bachelor in this remote station. My dear Josefina isn't a fancy cook, and those birds come out dry, when I fix them myself." He wasn't ready to ask me to cook for him, and I couldn't afford to appear anxious.

"The governor's used to eating at the Cattlemen's Club in Prescott and the best hotels in Tucson," he said. "Too bad we got no pheasant around here, chicken is so damn common."

"The key to cooking quail is to start with plenty of birds," I said, "so you can rip off the breasts and throw the backs and spindly legs to the hogs."

"We won't be short of birds. How would they be served in New Orleans?"

"I've heard that the Indians gather wild rice in a still-water pond down the river a couple miles. If you felt like sending a detail to get a few pounds, we'd have a place to start. A man might flour the breasts and lightly fry them, then wrap each one in bacon and jam them real close together in a pan and roast them hot for a few minutes in the oven."

The warden nodded knowingly.

"The rice would have to be ready when you took them out, so everything would be hot at the same time," I said. "Of course, we'd need a sauce."

"Don't think I'm forgetting what Jasper Sipes tried to do, and what you did to his brother." He drew closer, speaking very softly. When his hat brim hit the door, he took it off and leaned in until his face filled the tiny opening. "Mr. Sipes is tucked away in my little brown jug, across the yard," he said. "Test me, sir, and I'll chain you to a cactus outside the walls, to see you never get any closer to him than you are right now."

"Yes, sir," I said, "but I doubt that Brother Sipes would harm me. He certainly stands no risk from a newly born Christian, such as myself."

The warden walked away without answering.

Those on the expedition for wild rice cursed me roundly, and my reputation took a dive when it became known I was shamelessly kissing the warden's ass, and cooking for the governor. I could hear the muffled pop of shotguns all morning, as I finished cleaning up the roughly threshed rice. The warden sent me a hundred cleaned birds, with instructions to fix twenty for his party, and feed the rest to the guards as a special treat. I boiled down the quail backs and legs with some lard, to make a stock. Pike guarded his wine so jealously that a captain had to come to the kitchen and pour two cups directly into the pot. I tossed in a little flour, and strained it off. What the hell, it would have to do for sauce.

After supper, I set two breasts aside for myself, and sent a trustee to fetch Padre Nilos. When he came in I was eating my quail from a wooden bowl, and sipping coffee at the pine table next to the stove. I shoved the other bowl across the table, and nodded for him to sit.

"For your compassion toward the despised and imprisoned," I said, raising my coffee cup. "Will you eat with me, in the grace of God."

ALL GOOD MEN

He gazed fondly on the quail breast, bathed in sauce and covered with rice. "For your kindness, I thank you, brother. Do you mind if I take it with me, to eat later?"

Nobody could expect Jasper Sipes to be a good sport and die quietly, so I took the precaution of promising two quarts of mescal to the Mexicans on both sides of his cell, if they'd put a little extra spirit into their nightly singing. Any protest he made was lost in the howling and yelping of the *ranchera* ballads. I didn't have the liquor in hand to pay for the concert, but everyone knew I was a man of my word.

BURL LOCKHART'S IN TOWN

STEVE HOCKENSMITH

Lucas Harte," someone said. Behind, close. Practically whispering in Harte's ear. "Why, you thievin' bastard...you're still alive after all these years?"

Harte put down his beer and looked into the mirror behind the bar. It was a dirty little mirror for a dirty little saloon, and a crack ran through it from top to bottom. The break in the glass split the man standing behind Harte in two, making his features seem crooked, the halves mismatched. He was a thin man, gaunt even, dressed as Harte was—for the saddle, rough. But that was all Harte could tell.

"My name ain't 'Harte'," Harte said.

"Oh, yeah? Why don't you say that to my face?"

Harte's right hand was still on the bar, near his beer glass. But as he turned around, he pulled the hand in toward his body—and the Colt holstered to his hip.

"My name ain't—"

There was no use finishing. The man behind Harte knew it was a lie.

"Shit," Harte said when he saw the man's face. "You son of a bitch."

And they both laughed.

"Gunther Tietzmann." Harte clapped a hand on the man's shoulder. "I'll be damned."

"You got that right," Tietzmann said. "But *my* name ain't Tietzmann."

They laughed again.

"How long's it been?" Harte asked, his hand still on Tietzmann's shoulder. He could feel the tendons taut as rope beneath the lean man's shirt and skin. "Ten, fifteen years?"

"Hell, I can't even remember. When was it they…?" Tietzmann's grin wilted, his shoulders sagged. "When was it Frank and Smokehouse passed? Sixty-seven? Sixty-eight?"

Harte nodded, somber. "Yeah, something like that." He gave Tietzmann's shoulder a squeeze, then pointed at a table at the back of the room. "You wanna?"

"Now ain't a good time, but…hell, how could I not?"

"Glad you feel that way." Harte scooped up his beer and guzzled it down to the foam. "First round's on you."

A minute later, Harte and Tietzmann were seated side by side in the corner, both turned to face the batwings at the front of the saloon. The Phoenix was a small, dingy place, little more than a shack really, and there were only three other customers there. Two were hunkered at another table, conducting business in angry whispers. The third was stooped over at the bar, sullenly draining glass after glass as if there was a fire in his gut he could never put out.

The light that streamed in through the warped slats of wood that served as walls was slowly changing from twilight-orange to dusky-gray. The day was dying.

"So," Harte said, "what you been up to?"

Tietzmann shrugged. "Oh, you know—same ol' thing. You?"

Harte smiled slyly. "Same ol' thing."

"I figured as much. What do you call yourself while you're at it?"

"These days? This and that. Tommy Taylor, mostly."

Tietzmann's eyes popped wide.

"So…you heard of me, huh?" Harte said, his smile stretching, pushing his puffy cheeks up practically over his eyes.

"Course I have." Tietzmann hung his head. "Goddamn it."

"What?"

"I got bad news…Tommy."

When Tietzmann looked up, he flicked his gaze over to the saloonkeeper wiping glasses with a greasy rag, the huddled whisperers hissing at each other, the drunk doing his damnedest to get drunker. Then at last he looked at Harte again. Looked *into* him.

"Burl Lockhart's in town."

"Burl Lockhart…the Pinkerton?" Harte asked.

"I ain't talkin' about Burl Lockhart the Pope."

Harte picked up his beer and took a long drink.

"I just rode in this afternoon. Found me a room at a boardin' house," Tietzmann went on. "And the lady I rented a bed from, she says to me, 'Don't miss dinner, Mr. Adams—you'll be dinin' with a celebrity. *The* Burl Lockhart came in just before you did today. Why, he's in the room right next to yours, in fact. Two hotels in town, and he chooses to stay here. It's a real honor, don't you think?'"

Tietzmann spat into the dirt at their feet.

"'A real honor.' Shit," he said. "At first, I figured Lockhart was after *me*. I was gonna get myself a bottle of rye for the trail and clear out. But now that I know Tommy Taylor's in town…?" Tietzmann shook his head. "I'm sorry. He's here for *you*."

Harte took another drink. He was staring off at the mirror behind the bar, the crack that seemed to split the world in two. He said nothing.

"You know what?" Tietzmann said. "You oughta come with me. We'll put some miles between us and Kansas—head up to Montana, maybe. Then we can get back to work. Together. 'Same ol' thing,' just like in Texas after the war."

Harte tore his gaze away from the mirror.

"I ain't runnin'," he said.

Tietzmann sighed like he'd just lost a game he never thought he could win. "You always was the brave one, weren't you?"

"The smart and handsome one, too."

Both men made noises that were supposed to be laughter. It sounded more like they were coughing, gasping.

"Look," Harte said, "do you know who the town marshal is here?"

"I ain't never even been in Jetmore before."

"Well, you remember Beak Fitzhugh, don't you? Rode with Cal Hershey's bunch?"

Tietzmann nodded. "He'd still be wanted for killin' them rangers, wouldn't he?"

"Yeah. But George Thornton's not—and that's what he calls himself now. *Marshal* George Thornton."

Tietzmann grunted out another dry, mirthless chuckle. "Damn. They'll pin a badge on anybody, won't they?"

"I don't know...kinda makes sense to me." Harte tipped his seat back on two legs, his back against the wall. He was a burly man, and the chair beneath him groaned in protest. "Outlaws and lawmen, we're just two sides of the same plugged nickel, ain't we? A little thievin', a little bullyin', a little lyin', a little killin'. It's all in a day's work."

"Yeah, maybe. But that don't mean you can count on Beak to stand with you against Burl goddamn Lockhart."

"Badge or no, Beak still hates the big outfits and the Pinks," Harte said. "He's not gonna let the Cattlemen's Association send some assassin in here to gun me down. And the town'll back him up, too. Hell, half the squatters in this county are rustlin' themselves. It's safer to be a brand artist around here than a range detective."

Tietzmann shook his head. "That won't stop Lockhart. You've heard the stories. Just look at how he done Little Billy LaFollette. Tricked him into drawing first—right in front of the kid's own damn *church*! Almost got Lockhart lynched, but after the inquest he rode out free as a bird."

Harte leaned forward, bringing his chair down on all four legs again. He spread his hands flat on the table, too, as if bracing himself for something—a punch, a cyclone, an earthquake, worse.

"I ain't runnin' with you, Gunther," he said.

"Alright...I suppose that's just as well." Tietzmann took a prim little sip of his beer. "Lockhart'd track you down soon enough, anyway."

The two men sat in silence for a moment. Over at the bar, the drunk was still drinking, the saloonkeeper still spit-polishing dirty glasses that never got clean. The whisperers had left to do whatever it was they'd been whispering about doing. No one else had entered the Phoenix. It was a dive so low-down even the whores didn't bother with it.

"Did you see him?" Harte finally said, his voice low. He didn't look at Tietzmann. He was glaring at the drunk. "Lockhart?"

Tietzmann shrugged stiffly. Now he was giving the boozehound the eye, too. "I don't think so, but that don't mean nothin'. You know how he keeps his face out of the papers."

The souse at the bar noticed their stares. He was a nondescript man of perhaps fifty years dressed in the manner of a clerk or small-time merchant. He squinted at Harte and Tietzmann as if he couldn't quite make out their faces, was straining to see if they were smiling or frowning. He played it safe and flashed them a shit-eating grin.

He had half a dozen teeth left, at most, and those were as worn-down and brown as old tree stumps.

"Gentlemen," he croaked.

Tietzmann saluted him with his beer glass.

Harte slumped back into his seat.

"I know this much," Tietzmann said. "Burl Lockhart doesn't have to gum his mush."

"And that's about all we *do* know."

"Well, I bet you he doesn't have a peg leg, either. Or an eyepatch. Or green hair. Folks'd say so."

Harte turned his stare on Tietzmann.

"Sorry—it ain't funny," Tietzmann said. "How do you keep a feller from shootin' you in the back when you wouldn't even recognize him face to face?"

"The lady at your boardin' house has seen him. You could ask her what he looks like."

"Sure, I could. And then have her run straight to Lockhart himself." Tietzmann pursed his thin lips and spoke in the warbly, high-pitched voice of an old woman. "'Ooh, Burl—remember how you told me to let you know if anyone started askin' nosy questions about you? Well, guess what Mr. Adams just did. And him with the room right next to yours!'"

"Yeah, I know it's risky," Harte snapped. "But, dammit, we know where the man's beddin' down. There's gotta be some way we can...."

Harte's voice trailed off. But his mouth kept moving, curling at the edges, dimpling his round face.

"I remember that look," Tietzmann said. He sounded wary, as if Harte's smile was a hat on a bed or boots on a table—a bad omen.

"We don't need to know what Lockhart looks like," Harte said. "Cuz we know where to find him."

"Us...find *him*?"

Harte nodded.

"You can't be serious."

"We do it quiet," Harte said. "With knives. Two on one, it'd be easy."

"You...*cannot*...be...serious."

Harte's smile grew wider, becoming not just a toothy grin but a prod, something with which he could push, steer.

"Now, come on, Gunther. Show a little backbone here. You don't know Lockhart's after me. You've still got a hand in the game—he might be trailin' *you*. Either way, you or me, we could end it tonight...if we do it together."

Harte waggled his bushy brown eyebrows.

"Just like old times."

Tietzmann played with his beer glass a moment, tilting it this way and that, watching the suds rise up and slide down, rise up and slide down. Then he made a sound that was part sigh, part growl.

"Yeah...you always was the brave one. Shit."

He threw back his head and practically poured what remained of his beer straight down his throat. When he was done, he pounded the glass on the table.

"Alright. I'm in. But the next round's on *you*."

Over the course of the next three hours—and the next six rounds—there was no talk of Burl Lockhart. Instead, Tietzmann and Harte swapped gossip: where the wire was going up, where the easy pickings still were, which outfits were sending herds up which trails, who was buying cattle with blotched brands. And every so often one or the other would make a reference to the "old times" in Texas. "Frank would've laughed himself sick at that." Or "Now ol' Smokehouse, there was an artist. Give that man a runnin' iron, and he could turn a Bar 6 into a Diamond 9."

But there was no mention of the day the old times had ended. The day Tietzmann and Harte rode in with supplies—and found their friends hanging from the oak tree behind the cabin, each with a sign around his neck as well as a rope. "RUSSLER" on Frank. "THEEF" on Smokehouse. Two other signs had been left propped up against the oak's trunk. They each said the same thing: "KILLER."

Harte and Tietzmann never even dismounted. They spoke for all of half a minute, then wheeled around and galloped off without the packhorses. Headed in different directions. They hadn't seen each other since.

"Well, Mr. Adams," Harte said after finishing yet another beer, "it ain't gonna get any darker."

"I reckon you're right, Mr. Taylor." Tietzmann drained the last drops from his glass. "It's time decent folks was in bed."

In the ten minutes it took to walk to the boarding house, Tietzmann pissed once, Harte three times. They made their plans between stops.

"You've *got* a knife on you, right?" Harte asked.

"Of course. You?"

"Of course."

And then:

"What if he's not in his room?" Tietzmann asked.

"Then we settle in and wait for him to come back."

"Well, I'm gonna hope it don't play out like that. If I have to go up against Burl Lockhart, I'd rather do it when he's asleep."

And then:

"We oughta go in through the window," Tietzmann said. "The floorboards and doors in that place creak loud enough to wake the dead."

"The old lady'll get to test that out tomorrow mornin'. On Lockhart."

And then:

"This is it."

The house was small but pretty—one story, crisply painted, neat, with flowerbeds along the front porch and vegetables around back growing in lines as straight as soldiers on review. Even the water pump had been whitewashed, and it seemed to glow eerily in the moonlight.

There was no light at all in the windows.

"Over here," Tietzmann whispered, leading Harte to the back of the house. "Me." He pointed at a window, then crept on toward another. "Lockhart."

Tietzmann crouched down beneath the second window. Harte knelt beside him.

A black strip of nothingness about three inches tall ran along the sill. The window was open just enough for a breeze to slip in. Or fingers. The room beyond was a void, the kind of dark so deep it hurts a man's eyes to look into it.

Harte and Tietzmann stared up at the window, then at each other. Neither moved. Their plan was incomplete—one question remained.

"Who first?" Tietzmann said.

Harte swallowed spit. He looked like he wanted to piss again.

"You," he said softly. "You said the floorboards creak. You're skinnier than me. It should be you."

Tietzmann shook his head. Not like he was arguing. More like resigned.

"And you the brave one," he sighed.

"Me the smart one," Harte said.

"Right."

Tietzmann stood, slid his hands beneath the window and lifted. It rose four, five, six inches silently, smoothly—then suddenly jerked upward with a clatter.

Harte and Tietzmann jumped to either side of the window, both men reaching for their guns. They stayed pressed against the house for a full minute before Harte spoke.

"You hear anything?"

"I…I can't tell. Maybe…maybe snorin'?"

"Yeah…maybe." Harte jerked his head at the window. "Alright, let's get this over with."

Tietzmann nodded slowly and holstered his forty-five. The window was open high enough for him now. He took a deep breath and slithered through it.

And then he was gone, swallowed by the blackness beyond the sill. Harte waited a moment, then hauled himself in, too.

"Just hold still for a second, Gunther," Harte whispered as he came to his feet inside the room. His words came out so quiet he could barely hear them himself. "We'll do this together."

He drew his knife and took a step into the dark. The floorboards didn't creak.

"Lucas," Tietzmann said, his voice hoarse, strangled.

Harte turned toward the sound, seeing nothing.

Then Tietzmann spoke again. One more word. It sounded different this time, coming out hard, low, like the bitterest of curses—a curse he was aiming at himself.

"Tommy."

Harte saw the flash of light, heard only the beginning of the thunderclap. And then the bullet was tearing its way through his brain, and there was only oblivion.

The body toppled back against the window, then crumpled to the floor in a shower of shattered glass. Yet Harte never dropped the knife.

Tietzmann shot him again, twice. Because that's what startled men do. Not that Tietzmann was startled.

He walked over to the bed, pulled off his boots and got under the covers.

Down the hall, he could hear the old lady screaming. In a moment, he'd step out, calm her down, send the other lodger off to fetch Marshal Thornton. Beak would be pissed, but what could he do? It was self defense. Obviously.

There was a soft knock on the door.

"H-hello?"

It was Sears, the drummer who'd rented out the next room over.

"Are you alright, Mr. Lockhart?"

"I'm fine," Tietzmann said. "But I can't say the same for the other feller in here."

CANTICLE

DESMOND BARRY

Set on the porch, as the sun climbed above the red peaks distant, the boy orphan ran a fingertip along the line of letters that combined to reveal the ways and doings of the Nephites, and the Lamanites, and the Jaredites in that America once lost, or shrouded, or forgotten but now revealed by the Lord's Own Angel, who set down these doings in the holy book wherein the boy had learned his letters under the tutelage of Caleb Dunne, his guardian and saviour. The boy raised his eyes from the scriptures at the sound of hoof beat, the horses of a small group of men on the trail that would bring them to the door of Dunne's homestead. A lanky man led them, a man with sunken cheeks and a heavy grey moustache and eyes shadowed by the wide and drooping brim of a battered grey hat. The boy knew him as Jim Anderson, a lawman out of Silverton. The boy raised his hand in greeting and the small host, like marionettes pulled by the Lord's invisible strings, raised their hands as one, and at the same moment the footfalls resounded on the porch boards behind him, and Caleb Dunne appeared in frock coat and a round brimmed hat that shaded his blue eyes and the golden stubble on cheek and chin, and the hand of Caleb came to rest on the boy's shoulders.

Anderson reined in and likewise the bearers of bad news behind him.

"Carl Holden's dead," Anderson said.

The weight of the hand fell from the boy's shoulders.

"A good man, a decent man," Caleb said.

"Tobias Hunt got him. I believe you know him."

"Know of him," Caleb said.

The boy knew Hunt for one of the band that had run off some ten of Caleb Dunne's horses. Hunt, and a black man named Clay, and a man with a woman's name, Leonore.

"Holden heard that Hunt and Clay were in the Silver Belle and he thought he'd bring 'em in and ask about them horses."

"I had no proof," Caleb said.

"Someone must've warned Hunt," Anderson said. "He was waiting for Holden in the dark of the porch."

"I'm deeply sorry," Caleb said.

"Hunt and Clay escaped on foot. We got no idea where they gone. Maybe you'd like to accompany us to find them."

"Might be I find him easier my own self."

Anderson sat his horse a while.

"You might?"

"Leonore with them?" Caleb said.

"Nope," Anderson said. "Last we heard he was over in Creede."

"Been three days in a whorehouse," a weasel-faced man said and then he began a series of hisses, something that the boy thought might resemble laughter, as if the Weasel wished to embarrass Caleb. Caleb, in truth, was beyond embarrassment but the weight of his hand rested once more on the boy's left shoulder.

"You ever been in a whorehouse, boy?" Another man said that. His moustache and a goatee beard were liberally stained by tobacco juice, likewise the right lapel of his filthy duster. Hate in that voice, hate for Caleb, and for his guardian's creed.

"Boy's mute," Caleb said. "Ain't said a word since his folks was killed... not even to say his name."

And to the boy there arose in his mind's eye a vision, an infernal memory, the evisceration visited upon his father and mother, a vision lit by the flames of their broken wagon, like Gehenna erupted upon

Earth, and the boy's flesh was yet puckered and wrinkled where he had been pierced by a dozen heathen arrows in thigh, and calf, and hip, and arm. It was Caleb who had plucked out flint and shaft and had seared shut the wounds with red-hot blade to prevent a mortal bleeding. And then brought him home to foster.

"Voice don't work but his pecker might," the weasel said.

"Which whorehouse?" Caleb said.

"The Star," Anderson said.

"You know it?" Tobacco man said.

"Know of it," Caleb said.

Anderson's horse bent its head and rattled its bridle. A silence descended upon them. The boy discerned birdcall, the wind lift, a branch shift, the drift of straw wisps among the hooves of the lathered horses, Caleb's breath.

"I'll go over the mountain to Creede. Maybe Leonore will still be there, spending the money raised from the sale of those horses."

"Leonore ain't got a price on his head," the Tobacco Man said.

"Hunt's worth five thousand dollars," Anderson said. "Holden was a lawman."

"Find me something out," Caleb said. "Find me something that Leonore done, he can be held accountable for. Anything, big or small."

"It's Hunt I want," Anderson said. "Not Leonore."

"I'll bring you Hunt," Caleb said.

"You could bring him in alone?"

"I might could."

"Silverton folk want Holden's murderer," Anderson said.

"You'll have your killer. And I'll have recompense for my stock. But keep your men away from me, now, and keep 'em away from Leonore."

"Do you solemnly swear to uphold and administer the laws of the State of Colorado?" Anderson said.

"Up to a point," Caleb said.

"You are duly sworn as a deputy marshal of the State of Colorado," Anderson said. "Give him a badge."

The weasel-faced man dipped a hand in his pocket and pulled out a dull metal badge and tossed it toward Caleb and it clattered upon the boards of the porch. Anderson turned his horse and his

CANTICLE

followers all reined about and followed Anderson back towards the trail for Silverton.

"Get your traveling clothes, boy," Caleb said. "You coming, too."

Caleb picked up the badge and pocketed it in his frock coat. His hand guided the boy off the porch and into the warmth of the house where Caleb's first wife, big with child, stirred a pot upon the stove, and the second wife suckled a newborn girlchild, and the third wife yet suckled a boy of two, tow-headed, with bright blue eyes that stared over the curve of his mother's flesh nestling in the folds of her homespun shift.

"We'll be back directly," Caleb said.

He reached for his long-barrelled buffalo gun where it hung from the loftbeam, and set it against the wall near the commode. Then from a trunk beside the commode he took a plain leather belt hung with a pair of holsters and buckled the belt around his waist beneath his black frock coat. From a drawer in the commode he lifted a polished oakwood box and opened it to take from its velvet-lined interior a pair of Colts, and each revolver, which the boy had seen him clean and load only the previous day, as if in premonition of this moment, and Caleb slid them each one into a holster. Then, from the same trunk he took a 12-gauge shotgun, the barrels sawed off short and the stock, too, behind the handgrip, and he laid it on top of the commode. For the rifle he pocketed a box of .44-70 calibre shells and for the 12-gauge a box of birdshot.

"Caleb?" It was his first wife, Sarah, who spoke.

"The boy's coming with me," he said.

"He's a child," Naomi said.

She shifted the girl baby, trailing its spit from one full nipple to the other.

"He's seen more than most," Caleb said.

"You all take care, now," Sarah said.

The boy nodded and found his hat and his red and brown blanket coat and carried them in his hands, out the door, across the porch and across the yard to the stable, Caleb close behind him carrying the rifle and the 12-gauge.

"You'll see more in Creede," Caleb said.

In the chill of the late afternoon, they walked the horses through the mud of Main Street, past the tent-stores and the cribs of the whores, and the general stores and the miners' supplies hung above the boardwalk porches that listed above the puddled and manure-fouled thoroughfare. Miners and chancers and storekeepers lined the desultory streets while above the facades of the storefronts arose the rocky peaks, the hard redness of them among wisps of cloud and the darkness of the evergreens.

Caleb reined in outside The Star, a false-front bar with a sign in serif letters, and he indicated the hitching rail to the boy. The boy dismounted. On the porch, Caleb broke the barrels of the 12-gauge and loaded each one with a birdshot shell and snapped the shotgun shut.

"Follow close behind me, boy," he said.

The front doors of The Star were open. Pig-faced men, even at this early hour already bleary-eyed with drink, leaned their elbows on the rough plank bar. Card games were in progress at three of the tables. Slatternly women draped themselves among the drinkers and gamblers. One disengaged herself from the group at the bar, a small woman in black organza trimmed with red lace, her hips big and white breasts all but exposed to full sight. She tilted her high-piled, rat-tailed hair.

"That boy looking for a education?" she called.

The drinkers and the women laughed.

"He's getting one," Caleb said.

The skin on the boy's face burned. His lust rose.

A tall man, clean-shaven and hair oiled down, came from behind the rough bar. He waved a hand toward Caleb's shotgun.

"No need for that kind of ordnance in here, Caleb."

"I'll not disrupt your business, Jeremiah. Not unduly."

Jeremiah nodded.

"I'm looking for a man named Leonore," Caleb said.

Two heavy-set men distanced themselves from the drinkers and women at the bar and stood a short distance behind each shoulder of this man the boy now assumed was the bar owner. He did not know how this Jeremiah knew his guardian's name but he sensed the respect Jeremiah held for him, and Caleb for Jeremiah.

"I don't want any scores settled in here, Caleb," Jeremiah said.

"He'll walk out of his own free will," Caleb said.

"Upstairs, Room Three," Jeremiah said.

The eyes and slack jaws of the two bodyguards betrayed their surprise. But the 12-gauge in the hands of his guardian was capable of inflicting enormous damage on the human body. This the boy knew, and Caleb knew, and Jeremiah knew, and the bodyguards knew.

"Come with me, boy," Caleb said.

His guardian made his way to the stairs and began to climb them. Jeremiah returned to his station behind the bar; the bodyguards to their stations among the women; and the women draped themselves once more over the drunken miners while Caleb's boots trod down upon the stairs one by one and the boy's eyes followed, ever at the level of the worn heels.

Animal grunts and moans issued, muffled behind the closed doors on the landing.

Room Three. Caleb reached for the doorknob, twisted it and pushed the door open while he raised the 12-gauge. He crossed the threshold and the boy followed him into the room: a room with a bed, and strewn clothes, and a vanity table with a mirror and washstand and bowl.

"What in the hell...?"

Leonore was naked. As was the woman beneath him. She twisted away from under his body and kept mute witness to the dilemma of her interrupted customer.

"I believe you owe me," Caleb said.

"I owe you nothing, mister."

"You owe me for ten good horses run off my land over Silverton way."

The man sucked in a ragged breath.

"Now look..." he said.

He glanced beyond the cowering woman to where his guns hung over the seat of a straight-backed chair.

"Don't shoot that scattergun, mister," the woman said. "Please. This ain't none of my doing."

The boy saw that her breasts were small, wrinkled and empty sacks, each marked with a puckered brown cherry. She was a skinny and naked version of a woman, her loose skin yellow and liverish. She saddened the boy. She wasn't healthy like Caleb's wives.

"You have the money for the horses?" Caleb said.

"Hardly none left. We split it three ways and I been in here three days," Leonore said.

"I have a proposition," Caleb said.

"I'll not stop you making it," Leonore said.

"Your man Hunt shot a lawman over in Silverton. His head is worth five thousand dollars. You bring him in alive, you collect the reward and you pay me what you owe for the horses. The rest you keep. How's that sound?"

Leonore cocked his head, pulled the blankets tight around his waist.

"Five thousand?"

"Yep."

"That's a lot of money."

"Much of it's yours."

"Hunt's a partner."

"How'd you like to hang with him?"

"Cain't say I would."

"Then you'd just as well collect the money."

"That's logic."

"That's right."

"How come *you* don't want the money?"

"I want recompense for my horses. You know where to find Hunt. You don't want to hang, and in return you get your blood money."

"That's sound logic, preacher."

"You'll do it?"

"I'll do it."

"Take the man's guns, boy," Caleb said.

The boy edged forward and lifted the gunbelt from the chair.

The liverish woman smiled at him a coquettish smile, and he returned to his position behind his guardian, the weight of the guns in their holsters a strain on the muscles of his arms. But the greater strain was in the power of lust he felt for this naked and shameless woman that he could not touch.

"Where you reckon we'll find Hunt?" Caleb said.

"Hunt got a woman at a stage station in the mountains," Leonore said. "We could start there. If Clay's with him, I cain't take two."

"Don't want Clay."

"How you know I'll bring Hunt in?' Leonore said.

"I got a rifle in my saddle scabbard take your eye out at a hundred yards."

Leonore nodded.

"So you get Hunt," Leonore said, "and I get the money and go free?"

"Just as soon as you pay me what you owe me."

"I get the money?"

"You get the money, I guarantee."

"Let me get my clothes on," Leonore said.

Leonore sat still, the blankets gathered around him, waiting.

"I ain't decent," he said.

"I seen worse," Caleb said. "So has the boy."

And the boy knew that he spoke of his finding and that bloody memory mingled with his desire for the woman's body in a mist of red confusion.

Leonore swung out of bed, his manhood dangling.

"You see, boy. This act paid for with money is acceptable to the laws of men," Caleb said. "There's laws been passed to deny me this act with my three wives that we perform with love blessed by the Laws of God."

"Amen," Leonore said.

"Man's looking after your welfare, boy," the woman said. "You listen to him, now."

And the boy felt the fire aglow in his face and he stared at his guardian, the lantern light caught by the golden stubble on cheek and chin, his guardian who yet held the shotgun aimed at Leonore, immune to the nakedness of this fallen woman.

Leonore pulled on his pants and his shirt and his boots and he threw down a scattering of dollar bills on the bed for the woman.

"Be generous," Caleb said.

Leonore held up a handful of folding money.

"This all I got left," he said.

"Let it fall on the woman's bed," Caleb said. "I want you broke and hungry."

And Leonore scattered the green bills on the patchwork quilt, then picked up his hat and his tattered sheepskin coat and marched out of the room with the two muzzles of the 12-gauge shotgun trained on the small of his back, where their discharge, the boy considered, would likely sever his spine.

The stage station was nestled in a high valley off the trail that ran south toward Taos and Santa Fe. A farmhouse and a bunkhouse and a stable with a corral were surrounded by green meadow and the hillsides thick with pine. The boy counted seven horses on the upper meadow and two in the corral.

"What you aiming to tell 'em?" Caleb said.

"The laws got wind of where they at," Leonore said, "and one should go north and the other south. I'll get Clay to go north and bring Hunt back this way along the trail."

"You come out with Hunt an hour after Clay goes," Caleb said.

"My gun?" Leonore said.

Caleb pulled the Colt from his waistband and handed it over.

"It's empty," he said. "They your friends. Go on. You might load it down there but when you come back up here I'll kill you graveyard dead you reach for it, loaded or not."

Caleb drew his long-barrelled buffalo gun from the saddle scabbard.

"I plan to collect on Hunt," Leonore said.

He put his horse forward and went down the trail toward stage station.

"Settle down here, boy," Caleb said.

He dismounted and walked the grey into a brake of pines and tied the reins to a branch. Caleb tied his bay next to it. Then he climbed on top of a high red rock above the trail. A lone buzzard circled above the stage station and a flock of crows squawked and cawed in the broad spreading branches of a cedar tree close to the corral. The boy sat his ground at the base of the high rock while his mind filled with bloody and lustful visions and fretted over eternal damnation.

Within an hour, a black man came out of the farmhouse and went into the stable. Some ten minutes later he eased a roan out from between the barn doors. It seemed to the boy that Leonore was keeping his side of the bargain. And now his thoughts were taken by what Caleb would do when Leonore reappeared. A half-hour later, Leonore and another man came out of the house. A woman, pretty, around thirty years old, the boy guessed, waited on the porch until the two men rode out of the barn and waved back at her.

"That's Hunt," Caleb said.

He lifted the stock of the rifle to his shoulder and took aim.

"Pick up that scattergun, boy," Caleb said.

The boy hefted the short-barrelled shotgun into his hands. He did not want to use it.

"Stay down behind the rock now."

The boy could not see the approaching riders but he could hear the hoof-falls.

"Wait up, Leonore," Caleb called.

The horses stopped.

"What in hell?"

Hunt's voice, the boy thought.

"Unbuckle the belts, gentlemen. Let them drop."

The boy heard the weight of the weapons and the leather belts hit the trail.

Caleb slid down off the rock. He held the hunting rifle by the stock in his left hand and he had one of his Colt revolvers in his right. The boy came out from his hiding place to see what was going on, the scattergun levelled, muzzles facing the two riders. He did not know if he could pull the triggers.

"Leonore?" Hunt said.

"Sorry, old buddy," Leonore said.

"You turned me in."

"That I did."

"Take the belts, boy," Caleb said. "Put down that scattergun, now."

"You turned me in?" Hunt said.

"You're worth a lot of money, Tobias," Leonore said.

"Son of a bitch...you turned me in."

The boy laid the shotgun at Caleb's feet. He retrieved first one gun belt and then the other.

"There's rope in the saddlebags, boy," Caleb said. "Give it to Leonore and he can tie Mr. Hunt's hands behind his back."

Faces on the Silverton boardwalks turned their way, a murmur among the Gentiles as the four horsemen, Tobias Hunt with his hands tied behind, Leonore leading Hunt's mount, Caleb Dunne with the sawed-off shotgun across his pommel, and the boy on his grey, who walked among them along Main Street, as if he was there and not there both at the same time, a revenant escaped from that hideous dream of savagery wherein his father and mother were yet tormented day after day in memory's vivid vision that made the tongue in his mouth wordless.

They halted in front of the law office.

Caleb and Leonore dismounted. Leonore helped Hunt, encumbered as he was by the rope, from the saddle. The boy slid from the grey and secured his reins to the hitching post. A crowd had already begun to gather.

"That's the son of a bitch killed Holden."

Caleb turned his scattergun toward the crowd.

"He's under arrest. Leonore turned him in to me. He'll stand trial."

"No need for no trial. We know he done it."

"He's a goddamn Mormon, string him up, too."

The boy sensed the ugliness in the still-gathering crowd, violence there: hatred hovering among them, shadowy and demonic.

"March up the steps, Hunt," Caleb said.

"Get your whores to Utah, Dunne."

Leonore led Hunt up the steps and the boy followed Caleb and they entered the Silverton law office.

Anderson stood up behind his desk when they entered and the Weasel and the Tobacco Man, too, from curve-backed chairs they'd had leaned against wall and windowsill.

"Goddamn," the Tobacco Man said.

"This man come for his reward," Caleb said. He pointed at Leonore.

Voices were raised on the street. Shouts among the crowd they could hear even through the closed doors. The boy's hands began to shake.

"Leonore?" Anderson said.

"The same," Leonore said.

"God damn...turned in his own partner," Weasel said.

"I'll see him in hell," Hunt said. "Gimme a gun with one bullet and I'll do it now."

"Your gun days are over, Hunt," Anderson said.

He opened the safe behind his desk and stacked the reward money on the flat surface when he turned back to face them.

"Good green money," Leonore said.

"Ten horses at $300 a head makes three thousand dollars, I'd say," Caleb said.

Leonore's jaw hung slack, his eyes wide.

"Them's expensive horses."

"It was a mite inconvenient to collect my recompense."

"Pay the man his due," Anderson said.

"They'll want to hang you for a horsethief," Weasel said. "Them folks outside."

"I guaranteed his safety," Caleb said.

"With that scattergun?" Tobacco Man said.

"The same," Caleb said. Then he split his money into two piles. He slid one pile into his frock coat pocket and left the other on the desktop.

"That there is for Holden's widow," Caleb said. "Come on, boy."

"I'm coming with you," Leonore said.

"Safer that way," Caleb said.

"I hope they string you up and gut you," Hunt said.

"This is for you, Caleb," Anderson said.

He handed Caleb a sealed envelope.

"Obliged," Caleb said and slid the envelope into the inside pocket of his frock coat. Caleb's hand fell on the boy's shoulder and he guided him toward the door and through it. The crowd in the street had grown to scores, now. They stared at Leonore with hatred a moment but their intent was upon the man inside the office who had killed Holden.

"Bring him out, Anderson," they called. "Bring him out."

Caleb mounted his bay, the boy his grey and Leonore mounted his sorrel beside them. They eased their mounts through the crowd. They reached the level of the Silver Belle when a great roar went up behind them and they reined in and turned to see Hunt dragged from the law office and the rope go around his neck and through a pulley lashed to a roof beam above the boardwalk and the rope tied around the pommel of a saddle, and the horse backed up so that Hunt was hauled from his feet by the noose around his neck and he swung there, kicking and choking, his tongue thick and black, squeezed from the stretched mouth in his rapidly blackening face.

"Where you headed?" Caleb said.

"Safer in Creede, I reckon," Leonore said.

And the boy knew that Leonore would that night be letting his money fall upon the fevered bed of the liverish woman.

"We got work to do, boy," Caleb said.

"He's seen enough, Caleb," Sarah said.

"It ain't finished."

The boy knew so. He picked up his hat and blanket overcoat.

They rode over the mountain pass and into Creede and once more dismounted outside the brothel known as The Star.

"The wheel turns, boy," Caleb said. "Brings us round and round until we completed what we got to complete."

He had the scattergun in his hands again, and the envelope given to him by Anderson, now with its seal broken. The boy followed his guardian into the den of iniquity.

"Goddamn, you becoming a regular, Caleb," Jeremiah called.

"Unfinished business," Caleb said.

Leonore was seated at a table playing cards.

Caleb held the scattergun in his right hand and held up the leaf of paper in his left.

"You're wanted for horse rustling in the State of Texas," Caleb said. "I been authorized to arrest you by the State of Colorado."

"I guess that's the law," Jeremiah said.

Leonore came to his feet.

"Don't go for that gun, son," Caleb said.

But he did.

The scattergun roared and a great explosion of blood erupted from Leonore's right thigh.

"God damn!" Jeremiah said.

A high-pitched whine alternated by screams and foul deprecations and words formed in some hellish tongue issued from the throat of Leonore as he writhed on the floor. Caleb leaned over Leonore's twisting and bloody body.

"Get me a doctor," Leonore yelled.

The leg was badly torn, the flesh ripped away from the bone and great gouts of blood pumped up from the wound.

"That's tore apart an artery," Jeremiah said.

"Get me a doctor! Please," Leonore said, his voice a rasp.

"Wouldn't get here in time," Caleb said.

All around Leonore the wet redness pooled as he sat up on the rough plank floor and stared at the shot-torn thigh. And then he began to nod. And go pallid. And bend forward and then he was dead. And the boy shook his head at all this carnage that seemed ever his lot to witness since that day his mother and father died.

The boy closed his Book of Revelation and looked up as Jim Anderson rode up the trail to the Dunne homestead. Caleb came out upon the porch as Anderson reined in.

"Bad news, Caleb."

"You always bring bad news, Jim."

"There's a mob in town wants you out of here. And there's a law says I got to arrest you for having more than one wife."

"It was always coming."

"You got a choice…"

"No, I ain't."

"You going to Utah?"

"God's Law don't stand in this country no more."

"I don't know who writ which God's Law, Caleb."

"Wagon been packed a month or more," Caleb said. "I seen it coming."

"I'm sorry, Caleb," Anderson said.

"Let's go, boy. We better tell the women."

And as the cloud whirled above him and the sun blazed in the boy's eyes, new words of revelation echoed and shook inside him as if from some book not yet writ, or a book still hidden in a nether realm awaiting its moment to be revealed, and those words were known to the boy now by some holy or unholy second sight, and their letters appeared to him within the sacred light inside the bony dome of his skull, and formed themselves piecemeal in the cavity of his mouth like some dread American prophecy to be pronounced in tongues upon the slopes of these Colorado mountains where the sea of prairie ended, and the flotsam and jetsam of American life were thrown up, broken in all their beauty and vileness: miners, hustlers, whores, traders, bankers, rustlers and quacks, who grubbed from that red and rocky earth the ore of fortune or ill luck, addressed to them, these words that had never been spoken in any tongue at this moment known to man, words that now issued forth from the boy's unlocked throat, a clear and pure canticle in the language of God's own angels.

COLT

KEN BRUEN

Damn Colt 45.

Jammed.

Doggone it all to hell.

Darn thing is supposed to work every time and I clean it like I do my tin cup, plate, every evening.

I'd landed up in a one-horse town named Watersprings, and I ain't joshing you, one horse is what they had and that was mine, well, okay, I'm joshin you a bit here but my ride was the best, apart from the sheriff's and the owner of the saloon, who had three palominos sweet, sweet horse.

I've had my Sorrel since the Injun trouble and that baby, ain't never quit, no how.

I had me a thirst, been riding hard, real hard to get way the hell outa Arizona, they wanted me real bad in that godforsaken place. The why is a whole other yarn and I ain't gonna bother you none with that shit now.

Fuck no.

This here is about a gal.

Ain't it always?

COLT

I tethered my horse outside the rail at the saloon, couple a neer-do-ell's given me that slack eyes jaw look, I touched the brim of me beat up Stetson, said, "How de?"

Not too friendly, didn't want 'em getting no damn fool notions but enough to show I meant no injury, leastways I was pushed.

I took my Winchester outa its pouch, and I could see they knew it'd been well worn.

Make 'em think twice about foolin around some.

They done muttered some answer, I didn't detect nuttin there to reach for my colt so I carried on up to the saloon.

Real shitbird place, darn right.

Couple guys moseying at card playing but not more 'n a buck on the table. Big stakes, huh, but I noticed they was all carrying iron, watching me over them cards.

I seen 'em.

The bartender, big, burly, like a grizzly I seen one time up near Canada, too damn cold up there, and I had my Winchester, that bear in my sights and I swear, the beast turned, looked at me, like he was thinking, "I hurt you?"

I lowered the rifle, and never had a days regret, not a one.

He was kinda, I dunno the word...noble.

He sure a shotting was a big mother.

The grizzly behind the counter, gives me a slow eye, asks, "What's it gonna be partner?"

Could have said, "I ain't your partner mistah."

But no point touching trouble, one way or the damn other, the stuff done find me anyways.

I jacked my boot up on that brass foot rail, laid my Winchester lightly against the bar, said, "Whiskey."

Didn't put no please or nuttin on there, my daddy used to say, "Son, I ain't got a whole lot to teach you 'cept how to shoot, shoe a horse and this, don't start nuttin you ain't aiming to finish."

I ain't gonna lie to you none, I haven't always followed my daddy's saying, the reason I got me a bullet hole in my leg, drags a bit but I ain't bitchin, the other guy, he's not doing no walking, not no how's I see it.

Grizzly sets the bottle on the counter, shot glass, and it weren't durty but it weren't clean neither, I figured, the whiskey will wash it most ways.

I knock back two fast ones and damn, tasted real fine, like a ho after six months hitch in the State Pen.

He's lookin at my holster, goes, "That there a Colt?"

The fuck else it be?

Real slow, I reach, take it out, let him see it, don't let no man touch it, not unless he's got the draw on me and even then, well, he better be prepared to do more than mouth.

He lets out a slow whistle, said, "You rode with The Cavalry?"

The guy was whole lot smarter than he looked.

The Colt was Army issue, and the notches on the butt, an old horse soldier tradition, mine was riddled.

I nodded, not a story I wanted to share with some damn barkeep.

He reached out his massive hand, about to touch it and felt, rather than saw me stiffen, pulled back, asked, "You ever run into Custer?"

That prick.

I downed another shot, let it warm me belly, then real easy said, "Man never passed a mirror he didn't love."

Let it out there, see where he stood on that whole darn mess.

He poured himself a shot, downed it in one, grimaced, the whiskey of Custer?

He said, "He sure ran into one mountain of shit that day."

Okay.

Then he done told me about those fine horses he had and I gave him the face that asks..."*I say I was in the market for a horse?*"

I put a few bits on the counter and he asked, "You fixing to stay a few days?"

And when I didn't answer, it's real foolhardy to be asking a stranger his business these wild days, he added real fast, "Reason I ask is, we got us a hanging, folks coming for miles 'round, ain't often you gets to see a woman dangle."

I seen most stuff, lynchings, burnings, scalpings and I don't got me no taste for it, especially not the legal ones.

But I was interested, who wouldn't be and I repeated, "A woman?"

"Yeah, done shot her husband and now they gonna stretch her pretty little neck, see if they don't."

I dunno, I still can't get me a fix on it, I was aiming to get some chow, get my horse seen to and then hit out next day, I had business over in Shiloh and I was antsy to git movin but I asked, "She local?"

He was shaking his head, wiping down the counter with a greasy rag, said, "Hell no, outa Virginia, name of Molly Blair."

The whiskey stuck in me gullet and I'd to fight real hard to keep me face tight, I tipped my Stetson, said I might stick around for the rope party and he shouted as I reached the swing door, "Real purty little thing, shame to let all that fine pussy go a begging."

My hand went to my Colt, pure instinct, I would have drilled that sumbitch for two cents.

Outside, I had to grab me some deep breaths.

Molly, damn her to tarnation, the only gal I done ever loved.

I hawked me a big chunk of spittle and let it out on the boardwalk...looked round and could see the Sheriff's office down a ways.

Cussin nine ways to Sunday, I hitched my gun belt, headed on over, thinking, "The hell I had to go running off me fool mouth."

I glanced at my horse, tired as he was, tired as I was my own self, we could have bin outa there in two seconds flat, left her to rot, like she did me but...

Darn story of my life, I just can never mosey on the other way.

I put a chaw of bacca in me cheek, began to walk towards the jail, me fool heart thundering like the Injuns raining down on Custer.

Stepping up to the porch outside the sheriff's office, I heard loud hammering and looked to my left, sh-ee-it...how in all that's shottin did I miss seeing it?

The scaffold, ugly-looking thing but then, I guess, they ain't building 'em for purtyness.

Damn thing was near done, too, they was even trying out a sack of taters, body weight I guess, though Molly, a cup of sugar would have been about right with her.

Petite sweet thing I'd thought way back in Tennessee when I done first run into her.

Sweet?

Like a coyote in heat.

They let the bag fall, and it startled me, I had to shake me own self, get it tight.

I opened the door and a man was sitting behind a desk, cup of gruel going, cheroot dangling in his mouth.

Boots up on the desk and I thought, "Uh oh."

Frontier lawmen, a real mean breed of buzzard, they get that tin on them, they're as dangerous as a herd of buffalo in a Cheyenne Autumn.

He had him a belly there, a man who liked his vittles and his drinking if his flushed cheeks were any story.

Round thirty I'd hazard, and all them years, mean as can be.

He had him a smirk too, like he knew I wasn't bringing him no good news.

He got that right.

He drawled, "Help yah?"

Sounding like that was a darn fool notion.

I kept my hands loose, no threat showing, least not yet, said, "I'm kin to Molly."

He mulled that over then spat to his side, said, "That so."

Not a question.

I kept with it, tried, "Yessir, on my Momma's side, we ain't been real close or nuttin but I figured I'd better come, pay my respects."

He had a metal cup on the table and lazy as can be, he reached over, his cobra eyes never leaving my face, took his own time in a long swallow, making noises like a sow in heat, said, "Funny ain't it?"

What?

I went, "What?"

Then stuck on, "Sir?"

Let the beat in.

He blew a cloud of smoke at me, said, "The murdering bitch ain't mentioned no kin."

I gave a real slow grin, the *gee shucks* I keep for killing vermin, said, "Like I said sheriff, we ain't been real close."

He stood up, real sudden and I kept very still, he grabbed a bunch of keys, asked, "Well, whatcha waiting on son, you're real keen to visit with yer kin, am I right?"

Sumofbitch...*son*...I had a good ten years on him, I nodded and he led me back.

She looked even more damn beautiful than I remembered and before the sheriff could try his game, I said, damn near hollered,

"Coz, Momma done told me to come visit, see you be needing anything?"

He gave me the look then and his eyes showed most of what he was, a piece of trash with a Smith and Wesson, nothing no mo in that.

Molly, sharp as always, smiled, and I swear, even squeezed a tear out, shouts, "Cousin Lucas, I was believin my family washed their hands offa me."

I turned to the sheriff, asked, "Mind if I have me a moment with my kin?"

He minded, heck, he minded a lot.

He spat right next to my boots, said, "You got five minutes and I'll be right outside."

I done already said about me and my running off mouth and even now, I had to go, "That'll be a comfort sir."

His eyes sparked and he moved right in my face, drawled, real slow, "You sassing me boy?"

Like I was nigrah.

I shot men for less.

I heard Molly say, "Now sheriff, he's just a country type, don't know a whole lot how to behave round decent folk."

He thought about it, said, "I'll be talking some more to you boy."

He was fucking a nickel to a dollar on that.

Course, a lard ass like him, he ain't going to let it go easy, said, "I'll be needing that there Colt."

I gave it up, real slow, seeing another notch on the butt already and this time, it would be a whole lot of funning.

He made lots of grunting on his way back to his coffee.

I hoped it would choke him...slow.

She gave that radiant smile, that damn melt yer heart and yer senses, all in one, done make a fool outa a man everytime.

She reached out her hand, touched my arm, said, "You lookin real fine darling."

Ho to her heart.

I'd made me some gold offa a claim that was already staked out and I was looking to spend it, met Molly in a saloon and she not only took off with my stash but my dumbass heart as well.

Broke, hungover, I had me some real trouble to git on outa there with my skin.

I asked, "Why'd you fuck me over, wasn't I good to you?"

She lowered her eyes, said, "I was real young, real reckless, what do you know at 17?"

I whistled, went, "Boy howdy."

She was caressing my arm and I got riled, said, "You didn't know enough that leaving me without cash, could have got me killed, them fellahs in that saloon didn't take kindly to some greenhorn saying he couldn't pay the freight, they done give me a horse whipping, took my boots and ran my ass outa town."

She let her eyes melt in the honey way she had, said, "Lucas, I'm so damn sorry, can you forgive me?"

Dammit.

Then she said, "You gotta get me on outa here."

I laughed, not with any merriment or anything, asked, "And how you fixing on me doing that, that fat ass took my Colt."

Now her real smile showed, the smile of a woman who is one hundred years old and means to live another, said, "You telling me darling you ain't still got that derringer in your boot."

I always had that spooked feeling she knew things she never should have known and like a lovesick pup, I reached in my boot, took out the tiny pistol, two shots. She said, "Give it here hon."

The gun felt tiny in my hand, small as the focus of my thinking, I asked, "You're fixing to do what?"

A cloud passed briefly over them lovely features, then was gone and she asked, "You want to see them hang me, see me shit me bloomers as the rope bites in, you want that lover?"

I handed it over and she hollered, "Sheriff, git on in here."

He did and she shot him in the face.

Now her voice was hard as the Rockies in that big snow we had a time back, she said, "Get the keys."

I did and took my Colt back, turned to see her level the derringer at me, she said, "I'm sorry coz, but you'd only slow me down."

I pulled the trigger of the Colt and it jammed...you believe it, she gave me that almost sad look and pulled the trigger on the second load.

Took me right in the gut, she stepped over me, reached in my vest, took what money I had.

COLT

The Colt was lying a few feet from me, she glanced at it then stepped away, said, "They'll be coming, make sure it doesn't jam again."

And she was gone, I swear, leaving a trail of perfume that was warm as that first time I ever set my eyes on her.

The dead sheriff's dead eyes are staring at me and his cheroot is lying real close, if I could stop the blood for a moment, I might get a smoke before they come.

The Colt is a little outa reach and the damn thing let me down, you think I'm gonna trust it again.

Another inch, I might grab me that cheroot.

PIANO MAN

BILL CRIDER

I was just the piano man. Nobody ever paid any attention to me. My job was to play while the customers gambled and whored and drank. I never said much, but I'd watch and I'd listen. That's what I was doing the night a man named Morgan bet his daughter on a poker hand.

It was deep in the fall of 1880, and I was working in the Bad Dog Saloon near Fort Laramie. The glory days of the Oregon Trail were a long time gone, but people still came along, all the time. The fort itself had become almost civilized by that time, with boardwalks in front of the officers' houses and even a few trees that someone had planted to keep the place from looking so bare.

The Bad Dog wasn't anywhere near civilized, and it catered to a rough crowd: bullwhackers, trappers who thought there were still pelts in the mountains, whores, and gamblers who preyed on hapless pilgrims like Morgan, who'd started out too late in the year, got caught by an early snow, and was now down on his luck and hurting for cash. And drunk and stupid enough to try to win some in a poker game in a place like the Bad Dog Saloon.

"Play 'Nellie Was a Lady!'" some maudlin drunk yelled, and I did, moving right on to "Hard Times Come Again no More" after that, but all the while I had my eyes on Morgan's daughter.

She must've been about fifteen, with blonde hair, blue eyes, and an innocent face like an angel. She sat there with her chair against the wall, fifteen feet away from the table where her father was about to bet her on the cards he held.

"I ain't got enough money to stay in the pot," he said. He had a big voice to go with his thick neck and wide shoulders. The drunken desperation rolled off him in waves. "But I'm stayin' in. I'll bet the girl."

I glanced over at her when he said that. She didn't say a word, didn't even move. Just kept looking straight ahead out of those blue eyes.

Two of the other men at the table folded then. They were cold men, hard men, but that was a little too much even for them.

Ray Tabor didn't fold. He owned the saloon, and compared to him the snow outside was warm. He sat at the table in his wheelchair. It had a wooden frame, big spoked wheels, and a wicker seat. Texas Mary stood behind him. She was a whore but she worked for Tabor, like all the whores in the saloon, and she was his favorite. She was his whenever he wanted her, paying customers be damned.

He looked over at the girl and licked his thin lips. Then he looked at the pot.

"That's a hundred dollar bet," he said.

Morgan nodded. "The girl's worth it."

"I don't doubt it." Tabor smiled. "Very well, let's say you've called."

He fanned out his cards on the table.

"Full house."

Morgan swallowed hard. I couldn't see his hand from where I sat, but I figured it was something pitiful, a pair of threes maybe. Two pair at best. Morgan was a fool.

He didn't even show his cards. He stood up fast, knocking over his chair. His hand went for the pistol at his hip.

Texas Mary had moved around behind him, so I launched into "Rock of Ages," which would do, I figured, for his funeral song. Except Mary didn't shoot him with the little derringer she carried.

She hit him in the back of the head with a whiskey bottle before he could draw. He fell face-first onto the table, and broke his nose.

I played "Oh, Susannah," to get the boys in a jolly mood and take their minds off Morgan, who was pulled off the table and dragged out the door by the other two gamblers. They threw him out in the street, with Tabor looking at that little girl like a hungry dog looks at a meaty bone.

He spun his chair around and wheeled off to the back, toward the hall leading off to his room.

"Bring her to me," he said to Texas Mary, who smiled. She'd have more time to make money if Tabor was otherwise occupied.

She went over to the girl, who was staring at the door. Texas Mary took hold of her arm and pulled her out of the chair. She didn't want to come along and dug in her heels. Texas Mary slapped her a time or two, and that got her moving. She whimpered like a whipped dog and looked over her shoulder when Mary dragged her into the dark hall. Tears ran down her angelic face. Nobody made a move to help. They knew Tabor too well.

I played "Carve dat Possum" to cover the sound of the girl's crying, because someone's possum was sure enough about to get carved. Not that it was any business of mine.

I was a godly man once. My father was a preacher, and the first songs I played were things like "From Greenland's Icy Mountains," "Just as I Am, Without One Plea," "Fairest Lord Jesus." Nobody had to teach me. The music was just in me. If I heard the song, I could play it, and when I sat down at the piano and looked at the keys, it came out through my fingers. My parents thought it was a wonderful thing, a gift from God that would lead me to a life of service to the Lord.

It didn't turn out that way. As I got older, I found the call of the flesh far stronger than that call of the spirit, and I found that any number of lovely young women (and even more older ones) were eager to show their appreciation of my playing by letting me have my way with them after the services. That sort of thing did not endear me to the deeply religious husbands of many of the women. My fondness for the strong liquor, the only spirits I truly appreciated, did little to endear me to my parents, or to anyone else.

By the time I was twenty, I was a serious toper, and by the time I was twenty-two, I was a dangerous degenerate in my parents' eyes. I hadn't entered a house of worship in over a year. The only employment I could find was playing piano in saloons and whorehouses, and over time I was so overwhelmed by drink that even the more high-toned among those places wouldn't have me.

One morning I woke up lying on a pile of garbage in an alley somewhere. I didn't know the name of the town or how I'd gotten there. It was some time before I could even remember my name. I was so frightened by the experience that I vowed never to drink liquor or consort with prostitutes again.

It was a vow in vain, of course, as most vows of that kind are, but I did manage to achieve occasional sobriety, or at least the appearance of it. As to consorting with prostitutes, by that time the liquor had almost eliminated the desire for physical contact with the opposite sex, and I was convinced that merely playing piano in the vicinity of the soiled doves could do me no harm.

The piano was all I knew. Playing it was all I had left. I had to do it somewhere. Which more or less explains how I came to be in the Bad Dog Saloon.

"What do you think he does to her?"

That was what Frank wanted to know. Frank was the bartender in the Bad Dog, and when things were slow in the afternoon, sometimes he'd come over to the piano and talk or ask me to play "When You and I Were Young, Maggie" or "I'll Take you Home Again, Kathleen." He was a sentimental man, was Frank.

"It's not any of our concern, Frank," I told him, trying not to think about it.

"Yeah, I guess not. How about you playin' 'In the Sweet By and By.'"

I did, and he sang along in a passable tenor. I didn't join in. I don't sing, and for some reason I couldn't stop thinking about what he'd asked, even if it was none of my concern.

Morgan came back the day after he'd bet his daughter. Tabor had probably been expecting him because he'd told Hamp to stay close. Hamp was the bouncer. He was big as a bear and had only one eye. The lack of the other one didn't slow him down any when it came to knocking heads, and the eye–patch he wore to cover the hole added to his generally scary appearance. He liked to work with an ax handle, and he had it close by that day.

Morgan's nose was a mess. He was about as big as Hamp, and he didn't look scared, but that might have been because he was drunk again. Or still. He walked right up to Tabor and said, "I want the girl back."

Tabor was playing cards. He didn't even look up. He said, "You can't have her."

Morgan swayed a little on his feet. "You know it ain't right for you to keep her."

"I won," Tabor said. "You lost. Now get out of my saloon."

Morgan took an awkward step toward him, breathing heavily through his open mouth. "You fuckin' cripple."

Tabor spun the chair around and faced him.

Morgan stopped short and almost fell. He steadied himself and said, "I'll get the major at the fort, by God. He'll make you give my girl back to me."

"The major has no jurisdiction over me."

Tabor started to turn back to the table, and Morgan jumped for him, his big hands ready to strangle the life from him.

Hamp hit him with the ax handle in just about the same place Texas Mary had landed the whiskey bottle, only harder. I wondered if Morgan would ever wake up this time.

Tabor didn't give a damn. He told Hamp to take him to his wagon. "Pay somebody to drive him down the trail eight or ten miles and leave him."

Hamp nodded. He wasn't one to talk much. He picked Morgan up under the arms and dragged him out.

I don't think they expected to see him again. They thought he'd give up and move along.

They were wrong.

Tabor had broken both legs in a riding accident years before. They'd been badly set and never healed right. He could walk a little with the help of a couple of canes, but he seldom resorted to them except when he used the privy out back. Sometimes he didn't even go to bed. He just slept in his chair. When he wanted to bathe or put on his clothes, Texas Mary helped him.

All that changed when he won Morgan's daughter. She lived in his room and hardly ever came out. Morgan wouldn't let her leave. He owned her, and as far as he was concerned, she was nothing more than his slave. I knew it wasn't right, but what could I do?

Tabor let me live in a little room in the saloon on the floor with the whores. It wasn't much of a room, but it was better than sleeping in an alley, and up until now I'd liked it fine.

Not anymore. It was right over Tabor's room, and after I'd stopped playing for the night and gone up to sleep, I could hear them down there, Tabor grunting like an animal. I couldn't help thinking about the girl's innocent face and the indecent things he was forcing her to do.

The more I tried not to think about it, the more I did. Maybe it was my Christian upbringing causing my conscience to come back to life. I remembered my father's face in the pulpit, distorted and red as he denounced the sins of the flesh that I'd taken up with such enthusiasm. I wondered if he'd been right all along.

Or maybe it wasn't my upbringing. Maybe I wished the girl were doing those things to me.

Morgan came back. It could have been that his own conscience was consuming him. This time he brought someone with him, an older man named Tumlin, who should have known better than to follow a fool like Morgan.

They both had guns, but it didn't help them. Hamp used the ax handle to break the older man's arm just above the wrist, and his gun thumped to the floor, discharging a bullet that clanged into the railing of the bar.

Hamp twirled the handle so fast it looked like the spoke of a wagon wheel. Then he slammed the butt end of it into Morgan's soft belly, and all the air wheezed out of Morgan's lungs. It was followed by the remains of Morgan's last meal, which made a considerable stink.

Tabor was in his room while all this was going on. He never came out, and neither did the girl. I didn't know what they were doing in there. I didn't want to know.

"What're you gonna do with 'em?" Frank asked Hamp.

Hamp didn't say anything, just went to work on Morgan with the handle. Broke a few ribs, re-broke his nose. Knocked out some teeth. I sat and watched. It wasn't my place to interfere.

When he was finished, Hamp dragged Morgan outside and left him. The other man managed to get out on his own.

"You should've killed him," Frank said when Hamp came back inside. "He's not gonna quit."

Hamp shrugged. "Maybe he'll freeze to death."

"Yeah," Frank said. "Maybe he will."

Every night I had to listen to Tabor rutting with the girl. I thought about her hands, her red mouth. Her innocent face. I imagined Tabor's hands tangled in her blonde hair as he forced her head down on him.

I could have drunk myself to sleep. I don't know why I didn't. It couldn't have been because I wanted to hear. I know I didn't want that. That's what I told myself.

PIANO MAN

It was about a week later that Morgan came back one last time. It was early morning, about three or four, still dark outside. The saloon was quiet except for the creaking of the boards in the cold, and everyone was asleep except me.

I was awake because I'd found it harder and harder to sleep even after the sounds from the room below had stopped. I'd lie there and try to think about music, the songs I used to play in my father's church: "My Faith Looks up to Thee," "Jesus, Lover of my Soul," "Nearer, My God, to Thee," "Holy, Holy, Holy." For some reason the songs were a comfort to me, and my fingers moved on an invisible keyboard as the imagined melodies filled the dark room. Music had kept me sane for years, and it was calming to me even now.

Finally my fingers stopped moving. I still couldn't sleep, so I decided to take a trip to the privy. My bladder needed emptying, and maybe if I were more comfortable I'd drift off before dawn.

It was quiet in the saloon. All the girls were sleeping. I heard one of them snoring behind a closed door as I walked down the hall. Their customers were long gone. It being a week-night, there hadn't been too many of them anyway.

No sound came from Tabor's room, though it had been plenty noisy earlier. I tried not to think about that. I went past and out the back.

The alley was dark, the moon down already and the sky covered with heavy clouds. I didn't need light to find the privy. I could locate it by the smell in the shivery cold.

As I was about to open the door, I smelled something else. Coal oil. I turned from the door and saw movement out of the corner of my eye. It was like the shifting of a shadow, nothing more than that, and it was all the warning I got before Morgan hit me in the side of the head with a big fist and knocked me flat.

I didn't know it was Morgan who'd hit me, not until later, when I came to and he was tying my hands.

"What the hell?" I said.

"Shut up," he said and stuck something in my mouth.

It was a rag that tasted of coal oil, and I tried to spit it out. I couldn't. I choked and thought I might puke.

Morgan didn't care. He went about his business, soaking the base of the building with coal oil, stuffing more of the oil-soaked rags around in any cracks he could find and around the windows.

It didn't take him long. He came back over to me and stuck his face close to mine. He said, "You're damn lucky you ain't in there."

I could smell the liquor on his hot breath even with the rag in my mouth and under my nose.

"Teach that bastard he can't take my girl," Morgan said.

I didn't see how burning the place down and maybe killing everybody in it including his daughter would teach anybody anything. Maybe Morgan thought he could get her out.

He turned away from me and went back to the wall. I tested the ropes. A drunk man's not always good at tying knots, but these held. The rope wasn't tight, though. There was some play in it, so I started working at it.

Morgan struck a lucifer with his fingernail and set one of the rags on fire. It took a couple of seconds, but it burned fast after that. He went on to the others, and sooner than you'd think the whole wall was flaming. He stood back and looked at it with apparent satisfaction.

"I don't give a damn about the girl now," he said, looking around at me as if I'd asked. "The bitch coulda left him, but she didn't. She's ruined. She's no daughter of mine."

He turned back to watch the blaze.

She could have left. That was true. Why hadn't she? I didn't know, but I knew she wasn't ruined. Morgan was a bigger fool than I'd thought.

The ropes were coming loose, but I didn't think I'd get them off in time to do anything. Morgan looked back at me, and grinned. He bent down and picked up a hammer and a board and started to nail the board across the door.

The flames crackled, and I heard screams from inside. They'll go out the front door, I thought, but when I heard the shotgun blast I knew better.

Morgan tossed the hammer down, not far from where I sat.

"Old man Tumlin's out front," he said. "That bastard Hamp should never have broke his wrist. He'll keep 'em in there."

He would until someone stopped him, I thought, or until they got truly desperate. Maybe someone would stop him soon, but it would be too long for the people inside.

The ropes came loose. I pulled the rag from my mouth. I grabbed the hammer, jumped up, and hit Morgan in the forehead. He fell without a sound, and I flipped the hammer over to use the claw on the board. People pounded on the other side of the door, screaming in panic.

As soon as I ripped the board, the door flung open and knocked me backward and down. I was almost trampled as the whores came out, Texas Mary in the lead. Hamp's room was across the hall from Tabor's. Hamp was right behind the whores. Tabor and the girl were still inside.

I got up and asked Hamp about Tabor.

"Who the hell cares. Who did this?"

"Morgan," I said. "He's over there."

Hamp took a couple of steps and started kicking Morgan carefully and methodically. Then he came back to me and took the hammer that I still held. I didn't think Morgan would be getting up from where he lay.

The building continued to burn. The heat was intense, and everyone was backing away. There were no other buildings nearby, but people would soon be gathering from the fort and the trading post and the few stores. There wouldn't be anything they could do.

The girl was in there. Why hadn't she come out? The heat seared my face. Smoke rolled out the door. I didn't want to go in.

I had to. For once in my life I had to take action. I forced myself to go through the door. The smoke choked me, and the blazing heat singed my hair.

Tabor's room was on the right. I kicked the door open and went into the room. The girl was there, trying to help Tabor into the wheelchair, but she was having a bad time of it. They were both half blinded by smoke, coughing and hacking. Tabor couldn't stand or get his balance.

"Let me help," I said, but I knew even as I said it that I wasn't going to help Tabor. He could stay there and burn.

I pushed him aside, and he fell to the floor. I took the girl's hand and pulled her toward the door.

She jerked away, spitting at me like a cat. "We can't leave him!"

"What?"

"I love him! We can't leave him!"

She bent down and put her hands under Tabor's shoulders, trying to lift him. He got his hands on the seat of the chair and started to pull himself up into it.

Fire ran all across the ceiling above us. It was going to fall any second. I went to the girl and pulled her away.

"Leave him," I said.

She spit at me again and slapped me. I hit her on the point of the chin, and she collapsed. I caught her before she dropped to the floor and stumbled out of the room with her in my arms. I carried her outside through the smoke and got as far from the building as I could. She was struggling by then so I put her down. She kicked me in the shin.

"You bastard! I love him!" She rushed toward the burning saloon.

I'd thought she was a slave. She'd been nothing of the sort. She'd stayed with Tabor willingly. I'd had a stupid notion that she'd thank me for saving her, maybe move in with me, do the things she'd done with Tabor.

I laughed aloud. I'd thought Morgan was a fool, but I'd been the one. I let her go.

She didn't get far. Before she got ten steps, Tabor came flying out the door through the smoke. His chair stayed in the air for a second or two, then dropped, falling over on its side. Tabor rolled out and started pulling himself away from the building like an injured bug.

Hamp ran to him and picked him up. He carried him away, the girl clinging to his arm.

I sat down on the hard ground and watched the building burn.

There was nothing left of the Bad Dog the next day. Hamp, Tabor, and the girl stayed in Morgan's wagon. Morgan had disappeared at some point after Tabor came out of the building. I had a feeling that where Morgan had gone, no one would ever find him.

PIANO MAN

The whores all found places to stay. I didn't ask where. I stayed at the fort in the soldiers' barracks, but I couldn't do that for long. It was time for me to move on, to find another place where I could let the music that was inside me find its way out. It wasn't much, but it was all I had, and it would have to do.

Hamp came up to me when I left the barracks. "Tabor wants you."

"I don't work for him anymore. There's nowhere left to work."

Hamp gripped my upper arm and squeezed. Hard. Pain shot down to my fingers. I felt my knees go weak. Hamp didn't say anything. He didn't have to. I went along with him.

Tabor sat on the back of the wagon, his useless legs dangling. The girl sat beside him, holding his hand, her blonde head resting on his shoulder. Her eyes were closed.

"You left me to die in there," Tabor said.

He was burned on one side of his face. It was covered with some kind of salve. Some of his hair was missing. He looked like hell.

I would've run, but Hamp had my arm.

"I had to save the girl," I said.

She opened her eyes and looked at me. They were pure blue, sky blue, and as full of hatred as any eyes I'd ever seen.

"You fucking liar," she said.

Tabor smiled, though it must have hurt him. He said, "All right, Hamp."

Hamp slid his hand down to my wrist and dragged me to a barrel sitting by the back of the wagon. An ax handle leaned against the barrel.

"You want to help me?" he said, and the girl jumped down, smiling now.

Hamp forced my right hand down on the barrelhead. The girl picked up the ax handle.

"No," I said.

"Oh, yes," the girl said, raising the handle over her head.

"Please," I said.

She stopped, still smiling. "Say it again."

"Please."

"Fuck you," she said, and she brought the handle down.

All that happened a while back. I don't know how many times Morgan's daughter hit my right hand before she started on the left. I'd passed out long before then.

My hands are more like claws now. Looking at them, you'd never think they could have made music once.

The music's still in me. "Rescue the Perishing," "Onward Christian Soldiers," "Listen to the Mockingbird," "Oh Don't You Remember Sweet Alice, Ben Bolt?," "My Old Kentucky Home, Good Night."

The music's in me, but I can't let it out. Sometimes I think I'm going to pop like a boil the way it swells me.

But I can't play piano now. I can barely hold a drink without someone's help. I think I can hold a pistol, though. I won't need to hold it long, if only I can pull the trigger.

DESERT RECKONING

TREY R. BARKER

It gets under your fingers, this brown dirt. Sticks and clots like a man's blood after you've killed him close and personal.

While the emerging moonlight overpowers the dying sunlight, a painful cough leaves its stain on my lips.

For a moment, I wonder if the dirt isn't blood at all, but more tumors. Beneath each of my nails, at the tip of each finger, growing while I traveled the miles from Boston to this foul-smelling privy of a town. God knows how many more tumors there are now than when I got Palmer's telegraph.

"I'll be there stop Don't die until I get there stop I love you stop."

"I love you, too."

The old man, Topper, wearing tattered clothes that just manage to cover him, frowns. "Y'all say something, mister?"

A passing train—maybe Palmer's train—gives my answer. It fills the desert air with a roar somehow delicate, like Palmer's soft voice. Black smoke paints the evening air and smells like a burning homestead.

It isn't Palmer's train. And his grave dirt is just dirt.

Ignoring the pain keeping such close company, I listen for Palmer's voice. I dig and dig, and hear, rather than feel, my nails tear away. But it isn't enough pain to overwhelm the other pain, the other hurt.

While I dig, the moonlight finally settling heavy on the ground, I cry and my tears and sweat and blood soak the dirt I scoop out and toss aside.

"Wha'ch'all gonna do if you find him?" Topper asks.

Stopping, I stare into the moonlight, into the scrub and mesquite of west Texas, toward the tiny railroad stop a half-mile away. "You telling me he's not here?"

The old man, the nominal caretaker of the graveyard, shrugs. "Maybe is, maybe ain't. Somebody comes and buries a body, I got no idea who either of them is."

A gun fires then. Followed by another and another, from somewhere deep in the desert. Topper sucks his teeth.

"Shooting all the time. Cain't tell you how many times I woke up to bullet holes in my walls." He nods toward my forehead. "I seen that scar before. There's a whore in town, woman wants to be a nurse; the doctor lets her work. She came and got me."

Blood dripping from the tips of my fingers, I stand in the depression I've dug over the last hour or so. All I can smell is the dirt; grave dirt, death-dirt. The crumbling dryness of bones and a pine coffin.

"But I ain't so sure I'm talking about y'all's brother."

"Marshal Brack," I say.

Can I see Palmer through the dirt? Like looking through an opium haze, through a blast of fog, but yeah, I see him. Sharp cheekbones, strong chin, penetrating eyes. Well-muscled arms and back, bald head, and just a wisp of a mustache beneath that nose that had been broken so many times.

"Y'all ain't looking any too good, boy," Topper says.

"Not feeling any too good," I say, trying to stand tall though all I want to do is lay in his grave and see my brother again.

Truth is, I should be dead already. The tumors are everywhere. Yet there is another truth: that I'll keep going—damn the weakness—until I stare into Marshal Brack's dead eyes.

In the moonlight, my badge winks like a cheap whore.

"Brack's badge looks just like that," Topper says.

"I know."

"Gold with a five-pointed star. His name right smack in the middle. Don't say marshal or sheriff or nothing. Just his name... like that was the most important part." The old man licks his lips. "Brack's brother is a lawman, too."

"I know."

"Thought maybe you did." The old man shakes his head, heads for a shack standing at the edge of the bone yard like a lonely sentinel, comes back a few minutes later with a small shovel.

"Got some digging tonight?"

"Ain't I?"

"About a half-mile?" I ask. "To Midway?"

"Yeah."

I toss him a double eagle. Surprisingly, he tosses it back and I nod as I climb from my brother's grave, setting my eyes on the faint glow across the flat nothingness. Then I try to climb into the saddle. My foot slips, my right hand loses grip. I hit the ground hard.

"Y'all need some help there, cowboy?" Topper asks, helping me back to standing.

I wave him away, but after failing twice more to mount the animal, I swallow down my meal of anger and embarrassment and let him shove me atop the horse.

He says something—maybe a warning to stay away from Brack, maybe an apology for my brother's death—but it's covered by the noise in my head, a buzz and grind, like a blacksmith's tool against raw metal, that I believe it the noise of brain tumors.

After coughing, after wiping my blood on the brim of my hat, I spur my horse and ride to Midway.

The windmills sound like metal soldiers. They bang and clang in the dark, their blades stumbling along in the weak breeze, water trickling through their pipes and into the tanks. Just barely, nearly hidden beneath the air's dirt smell, I get a whiff of water. It doesn't smell how Palmer said the Pacific Ocean does. It smells rotted, like water standing in the summertime.

This place is just a water stop. Halfway between Fort Worth and the rest of the world. Trains come through, fill up their tanks, drop a few passengers, maybe pick up a few. That I can see through the haze of a hot summer night, Midway only has a few saloons, a general goods store, a few businesses. There's a doctor's office—where they took Palmer.

There is more shooting, but it fades quickly. Beneath it, I hear a growling dog and laughing men. When I spot them, still winded from the few minutes I dug at Palmer's grave, they ignore me, riveted on the dog.

And the man tied to the dog.

Even from here, better than thirty feet away, all of them stink like a brewery.

"Get 'im, hoss," one man shouts. "I got another V-spot says that damn dog kills him."

"Lay it down, boy," another says.

One of the man's hands is tied to the dog. The other is free and he uses it to slash at the animal with a knife while the mutt snaps and claws at him. Both scream, both bleed.

A block further, I tie my horse—a giant black I named after my brother—and slip into a tavern. When I step in, when I close the door and they look at me, I feel the hatred. Not for me because they have no idea who I am, but for Me, the darkie with balls enough to come inside their lair.

"What the hell you doing in here?" the barkeep asks.

Opening my vest so they can see, I order a shot.

"That a badge?" an old man asks. "Guess they givin' badges to anyone." A few other men—and not a few women—mutter in agreement.

The bartender hands me a shot and I pay him, the coin disappearing into his apron. May not like the color of my skin, but he's damn sure interested in the color of my money.

"I'm looking for a fellow lawman." I don't speak loudly but my voice carries to everyone. "Marshal Brack. I got some troubles in my county, heard he might be able to educate me on how to handle it."

It burns the barkeep that I'm here. I can see it in his body language, in his eyes, hear it in the way he talks to customers, the way they talk to each other. Maybe the man at the piano plays louder. Maybe the couples dance more frenzied. Maybe the two hounds hunkered in the far corner bare their teeth.

Mostly, they're all looking at me.

Just like my family, my neighbors and friends. Just like those first awful days after Doc Henson's pronouncement. Everyone staring, no one with the right word or the right thought. There had been times I would startle awake and realize again, as everyone stood over me as though they were at a dead man's viewing, I was the only one sick; outcast by virtue of ill-health.

Everyone had been unsure, scared more for themselves—for their doubt about their own mortality—than for me or the cancer eating me from my soul out. Except my brother. From across the country, he had acknowledged my cancer, had shaken hands with the uncertainty of what time I had left. He didn't ignore the sickness, he just chose to not let it define us.

"Another, *marshal?*" The barkeep slides his sneer across the word "marshal" until it sits like a pile of horseshit in his mouth. "Gotta drink or get out. This is a drinking establishment, don't allow no loitering."

With a shrug, I order another shot. "Nice little town you have here."

"We aim to keep it that way, too," a woman says. "We got laws here, marshal, and they keep to. Don't matter who you are: the President—" She says it as though there were ever a chance that an American president would come from this pisshole. "Down to Topper."

"A decent old man." I knock back the first shot in a swallow. "He's doing some work for me."

"All that old coot knows how to do is dig graves."

I nod.

The woman clears her throat. "Anyway, we all follow the law."

"Well, that's good," I say. "Guess I'm wondering if I'm breaking one right now. Maybe one has to do with caste."

At home with family in Boston, I was an outcast by dint of being sick, here I am an outcast by virtue of being Negro.

"Marshal or not," the bartender says. "Watch that mouth, boy."

I nod. "I'll be out of your town soon enough. Just need to take care of a little business."

"With Marshal Brack?"

"Sure, that. Had some other business, too." I nod toward the cemetery. "Had to lay some flowers down."

"Whose grave?" the barkeep asks.

"My brother's."

The air thicks up. Might have been tense moments ago but that's nothing compared to now. Sweat covers their faces like late-night rain on Boston's dirty streets and maybe it's heat but maybe it's fear.

The dog squeals then—a screech that fills the air like a tornado storm and reminds me of a man I once heard stabbed in the gut—and I guess the tied man finally got the better of it.

The bartender nods. "Ol' Sherry'll have fresh meat for lunch tomorrow."

Someone laughs but mostly they're quiet. Their knowledge of who I am splits my skin open like a whip against my back. These people, the card sharks and piano man, the dancing girls and fucking girls upstairs, they all understand now who I am.

"Y'all bringing us trouble, y'all get more than you can handle, boy."

"It's *marshal*," the woman said.

"Maybe it's *sheriff*," another man said. "Somebody elect you, boy? You got some county somewhere had enough niggers to elect one'a they own?"

"Cain't be a Texas county," some old man says. "We got enough sense to keep 'em outta here."

"Guess we showed that at Brack's trial, didn't we?" the barkeep says.

They want me to say something, to get angry or violent. But I'm quiet and my silence offends them. It also touches them with a finger of fear as a train slides through town. Maybe this one is Palmer's train. He had gotten himself a porter's job, running east out of San Francisco through Phoenix and Midway to New Orleans. Then northeast toward Boston.

"Making good time stop A few more days I'll be there stop."

He couldn't afford the trip without working the train. Him working the wharves in San Francisco and me, dying in Boston, torn down by pain that clamped itself onto my bones and muscles, by bloody coughing that hadn't let me pass a decent night's sleep in months.

"Have a trial recently?" I ask.

Some of the customers frown, surprised. "Yeah," an old man says. "Ain't that why y'all here?"

"Here to see Marshal Brack. I got some trouble in my county. I want to ask his advice."

The bartender frowns. He doesn't believe me but doesn't know what else to believe. Eventually, after the piano player starts up again, after the dancing begins anew, after the headboards upstairs start banging against the walls again, he shrugs. "Don't know where he at right now. Try him tomorrow morning…at the jail."

"Good enough. I appreciate your help."

I toss Topper's double eagle on the bar and leave. Even with the music and dancing, with the gambling and drinking, even with all the noise, my boots bang against the dirty floor. A shuffling sound, I realize, because I'm limping.

But the sound reminds me of Topper's shovel, biting into the dirt.

Tomorrow.

The world is filled with tomorrows and none are worth a damn, at least for me. Tomorrow has some bit of hope attached. Things will be better tomorrow. I'll have a decent job and a good, solid wife. Tomorrow I'll have my health back or a brand new baby boy or a string of ponies.

Tomorrow I'll see my brother when he steps off that train.

Except all the tomorrows were long since smashed beneath a quiet doctor's words. And seeing Palmer tomorrow—when he gets off that train—had been stolen by two bullets from Marshal Brack's gun.

I leave the horse at the bar, knowing I can't climb up. There is so little strength left in my blood and bones that I torture myself with the thought of not even being able to lift my gun when I find Brack. And I wonder if the smell stalking the dirt streets of this nice little water stop, that rotten meat stink, comes from around me or inside me.

Coughing, bleeding through my mouth, I stop behind a two-story clapboard building. Topper said if Brack wasn't at the bar, he'd be here. Five windows across each floor and all are open. I get a whiff of perfume and of stew, of fresh bread. But I also hear the girls in those rooms and all the cowboys sweating over them.

I hear the violence, too. A slap, flesh against flesh, followed by a woman's moan.

"Why'd you do that?" Hers is a thin voice, full of the same begging and pleading I heard in my own voice after Doc Henson. "No more. I'll be good, Marshal, I promise."

"Damn straight you'll be good."

Then the sting—again—of flesh on flesh. No other sound like it in the world. A man might never have heard the sound before, but the first time he does, he knows it exactly.

Like the tumors. A man might never have had one, might never have seen one, but as soon as it explodes beneath his skin, as soon as it presses against his heart and lungs, he understands fully.

The woman yelps and falls to the floor. Or to the bed. Or against the wall. I don't know exactly.

"Damn right y'all be good...many times as I want."

"Damnit, leave me alone." A scramble, then: "Don't touch me."

Then the moment of her independence is gone, crushed beneath another thump, flesh against quivering flesh.

From other windows: moans and pleas, negotiations, haggles and harsh kisses. A cavalcade of sounds, pinching and boxing my ears. Maybe there are soft sounds, too, whispered 'I love you's,' or promises of marriage, but they're covered by a tinge of possible violence.

A breeze carries the smell to me again. Dry like dirt or rocks, like a man's empty bones. Dry like the desert into which I've ridden, covering—for the moment—the other smell, the stench of sickness that clings to me like melancholia. And beneath all that, at the backdoor of this place, the stench is also stale sweat, dirty clothes, unwashed bodies. It is fetid sex and rancid food with blood as a garnish. It is the stench of booze both to get the women drunk and clean up after the late-night abortions.

I grab the latch, shove against the door. It doesn't move. I push, push some more, and still it doesn't move.

"A little weak tonight, honey?" a woman's voice asks. She opens the door, frowns.

She doesn't expect a Negro.

"We don't serve men like you." Black bruises surround both her eyes, no doubt payment from a customer, and does she see the irony? She will make no money for a few days because of her blackness yet she will refuse my money because of my blackness.

When I flip the eagle toward her, it catches the candlelight, winks at both of us.

"I ain't fucking you for this."

I set a second and third coin on the sideboard next to us. "Still ain't getting none'a me."

"Not the taste I'm looking for. Brack."

Her breath stops, hanging in the hot air between us. Is that what my brother sounded like when he stopped breathing? "He'll kill you."

"Pretty close to dead already."

It takes another coin before she casually holds up four fingers while slipping out the door. Yeah, she gives me the answer I want but come the next hour, when Midway tears itself inside out looking for me, she'll be as indignant and angry, as righteous and blood-thirsty, as everyone else.

Just with a few more coins. Maybe she'll use the money to get out of town, to get back to her parents or her sisters or brothers, to get away from these men. But as I mount the stairs, headed for room four, I see her through the window, handing a dark-skinned Mexican a coin. He shakes his head. She hands over another and he gives her a package wrapped in brown paper.

She's not going back to Mama. She's going to find a dark corner that smells of piss and shit; she's going to spend the next few days believing she is with Mama.

I stop on the stairs, my head light, dancing like a drunken hostess. My hands shake, maybe fear of Brack and maybe the sickness, it's hard to know which. Regardless, my face is quickly covered by a little girl's tears, as it is most every night anymore.

I cry because I am dying. And because Palmer is already dead.

The whore doesn't even look when I enter. Maybe she's used to interruptions, or to multiple customers at once. Whatever, she leans to the side, allowing the man beneath her to see around her breasts and shoulders, allowing the man—the marshal—to see who has come for him.

When Brack sees me, sees a Negro not only in his town but in his lover's suite, anger flashes in his eyes. "Fucking nigg—"

He shoves her to the floor as he stands. He has no badge other than his member standing long and still hard. "What the hell are you doing here, boy? You best turn your ass around, get outta this room, mosey on down the road."

"In a while."

"In a while? You don't get out now, you ain't gonna have a while." His eyes narrow. "You know who I am?"

"I do." My gun pins him to the far wall, opposite side of the room from his Peacemaker, snug and terrible in its brown leather belt, hanging useless on the bedpost. I've no problem with shooting him, though I'd rather do it by hand, close and personal.

"Do you know who I am?" I ask.

"Some fucking idiot, bent on a hard death."

The woman, still pretty in spite of Brack's mileage, nods. "I do."

I frown. "What?"

A thin, pale finger traces a cross on her forehead. "I seen that before. He told me your old Master Thomas did it...in South Carolina. When you were little boys."

"To mark his territory," I say. "Like a dog pissing on a bush."

"Woman, shut the hell up." Brack takes a step, but my gun shoves him back. "Why you smiling? Get that grin off your face, stupid bitch."

She strides to him, her anger making his nothing more than childish petulance. "I told you to leave me alone."

He grins. "Oh, something bad's gotten into you, woman. After I've killed the nigger, I'll get some work done on you, too."

Rather than shrink from his venom, she spits in his face. "I knew you'd get here," she says to me. "Palmer told me." Her eyes cast down to the floor. "Told me you were sick, too."

"I am."

"So was my mother. It killed her slow. She hurt all the time. You?"

I nod.

"She wanted a quick death, but it didn't happen that way."

"Yeah, me, too."

Brack sighed dramatically. "I hate to break up this little... whatever it is. But we got a problem here." He clenched his hands to fists. "Listen to me, boy, you done gone a heap too far. But you shuck-ass outta here now—and I mean right now—I won't kill you."

I ignore him, concentrate on her. "You're the nurse."

With an embarrassed nod, she says, "I hope to be. I like seeing babies born the best." She shrugs. "Don't know why I said that. I was there when Palmer died. He told me all about you. He said you'd come."

"How'd he die?" I ask, something thick and powerfully painful in my throat.

"Shot."

I shake my head. "*How* did he die?"

Understanding flickers into her face. "Died good. Managed to stay alive for three hours. Last things he said were all about you."

"Dying and he's worried about me."

"'Cause you're sick."

Brack nods, understanding now exactly who I am. "The nigger I killed. The train porter." A laugh, severe and brittle, broke through the room. "Y'all cain't do nothing about that, I was acquitted."

"I don't really care about trials."

A corner of his mouth curls like a snake. "You'll care about this: I'm the law."

I let him see the badge. "So am I."

His laugh grows, the sound of a violent summer squall. "Ain't no darkie never been no law." When he smiles, his laugh dead, all I see is teeth, flashing like the dog near the livery. "And no whore ever gonna be a nurse."

"Whereas you're the marshal," I say. "You're in charge."

"Damned right."

"And you got a problem with uppity negroes."

"I got a problem with *all* negroes."

I show him the badge again and after a few long breaths, he stares at me. "Where'd you get that badge, boy?"

"Found it on a dead man." I take a step toward him. I'm not going to shoot him, I want to taste his breath, feel his terror. I want to feel the moment his blood stops.

"My brother, motherfucker. So, tit for tat…I kill, you kill."

At the Midway stop, Brack had tried to barrel his way onto the train without a ticket, tried to push past Palmer. Palmer had refused to let the man on, had, in fact, shoved him to the ground.

"I'm not done killing," I say.

"Me, either." Brack snorts. "Should'a seen his face. No son of a bitch, sure as hell no son of a bitch oughta still be wearing chains, keeps me off the train."

Two shots to Palmer's head and I still don't understand how he survived even for a few hours. Brack's brother didn't fare so well. No extra hours or minutes. Two shots and he was done.

"Since you don't care for trials, we'll just handle this here and now," Brack says. Straightens himself, still naked, takes a step or two toward me. "Just gonna kill you straight out, leave you for the coyotes."

I raise the gun, gently pull back the hammer.

Hesitation, but only long enough for a cough to wrack me, for me to lower my head from the hurt. The gun wavers, as I've always known it would, and he's on me.

No punches, no blows, no kicks. His bear paw wraps around the gun barrel, shoves it down even as he spins me around. Before my cough is over, I'm pinned against the wall, my right arm painfully behind me, my gun useless.

They'd put Brack on trial, these people of Midway. Put him on trial because the circuit judge had demanded it. But then had acquitted him.

"*He weren't nothing but a nigger. They gotta learn to keep their place.*"

"Guess maybe you are done killing," Brack says. His breath is hot, putrid on the back of my neck.

"Son of a bitch," she whispers, standing at the bedpost.

"Looks like you bet on the wrong horse," Brack says to her. "Don't worry, I'll have time enough for you, I'm almost done here."

As am I. I've never wanted it to end here, in a shitty room in the middle of a shitty water-stop. But I can feel it in the air, can smell Topper's freshly turned earth. I'd hoped that earth was turned for Brack, but maybe I was wrong about that.

My legs are weak, as weak as my hands had been trying to pry Palmer out of the dirt. Brack still holding me, I slump, bang my face against the wall. Why resist? It's time to see Palmer.

Instead, there is a shuffle, a scuffle, and Brack slides to the floor behind me.

She stands over him, the tip of his own gun bloody where she laid it against his head. She turns away from me and I take my gun from Brack.

"Are you going to kill him?" she says.

I fire twice, as Brack had done on that train platform. He'd given our family two bullets and now I've given them back.

"They'll lynch you," she says.

I had expected Brack to kill me. No, untrue. I had expected to die on the trail from Boston. I had never expected to make it this far.

"I'm dead already."

"Like my mother."

I nod. "Slow and painful."

In the tiny room, with the moans of the bought all around us, the click of the hammer of Brack's gun is terrifyingly loud. She understands, this woman who has seen both death and life, that she will be the hero, that the town will hold her up as their savior for killing an uppity nigger who killed their beloved marshal.

But she also understands that she can be mine, as well.

It is time to see Palmer.

LUCKY

HARRY SHANNON

J oe Case slept sitting up for three nights running, long Henry rifle across his dirty knees. No fires. He ate dried beef and biscuit at dawn before urging the mare on through the rocks, always moving west. When he finally hit a sudden stretch of flat, grassy ground well before sunset it was a welcome change, but Case didn't think of it as lucky. A man made his own luck. This was likely the edge of someone's spread, and other folks generally meant trouble.

Case got to the edge of a thick clump of Cottonwoods. He stretched, turned in the saddle, and took one last look back at the jagged ridge line. The air smelled of burned metal. A thin spiderweb of lightning tattooed darkening clouds. He saw no sign of the three angry cowboys who wanted him dead. Case had gunned down their friend after a drunken card game. He'd been on the run for more than a week, but the only thing following him now was a steadily weakening storm.

A few seconds later thunder growled and the sky spat. A few thick drops of rain drummed along the brim of his hat. Case rode on, and soon could hear the music of a nearby stream growing wider and deeper as the mountains overflowed. He licked his parched lips.

LUCKY

The mare whinnied softly, smelling that fresh water. Case stopped, patted her head, sat listening to faint wind in the trees, something furry rustling in the tall grass. A 'po will whistled from a clump of manzanita maybe a quarter mile below. Finally another horse answered the thirsty mare. Just one? Thirsty but cautious, Case loosened the Henry, left the tree line and let the mare walk.

The storm hung itself up in the hills like a drunken Mescalero, and for a time just kind of spun in a circle as if unable to decide which way to go. Case was happy to beat it down the hill. The creek was louder now, off to his right. He got to the edge of a thick orchard, dismounted and walked, the horse in between as a shield. He looked around, squinted. The afternoon shadows were lengthening steadily, stroking the damp earth. Sunset was maybe an hour off, tops.

When he entered the darkening trees, Case felt his small hairs flutter, a gut instinct acquired after years of calculated risk. He knew there was no way the cowboys could have gotten around and so far in front of him. If this was a trap, it was someone else. *Apache, maybe?* Case fondled the rifle.

He found the other pony, a gaunt palomino, tied to a dead trunk. She nickered again. Could be she was thirsty. If so, she'd been tied up for a while. He knelt in the dirt and read the ground. Signs of some kind of struggle, boot heels mixed in with bare feet, hooves, some moccasin tracks here and there. No blood.

Case got up, went to the palomino. Eyes on the trees, he loosened the knot and let her go free. She trotted into the brush and he heard her crash down into the stream bed to drink. Case let his own horse go next, and moved away and down. He went flat to have himself a look-see and edged into some mud, rifle ready. Peered over the edge of the bank, looked down.

To the northeast he saw a waterfall that pretty much sealed off that side of the mountain. Then the ridge line he'd come over some time before. Across the stream, woods. He looked south, scanning the banks as his vision shifted. More tracks, a lot of them going back and forth and in and out of the water on the opposite side, but hard to say how many horses from this far off. Case rose a bit, moved his head. Some motion caught his eye and he hunkered down again.

Closer to the bank, a young white woman stood knee-deep in the freezing water. Case couldn't quite take it in at first, but then realized she was busily washing herself between the legs. He crawled closer. Her clothing was torn, and someone had bloodied her a tad. Even from yards away it was plain she had bruises and scrapes. Case watched her for a while. He wanted to be sure she was alone, that he hadn't just stepped in a pile of shit. The sight was easy on his eyes, anyway. He hadn't been with a woman in weeks, and this one had a nice, ripe body.

The horses drank their fill and clopped away to munch grass a bit further down the bank. The woman finally looked and saw her own mount moving, then looked again and jumped back at the sight of a second horse. Something seemed to fill her with terror. She stumbled through the water, sobbing, and moving faster than he would have dreamed possible, came right up the mud and ran into Case, who was just getting up off his knees.

"Easy, lady." Case hadn't said a thing for nearly a week, almost didn't recognize that croak as the sound of his own voice.

The woman started flailing in desperation, not even bothering to scream, or maybe she was already all screamed out. She kicked and scratched, but Case wore trail gloves and long sleeves, so she couldn't hurt him. Not until she went for his weathered face. Scratched him. Then Case wrapped her up and flung her down flat into the wet grass. He fell on top. That made her even crazier, and so Case figured he was going to have to knock her out, but then it hit him to just treat her like a scared animal. He backed away and made a show of lowering his long rifle.

"Ain't fixing to hurt you."

The young woman glared, her fine nostrils flaring. One plump breast peeked through that torn blouse like it wanted to say howdy. Case finally looked down and away. The girl shifted her clothes. He chewed his lip, drew the rifle close as a lover and lowered his voice to a whisper.

"Gone?"

She shook her head briskly, shrugged. *I don't know.*

Case looked around again, listening, and then looked back at the woman. Whispered: "Apache?" Case figured if it was Indians, they were likely still around, and then he had indeed stepped in it.

LUCKY

The woman just stared at him. She was panting for air. Case wasn't much for being a gentleman, so he couldn't help but notice again that she was a real looker. Her red-rimmed eyes were china blue. Finally, she answered in a voice probably gone hoarse from screaming.

"He raped me."

"Who?"

"Chato. Our hired hand."

"Just the one raped you?"

"That's not enough?" She glared. "All you men can all go to hell."

Case smiled, thinly. "Already been there, lady. And I only asked because of all the tracks."

"My husband Robert was here...before it happened. We got in an argument and rode around in a circle yelling. We were both hopping mad."

"He coming back, your husband? This Robert?"

Her eyes narrowed with suspicion. She nodded, briskly. "Any minute, and he'll kill that bastard Chato sure as rain." She was lying.

"Fair enough. You won't be needing me, then." He got up and went down to the water, drank greedily and filled his canteen. The woman moved around as if going toward her own pony. It was silent a full minute too long. Case looked up the bank. The woman was standing there, all alone, holding herself.

"Sir, could I impose on you to stay with me a spell? Just until my nerves settle down?"

Case washed his face and hands in the stream without answering and wondered at his fortune. He closed the canteen, went back up the bank, caught his horse and led it back. He took a bottle of whiskey from his saddle bags, wiped the top and offered her a drink. The woman refused at first, but then accepted. She drank, grimaced, shuddered but took a second pull. Case liked that about her, the toughness. He took a sip himself. The alcohol sparked in his gut.

"My name is Jackson," Case said. The lie came easy.

"Muriel." She licked her lips. "I thank you for the drink, and for your kindness."

Case moved a bit closer, gauged her reaction. She accepted a third shot of whiskey, and by now her features were softening. *A man makes his own luck.* Case smiled, spoke gently.

"Muriel, how long has it been since he passed away?"

Her eyes filled. "I pray you will not hurt me for being honest with you, sir. My poor husband has been dead for nigh on half a year."

"And this Chato, he worked for you?"

"Two years and a bit."

"Well, then." Wind made the nearby trees moan, and a burst of thunder shook the ground. The horses neighed. "Why don't you tell me what really happened?"

Muriel looked away for a long moment. Thunder boomed in the foothills. "Chato tried a few times before. I always said no. He brought some Mexican boys here to help slaughter the lambs. They drank Mescal last night and well into the morning. I got scared and rode out thinking I'd go to town, stay with the preacher and his wife. They followed."

Case watched her talk, the way her body moved. "Go on."

"He raped me, sir. And did so in front of the others. I think it was only him, but I passed out after a while, so I can't be sure. When I woke up they were gone. I was bound, but wiggled free just before you arrived." She looked up and deep into his eyes. "Chato, he'll be back soon for more, I can feel it. Please. Don't let him touch me. Not again. Can you stay here, or maybe follow me into town? I can pay."

Case shrugged. "No offense, Muriel, but this is your trouble on the hoof, and this ain't my business."

She stepped back, trembling. Her eyes cut him into thin slices of jerky. "What kind of man are you?"

"A survivor."

"A pig."

Case sighed and made as if to leave. The woman said: "No."

He looked at her. Muriel's eyes glistened. "I have a good-sized ranch here, sir. And I can make it...worth your while."

Did she mean what she seemed to mean? Case wasn't sure, but his belly tingled. She started to speak again. Case waved his hand for silence. He listened intently. "Someone is coming, riding hard."

"Please, help." Muriel said again, even more urgently. "Stop him."

Hooves. A rider appeared on the ridge line, turned sideways. A big man, hunched over in the saddle. He saw the two of them down below, stared long enough to take it all in and then began to whip his horse. Lightning creased the blue-black sky at his back.

Case weighed the distance to the trees, considered his chances. Meanwhile the rider raced down the slope, came closer and closer. Case felt his pulse quicken. He fondled the Henry, looked at the woman, then back at the approaching man.

"Help me!"

Case jumped back, startled. Muriel was now turning in circles, tearing at her clothes, shrieking in terror. "Help me, please! Kill him!" She glared at Case, back at the rider, back and forth.

The approaching rider drew a gun from his waist and fired. Dust rose not two feet away from Case's left boot. He aimed the Henry without thinking and pulled the trigger. The big gun slammed back into his shoulder BOOM. The horse kept on coming, but now there was nothing but empty leather on his back. Behind him on the ground only dust rising and a pair of worn boots pointing up.

Muriel stopped screaming and sat down in the dirt as if stunned. Case shaded his eyes against the lowering sun to see if the rider was still moving. He wasn't. The empty horse slowed down, cruised to the east and headed for the stream. The woman pointed at the body.

"Is he...dead?"

"Stay here."

Case walked close enough to see the gaping hole in the rider's chest. Gore covered his head and shoulders.

Case returned to the clearing and stared at the exhausted, nearly naked woman. He nodded. Something odd came over her. She seemed more aroused than shocked. Case read seduction in her eyes. He shook his head.

"What kind of a woman are you?"

"Grateful."

She stared, one hand toying with the shredded blouse, as if daring him to take her right then and there, with a dead man cooling not thirty foot off. Case considered that idea, decided it had merit.

"Well, I'll be damned."

He set the Henry down against a flat rock. *What the hell, right?* He undid his belt buckle, feeling a bit foolish, but fully aroused regardless of the circumstances. He got down on one knee, reached for her breast.

The first bullet missed his heart and took him in the left shoulder. The impact knocked Case backwards into the dirt. Then he heard the sound, loud and pretty close by. Case landed on his back with his pants half off and immediately went into shock. The world got silent and slowed down some. He watched Muriel. The woman was back on her feet, screaming again, pointing his way this time. Faint, from very far away, Case heard her saying *shoot him Chato he killed my husband and raped me the murdering son of a bitch kill him Chato kill him please...*

Case saw the squat Mexican now, the one called Chato, and hell, it was just some old man with silver hair. He came from the other side of the orchard, deftly riding bareback on a palomino, aiming his long rifle right at Case's chest. Chato wore moccasins. His brown face was tight as a fist, murderous rage danced in those dark eyes. He was buying her whole story hook, line and sinker.

Case coughed, swallowed blood. She'd seen him coming from over a mile away, had plenty of time to work things out. He tried to speak, to warn the old man about her, because just before Chato blew his head off, it finally hit Case what kind of woman this Muriel was.

The kind who made her own luck.

GOING WHERE THE WIND BLOWS

JAN CHRISTENSEN

It wasn't that she liked whoring. But what else could a gal do? She'd come to San Francisco with a man who'd promised to marry her right after they arrived. He had the temerity to be shot dead in the lobby of the Occidental Hotel where they were staying, quite properly, in separate rooms.

She'd watched it happen, and the scene ran through her mind over and over again. They'd just descended the grand staircase when a man stepped from behind a pillar in the lobby. He was crouched low, so it was hard to see how tall he was. He wore a red bandana across his nose and mouth. He'd shot Bill twice— once in the stomach, and once in the head—then run out the front door. The only other person in the lobby was the room clerk. She'd known right away that Bill was dead, but she pretended to try to help him while she checked his pockets. All empty. The clerk stood in shock. No one chased the gunman.

Soon the sheriff arrived, bent over Bill and pronounced him dead. He'd straightened up slowly, looked her up and down, then led her over to a corner of the lobby were they sat facing each other while he questioned her.

He was one of those skinny men who grows a paunch as they get older. She thought he was perhaps forty. He wore scuffed boots, tan pants with gun holsters on his worn belt, a blue shirt with no collar, a navy vest, and a cowboy hat rimmed with sweat which he held on his knee as they talked.

"Name?"

"Rita Mae Wilson."

"You're new in town. Where you from?"

"Denver."

"Name of the victim was Bill Reynolds. You came to San Francisco with him?"

"Yes. We were going to get married next week." Rita Mae took an embroidered handkerchief from the cuff of her sleeve and dabbed her eyes. She noticed the sheriff wore a gold wedding band.

He gave her a skeptical look. "What was Mr. Reynolds planning to do in San Francisco?"

Well, she couldn't tell the sheriff that Bill and she planned to rob a few banks. *Thou shalt not steal.* Her mother's voice was counterbalanced in her head by Bill's. *But it's so much fun, isn't it?* "We were on vacation," she told the sheriff primly.

"What did Mr. Reynolds do while not on vacation?"

"He was in banking."

"Uh huh." The sheriff pulled an old, worn metal pocket watch from his vest and checked the time. "I'm afraid you'll have to stay in town until I learn more, Miss Wilson. I'll be in touch." He stood and went to talk to the desk clerk.

Bill had held all the money, and none of it was on him. What had happened to it? Until she found out, she was stuck here, stuck whoring, and mad as hell. Almost mad enough to try holding up a bank on her own. But something held her back. Some cautious little voice in her head told her to take it slow, to see if she could recover the money and get the hell out of San Francisco. No one else would hire her. At best, she might bring bad luck, or at worst, they thought she might be a murderess.

Her first client of the evening had not had a bath in who knew how long, his teeth were rotting, and his beard the scratchiest she'd ever felt. At least he didn't want anything kinky. Just straight sex. She took the money he handed her when he'd finished, no tip, she noticed, and was glad to see his back as he left her pathetic little room at the top of the stairs in the whorehouse. Sure, it was the best whorehouse in town, and she had the best room, but it was still pathetic.

After getting dressed, combing her hair and putting on her red high heels, Rita Mae made her way downstairs to the bar.

Miz Halley stood in her usual place behind a tall desk. There were only three other working girls, usually not enough for the number of customers. None were in the bar, so they must be busy. Miz Halley neither smiled nor frowned at Rita Mae, just gave her a slight nod. A short, stout woman, her round face had two chins and the beginnings of a third. Rita Mae found her to be businesslike and practical. No warmth, but no censure, either.

Jimmy gave her his usual hound-dog look, and Rita Mae gave him her usual faint smile, not wanting to encourage him in any way. Without her asking, he poured her a Martinez. Jimmy had stolen the recipe from Jerry Thomas over at the Occidental Hotel. She particularly liked the cherry at the bottom of the glass, nicely coated with the gin and sweet vermouth.

She'd been here a week, and had learned almost nothing about what had happened to Bill. The sheriff wouldn't tell her anything, and the other men tended to cluck her under the chin or pat her on the head when she asked questions. *Ask and it will be given to you; seek and you will find; knock and the door will be opened to you.* Her mother's voice, quoting the Bible, rang in her ears. Well, Rita Mae had asked and asked, but nothing she wanted had been given to her until Bill came along, and now he was dead.

If only she weren't so damned cute. She hated her "button" nose, huge blue eyes, the full lips, and the dark blond hair which had a curly mind of its own. Of course all that and her curvy figure made it easy to ply the whore trade, but no one took her seriously. The education her father had been so insistent she have, and all the reading she'd done all those years, had been of no use in her present situation, nor had it been since her parents died in a carriage accident four years ago, leaving her educated, but penniless.

The place was almost empty, and Rita Mae had almost finished her drink when a rather short, slender man sat down next to her at the bar and ordered a whiskey. Then he turned to her and said, "You look lonely."

She stared at him. That was a new line. Most men weren't looking at her to try to figure out how she might be feeling. Certainly, none of them cared. Of course, it might be because of where she hung out.

She didn't know how to answer him, so she shrugged. But she inspected him under lowered lashes. He had interesting hazel eyes, light brown hair, a slightly crooked nose. And nice lips. Her gaze lingered on those lips, then she looked down at her cocktail.

"You're also new here," he said.

"Got into town about a week ago," she answered. "But I haven't seen you before."

He stared at her, and she realized she'd spoken too boldly, as usual. Avoiding his stare, she took a sip of her Martinez.

"I travel a lot," he said.

"Oh, a drummer?"

"Sort of."

He's lying, she realized, and her guard went up. "What does 'sort of' mean?"

His smile was easy. "It means I sell myself—I'm an actor. Came into town with the Cisco Players. We're doing *Taming of the Shrew.*"

An actor. She'd met a few. Full of themselves and always broke. She returned to her drink, all interest in the man gone.

When she glanced back at him, she saw his puzzled look. Perhaps he was used to women falling all over him. She was too practical for that.

"What brought you to San Francisco?" he asked.

"I came with my fiancé. He met with an unfortunate accident."

"Oh, I'm sorry to hear that. What happened?"

She shrugged. Until she had another customer, she had nothing else to do. She didn't imagine he'd be a customer—he probably got all the women he wanted. "He was shot in the lobby of the Occidental Hotel. You may have heard about it."

"No. Is he all right?"

"He's dead."

His eyes widened slightly, then he looked away from her. "I'm sorry to hear that."

"Yeah. So was I. He had all our money on him, and it's disappeared."

"That's too bad."

The guy was full of platitudes.

"I thought so," she said. "That's why I ended up here."

She watched his face. First he swallowed hard, then he frowned, then he tried to make his face a mask. To cover, he took a sip of his whiskey. Not a great actor. She wondered about that.

"When's the first performance of the play?" she asked.

"Um, Friday night."

"And what part do you play?"

"Um, Petruchio. You know the plot?"

She couldn't hide her surprise. "The lead? Yes, I know the play. Petruchio marries Kate to tame her. It's not clear whether he loves her or not, or just considers marriage a convenience."

"What do you think?"

"Well, I'm a woman, so I think he loves her."

He nodded and signaled Jimmy for another drink. "And that's the way we play it. We think the audience is more satisfied with that interpretation."

Maybe he really was an actor. Maybe he did better on the stage than in real life.

The bar doors swung open and a huge man Rita Mae had never seen before walked in, his footsteps loud on the wooden floor. He stopped just behind Rita Mae and put his hands on her shoulders. "You're new," he said, his voice rumbling in her ear. "Let's go upstairs."

She turned toward him. "Buy me a drink first?"

"I don't work that way," he said. He took his hands off her shoulders and took her arm.

Rita Mae slipped off the barstool. For some reason, she couldn't look at the actor. *I'm not ashamed*, she told herself. She had to do this to survive.

"I'm Jake," the man said as they climbed the stairs. "Been out prospecting, but first thing I do when I get back to town is get a bath, a shave, and a haircut. Next thing I do is come to Miz Halley's for one of her delightful women. Then I have a drink. If you're nice, I'll buy you one. After."

A man who had his own set of priorities. She was thankful he'd had a bath.

She got a better look at him after they entered the room. Seductively, she began to remove her clothing. He stood, arms crossed, leaning against the door. A slow smile crossed his lips when she removed her corset. He was ruggedly handsome, and she suppressed the slight tingle she felt when he let his eyes roam over her body. When she was finished undressing, she sat on the edge of the bed and watched him undress. He placed his gun on the nightstand first, removed his boots and the rest of his clothes and got into bed, pulling her close.

He surprised her when he took her gently, even trying for a bit to arouse her. He gave up soon enough when she didn't respond. When he finished, he rolled off her to lie on his back. She eased herself off the bed and began to get dressed.

"You promised me a drink," she said. She felt thirsty and suddenly very tired.

He grunted.

When she finished dressing she looked at him and saw he'd fallen asleep. She sighed and shook his shoulder.

He came awake with a start and went for his gun on the nightstand. She took a step backward, then said, "It's only me. How about that drink?"

Jake looked at her with bleary eyes. "Sorry. Haven't slept in a bed in so long, forgot how comfortable they are."

He stood up and stretched. He was one hunk of a man, even unaroused. She looked away and went to the vanity to comb her hair. *Stop judging by mere appearances, and make a right judgment. Quiet, Mother.*

She heard Bill's faint laughter in her head, saw his smiling face.

When they arrived downstairs, she was surprised to see the actor still at the bar. He wouldn't look at her when she sat down next to him. His eyes were bloodshot, and his words slurred when he ordered another drink.

She ordered a Martinez again. Jake sat on her other side, and she could feel his body heat.

She turned to him. "Have much luck with the prospecting?" she asked.

"Not lately. Did a couple of years ago, but blew it all on gambling and women. I can feel my luck's about to turn anytime now, though."

That's what they all say, Rita Mae thought.

The sheriff came through the swinging doors, looked around, and approached Rita Mae. She stiffened on the barstool.

"Where's Miz Halley?"

"I...I don't know. Around, I guess. I haven't seen her in a while."

The sheriff looked at Jimmy, who shrugged. The sheriff walked down the back hallway, boot heels loud on the wooden planks. Rita noticed he had new boots, all shiny. Was that snakeskin?

A few minutes later he came back, his skin pale. He wiped his face with a red bandana, stuffed the cloth back into his pocket and walked right over to Rita Mae. "Where you been all evening?" he asked.

"Why, right here, Sheriff. What's wrong?"

"Miz Halley's dead. Shot in the head."

Rita Mae gasped and put her hand over her open mouth. She felt suddenly sick and almost toppled off the barstool. Jake caught her and held her.

Two of the other girls came clattering down the stairs, heads bent together. When they reached the last step they giggled, but stopped abruptly when they saw the sheriff.

He gave them a glum look. "Where have you ladies been?" he asked.

Both hunched their shoulders slightly, and their eyes darted around the bar. "We were upstairs," Lulu said. She had a doll-like face and blond hair which she curled into an intricate fashion. Rita Mae often wondered how she kept it looking so good after all the time she spent in bed.

"Together?" the sheriff asked.

"Yes. Miz Halley gave us the evening off, it being so quiet an' all."

"Miz Halley won't be giving you any more time off. She's dead. Murdered. You know anything about that?" The sheriff leaned casually against the bar but Rita Mae noticed he still looked rather ill. He had everyone's attention, and the room was the quietest Rita Mae had ever heard it.

Jimmy gave the bar a swipe with his cloth and glared. Rita Mae suddenly realized they were all out of jobs. What was she going to do now? With four of them out of work, it was going to be hard to whore somewhere else.

Tinkling laughter broke the silence. At the top of the stairs, Fanny stood with Homer, their arms entwined. Rita Mae had taken an instant dislike to Fanny when they met, and she was pretty sure Fanny felt the same way about her. Homer was a regular who preferred Fanny, but if she was busy, he would go with any available girl. So skinny he looked frail, Rita Mae had felt his strength the one time he'd bedded her. He'd been crude, and she'd had to tap down the sudden flair of hatred she'd felt toward him when he'd grabbed her arms and pinned her to the bed, then kissed her roughly. He'd been rough as he rode her, as well, and she gritted her teeth for a while, but then she said, "Be careful with the merchandise. It's all I've got to survive."

He paused for a moment, then gave a bark of a laugh and continued on as if she hadn't spoken.

As she looked at Homer and Fanny now, she decided they deserved each other.

She almost felt sorry for the sheriff. He looked a bit lost. She saw the effort it took for him to pull himself together. "I want to know where each of you was every minute of this evening," he said, his voice louder than it needed to be.

No one spoke.

He looked at Rita Mae who suddenly wondered if there was a connection between this murder and Bill's. She closed her eyes, rocking on the barstool.

What, after all, did she really know about Bill? Other than he was the most exciting man she'd ever met, and the most handsome? He'd entered the general store in Denver where she was clerking after her parents' death and changed her life. He'd never spoken much about his past, only that he'd been born in Manhattan and that he'd been roaming around the country since he'd turned sixteen. It hadn't taken him long to lure her into helping him with the bank jobs. The excitement gave her an incredible high. She'd known since she was sixteen that her father was a small-time crook who robbed people when the opportunity came along. The rest of the time he tutored rich people's children. Perhaps the thrill of thievery was in her blood. Bill had made her feel more alive than she ever had. A wave of grief coursed through her as she sat in the grimy bar with three whores, their customers, a bartender, the sheriff, and the murdered madam in a nearby room. She shuddered and felt a strong need to flee.

The bar doors crashed open and one of the deputies rushed in, out of breath. "Sheriff, there's a gun-fight down by the corral. You better come quick."

Scowling, the sheriff barked, "No one leave the bar," and ran out with the deputy.

Everyone remained quiet. Glances darted towards the hallway. Rita Mae felt an insistent pull to go see for herself. She climbed down from the barstool and walked toward the doorway leading down the hall. She felt someone behind her, but she didn't bother to look. She stopped abruptly as soon as she could see into the madam's office. Feathers were everywhere. They covered the floor, the desk, and stuck into Miz Halley's hair. As Rita Mae put her hand up to cover her mouth, a feather flew lazily down from a picture frame and landed on Miz Halley's outstretched hand.

"Silenced the bullet," Jake said behind her. She gave a start and bumped into him.

"What?" she asked and turned around. Behind Jake she saw the actor. His eyes were wild-looking.

"Whoever did it used a pillow so no one would hear the shot," Jake explained.

"Oh." She turned back around and studied the room. The madam sat with her head between her arms which were stretched out on the desk. Nothing in the room seemed disturbed except for the pillow and the empty safe, door wide open, in the corner.

No one entered the room. Instead, they turned and walked back to the bar where the others sat and stared at them.

"Not much to see," Jake said. "Whoever did it knew enough to use a pillow to muffle the sound of the gunshot."

One of the other women gasped. The three of them were sitting at one of the booths, Homer squeezed in with Fanny on one side, and Lulu and Lisbeth opposite.

Jimmy was busy behind the bar, mixing a fancy gin drink for the whores and then pouring straight whiskey into a glass for Homer.

Rita Mae's head buzzed. A bit too much liquor, a bit too much lousy sex, and a bit too much murder. She took the same barstool she'd been using since she started work at the whorehouse, put her elbows on the bar and heaved a huge sigh. Jake sat down beside her and ordered a whiskey. Jimmy gave Rita Mae an inquiring look, but she shook her head.

"Who would want to murder Miz Halley?" Rita Mae wondered aloud.

Jimmy stopped wiping a glass. "Makes no sense. We all lose our jobs. She never kept a lot of money here—put it all in the bank every morning. More here in the till than in her office."

"She must have known something," the actor spoke up. "Something someone didn't want anyone else to know. Maybe she was blackmailing someone."

The rest of them looked at him with interest.

"You have personal knowledge of such a thing?" Jake asked.

"No! No, of course not. I just got into town yesterday. I'm just speculating."

But from his manner and tone of voice, Rita Mae had the idea that he knew more than he was saying. She studied him for a moment. He sat loose-jointed, relaxed, on the bar-stool. Perhaps a bit drunk.

"You ever been in San Francisco before?" she asked.

The actor glanced at Jimmy, then looked Rita Mae in the eye. "Nope."

Jimmy stirred behind the bar.

"You know," Rita Mae said sweetly, "you've got to be the worst liar I've ever met. I can't believe you're an actor." She turned quickly to Jimmy. "You've seen him here before, haven't you?"

Jimmy wouldn't look at her. "None of my business. I would never call a customer a liar." He turned his back and fiddled with some bottles on the shelf against the mirror.

"Who are you?" Rita Mae demanded. "I don't even know your name."

"My name is Shane McDaniels."

"Oh," Rita Mae said, her breath coming out in a whoosh. "You're Bill's best friend."

"Was," Shane said, his tone bitter.

"But why didn't you tell me right away?" Rita Mae asked.

"I wasn't sure I could trust you."

"Oh."

"What made you change your mind?" Jake asked.

"Who says I have?"

Rita Mae clutched her throat. "I loved him," she said. "I would never do anything to hurt him." Tears came, bitter and sad and lonely. "I loved him," she whispered.

Jake put his arm around her shoulders. He glared at Shane. "You can tell just by looking at this little lady that she would have nothing to do with murder."

Shane snorted. "You don't look the naive sort. She had a lot to do with bank robbing and whoring. Why not murder?"

Jake stood up, his hand on his gun in its holster. "Watch yourself now."

Shane shook his head. "You gonna defend the little lady's honor?" His tone was so sarcastic that Rita Mae cringed.

She stood up. "Please stop. Stop! Just help me find out who murdered Bill. Maybe the same one who killed Miz Halley."

Jake took his hand away from his gun. Rita Mae could feel the tension in the bar ease. One of the other whores picked up her glass and took a noisy sip. Jimmy poured himself a beer.

"How'd you get the acting gig?" Rita Mae asked McDaniels.

"They were short a player. I'm not that bad." His tone was defensive.

Rita Mae raised her eyebrows at him, then looked around the room. Who killed Bill and Miz Halley? Was it even the same person? And where was the money Bill was carrying?

She turned quickly to Shane. "How'd you know Bill was dead? You came here because you knew, didn't you?"

Shane averted his eyes. "I got a telegram. Unsigned."

"Who did Bill know in San Francisco? I thought he was a stranger here."

"He'd been here a few times," Shane said.

"Oh."

"Used to come in here," Jimmy said with a smirk.

Rita Mae gaped at him. "You never told me that."

"Didn't want to speak ill of the dead." Jimmy gave her an odd look.

"Then he knew Miz Halley," Rita Mae said.

"Knew Miz Halley. Knew all the wimmen here. Knew the sheriff. Sheriff kept an eye on him, didn't trust him."

But when the sheriff had questioned her, he'd acted as if he didn't know who Bill was.

Bill's money gone, and the safe empty in Miz Halley's office. Had Bill asked Miz Halley to hold their money? He wouldn't put it in a bank, of course.

"Knew Miz Halley rather well," Shane said. "She was his mother."

Rita Mae gasped.

"Probably why she took you in. I bet no one else would."

"True," Rita Mae said and turned to Jimmy. "Why didn't you tell me? Why didn't Miz Halley? Bill said he was from Manhattan."

"His father lived there," Shane said. "Probably didn't want to tell you his mother ran a whorehouse."

Rita Mae sat in stunned silence. She and Bill had said how much they had in common—fathers who were thieves, although Bill's did a lot better than Rita Mae's. Housewife mothers. That was a laugh. His a madam, and Rita Mae's a demanding woman who was never satisfied with what she had and used her piousness to cloak her illnature.

Well, what did it matter now? Of course Bill would have asked his mother to hold the money. It had been sitting in her safe all this time. Who else would have known there was a huge amount of money in that safe?

She looked at Jimmy. He didn't seem the type, but you never knew. Bill might have told, or bragged, to Shane. Neither of them had been honest with her.

The three whores had loosened up after a couple of drinks. Their laughter grated on Rita Mae's nerves. Would any of them have known about the money? Rita Mae didn't think Miz Halley would have trusted any of them with that kind of information.

"What else don't I know?" Rita Mae asked.

Jake cleared his throat. "Sheriff and Miz Halley had a thing going."

"What?" The idea of them together made Rita Mae shudder.

Jake laughed. "Strange bedfellows, for sure."

"Isn't the sheriff married?" Rita Mae asked, remembering his wedding ring.

"Thirty-some years," Jake said cheerfully.

Thou shalt not commit adultery. Yeah, Mom, I know. But it wasn't me!

So who was the most likely to know about the big bunch of money in the safe? The sheriff, of course. Miz Halley wouldn't tell her bartender, or her whores.

Shane stirred on his barstool. But Bill might have told Shane.

The bar doors swung open, and the sheriff and his deputy entered. They smelled of horseflesh and sweat.

"Everything okay down at the corral, Sheriff?" Jake asked.

Shaking his head, the sheriff hooked a chair with his foot and sat down heavily. "Sometimes I think liquor should be outlawed," he said.

The deputy sat down opposite his boss. "Couple of beers, Jimmy," he said, grinning at the sheriff.

"Those new boots?" Rita Mae asked the sheriff.

He looked at them proudly. "Yep. Just got them the other day."

"Nice," Rita Mae said. "You get a new watch, too? I see the chain is real shiny."

The sheriff pulled out the pocket watch and held it up for everyone to see. The cover showed an eagle holding a shaft of wheat.

"Pretty," Rita Mae said. "You come into some money, Sheriff?"

Quickly, the sheriff slipped the watch back into his vest pocket and took a sip of his beer. "No. Been saving up for a while."

"I see," Rita Mae said. "Been buying anything else lately?"

The deputy snorted. "Only a new house."

"What?" Rita Mae said. She stood up and walked over to the sheriff. "You took Bill's money, didn't you? I bet Miz Halley gave you some, but you decided you wanted it all."

"That's ridiculous," the sheriff sputtered. "I'm the lawman in this town, and I abide by the law."

"Used to maybe," Rita Mae said. "But you had no compunctions disobeying one of the ten commandments—the one about adultery. Why not another?"

Thou shalt not steal. Rita Mae stared at the sheriff. She herself was a thief, and a whore. Would murder be the next step?

The deputy was a bit slow, but he drew his pistol and pointed it at the sheriff.

GOING WHERE THE WIND BLOWS

The sheriff was a lot faster on the draw. Jake stirred behind Rita Mae, and she glanced back to see him pointing his own gun at the sheriff.

The sheriff changed the position of his aim so his pistol pointed directly at Rita Mae. "No one move, or she gets it," he said. He stood up, the chair crashing behind him. He began to back away, but Rita Mae jumped forward.

"No! You killed my Bill!"

"He was nothing but a low-down thief, and so are you. Not to mention a whore."

Gunfire erupted. Rita Mae heard at least three shots, maybe four. She realized she was falling, but didn't really feel the floor when she landed. Her side hurt. She put her hand over it and felt something sticky, like molasses.

She looked up and saw several faces looking down at her. Jake looked sad. Jimmy, Shane, Homer, and the deputy shocked. The other whores scared. Where was the sheriff? She turned her head to the side and saw him lying in a pool of blood, his eyes staring sightlessly up at the tin ceiling.

Blood. Blood was what she'd felt on her dress, and she knew she was dying. She'd always hated her mother and her fake piousness. But now she realized it had given her mother inner strength. Rita Mae had always just gone where the wind blew. She panicked. She didn't want to die...

Her mother's voice sounded for the last time in her roaring ears.

The wages of sin is death.

Rita Mae let go, and Bill's voice drowned out the other.

Blow with the wind, darlin'. Just blow with the wind.

THE OLD WAYS

ED GORMAN

There had been a gunfight earlier in the evening, but then, in a place like this one, there usually were gunfights earlier. And later, for that matter.

The name of the place was Madame Duprée's and it was one of the big casino-drinking establishments that were filling the most disreputable part of San Francisco in this year of 1903. The Barbary Coast was the name for the entire district and, yes, it was every bit as dangerous as you've heard. Cops, even the young strong ones, would only come down here in fours and sixes, and even then an awful lot of them got killed.

The way I got this job was to get myself good and beaten up and tossed in an alley behind the Madame's. One of her men found me and brought me to her and she asked me if I wanted a job and since I hadn't eaten in three days I said yes and so she put me to work as a floater in her casino. What I did was walk around with a few hundred dollars of Madame Duprée's money in my pockets and pretend to be drunk. Inevitably, rubes would spot me as an easy mark and invite me into one of their poker games. Thanks to a few accoutrements such as a holdout vest and a sleeve holdout, I could pretty much deal myself any cards I wanted to. Eighty-five percent of my winnings went back to Madame Duprée. The rest I kept. Not bad pay for somebody who'd been raised on an Oklahoma reservation and saw three of his brothers and sisters die of tuberculosis before they reached eight years of age. I'd gotten my memory back and wished I hadn't.

What Madame Duprée didn't say—didn't need to say, really— was that an Indian was a perfect mark because he was held to be the lowest form of life in these United States, even below that of Negro and Chinaman. What rube could possibly resist taking money from a drunken Indian? Or, for that matter, what Indian could resist? You saw a lot of red men along the Barbary Coast, men who'd worked or stolen their way into some money and now wanted to spend it the way white men did. The Barbary was about the only place in the land where no distinction was made among the races—if you had the money, you could have anything any other man could have. This included all the white girls, some of whom were as young as thirteen, though this particular summer a wave of various venereal diseases was sweeping the Barbary. More than six hundred people had died so far. A Methodist minister had suggested in one of the local newspapers that the Barbary be set afire with all its "human filth" still in it. I wasn't sure that Jesus would have approved of such a proposal, but then you never could tell.

Tonight's gunfight pretty much started the way they all do in a place like this.

On the ground floor, Madame Duprée's consisted of three large rooms, the walls of which were covered by giant murals of easy women in even easier poses. As you wandered among the sailors, the city councilmen, the crooked cops, the whores, the pickpockets, the professional gamblers, the farmers, the clerks, the disguised ministers and priests and even the occasional rabbi, the slumming socialites, and the sad-eyed fathers looking for their runaway daughters, you found gambling devices of every kind: faro, baffling board, roulette, keno, goose-and-balls, and—well, you get the idea.

Tonight a drunken rube suspected he'd been cheated out of his money. And no doubt he suspected correctly. He got loud and then he got violent and then as he was being escorted out one of the side doors by a giant Negro bouncer with a ruffled white shirt already bloody this early in the evening, he made the worst mistake of all.

He pulled his gun and tried to shoot the bouncer in the side. And the bouncer responded by drawing his own gun and shooting the man's gun away. And then the bouncer threw the man through the side door and went out into the dark alley.

Everybody who worked here knew what was going to happen next. Every bouncer at every major casino in the Barbary had a specialty. Some were especially good with knives and guns, for instance. This man's specialty was his strength. He liked to grab the top of somebody's head with his giant hand and give the head a violent wrench to the left, thereby breaking the neck. I'd seen him do it once and I couldn't get the sight out of my mind for a couple of weeks afterward. The funny thing was he was called Mr. Stevenson because late at night, at a steak house down the street, he read Robert Louis Stevenson stories out loud to anybody who'd listen. Mr. Stevenson told me once, "I was a plantation nigger and my master thought it'd be funny to have a big buck like me know how to read. So he had me educated from the time I was six and a couple of times a week he'd have me come up to the house and read to all his friends and they just couldn't believe I could read the way I did." That gave us something in common. An Oklahoma white man who ran the town next to my reservation put me through two years of college. I probably would have finished except the man dropped straight down dead of a heart attack and his son wasn't anywhere near as generous.

That was how Mr. Stevenson and I were the same, the education. How we were different was his physical strength.

After Mr. Stevenson finished with the rube, I got myself a good cigar and wandered around in my good clothes, weaving a little the way I did to let people know that I was a drunken Indian, and I got pulled into three different games in as many hours. I won a little over four hundred dollars. Madame Duprée would be happy—at least she would be if she'd gotten over her terrible cold, which some of us had come to suspect was maybe something more than a cold. Be funny if one of the owners died of venereal disease the way their girls and their customers did.

Around ten, I saw Mr. Stevenson working his way over to me. He wore his usual attire, a bowler perched at a rakish angle on his big head, his fancy shirt with the celluloid collar, and a sparkling diamond stickpin through his red cravat.

"You catch a drink with me?" he said as he leaned over the table where I was playing.

"Something wrong?"

He nodded. He had solemn brown eyes that hinted at both his intelligence and his anger.

"Five minutes."

"You know that coon?" one of the rubes said after Mr. Stevenson had left.

"Met him a little earlier. Why?"

The rube shook his head. "Scares the piss out of me, he does. I heard about how he snaps them necks." He shuddered. "Back in Nebraska, you just don't see things like that."

I finished the hand and then joined Mr. Stevenson at the bar. As always, he drank tea. He took his job very seriously and he didn't want whiskey to make him careless.

I didn't much worry about things like that. I had a shot of rye with a beer back.

"What's up, Mr. Stevenson?"

"Moira."

"Oh."

There was a group of reservation Indians who had collected in the Barbary over the past two years or so. Maybe a dozen of us, all employed in various capacities by the casinos. One was a very beautiful Indian girl who'd been called "Moira" by the Indian agent where she'd grown up. Mr. Stevenson was sweet on her, and in a terrible way. He'd go through periods where he couldn't sleep; you'd see him standing in front of her cheap hotel, staring up at her window, doing some kind of sad sentry duty. Or you'd see him following her. Or you'd see him sitting alone in a coffeehouse all teary-eyed and glum and you knew who he was thinking about. Or I did, anyways. I'd gone through the same thing with Moira myself. I'd been in bitter love with her for nearly a year but then I'd passed through it. Like a fever.

Not that you could blame Moira. She was as captivated by another reservation Indian named Two Eagle as we were captivated by her. Did all the same things we did with her. Followed him around. Bought him gifts he didn't want. Wrote him pleading little notes.

Then they got a place and moved in together. Moira and Two Eagle, but word was things weren't going well. He was one of those

Indians too fond of the bottle and too bitter toward the white man to function well. Kept a drum up in his room and sometimes in the middle of the night you'd hear it, a tom-tom here in the center of the Barbary, and him yowling ancient Indian war cries and chants. He was fierce, Two Eagle, and he seemed to hate me especially, seemed to think that I had no pride in my red skin or my ancestors. I returned the favor, thinking he was pretty much of a melodramatic asshole. I was just as much an Indian as he was. I just kept it to myself was all.

Only time I ever liked him was one night when I ran into him and Moira in a Barbary restaurant, real late it was, and Two Eagle gentle drunk on wine, and him telling her in great excited rushes about the old religions of ours, and how only the red man—of all the earth's peoples—understood that sky and sun and the winds were all part of the Great God spirit—and how a man or woman who knew how to truly speak to God could then address all living creatures on the earth, be they elk or horse or great mountain eagle, for all things and all creatures are God's, and thus all things in the world, seen and unseen alike, are indivisible, and of God. And he spoke with such passion and sweep and majesty that I could see tears in his eyes—and I felt tears in my own eyes…and I saw that there was a good side to his belligerent clinging to the old ways. But his bad side…

Moira liked white-man things. Back when she'd let me take her to supper a few times, we'd gone for a long carriage ride by the bay and she'd enjoyed it. Then we went up where the fancy shops were. She made a lot of little-girl sounds, pleased and cute and dreamy.

This was the part of her Two Eagle hated. By now he'd got her to dress in deerskin instead of cloth dresses, her shining black hair in pigtails instead of tumbling tresses, her face innocent of the "whore paint," as he pontifically called it. He worked as a bouncer in a place so tough it might have given Mr. Stevenson pause, and she worked behind the bar in the same place. Pity the man who got drunk and started sweet-talking Moira. Two Eagle would drag him outside and make the man plead for a quick death.

Now that I was over Moira, I didn't especially like hearing about either of them. But you couldn't say the same for Mr. Stevenson. He was as aggrieved as ever, all pain and dashed hope.

"She went out on him."

"Oh, bullshit."

"True," he said. "Few nights ago. They got into a bad fight and he kicked her in the stomach. He didn't know she was just startin' to carry a baby. Killed the baby and nearly killed Moira, too."

"The sonofabitch. Somebody should kill that bastard."

"You haven't heard the rest of it."

"I'm not sure I want to."

"He wants to cut her."

"Cut her?"

"The old ways, he says. What the Indians used to do back when I was on the plantation. When a woman went out on a man like that. You know—her nose."

"That's crazy. Nobody does that shit anymore."

"He does. Or at least he says he does. You know how he is. All that warrior bullshit he gets into."

"Where's Moira?"

"That's the worst part. She thinks she's got it coming. She's just waitin' in her room for him to come up and cut her. Says she believes in the old ways, too."

I shook my head. "That sounds like Moira." I took my pocket watch from my breeches. "I've got some time off coming. I can tell Madame Duprée I'm going for the rest of the night."

"You're tough, man, but you aren't that tough. Two Eagle'll kill you." He showed me his hands. How big they were. And strong. And black. "Fucker tries to cut her, I'll take care of him." He nodded to the front door, his bowler perched at a precarious angle. Sometimes I wondered if he had it glued to his bald head. "Let's go."

We went.

Making our way along the board sidewalks this time of night meant stepping over corpses, drunks, and reeking puddles of vomit and blood from various fights. Every important casino had a band of its own, which meant that the noise was as bad as the odors.

It was raining, which meant the boards were slick. But we walked fast, anyways. Two Eagle had a couple of rooms on the second floor of a livery stable. Moira lived there, too. She'd waited a long time for him to marry her. I figured she'd wait a lot longer.

A drunken rube made a crack about Mr. Stevenson, but if the black man heard, he didn't let on. Just kept walking. Real quiet and real intense. Like he had only one thought in the entire world and everything else just got in the way. Moira can make you like that.

The Barbary looked pretty much as usual, a jumble of cheap clothing stores for drunken sailors, dance halls where the girls were practically naked, and signs that advertised every kind of whore anybody could ever want. There was a new one this month, a mulatto who went over four hundred pounds, and a lot of Barbary regulars were giving her a try just to see what it'd be like, a lady so fat.

Half a block away you could smell the sweet hay and the sour horseshit in the rain and the night. Closer, you could hear the horses roll against their stalls, making small nervous sounds as they dreamed.

We went up a long stretch of outside stairs. The two-by-fours were new and smelled of sawn wood, tangy as autumn apples on a back porch.

Stevenson didn't knock. He just kicked the door in and stepped over the threshold. The walls inside were stained and the floors so scuffed the wood was slivery. She'd put up new red curtains that were supposed to make the shabby room a home but all the curtains did was make everything else look even older and uglier.

Moira, sad beautiful Indian child that she was, sat in a corner with her head on her knees. When she looked up, her black eyes glistened in the lantern light. She wore a deerskin dress and moccasins. The walls were covered with the lances and shields and knives and arrows of Two Eagle's tribe. He liked to smoke opium up here and tell dream-stories about ancient days when the medicine men said that the bravest warriors had horses that could fly. But the toys on the wall looked dulled and dusty and drab. Every couple of weeks he had his little group of Barbary-area Indians up here, Moira had told me once. The last stand, I'd remarked sarcastically. But she hadn't found it funny at all.

"This is crazy shit, Moira," I said. "We're gonna get you out of here before he comes back."

She had wrists and ankles so delicate they could make you cry. She stood up in her red skin, no more than ninety pounds and five feet she was, and walked over to Mr. Stevenson and said, "You don't have no goddamn right to come here, Mr. Stevenson. Or you either," she said to me. "What happens between Two Eagle and me is our business."

"You ever seen a woman who's been cut?" I said. I had. The man always took the nose, the same thing the ancient Egyptians had taken, just sawed it right off the face, so that only a dark and bloody hole was left. No brave ever wanted a woman who'd been cut, so many of the women went into the forest to live. A few even drank poisoned wine to end it quickly.

She looked at Mr. Stevenson. "We don't have no whiskey left."

"So the nigger goes and fetches you some, huh?" he said in his deep and bitter voice.

"I need to talk to Jimmy here, Mr. Stevenson, that's all. Just ten minutes or so."

He brought up his big murderous hands and looked at them as if he wasn't quite sure what they were.

"Rye?" he said.

She smiled and was even more beautiful. "Thanks for remembering. I'll get some money from Two Eagle and pay you back."

"I don't want any of his money," Mr. Stevenson said, and fixed her with his melancholy gaze. "I just want you."

"Oh, Mr. Stevenson," she said, and gently touched her small hand to his wide, hard chin. Sisterly, I guess you'd say. She was like that with every man but Two Eagle.

"You don't let him lay a hand on her," Mr. Stevenson said to me as he crossed the room to the door.

I brought up my Colt. "Don't worry, Mr. Stevenson."

He glanced at her one more time, sad and loving and scared and obviously baffled by his own tumultuous feelings, and then he left.

"Poor Mr. Stevenson."

"He's a decent man," I said.

"Kinda scary, though."

"Not any more so than Two Eagle."

"I just wished he understood how I felt about Two Eagle."

"Maybe he finds it kind of hard to understand a man who kicks a woman so hard she loses the baby she's carrying—and then wants to cut her nose off."

"He didn't mean to kick me that hard. He was real sorry. He cried when he saw—the baby."

I went over to the window and looked out on the Barbary Coast. One of the local editorial writers had estimated that a man was robbed every five minutes in the Barbary. At least when it rained, it didn't smell so bad.

I turned back to her. "I want to put you on a train tonight. For Denver. There's one that leaves in an hour and a half."

"I don't want to go."

"You know what he's gonna do to you."

Her eyes suddenly filled. She padded back to her corner and sat down and put her head on her knees and wept quietly.

I went over and sat down next to her and stroked her head as she cried.

After a time she looked up, her cheeks streaky with warm tears that I wiped away with my knuckles.

"He caught me."

"It's not something I want to hear about."

"I was so mad at him—with the baby and everything—that I just went out and got drunk. Didn't even know who I was with or where I was."

"Moira, I really don't want to hear."

"So he came looking for me. Took him all night. And you know where he found me?"

I sighed. She was going to tell me anyways.

"Up in some white sailors' room. There were two of them. One of them was inside me when he came through the door and found me."

I didn't say anything. Neither did she. Not for a long time.

"You know what was funny, Jimmy?"

"What?"

"He didn't hurt either one of them. Didn't lay a hand on them. Just stood there staring at me. And the guy, well, he pulled out and picked up his clothes and got out of there real fast with his friend. It was their own room, too. That's what was real funny. By then, I was sober. I tried to cover myself up but I couldn't find my clothes, so I went over and held Two Eagle just like he was my little boy, and then he started crying. I'd never heard him cry before. It was like he didn't know how. And then I got him over to the bed and I tried to make love to him but he couldn't. And he hasn't been able to since it happened, almost a week now. He's not a man anymore. That's what he said to me. He said that he can't be a man ever again after what he saw. And it's my fault, Jimmy. It's all my fault."

I wanted to hate him, or her, or myself, I wanted to hate some-goddamned-body, but I couldn't. It was just sad human shit and at the moment it overwhelmed me, left me ice cold and confused. People are so goddamned confusing sometimes.

She laughed. "You and Mr. Stevenson must have some conversations about us, Jimmy."

I stood up, reached back down, and took her wrist. "C'mon now, I'm taking you to the train."

"You ain't takin' her nowhere."

A harsh, quick voice from behind me in the doorway. When I turned I was looking into Two Eagle's insane dark eyes. I'd never seen him when he didn't look angry, when he didn't look ready for blood. He wore a piece of leather tied around his head, his rough black hair touching his shoulders, his gaunt cheeks crosshatched with myriad knife slashes. His buckskin outfit gave him the kind of Indian ferocity he wanted.

He came into the room.

"Why can't you be true to our ancestors for once, Jimmy?" he said, pointing his Colt right at my head. "Cutting her is the only thing I can do. Even Moira agrees. So why should you try to stop it? It's our blood, Jimmy, our tribal way."

"I don't want you to cut her."

His hard face smiled. "You gonna stop me, Jimmy?"

He expected me to be afraid of him and I was. But that didn't mean I wouldn't shoot him if I had to.

And then Mr. Stevenson was in the doorway.

Moira made a female sound in her throat. Two Eagle followed my gaze over his shoulder to the huge black man in the doorframe.

"You're smart to have him around, Jimmy. You'll need him."

Mr. Stevenson came into the room carrying a bottle of rotgut rye in one hand and a single rose in the other. He carried the flower to Moira and gave it to her. Then, without any warning, he turned around and backhanded Two Eagle so hard the Indian's feet left the floor and he flew backwards into the wall. The entire room shook.

Mr. Stevenson wasn't going to bother with any preliminaries.

He went right for Two Eagle, who was trying to right his vision and his breathing and his ability to stand up straight. He'd struck his head hard when he'd collided with the wall and he looked disoriented. Bright red blood ran from his nostrils.

Mr. Stevenson grabbed him and it was easy to see what he was going to do. Maybe he thought that this would ultimately give him his first real chance with Moira, killing Two Eagle by snapping his neck.

"No!" I shouted.

And dove on Mr. Stevenson's back, trying to pull him off Two Eagle.

But it was no use. I clung to Mr. Stevenson like a child. I could not even budge him.

By now he had his hands in place, one on top of Two Eagle's head, the other on the bottom of his neck—ready for the single wrench that would kill Two Eagle.

Two Eagle used fists, feet, even his teeth to get free, but Mr. Stevenson paid no attention. He was setting himself to perform his most magnificent act...

Moira shot him once in the side and then raised the gun and shot him once on top of the head. His scalp flew off and affixed to the wall by pieces of sticky flesh and bone.

The funny thing was, he kept right on going, as if he refused to acknowledge what Moira had done to him.

Getting ready to snap Two Eagle's neck—

And then she ran closer, shrieking, and shot him again, and this time not even Mr. Stevenson could refuse to acknowledge what had happened. Blood poured from his ears.

An enraged Two Eagle was now able to bring his hands up and seize Mr. Stevenson's throat, holding tight, choking him, as the big black fell over backwards, Two Eagle riding him down to the floor and then grabbing the gun from Moira's hand.

Two Eagle put the barrel of the .45 to Mr. Stevenson's forehead and fired three times. Didn't seem to matter to him that Mr. Stevenson had died a little while ago.

With each shot, Mr. Stevenson's head jerked upward from the coarse board floor and then slapped back down.

Two Eagle was calling him nigger and a lot of other things in our native tongue.

Then he was done, Two Eagle, pitching forward and lying facedown on the floor, very still for a long time.

I got up and straightened my clothes and picked up my gun from the floor where it had fallen when I'd jumped on Mr. Stevenson.

Moira said, "You two shouldn't have come up here."

"I guess not." I nodded to Mr. Stevenson. "He was trying to help you was all."

"It wasn't none of his business and it ain't none of yours, either."

"I guess he didn't see it that way. Seeing's he loved you and all."

"A nigger," Two Eagle said, getting up from the floor suddenly. "A nigger, lovin' Moira. Maybe you think that's all right, Jimmy, but then you gave up bein' a true man a long time back."

And then he went for me. Couldn't help himself. He still had all this fury and it had to light somewhere.

So he came at me, but he was stupid because he didn't look at my hand.

I felt his powerful arm wrap around my neck. I smelled his sweat and whiskey and tobacco.

He pushed me back against the wall.

And that was when I raised my Colt and put it directly to his ribs and fired three times.

He was dead before he hit the floor.

She was screaming, Moira was. That was about all I can tell you about my last few minutes in the room. She was screaming and Two Eagle had fallen close by Mr. Stevenson and then I was running. That's about all I can remember.

Then there was the night and the rain and I was running and running and running and tripping and falling and hurting myself bad but no matter how far or how fast I ran, I could still hear Moira screaming.

WEEK LATER IT was.

I was back doing my nightly turn at Madame Duprée's, winning upwards of five hundred dollars this particular night, when I saw Lone Deer come in the side door by the faro layout.

She looked frantic. I figured it was me she wanted.

Being's as we were waiting for some liquid refreshments at our table, I got up and went over to her.

When I reached her, she said, "She's goin', Jimmy. Leavin' us. Twenty-five minutes, her train leaves. I didn't find out till half an hour ago myself. Thought I'd better tell you."

"I appreciate it."

I suppose, like Mr. Stevenson, I'd had the idle dream that Moira and I would be lovers now that Two Eagle was gone. I didn't have to worry about any recriminations from the law getting in my way. A dead nigger and a dead Injun on the Barbary Coast don't exactly turn out a lot of curious cops. They're just two more slabs down at the morgue.

I figured I'd give it a few weeks and then go see her, tell her how what I did was the only thing I known to do—kill him to save my own life. And then I'd gentlelike invite her out for some dinner and...

But that wasn't to be. Not now.

Moira was leaving.

"You'd better hurry," Lone Deer said. And then took my arm and drew me closer. "There's something else I need to tell you."

LESS THAN TWO minutes later I was running toward the depot. It was crowded and the conductor walked up and down all pompous as he consulted his railroad watch and shouted out that there were only a few minutes left before this particular train pulled out.

I found her in the very back of the last coach. The car was barely half full and she looked small and isolated there with the seats so much taller than she was. Moira. She'd always be a child.

I dropped into the seat next to her and said, "Lone Deer told me what you did."

"I wish she wouldn't have. I didn't want nobody to see me off."

"I love you, Moira."

"I don't want to hear that. Not with Two Eagle barely a week dead. Didn't I betray him enough?"

I'd seen the soldiers drag my grandfather from the reservation one day when I was very young. They were taking him to a federal penitentiary where he would die less than two months later at the hands of some angry white prisoners. I could still feel my panic that day—panic and terror and a sense that my own life was ending, too.

That's how I felt now, with Moira.

"But I won't betray him no more," Moira said. "You can bet on that."

"Is that why you did it?"

"Why I did it is none of your business."

I looked at her there in her black mourning dress and black mourning hat and black mourning veil, a veil so heavy you couldn't make out anything on the other side.

"No man'll ever want to bother me again. I made sure of that."

I was tempted to lift the veil quickly and see what she looked like. Lone Deer had said that Moira had used a butcher knife on her nose and that nothing remained but a bloody hole.

But then I decided that I didn't want to remember her that way. That I always wanted her to be young and beautiful Moira in my mind. Every man needs something to believe in, even if he knows it's not true.

"You got a ticket, buck?" the conductor asked me. Ordinarily, I'd take exception to his calling me "buck," but at the moment it just didn't seem very important.

I leaned over and kissed Moira, pressing her veil to her cheek. I still couldn't see anything.

"Hurry up, buck. You get your ass off of here or you show me a ticket."

I squeezed her hand. "I love you, Moira. And I always will."

And then I was gone, and the train was pulling out, all steam and power and majesty in the western night.

Then I walked slowly back to Madame Duprée's where I got just as drunk as Indians are supposed to get.

IN SOME COUNTRIES

JERRY RAINE

The day's work was over and the sun was sinking on the horizon. Inside the kitchen Woody Granger was eating supper on his own. He usually ate with the Cutter family but he'd been late coming back from the field where he'd been fixing fences all day and the family was next door in the living room playing cards. Woody preferred eating on his own though. He wasn't much of a conversationalist. Never had been, never would be. He was a sixteen-year-old orphan drifting through Tennessee, getting work where he could.

He finished his cup of coffee and carried his dishes to the sink. The living room door opened and Harold Cutter came in. He was a large red-faced man with thick hairy arms and a belly that hung over the belt of his jeans. Woody was a bit scared of him because he could never tell what kind of mood his employer would be in. Sometimes they would joke together, and other times, when either the work was too hard or the sun too hot, they would nearly come to blows.

"Do you want to come with me tonight, Woody?" Harold asked, as he made his way to the pantry.

IN SOME COUNTRIES

Finishing his dishes, Woody said over his shoulder "Okay," when he really wanted to be going back to his room.

Harold came out of the pantry carrying a bucket with a chopper and two large knives inside. Woody's heart dipped. He dried his hands and Harold pointed to a lantern that was sitting on the table. "Carry please," he said, then they walked out into the yard.

At the sound of the screen-door slamming, six dogs sprang out from under bushes and chairs and came running towards their master with heads bowed low and tails wagging. Woody smiled at them and patted Mickey, the eldest.

"Are we taking the horses?" Woody asked.

"No, we'll walk," Harold said. "The sheep are only in the home paddock."

Woody was disappointed. He always liked riding, especially at night. He walked alongside Harold and threw sticks for the dogs. His favorite was Snowy, who was in fact black. He also had a soft spot for Skunk, a grey and white streaked dog who was permanently chained at the back of the house. Skunk was a sheep killer and was very rarely let off his leash.

Ten minutes later and they were at the home paddock. Harold unlocked the gate and they all went through, the dogs getting excited when they saw the hundred or so sheep in the distance.

They walked to a large tree in the centre of the field. The tree had no leaves and the branches were wrinkled and crooked like the fingers of an old man. Hanging from one of the branches was a large hook and the bottom of the trunk was stained with dried blood. Harold left his bucket by the tree and called out to the dogs.

"Get back! Get back! Fetch 'em up! Fetch 'em up!"

The dogs ran towards the herd, some going right and some going left. They got right behind the sheep and barked at them and nipped their legs. The herd moved slowly forward.

Harold and Woody waited by the tree. The sun was almost down and soon it would be dark. Woody lit the lantern and hung it from a branch.

"Just watch what I do this time," Harold said, "and next time you can have a go yourself. Just give me the knives when I tell you."

Woody had only been working on the farm for six months. He'd been down on his luck, sitting in a bar in town, wondering where to go to next, when he'd overheard a conversation about work. He'd walked the five miles to the Kerren Ranch and started work straight away. He was the only person the Cutters employed.

Woody watched as the sheep came nearer and soon they were surrounding the tree with no escape, the dogs keeping them in a neat circle.

Harold walked into the middle of them still calling to the dogs, but not so loudly now. He pushed and prodded, looking for the right sheep, then grabbed one round the neck and dragged it over to the tree.

"Okay Woody," he said.

Woody took one of the large carving knives from the bucket and gave it to him. Harold had the sheep lying backwards between his legs with his strong hands around its neck. He took the knife and started cutting into its throat. It made a crunching noise as it cut through the main arteries and Woody winced as he saw the blood coming out. It ran dark red down the sheep's stomach and then as the knife went deeper it started to bubble in the deep cut and now and then a small fountain would squirt on to the ground. The sheep's eyes stayed open for what seemed like a long time and then they shut and Harold let the body fall. It lay on the ground with the blood spreading into the ground, and then its back legs twitched and the animal was still.

Harold wiped his bloody hands on a tuft of grass and went back to find another sheep. He killed this one the same way and then he told the dogs to back away. The sheep slowly wandered back to where they had been before, minus their two friends that lay at the foot of the tree.

Woody watched Harold go to work on the sheep. His arms were now covered with blood as he chopped off the two heads. Then he skinned the two animals by slitting open their bellies. The dogs were sniffing and looking anxious, eager for the innards that Harold would eventually give them.

"Give me a hand here, Woody," Harold said. Together they lifted the first sheep and hung it upside down from the hanging hook. Woody turned away from the smell as Harold cut out the stomach, bright green chewed grass falling from a split. He threw it to the dogs along with the intestines. The dogs gathered around hungrily and ripped the flesh to bits. Woody was disappointed to see Snowy joining in the fun.

IN SOME COUNTRIES

Harold continued cleaning out the carcass and took it off the hook and laid it out on an old rug that was lying behind the tree. Then they hooked up the second sheep and Harold went to work again.

"It's pretty easy," he said, "once you get used to the smell. The smell's the worst bit."

"Yeah, it doesn't smell too good," Woody said.

They took down the second sheep when the carcass was clean and placed it alongside the other one on the rug. They also placed the two skins on there. Although they were bloody and dirty they would be put on the shed roof and later on when they were dried out and stiff, they would be sold.

They each took a corner of the rug and started pulling it and the sheep back toward the farm. It was slow going and Harold kept shouting at the dogs to move away as they were now getting interested in the good meat.

"I usually just kill one sheep," Harold said, "but with you here I can pull an extra one back. When we've eaten this lot I'll let you kill the next two."

Great, Woody thought to himself. *I'll be looking forward to that.*

When they were back at the farm they lifted the carcasses onto one of the water tanks where they would be out of reach of the dogs. They would stay there until morning when Harold would cut them into smaller chunks and his wife Molly would then put them into storage.

From a tap in the garden the two of them washed their hands and shook them dry. They stood in the kitchen light that came across the veranda. The dogs had crept back to their bushes and chairs to sleep.

"You can knock off now, Woody," said Harold. "I'll see you in the morning."

Woody said okay, and tried to smile, but the dead sheep smell was still with him. Harold sensed how he was feeling and grinned.

"You'll get used to it," he said, and patted him on the back.

Woody went back to his room, but before he reached it, he doubled over and puked in the bushes outside.

The next day Woody was back in the field fixing fences again. He was wearing a hat to keep the sun off his face. Just last year, on one of the other farms he'd worked, he'd been digging a ditch all day and telling the time by looking at the sun. When he'd returned to his lodgings he'd had a terrible pain in his eyes, like someone had thrown sand in them. Much to the amusement of the other workers he'd spent the whole of the next day lying in a darkened room. They'd told him he had sunstroke. Eventually the pain had disappeared, but he'd learned his lesson.

At lunchtime, Woody saw a horse approaching, and as it came nearer, he was pleased to see the rider was Harold's daughter, Jane. She was fifteen years old, pretty, with long blonde hair. She climbed down off her small horse, and carried over a bag lunch for him.

"Hello," Woody said shyly. "How are you?"

"Fine Woody," said Jane. "Have you recovered from last night?"

Woody decided to play it dumb. "Recovered from what?"

Jane handed him the bag of food. She was wearing a white dress with a flower pattern on it, a straw hat on her head. "The killing of the sheep. I heard you puking after."

Woody felt embarrassed. Jane's room was just behind his. He shrugged. "So I puked. So what?"

"You'll never be a farmer if you can't kill a sheep."

"Who says I want to be a farmer?"

"What are you doing here if you don't want to be a farmer?"

"I need the money. When I've saved a bit, I'll do something else. Like maybe rustle cattle. Or rob trains."

Jane laughed. "Just keep dreaming Woody. We all need our dreams. I have to get back. My dad said to come straight home."

Woody watched Jane walk back to her horse and climb on. He looked down at the lunch bag and started opening it.

"Woody?"

He looked up and Jane was sitting on her horse. Only now she had her skirt pulled high up on her thigh and she was rubbing her leg. "Do you think I have nice legs?" she asked.

Woody was so shocked he didn't know what to say.

IN SOME COUNTRIES

"If you kill a sheep for me, Woody, I'll let you see more," and then her dress fell back into place and she was riding away.

Woody was stunned. He looked at Jane until she was almost out of sight. Then he looked down at his lunch bag but he didn't feel so hungry anymore.

Woody kept thinking about Jane's leg for the rest of the day. What did she mean exactly by saying she'd let him see more? Was she going to let him go the whole way? He was still a virgin and wasn't sure he knew exactly what to do. Maybe he should just forget the whole thing. Maybe she was just leading him on. And what did she mean by "kill a sheep for me"? Was this some kind of test of his manliness? Or was she trying to lead him into trouble.

Woody worked hard on the fence and then started walking home. At the dinner table that night he couldn't keep his eyes off Jane. She kept smiling at him and even winked one time. Her younger brother Billy did most of the talking, so Harold and Molly were easily distracted.

When the dishes were done Woody went back to his room. Evening times always passed slowly. His room was only big enough for a bed and a wardrobe and was right next to the back veranda. On the other side of the veranda was the washer room, and several times he had watched Jane in there, washing clothes in the sink.

He still thought of her words. "Kill a sheep for me." What was that meant to mean? Was he meant to bring the body back to her room and lay it out in front of her? What kind of sick person was she? Or would just the head be enough? Bring me the head of a sheep and I'll let you see my body. He wished she'd been clearer in her intentions. He lay on his bed and looked at the ceiling.

After an hour of turmoil he could wait no longer. He left his room and edged round to the veranda. He crept on to it and looked into the kitchen. It was empty. He eased open the screen-door and crept into the pantry. He took a large knife and slid it under his shirt. Then he crept outside.

His heart was pounding with excitement as he made the short walk to the home paddock, the carving knife now stuck down the belt of his jeans. He had decided to kill a sheep and bring the head to Jane. Then she would show him her body. Then he would see what would happen next. He quickened his pace.

He found the herd easily, a grey moving shape in the dark. He walked slowly up to them, but they heard him coming and moved away. He tried running at them but they ran away, faster than he'd thought they could be. He stopped to catch his breath. He tried again. They ran away again.

It took him ten minutes to finally catch one, and he was so angry and frustrated he just plunged the knife straight into the sheep's chest. It seemed to have little effect, so he stabbed it in the neck and then stabbed it again. Eventually the bleating animal was still.

Woody sat on the grass next to it, catching his breath. Sweat was pouring off him and he was covered in blood. He looked at the sheep and immediately felt guilty. Why was he doing this? Taking away a life just so he could see Jane naked? He felt the same revulsion he'd felt last night. He felt his supper starting to come into his throat. He moved away from the sheep and sat down again. Then he lay on the grass and looked at the stars. He waited until he'd cooled down. There was no way he could cut off the sheep's head. He would just make his way home and forget the whole thing. He would have to throw his bloodstained clothes away.

He left the sheep where it lay. When Harold found it tomorrow maybe he would think a wolf had done it. Woody left the paddock and made the walk home, the knife stuck down into the belt of his jeans once again.

He approached his room from the privy side, where no one could see him. He walked on the path where Skunk was tied up, but as he approached, Skunk began to growl.

"It's only me Skunk," Woody said softly.

But then Skunk barked loudly and ran straight for him, his chain rattling as it took up the strain. Woody took a step backwards and then Skunk made another charge. This time, to Woody's horror, the chain broke and Skunk was on top of him. He wrestled with the dog as it went for his throat. Skunk was going berserk and Woody didn't know why. He thought that maybe it was the smell of the sheep's blood. Then he remembered the knife in his belt. He managed to get it free and he slammed it into Skunk's side. The dog whimpered and fell off him on to the dirt. Then Woody passed out.

When he came to, Woody didn't know where he was. He was lying on his back on something hard and he didn't recognize the ceiling. He turned his head and looked around. A sofa and some armchairs. A chest of drawers. A cabinet for plates and cutlery. He was in Harold's living room.

He was lying on a table. He had an incredible pain in his left arm. He looked down and wondered if he was imagining things. He looked down again. His left arm was covered in a white bandage but it was much shorter than it used to be. He tried to wriggle his fingers but he didn't seem to have any. His hand just wasn't there anymore.

Feeling a panic sweep over him he rolled off the table and put his feet on the floor. He held his two arms out in front of him but the left one was nearly a foot shorter.

"NO!" he screamed, and staggered out of the room.

He was in his own room now. Sedated.

He stayed there for a week while the pain in his arm lessened and his neck healed. But he wasn't too worried about his neck, he was worried about his missing hand. How was he going to get work now? No one would employ a one-armed man. Maybe Harold would be kind and keep him on. He would have to have a talk with him real soon.

Molly brought him his meals. He hadn't seen Jane at all. He tried talking to Molly as she fed him, but all she would say was that his hand had been mangled by Skunk. Skunk was dead of course. She didn't mention the dead sheep.

Another week passed before Harold came to his room. Woody was sitting up in bed and Harold pulled up a chair and sat down.

"How's it going, Woody?" he asked.

"Not too good," Woody said. "What happened to my hand?"

Harold looked down at the floor and didn't meet his eyes. "Skunk got a hold of it. Chewed it all up. The doc said he couldn't save it."

"Are you sure?"

Harold looked up. "Sure about what?"

"Sure that he couldn't save it."

"Sure I'm sure. I saw it myself. It's just bad luck, that's all."

"Shit," Woody said. "I don't even remember Skunk attacking my hand. All I remember is him going for my throat."

"Well, it probably happened too quickly for you to remember. You probably passed out before he did it."

"Maybe," Woody said.

They were silent for a minute and then Harold cleared his throat. "I'm going to have to let you go, Woody."

Woody had suspected as much. He nodded.

"After all," Harold continued. "You won't be able to do much with one hand."

"I know," Woody said. "I'm no use to anybody now."

They were silent again.

"Sorry," Harold said, and then he stood up and reached for the door.

The day before he left Woody asked Harold for just one thing. He asked him for a pistol with just one bullet in it.

Harold said okay, but asked him why just one bullet?

Woody said, "Eventually I'll probably have to shoot myself because I won't be able to get any work. When I do it though, I want to be sure that I'm doing the right thing. If I have six bullets I'm likely to do it when I'm drunk. If I only have one bullet I won't know which chamber it's in when I'm drunk and the feeling will pass. If I kill myself I want to be sober, just so I'm sure that's really what I want to do."

Harold looked at him with a little more respect in his eyes. "That's a good idea, Woody, a good idea."

Woody walked down the road away from the farm, his few belongings in a bag over his shoulder. From the front veranda Harold and Molly watched.

"Do you think he'll be okay?" Molly asked.

"I don't know," Harold said. "I really don't know."

"He was a nice boy," Molly said. "I wish you hadn't cut off his hand."

Harold didn't look at her. "He shouldn't have killed that sheep. I can't afford to have sheep killed for nothin'."

"Oh, I think you know very well it wasn't for nothin'."

Harold looked at her. "In some countries they cut off your hand if you steal something, you know. He killed a sheep. I don't see what the difference is."

Molly gave him a scornful look. "In some countries. But we're not in those countries. We don't have to do things those ways."

"The real problem," Harold said, "is that daughter of yours. That makes three we've had to get rid of because of her. This can't go on forever. We're gonna have to talk to her again."

And then he walked back inside the kitchen.

THE CARTOONIST
(A Western Melodrama in Five Scenes)

JON L. BREEN

Scene 1

(The Office of the Adcock City *Clarion*)

"Sit down, Terrence, sit down," said editor Horace Millstone, offering his visitor a chair opposite his cluttered desk. "Press isn't running, so we can hear ourselves talk. May I offer you something to tamp down the dust of Main Street? I have a bottle of good rye whiskey in my bottom drawer here." He winked. "Journalistic custom, you know."

"No thanks, Mr. Millstone," said Terrence Webb. "I like to keep a clear head when talking business."

"Certainly, my boy. A sound policy for a young man. For an old man, too, I venture, though harder for this old man to follow. Now before you say anything, I know why you've come."

"You do, sir?"

"Certainly. Might as well bite the bullet, take my medicine, swallow my pride. But dear me, that makes of pride a medicine, does it not? Beware of metaphors! They are words in their most seductive attire, ensnaring us with beauty and promise like one of Flossy Beaudine's painted ladies at Dismas Craven's saloon, eh? But the pleasures of words are longer lasting than the pleasures of the flesh. After my dear late wife, after my lovely daughter, I love the English language beyond all else."

"That is obvious from the eloquence of your editorials, sir."

"It is generous of you to say that at a time when you undoubtedly would like to measure a length of rope, encircle my wattled neck, find a stout-limbed tree, and reserve for me a weedy plot in the farthest corner of Boot Hill."

"Sir, I would never—"

"I know you wouldn't, my boy. Forgive a garrulous scrivener his habitual hyperbole. But let us get to the crux of the matter: your advertisement in last week's *Clarion*. I must explain about my assistant, Joe Betts, a commendable fellow in many ways, generally efficient at the setting of type, tireless at the running of the press, but a bit too enamored of strong beverages. I once admonished him for unauthorized withdrawals from my rye bottle, but I cannot control what he consumes before reporting for work or what he may conceal in his commodious pockets. Joe Betts was having, shall we say, one of his bad days. And that is how it happened that your advertisement was published upside down. Ultimately, however, the fault is mine. I am the editor after all, and I should have noticed it. All I can offer is sincere apologies and a free ad in this week's paper."

"That's kind of you, Mr. Millstone, but not at all necessary. Seven people came in to tell me my ad was upside down, and four of them wound up sitting for photographs. If anything, I feared you would raise your advertising rates."

"My relief is manifest. And I'm pleased your business is flourishing. We need young men like you in Adcock City to bring us culture and new ideas, to facilitate our march to civilization. What brought you West to begin with, if I may ask?"

"As so many, I came to forget."

"A woman?"

"Must it always be a woman? But yes, in a manner of speaking. She was beautiful, and I thought I loved her, but she betrayed me. She was the kind the French would call a *femme fatale*, who squeezes everything she wants out of a man and discards him like a soiled handkerchief. Women I find are more honest here in the

West. They're either frankly wicked like those saloon girls or good and pure like...but that's not what I came here to talk about."

"I won't press you for personal details, my boy. Keep the past in the past, and look to the future. Well now, you don't object to your ad and you haven't tried to convince me to pose for your remarkable camera, so to what do I owe the pleasure of your visit?"

"I have an idea that might help the paper and might help the town."

"You think it needs help?"

"The paper or the town?"

"Either one."

"You're a better judge than I of whether the paper needs help, Mr. Millstone, but the town surely does. I think you can see that."

"Terrence, as a newcomer to Adcock City, you may not have the perspective of one who has been here from the beginning. I published the first editions of this newspaper out of doors on a hand press. Now I have this fine office and this modern equipment. I have seen Adcock City grow from a wild-and-wooly stop on the railway, a place of rowdiness and shootouts and lawlessness, to a real community, a place of purpose, variety, morality, fine sentiments, law and order. With these qualities come snobbery and social distinctions, I'll admit, but these are inevitable barnacles on the hull of civilized society. I have not witnessed a shooting on Main Street in nearly a year. Women and children can walk our streets in safety. We have churches, schools, and shops that cater to the most delicate and discriminating of tastes. We have a theatre that offers us high-class entertainment from the East. The immortal words of Shakespeare are spoken on our wild western stage." With a wink, he added, "We even have enough business to support a portrait photographer. I think Adcock City is a success."

"But at what cost, sir?"

"What do you mean?"

"Benjamin Adcock runs this town."

"Well, after all, he built it. He and his father."

"That doesn't make it his personal property. He looks down on us all from that fine house of his."

"It is no crime to be rich."

"No, but it's hard to get that way without committing a few crimes along the way. Every business in this town pays tribute to

Adcock. He runs the gambling and the prostitutes indirectly, but everybody knows it. He takes what he wants from people who don't have the will or the means to fight him. If anyone dares to cross him, he sends them a message in the form of a bullet. Out on the range, of course, not here in the city where we can see it happen and might feel compelled to do something about it. He does all of this while you're writing editorials about street cleaning and building standards."

"Are those matters of no significance to the community? And, more to the point, are not they part of the everything Ben Adcock controls?"

"They are, sir, and I'm not saying they aren't important—"

Millstone raised a hand. "I take your meaning, Terrence. You think I am afraid of Ben Adcock. Perhaps you even think I am on his payroll and am allowed to write the occasional critical editorial to conceal that fact. Is that what you believe?"

"No, Mr. Millstone. I think you're one of the few honest men in this town. I think you've just been waiting for the right opportunity to go after Adcock. I've talked with May about you, you see. We went riding in a borrowed rig, with your permission, as I'm sure you remember."

"With a proper chaperone in the person of my long-suffering sister-in-law, of course. Thank God my daughter is sensible."

"She is all of that, sir. Too sensible to welcome the attentions of this Eastern dude. She tore her dress alighting from the rig, as she probably told you, but I fear by that time the battle was already lost."

"I am sorry she has rebuffed your attentions. Between us, I would have placed you among the better prospects Adcock City offers a young woman seeking a husband, but May has a mind of her own and I would never deny her its free exercise. I only ask that she be kind in her personal dealings."

"Sir, I assure you she closed the door on my entreaties in the kindest possible way."

"Perhaps you have given up too easily. When you had the opportunity to exchange words with May, perhaps her father's editorial plans were not the ideal choice of topic."

"We did not discuss your editorial plans, Mr. Millstone, but she gave me a sense of something more important, your character. You are a brave man. A man who won't shy away from a fight."

"Men strive to be heroes to their children, but maintaining such exalted rank can be a chore. Anyone in the sort of wide-open town Adcock City used to be is aware of danger all around him and must be prepared to face it down. Do you keep a firearm in your photographic studio, Terrence?"

"No, sir, I have not felt it necessary."

"Well, I still keep a handgun in my desk, but now I think of it mostly as a relic of how things were before civilization came to make us soft by small degrees, so gradually we don't even realize it is happening. What exactly are you proposing?"

"Not a gunfight on Main Street, sir, I assure you. Have you heard of a man named Thomas Nast?"

"I have."

"I admire his work."

"As do I."

"Photography makes me my living, and I'm convinced it will take the place of drawing, painting, and sculpture in its ability to render an accurate visual depiction of people and places. But the art of the cartoonist, the caricaturist, can accomplish things photography never can. A friend back east has been sending me copies of *Harper's Weekly*. Mr. Nast has effectively used the power of his drawing to bring down the corrupt dictator who ran politics in New York, Boss Tweed of Tammany Hall. I'd like to do the same here in Adcock City, Mr. Millstone."

"You wish to bring down Boss Tweed?"

"No, sir. As I think you realize, I wish to bring down Boss Adcock."

Terrence Webb opened the portfolio he had brought with him and handed several drawings across the desk to editor Millstone, who looked at each in turn, pursing his lips judicially. They depicted Ben Adcock as circling vulture, as puppet master, as schoolyard bully, as debaucher of women, as overfed giant with locally prominent citizens looking out of his greatcoat pockets. Facial features were comically exaggerated, but the overall effect was too troubling and truthful to be funny. Millstone passed the drawings back.

"Sir," he said, "you have called this sleeping journalist to duty. Of course, these must be published and they shall be published and damned be the consequences. But I shall oil my gun, and I might suggest you acquire one of your own."

Scene 2

(The Parlor of the Millstone Home, Two Months Later)

May Millstone, attired in black, sat opposite Terrence Webb. Her Aunt Matilda, sister of her late mother, knitted in a discreet corner, far enough away not to intrude on the conversation but close enough to maintain propriety.

"This is such a beautiful room," Terrence said.

May smiled wryly. "It was what Father wanted for me: a room indistinguishable from a fashionable Eastern parlor. We must have a piano. We must have expertly crafted tables and chairs in the finest woods, all polished to a high gloss. Some things were sent by ship between the great craftsmen of Europe and our Eastern ports; all traveled by rail between the dealers and this dusty town. I selected the furnishings from catalogs, but the impetus for the project all was his. I love what my father gave me, but I would give it all to have him back, sitting in that chair, enjoying his pipe."

"Is there anything more I can do, May?" Terrence asked.

"Father is in the ground," the young woman said. "You have done enough."

"You blame me for his death, don't you?"

"Unless it was your hand that pulled the trigger, no. Father made his decision to confront the powerful while careless of his own safety. You bear no responsibility."

"And yet you regret his acceptance of my cartoons."

"How could I not regret it? But men do what they believe they must."

"One thing is certain, May. The *Clarion* must continue."

"And so it shall, I assure you. Indeed, I have hired a new editor who will arrive soon from St. Louis."

"Then I shall present my future work to him."

"No, please. There will be no more cartoons, Terrence."

"The best memorial to your father would be to continue the work he started."

"I want no more memorials. I did not summon this new editor to join my father on his office floor in a pool of blood, and I want no such fate for you either. Take your photographs, build your business, and we shall gladly publish your advertisements. I shall do my best to continue the *Clarion* as a responsible weekly newspaper, without courting trouble."

"Has Sheriff Wimbush any idea who killed your father?"

"My father is just as dead whoever killed him."

"And don't you want his killer brought to justice?"

"Is God's justice not enough?"

"To satisfy men, and to satisfy the needs of a civilized society, no, God's justice generally is not enough."

"You know, Terrence, I nearly refused to receive you today."

"Why?"

"I have seen that second group of cartoons you submitted to Father the day before his death. Some of them were horrible."

"Badly drawn?"

"No, not badly drawn. But one in particular struck me as offensive, and I think you know the one I mean."

Terrence looked down at his lap. "May, I didn't know you had seen that drawing. May I assure you neither you nor your father was intended to see it?"

"Oh, I'm quite sure of that."

"Truly. It was included by mistake."

"By mistake. And is that supposed to make me feel better about it?"

"No insult was intended. You must have noticed I did not distort your face as I usually do in caricature. I rendered your beauty as accurately as my poor talent permitted."

"If that was your idea of beauty, it was most superficial. Father was outraged by it. I was almost afraid he would do you some injury. I did my best to calm him down."

"I regret I was misunderstood by you both. I regret also that I did not have the chance to speak to him again before his death and do something to ameliorate the misunderstanding."

"Thank you for calling, Mr. Webb. You may consider your obligation completed."

THE CARTOONIST

Terrence stood up stiffly. "Very well. Then I take my leave of you. And again, remember I am at your service."

"Your service is not required, sir."

Scene 3

(The Office of the Sheriff, the Next Day)

"I'm going to listen to whatever you have to say to me, Webb," said Sheriff Clint Wimbush, "'cause you're a citizen and you have a right to my attention. But that don't mean I got to like you or your goddamn cartoons. I especially didn't like that one where you show Mr. Ben Adcock wearing that big old coat with various local citizens stickin' out of his pockets. One of those people has a star on his chest and looks not a little like me. You are lookin' at one honest lawman, and I ain't in nobody's pocket."

"Perhaps not," Terrence said. "But is not part of your duty the suppression of vice?"

"Let me tell you about vice. We still got lads comin' in from the ranches, comin' in off the prairie, comin' in off the cattle drives, want to have some fun, and a big part of the business of our town is to give 'em what they need. I don't mind gamblin' if it's honest gamblin'. I can live with whorin' if it's honest whorin'. I want a safe town for the folks that live in it, which is what we got. A pure town is more than you can ask out here in the West. If you want purity, you'd best head back East, where things might suit you better. There, now. I've said my piece on that."

"You have indeed. Sheriff, the reason I came—"

"Just one more thing. I hear you been visitin' May Millstone. I don't like that."

"I think it's up to the lady who she receives in her own home, Sheriff. Properly chaperoned by her maiden aunt at all times, may I add."

"Not necessary to add. They're right moral folks."

"Sheriff, do you and May have some kind of understanding I'm not aware of?"

"Nope," the Sheriff said with a hint of wry smile. "No understanding except that she sees no future with a lawman. But she's a fine woman."

JON L. BREEN

"I can only agree."

"Good. Now, what are you doin' here?"

"I want to know who killed Horace Millstone."

"No more than I do, but that's a tough one. We know he was shot with his own gun, which he kept in a desk drawer, the drawer right above his rye bottle. The gun was left at the scene. Nobody saw who fired it. After your cartoons appeared"—the Sheriff punctuated his disgust by making a well-aimed deposit in the spittoon in the corner— "there should be a long list of possibilities."

"Starting with Ben Adcock."

"Not on the list."

"How can that be? He's the most logical suspect."

"It ain't his style. He wouldn't do it the way it was done."

"Not personally, no. But if he sent one of his men, he would be no less guilty."

"Webb, we both know such dirty work as gets done—and nobody's ever proved Ben Adcock is behind any of it—gets done out on the range, not in town."

"But Editor Millstone rarely would be found out on the range."

"He worked funny hours. It wouldn't be hard to kidnap him and take him out on the range late some evening without being seen. And even if Adcock, or somebody, sent a killer to do the job, that killer would carry his own gun, wouldn't he? I don't see a hired gunslinger relyin' on grabbin' his victim's gun out of a desk drawer, do you? I think we're looking for a killer that doesn't normally pack a gun. A killer that's not used to killing, maybe."

"So who else have you considered?"

"How 'bout Joe Betts, the editor's drunken assistant? He found the body, came runnin' down Main Street to tell me about it. You'd be surprised how often a shooter winds up reportin' his own crime."

"Well, at least he might know where Millstone kept his gun. But what motive would he have?"

"Millstone was always threatening to fire him."

Terrence shook his head. "Betts seems unlikely to me, Sheriff. Who else is on your list?"

"Well, there's Dismas Craven, little twerp who runs the saloon."

"He's barely big enough to lift a gun, and his hands shake all the time."

"Yeah, I know. And he'd hardly go out on his own, wouldn't have the nerve."

"Maybe somebody else I drew in the cartoons—"

"To tell you the truth, Webb, I'm not convinced your lousy cartoons were the motive at all. If Ben Adcock or somebody working for him wanted to kill the editor, why would they wait till half a dozen of the cartoons had appeared in the paper? The damage was done by then. I'm thinkin' there might be more of a personal motive."

"Then you're back to Betts. Who else is there? Mr. Millstone was well liked in this town. Don't you have anything else to go on?"

"What'd you have in mind?"

"I don't know. You're the lawman. Was anything left at the scene that might suggest who did it?"

"Funny you should mention that. There was one thing, yes." The Sheriff opened his desk drawer and drew out a small piece of cloth, showing it to Terrence in his open palm. "Any idea what this is?"

"Looks like it was torn off a lady's dress." Terrence turned it over. "Some kind of stain on it. Dried blood?"

"Yup. It was lying near Millstone's body."

"Then you think a woman shot him?"

"No, but a woman must have been there when he was shot or shortly after."

"And hasn't come forward?"

"Nobody's come forward, no."

"Don't under estimate the weaker sex, Sheriff. I know from experience that there are women in this world who devour men like a black widow spider disposing of her mate, evil women, and some of them wouldn't stop at murder. They don't usually carry their own sidearms, so going after something near at hand on the scene would make sense. Flossy Beaudine had reason not to like my cartoons, didn't she? She wouldn't have any moral qualms about murder, and I think she's strong enough to take matters into her own hands, not wait for a man to do it for her."

"Naw, Flossie wouldn't have done this."

"Perhaps you know her better than I. But I can't think of any other woman who might have done it, can you?"

"Unless it was one of her girls, but—"

"Why'd you stop, Sheriff? You got something?"

"You said yourself it had to be somebody who would know where Millstone kept his gun. Flossie wouldn't, and her girls wouldn't, but what woman would? Could it be...? Naw, that's impossible."

"What are you suggesting?"

"What about the women in his own household?"

"You mean Aunt Matilda? You must be joking."

"Well, no, I can't really picture that. But she wasn't the only—"

Terrence Webb leapt to his feet, knocking over the chair he'd been sitting in. "You're accusing May Millstone of murdering her own father?"

"Naw, no such thing. I was just thinking out loud."

"She might be interested to know you consider her a suspect."

"I told you to stay away from her."

"And I'm telling you she deserves better than such crazy accusations."

"I never made no accusations," Sheriff Wimbush said, but Terrence Webb was already out the door and marching down Main Street.

Scene 4

(The Millstone Parlor, That Evening)

"It was good of you to see me again, May," Terrence Webb said. "But where's your Aunt Matilda?"

"She got a note by messenger late this afternoon. A friend of hers is sick, and she went to see to her."

"Leaving you all alone in this big house?"

"I feel quite safe here."

"Just the same, I hope you wouldn't let any other man in without a chaperone."

"Spare me your concern, Terrence. You see me as a black widow spider, don't you? Why should I not welcome the male of the species into my parlor?"

"I told you, May, I just used your face in that drawing. I wasn't commenting on your own sterling character."

"You said that, yes. Very convincing you were."

"In all seriousness, May, you should have a firearm to protect yourself. I know Adcock City has advanced toward civilization by leaps and bounds, but still, a woman alone in a house..."

"I have a firearm."

"Show it to me."

"Why?"

"To relieve my mind. Please."

May disappeared into another room and returned with a small revolver in her hand.

"Good. Don't point it at me, but reassure me that you know how to use it."

"I certainly do." May put the gun down on the table between them.

"May, I came here to warn you. Sheriff Wimbush suspects you of murdering your father. I tried to tell him how absurd that is, but I don't believe I convinced him. What motive could you possibly have?"

"None at all. I loved my father."

"But once his mind starts turning it over, there's no telling what wild theories Wimbush might come up with. Maybe you duped your Aunt Matilda and entertained men in secret when your father was hard at work at his newspaper. Maybe you're the sort of woman who hides behind a façade of propriety and gentility, lures men to the brink of madness with your virginal innocence, causes them to sell all they own, then rejects them and laughs at them and drives them to suicide or if they're lucky—do I mean lucky? I'm not sure—drives them away. Drives them West."

"Did that happen to you, Terrence?"

"If it happened to me, I wouldn't let it happen again, I can tell you that."

"Is that the Sheriff's theory you were just describing or your own? When did you develop that twitch in your right eye? Terrence, you're frightening me! No, don't come any closer."

May reached for the gun on the table between them, but in one quick movement, Terrence wrested it from her hand.

"I saw you that day after I left the newspaper office," he said, a glint of madness in his eye. "I saw who you were talking to, and I realized then what kind of woman you really are."

"Because I was talking to someone on a public street in broad daylight? I talk to many people."

"I never meant your father to see that drawing, but once he did, I thought he would see what you really are. But he was blind, a loving father to the last. He got angry that night I went to see him. He wouldn't believe a word against you. He said he wouldn't run any more of my cartoons and he'd see me run out of Adcock City. Some brave crusading journalist your father was, unable to accept the truth about his own daughter. I felt sorry for him, but I had to—no, that's not right, I didn't kill him. You did, May, by being the kind of soul-devouring vampire you are. And when you killed him, you left a little clue at the scene, that bit of cloth that tore on the rig the day we went riding with your Aunt Matilda."

"You kept that?"

"I treasured it. I carried it with me in my pocket all those days since. At first, it was as a part of the woman I could never have, but later I saw how I could use it. I'll bet the dress you wore that day is still hanging in your closet. I see from your expression that it is. When that cloth is matched to the dress, everybody will believe you killed your father. When I came here today, outraged at the Sheriff's insinuation and intending only to warn you, you drew this gun on me. Naturally, I had to defend myself. We struggled, and I accidentally shot you. I didn't mean to kill you but it was clearly self-defense."

She moved toward him, reaching for the gun.

Terrence Webb rose from his chair and took aim.

A shot rang out.

May collapsed back onto the settee.

Terrence Webb fell dead, the Sheriff's bullet finding his heart and killing him instantly.

Scene 5

(The Millstone Parlor, the Following Day)

"You'll be all right now, won't you, May?" Sheriff Wimbush said.

"Yes, Clint. What the doctor gave me helped me sleep, and when I woke up...well, it was a new day. A day I almost didn't live to see. How did you happen to turn up at just the right time?"

"If I'd figured things out a little faster, I wouldn't have cut it so close. The key was this: there was nowhere in the newspaper office for that piece of cloth to get torn off your dress and wind up lyin' in your father's blood without you bein' aware of it. It had to have been planted to implicate a woman in the crime. And then I remembered how Webb was directin' the conversation when we talked. Seemed like he knew I'd found something at the scene and just wanted me to say it. He pushed me to consider you as a suspect—though I didn't, not really—and then pretended to be outraged by the idea. I think Webb came here last night planning to kill you. Probably he sent that phony message to get your Aunt Matilda out of the way."

"I should have known, too, when Terrence came here the first time. He'd drawn a horrible cartoon of me as a black widow spider, surrounded by prominent citizens I had supposedly lured into my web. You were among them and Ben Adcock was among them, and so many others, some of whom I've never even met. How he got those ideas about me I can't imagine. Then he accidentally—he said it was an accident—gave the drawing to my father with his second batch of cartoons. He could have ruined my reputation forever. When he made his condolence call and I confronted him about the drawing, he didn't know I had seen it, but he seemed to know my father had seen it, and yet he denied having spoken to my father after he turned the second set of cartoons in."

"May, I was almost too late. If I'd come through that door a few seconds later, you'd have been dead."

May put her hand on his and said, "Clint, I'll be forever in your debt. Poor Terrence Webb—I do feel sorry for him now. He was sick, tortured by his past. God rest him."

The Sheriff gazed into her eyes and said, "I don't know what kind of crazy ideas Webb got in his mind, May, but I know what kind of woman you really are. Do you think you could reconsider bein' married to a lawman?"

Her eyes were moist as she looked back at him. "Clint, you're so sweet, but I've been through a lot. Things have happened so fast. You'll have to give me some time."

JON L. BREEN

News item from the Adcock City *Clarion*

In the most elaborate and well-attended wedding in this city's short history, May Millstone, daughter of the late founder of this newspaper, became the bride of the city's leading citizen, Mr. Benjamin Franklin Adcock.

DURSTON

NORMAN PARTRIDGE

The whore wouldn't take his money.

That didn't matter to Durston. He took what he wanted anyhow, and he took it the way he pleased. Now she was over on the other side of the bed with her back to him, her shoulders heaving the way you'd expect. Making those little mewling sounds the way they do.

All of a sudden Durston wanted to hit her again. That's how angry he was. Bottled up in this tinderbox whorehouse, flatbacked on a sodden excuse for a bed in the shadows and the midnight heat. Just him and her and a bottle of mescal.

And the dead man, hanging there in the rafters.

The dead man, scuffed boot heels swinging over top of them as they lay together in that bed.

Pitch Dunnigan twisted in the dark, the rope around his neck groaning in a way the whore never could. Durston didn't have to look up to see his dead partner's face. Didn't have to suck wind to smell the stink of the leavings that had stained the dead man's britches as the rope snapped taut around his gizzard, didn't have to listen to hear the bitter words that scalded Pitch's rotting brainpan—words that'd never travel the bellows of breath thanks to a hemp noose.

For another man, that last thing might have been a small favor afforded by the hangman's tool. But Durston wasn't another man. Pitch Dunnigan's words found him as sure as a tick finds something that's warm and pumping blood. Durston heard the dead man the same way he saw him, the same way he breathed him...with no need for quiet or mescal to aid his visions, and no need for the goddamn light of day.

But the night could only stretch so far. The gunman knew that. He'd done what he'd come here to do—dead man be damned—and he wouldn't linger in some whore's bed now that he'd put backside to the deed. Soon enough there'd be other deeds that needed doing.

The first splash of morning light found the cataract glass set in the window. The floor took up the light the same way it took up dirty water, drank it between splinters and cracks. But the light that made it past the floor streamed across the sheets and found Durston and the whore...and then it made higher ground and found the polished Mexican spurs attached to Pitch Dunnigan's swinging heels.

And so came the start of another day.

Durston swung his ass out of bed. He dressed, grabbed mule-ears and pulled on his boots. That done, he snatched a knotted rawhide pouch off the nightstand and holstered his gun.

He walked to the door, putting his back to the room. Didn't make much difference. Behind him, the hangman's rope still complained, and the whore still moaned. That was just the way it was. Durston understood that. In life, there were some things you just had to choke down until you could get shed of them...like a twisting rope, a moaning whore, or the forty double eagles scarred by a sheriff's knife that lay silent in the rawhide pouch fisted in Durston's right hand.

The man at the bar looked like something you'd see in an old mirror. Must have been he was some kind of cripple. Durston didn't know exactly what kind, nor did he care. What he cared about was untying the knot around the rawhide pouch.

"Want to settle up for the woman," Durston said, "and the room."

The barman's cheeks went sallow, like someone had wiped his looking-glass face with a rag. "That ain't necessary, Mr. Durston. It's on the house."

The gunman grinned. Sure, that's exactly what the cripple would say. He'd heard the stories. Everyone had. About the gunsmith down in Denver who'd blown his brains out after Durston paid him with those scarred double eagles, and the gentleman gambler who'd slit his own throat in a plush indoor privy after winning a pot seeded with the same, and the woman over in Silverton who'd stolen a few of those twenty-dollar gold coins from Durston's rawhide pouch while he slept like Rip Van Winkle.

The fate of that bitch wasn't something you'd want crawling around in your brainpan, not even in the light of day. But Durston could see it in there, wriggling around behind the looking-glass man's rheumy eyes. That's why Durston had known the man wouldn't accept his coin before he even put tongue to the offer.

Not that Durston intended to pay the man.

In truth, that wasn't what he intended at all.

Still, this thing had to go a certain way. Durston untied his poke. Tipped a scarred double eagle into his callused hand. Slapped it on the counter like he was driving home a nail.

"Please, Mr. Durston. There ain't no need—"

"Yes. There is."

Durston grabbed the man and yanked him over the bar the way you'd yank a dead cornstalk from a field. The scarred coin hit the floor rolling, but it didn't roll far. Durston snatched it up and jammed it into the man's pocket, and the cripple's looking-glass face clouded over as if Satan himself had steamed it with a sulfurous breath.

The man dug into his pocket with shaking fingers.

Again, Durston's coin hit the floor.

Durston stared down at it.

"All right," the gunman said. "If that's the way you want it."

He snatched up the scarred double eagle. The damn thing was wet. So were the cripple's britches. Mr. Looking Glass had piddled his pants like a child, but that didn't matter to Durston any more than the whore's whimpering had mattered. There wasn't a hard yard of difference between those things. They were less than piteous to a man like Durston, just so much chewed cud in the mouth of the world.

The gunman's fingers curled around the wet coin.

The pissed-on cripple started bawling like a kid.

To hell with that, Durston thought.

To hell with that.

Durston took his time.

Ten minutes later came the sound of busting glass.

Wasn't the looking-glass man that went to pieces, though. Was the big plate-glass window that fronted his saloon. And what did the damage? Why, that scrawny little bastard going through it head first, of course.

Durston's palms hit the batwings and he stepped outside. Busted glass crunched under his heels. Looking-Glass lay there among the shards, red cracks jagging across his bruised face like he'd been shattered but not quite broke to bits. Durston didn't pay the cripple any mind. He didn't bother to watch the twisted little bugeye crawl away, didn't bother to note the smear of blood he left behind any more than he'd linger over a trail left by a slug.

His attention was directed elsewhere. Already, folks were running up the street towards the sheriff's office. Stepping off the boardwalk, the gunman watched them go. Women, kids, men... Durston wasn't worried about any of them. He never worried about anything that showed its back as soon as trouble reared up on its hind legs and snorted. Just wasn't worth his time.

But it was comical to watch. Men trying to look like they meant business while beating a hasty retreat. Kids who wanted their first look of dark doings getting yanked along by their mothers. And the women...why, the women were the best. Durston enjoyed watching their asses as they fled. All that gingham and calico pumping in furious motion. Why, one gal looked like she had a couple of bushels of apples hidden up under her skirts. Durston could almost hear a clock ticking in his head as she hurried up the street.

Tick tock tick tock tick tock tick tock...

It was quite a sight. For about half a minute.

Then another sound caught Durston's attention.

A sound he couldn't ignore.

A twisting rope.

The sound came from behind, just above Durston's left shoulder. He smelled the familiar stink as he whirled, knew what he'd see even before he laid eyes on it. Pitch Dunnigan, hanging from the saloon's second floor balcony. Stretched gizzard gone to black, bloated tongue and face gone to purple, all except those stark staring blue eyes that spoke every word locked up in the dead man's brain.

Durston clutched tight to his rawhide pouch. He told himself that this vision of his dead partner was no more real than a mescal dream, but that little message was denied by his eyes, and his ears, and even his goddamn nose, and Durston's guts stretched as tight as newly strung barbed-wire as a result. Because Dunningan's corpse was *right there*, hanging in front of him. Durston couldn't deny that. It was part of the reason he'd ridden two hundred miles to this place, part of the reason he'd come with those forty double eagles scarred by a sheriff's knife, knotted in a rawhide pouch.

That goddamn sheriff.

That goddamn Ed Hauser.

Durston meant to make that bastard pay. Only that wasn't right. The bastard had already paid, and then some. What Durston wanted was something different. What he wanted was—

Right at his heels. A couple of deputies—the same two that had brushed off Durston the day before at the sheriff's office. One of them yanked Durston's pistol from his custom rig before the gunman even sensed that the man was behind him. The other took hold of Durston's shoulder and spun him around like a kid's wooden top.

Both deputies were big. They were a pair of prairie farmboys, the kind Hauser always hired. But they didn't surprise Durston. He'd made his play, and just as he'd hoped it had come to this.

"Like I told you boys yesterday," Durston said, "I want to see Hauser."

"You'll see him pretty damn quick," one of the deputies said.
The other one didn't say anything.
Leastways, not with his mouth, he didn't.

Durston spit a tooth on the café floor, but that didn't slow Hauser down any. The big man chewed heartily, the dull percussion of his powerful jaws offset by the precise sounds of knife and fork working over the rare steak that covered three-quarters of his breakfast plate. Not the kind of sound you'd expect to notice but there was really no way to avoid it—the café was empty except for the sheriff, his corn-fed deputies, and Durston down there on the floor.

"You want to talk to me so badly, well, here I am. Get to talking, Mr. Durston."

"You're a hard man to see."

"Not so hard if a man's willing to make a real effort."

Durston had to grin at that, and though it felt like hell, he was glad there were enough teeth left in his head to do the job.

"I'll give you this, Durston. You don't take *no* for an answer. Though I'm certain Dan Wagner wouldn't think much of your method of gaining my attention."

"Who the hell's Dan Wagner?"

"He's the man you tossed through that window."

"Man?" Durston guffawed. "*Crippled little shitstain* is more like it."

Hauser laughed, swallowing the sound with a bite of steak. Durston spit. There was more blood in the saliva than he liked. When he looked up, the square-headed German was staring down at him, or maybe Hauser was staring at that red spit-blot on the floor. Staring, forking Mexican eggs into his mouth. Quickly. Mechanically. Like he was feeding a furnace.

One thing was sure—this bastard didn't let things slow him down much.

Neither would Durston.

He reached into his pocket, took hold of the rawhide pouch.

"Take this back," Durston said.

"That's what you want to see me about?"

"Yes."

"Then you just raised a bushel of hell for nothing."

"Listen here—"

"No, Mr. Durston. You're the one who needs to listen. You were paid for services rendered. You betrayed your partner. I strung up Pitch Dunnigan and watched him kick. That's the story, *entire*."

"You know there's more to it than that."

"I've heard some empty-headed talk, but I'm not much interested in fairy tales. The way I see it, it's simple: I gave you cash on the barrelhead; you sold out your friend. And that's the end of it."

"I know damn well good enough what I did. That's not why I came—"

"But that's all there is to it, Mr. Durston. The rest is embroidery. If you want to salve your guilt in superstitious wallow, that's your choice. But if that's the case you're as much a fool as those cowards out there who ran from your miserable shadow."

Durston stiffened. By God, he wouldn't take this. To be talked to like a half-shingled idiot by this smug bastard, when Durston knew Hauser had done *something*. Exactly what, Durston wasn't sure. But something…*something* had been done…and it had to be Hauser was the one who'd done it. Couldn't be any other way.

Durston dumped the gold coins on the floor. Shiny tails, scarred heads. The sound of the sheriff's knife working over the steak scraped against the silence, blade slicing against that china plate the same way the big German's Bowie had worked over the coins.

Behind Durston came the inevitable sound of a twisting rope. Then the familiar stink washed over him, and—

"Put your money away, Mr. Durston."

"By God, I won't."

"Believe me, you will."

"But these damn coins. The way you marked them with that Bowie knife—"

"Maybe I wanted people to know what kind of a man they were bartering with."

"And now those people are dead."

"That's what folks say, but folks say all sorts of things."

"Yeah. Sometimes they even tell the goddamn truth."

Hauser shook his head. "Look here—you got fifty gold pieces, Durston. Judas Iscariot got thirty pieces of silver. He ended up at the end of a rope the same way Pitch Dunnigan did, only it was his hand got him there…his hand and his brain. If you can't stand the fit of your skin with that money in your pocket, that's not my affair."

Durston boiled. "My skin suits me just fine, dammit. This ain't got nothing to do with *me*. That's not why I'm here. I came for *answers*."

"I believe you've had them."

"And I believe I haven't had a single goddamned one."

Durston gained his feet. The corn-fed deputies were right there with him, but Durston didn't care. Sheriff Hauser mopped up eggs with a tortilla, took a bite and chewed. He stared at Durston, not saying a word. As far as the sheriff was concerned, there were enough words hanging in the air already. And then Hauser took up his knife and fork, and the sound of those tools working across that china plate made it seem that the sheriff was cutting up his own words, and Durston's.

That was when Durston realized that words didn't matter.

The way he saw it, they never did.

There was a clutch of woods outside the town. That was where the deputies took Durston. They'd used their fists on him the first time around, so this time they used their feet—kicking his ribs with scuffed boots, going to work like kids bent on stoving in a busted-down chicken coop.

Durston tried hard not to squawk like a fox-gnawed hen, but there was only so much a man could stand. The grunts started low and deep in him, and by the time they reached his throat he knotted them into sharp whistling gasps, but those boys knew how to kick, and where, and they sighted down the spot where Durston's complaints were born and they kept on working, clubbing muscle and bone with more of the same bound up in hard leather boots.

Soon enough screams crossed Durston's lips. It went on like that for a while, until Durston didn't have a single scream left in him. Finally, he curled into a whimpering ball. That was when the deputies stopped. But even minus punishment, Durston couldn't keep from wincing. His guts were bucking something awful, threatening a foul surprise.

It came soon enough.

Durston's bladder let loose, and he pissed himself as he lay there in the dirt.

"Well, hell," one of the deputies said. "Look at him."

They didn't say more. The deputy who'd spoken tossed Durston's rawhide pouch in the dirt, and then both men turned away and followed a path through the live oak grove. Gnarled shadows twisted across Durston from the trees above, and sunshine found him too, but it seemed that the shade fell in all the wrong places. The gunman couldn't stop shivering.

It took awhile, but soon enough Durston realized it wasn't the shade that made him shiver.

Was a sound up in the branches that did that little trick.

The groaning of that goddamn rope.

Durston pounded the ground with a fist, but he did not waste a single moment thinking of Pitch Dunnigan. No. He thought about Ed Hauser instead. Thought about that bastard sitting there, eating his goddamn steak while he lectured Durston on the workings of the world.

Talking about *superstitious wallow* and *fairy tales* and *embroidery*. Talking about *Judas Iscariot* and *the fit of Durston's skin*, for God's sake. As if the whole goddamn deal had boiled up from Durston's own guts, as if that was where Pitch Dunnigan lived now that he'd drawn his last breath.

Durston nearly laughed, thinking of the things Hauser had said. He rolled over and stared up into the tree. *Goddamn right.* There was Pitch Dunnigan. *Right there.* Not squirming around in Durston's guts. Not locked up in his brain. He was *right there, hanging in that goddamn tree.*

And maybe Durston was the only one who could see him, but that didn't change the fact that the bastard was there, any more than it changed the fact that there was more to this deal than a strung-up spectre. All Durston had to do to prove that was look down in the dirt, because there was the rawhide pouch. *Right there.* The gunman snatched it up, heard gold coins dancing inside. Those twenty-dollar coins were real enough, and Durston knew what they had done and what they could do, just as he knew the identity of the man who'd scarred them with a Bowie knife.

Goddamn right he knew. Durston untied the pouch, spilled coins into his hand. There was no denying them. They weren't ghosts hanging in a tree. There was no explaining them away. They were *right there*, goddamn it. *Right there* in his goddamn hand.

It took until twilight, but Durston managed to get on two feet. That it took him some time to do the job was okay. It gave him a chance to think things through. And Durston did have some thinking to do, because he'd not be broken by another man's fists or boots. He'd not be broken by the stink of his own piss fouling his clothes. Those things might nail down the corners on another kind of man, but they wouldn't nail down the corners on a man like Durston.

No. Durston saw that clear, the same way he saw his life. With some things, you just had to tighten the cinches and ride on through. With some things, there wasn't another way to play it, not if you wanted to get where you were going. So you boxed up those things the same way you boxed up the things you did in a whore's ten-by-twelve room, and you locked them in there with the shadows where no one else could see them.

And, hell. Things go the way they go. You ride on through. You get where you're going, and to hell with the rest of it.

That was Durston's way.

Pitch Dunnigan twisted above him in the darkness.

Durston sat listening to the sound of the rope.

He waited as night came on.

When it closed around him, he was all done waiting.

The sheriff's house was a good bit out of town, but so were the woods where Durston had taken his beating. It took him awhile to close the distance between the two, what with the shape he was in and the fact that Hauser's deputies had taken both his horse and his pistol.

But by the time the moon hung high in the sky, Durston had a stolen mount and a dead man's sawed-off shotgun, which were all the tools required to run the play he had in mind. Now all he needed was to get Ed Hauser at the other end of that street howitzer, and Durston didn't think that was going to be a problem. The way he figured things, there was only one place a man like Hauser would be when the wolf's hour rolled around.

Durston crept down a neat little path that forked away from the sheriff's back door.

One-handing the sawed-off shotgun, he yanked open the door to Hauser's outhouse.

The sheriff's head jerked up, moonlight shining in his startled eyes.

"How in the hell—"

"Was easy to figure, really," Durston said. "Steak, eggs, tortillas...a man eats a breakfast like that, he's sure to end up on the shitter before the night is through."

Hauser started to rise. "Listen here, you crazy bastard—"

Durston lashed out. The shotgun split one of Hauser's cheeks like an overripe plum, and his ass found the shitshaft hole as quick as could be.

"I won't stand for that kind of talk," Durston said.

Hauser shook his head dizzily and didn't say another word.

"I've come to finish our business," Durston explained, reaching into his pocket for the rawhide pouch. "Now, you put out your paws and get them open. You're taking back these coins, and then you're going to goddamn well tell me if there's anything else needs doing to square this deal."

"There's nothing I can tell you, Durston. And if you think any different you're a damned fool—"

"I warned you once." Durston said, and again he lashed out with the shotgun. But Hauser was ready for him this time. The sheriff's big hands flew up and closed around the twin barrels just as they cracked against his skull. With the bag of gold coins clutched in one hand, Durston only had five fingers wrapped around the stolen weapon, and Hauser was a powerful man and a frightened man, and his big hands grabbed that gun for all he was worth and he wrestled it toward him, and—

Durston's trigger-finger jerked.

Both shotgun barrels cut loose.

Muzzle-flash illuminated the outhouse for one brief moment.

In that moment, half of Hauser's head disappeared. So did a good piece of the wall behind him. The sheriff's body jerked back, slamming against splintered boards, and then it flopped forward, his big hands slapping his naked white thighs as if applauding.

The applause didn't last. It couldn't. A few final twitches and those dead hands lay there in the sheriff's lap, pooling moonlight and blood. Swearing under his breath, Durston untied the rawhide pouch. He dumped scarred coins into Hauser's open palms. Some of them stayed there. Others dropped into the darkness below. Durston swore, not so quietly now. He balled the rawhide poke in his fist and tossed it at the remains of Hauser's head.

There.

One dead, lying bastard in front of him.

One rawhide poke, empty.

Forty coins returned to the hands that had scarred them.

That put an end to it.

That had to put an end to it.

Durston grit his teeth and promised himself it was so. He hurried up the path. A few minutes later he was in the saddle, riding away from Hauser's place on the stolen horse, and he did not spare the animal his spurs. He was glad of the dark as he rode, glad he could not see the treetops or the things that might hang in them. When he crawled off the saddle as dawn broke he was far away, high on a mountain ridge with aspen all around him. And the only things that hung from their branches were golden leaves, and even though the leaves were as round and shiny as twenty-dollar gold pieces, the morning wind whispered through them like music sent down from above, and to Durston it was as pleasing as the sound of coins falling into a dead man's hands.

He slept through the morning.

He slept through the afternoon.

When he awoke at dusk, a shadow hung in the golden leaves...a shadow with stark staring blue eyes. And Durston knew that it was just a shadow. He knew it, but that didn't change a goddamn thing.

Because even if it was just a shadow the damn thing was there, *still there* in spite of all the things Durston had done, and he opened his mouth at the sight of it but there were no words in him, there were only sounds, and they were the kind of sounds most men heard rarely, or not at all.

Unless they were men who worked in a slaughterhouse.

Unless they were men who swung a hammer.

The rope wasn't quality, but Durston wasn't a heavy man. He figured it was strong enough to do the job. And so he spun a good twenty feet of it from the spool before cutting it off, because he wasn't sure just how much rope the job would take.

Coiling the rope around his arm, he carried it to the front of the store where the shopkeeper waited. The man went white at the sight of Durston. He went whiter still as Durston placed the makings of his own suicide noose on the counter and reached for his money poke. The gunman nearly laughed as he did that, because it wasn't really his money poke at all. The goddamn thing wasn't even made of rawhide. It was velvet, and fine and heavy, and he'd taken it from a gutshot banker that very morning.

The truth was that Durston hadn't even touched the coins in that purse. They certainly hadn't been scarred by Ed Hauser's Bowie knife. Of course, that didn't matter to the clerk. Like most men, he believed what he wanted to believe.

"I won't take your money, Mr. Durston," the clerk said.

"I figured you wouldn't, you rattle-brained bastard," Durston replied.

He grabbed the rope off the counter.

And then he reached for his gun.

EMMA SUE

DAVE ZELTSERMAN

Emma Sue's maybe the prettiest gal I've ever seen. I thought so when we were both young and I was courting her, and ten years later I still don't think any differently. She's still a small little thing, no more than eighty-five pounds soaking wet. Her hair's still the same color as fresh-cut hay, and with it rolled back in a bun as she usually wears it, it leaves her face so small. As smooth and pink-hued as her skin is, most men would have a difficult time guessing that she was any older than the seventeen-year-old gal I talked into marrying me all those years earlier. Most men looking into her clear blue eyes would have no idea about how hard a life she has led since becoming my wife.

Not that there hasn't been some happiness in our lives. I love her enough that I'd cut out my heart for her and I'm pretty sure Emma Sue would do the same for me. But it's been hard for the two of us the last ten years with all the obstacles the good Lord has put in our way as we've tried to run our sheep ranch. The first year a fire burned down our barn and half of our home. I was still rebuilding the barn when an early cold spell hit and wiped out a third of our herd with pneumonia. Emma Sue and I were still struggling to recover from that when three years later a twister struck and tore down both the new barn and most of our fencing. We lost half of our sheep 'cause of that tornado, and six years later were still working ourselves ragged each day to overcome all of that when the final blow was struck. Three months ago a cougar got into our sheep pen and went into a killing frenzy. I should've heard the sheep's bleating, but I was just too bone weary to make sense of their cries. Emma Sue lying next to me slept through it all, dead to the world after spending sixteen hours that day first doing her chores and then tilling the soil and planting hay for the fall. Me, I heard the ruckus, but didn't make sense of it until it was too late. By the time I got my rifle and made it to the pen, the cougar was mauling my last standing sheep after killing all eighty head in the herd. I dropped the cougar with two rifle shots, but it was too late to help me any.

A month later critters even more kill hungry than that cougar took our ranch. The bankers who held the note to our property. I had an offer to work as a ranch hand at the Double Bar, and was able to get Emma Sue a job washing and cooking there, but she would hear none of it.

"If we took those jobs we wouldn't be together," she stated flatly.

That was true. We'd be in different bunk houses. I hated the idea of it since it meant something special having her small body next to mine each night even if we were too exhausted to do much more than feel each other breathing. It gave my life some meaning. But I tried explaining that we didn't have much choice in the matter, and after a few years we'd save enough money to try our luck at ranching again. She told me that nothin' was going to make her sleep apart from me and that we did have another choice. She told me how we were going to make enough money to buy ourselves a farm since she didn't want nothin' anymore to do with sheep. The thing with Emma Sue is she's as tough-minded as she is pretty. As much as I didn't like what she was saying I knew I had no chance of talking her out of it and reluctantly went along with her.

We rode out to Tulsa after that. Before we entered Luke Jacobs' Hardware Store, Emma Sue told me we couldn't leave any witnesses.

"The two of us will be caught if we do," she said. "Even if we wear handkerchiefs over our faces, they'll find us. A man and woman robbing the store with me being as small as I am. We have no choice, Bo."

I didn't like it. I didn't see what Luke or his customers ever did to us to deserve what was going to happen to them. Weakly, I suggested we rob the bank that took our ranch instead. She shot me a fierce look. "We do that we'll get caught. Banks can hire posses. No, Bo, this is what we're doing." I knew looking into her eyes there was no use arguing, and besides, I had to admit I didn't see much point in anything if we had to live apart from each other.

As a concession, Emma Sue watched the hardware store from a distance, waiting for when she thought it would be mostly empty. It would be hard for anyone to recognize Emma Sue standing there with the bulky sheepskin coat she was wearing and her cowboy hat pulled low over her eyes so it hid her golden hair. Someone giving her a quick look might even think she was a small man. When Emma Sue signaled, we both strode towards the store from different directions. Emma Sue entered first. When I entered the store I saw that Luke was an old grandfatherly-type with white wisps of hair and a cheery smile. He nodded to me and continued with his pleasantries towards Emma Sue. Outside of Emma Sue and Luke, there was a man about my age studying a shovel. Before I realized it, Emma Sue took two Colt .45s from her coat and trained them on Luke and the customer. I stood mostly in shock at the sight of it.

"What are you waiting for?" she asked, her small knuckles bone-white as she gripped the guns. Luke had frozen up as much as me. The customer with the shovel looked like he was thinking about trying to swing at us. "Oh for lord sake," Emma Sue swore. She shoved one of the pistols in my hand, and I stood dumbly watching as she unsheathed a knife, walked over to Luke and cut his throat as matter-of-factly as if he were a lamb for Easter dinner.

The customer with the shovel decided then he better take action. He swung the shovel back as if he were going to try to knock Emma Sue's head off. I shot him in the belly and he sat down hard on the floor. He looked up at me for a brief moment and then stared at his hands as his guts leaked through them. Emma Sue shot me a disgusted look. She walked over to the dying man and cut his throat also. After that she found the cash drawer and emptied it.

EMMA SUE

"If you hadn't just stood there you wouldn't have had to fire any guns and brought us attention," she scolded me in a breathless whisper. "Now get moving!"

As we agreed earlier, I left the store first. My gunshot hadn't attracted any interested parties. I got on my horse and waited until Emma Sue left. I watched as she rode off, flashing me just the barest of looks. A half hour later we met up, all the while my heart was racing with worry over Emma Sue.

"Why'd you freeze back there, Bo?" she asked me.

"Those two back there didn't deserve killing."

"Life is full of suffering," she said. "I'm just sick of it being us all the time. Bo, we're just doing what we have to. It would kill me having to live apart from you, and I'd think it would kill you having to do the same. I ain't going to let that happen to you."

I nodded 'cause I knew she was right. "How much was in that cash drawer?" I asked.

"Eight hundred dollars."

Eight hundred dollars was more than we had thought going in, but I still couldn't help being disappointed. We figured we needed three thousand dollars to start over, and this meant we'd have a lot more killing to do before we were done.

"It's a good start," she said. "In a week we'll ride out to Chandler."

"You ain't doing no more killing," I said.

She gave me a hard look then, her blue eyes piercing deep into mine. "As long as you have the strength to do what has to be done," she said at last.

"I'll have the strength," I said.

We spent the next four hours riding to Muskogee. We didn't talk much during the ride, and I tried hard not to think of Emma Sue cutting those two men's throats. We lived it up in a hotel the next week, but I couldn't get myself to touch Emma Sue. She didn't say anything, being too proud a woman, but I knew it hurt her. And I knew it wasn't right on my part. She did what she did for me. But news had spread about the slaughter at Luke's, and I just couldn't quite look at Emma Sue the same way, at least not until we rode off to Chandler. By then I had accepted what had happened, and as we exchanged glances I could see that she knew there were no longer any problems between us. We stopped at the town of Sapulpa, checked into a fancy hotel they had there and made up for the past week. The next morning we rode straight to Chandler. When Emma gave the signal, I strode straight into the Chandler General Store, and without breaking stride got behind the storekeeper and cut his jugular. There was a woman in the store and she started screaming. Emma Sue had her gun pointed at her, and I could see her knuckles growing whiter but I'd be damned if I let her do any more killing. As savage as that cougar must've been with our herd, I was on that woman damn near cutting her head off. When I looked up Emma Sue was emptying the cash drawer. Before either of us could move a boy entered the store. He was skinny, no more than ten, and had a big grin on his face until he spotted the carnage and made sense of it. The grin disappeared then and his skin paled to the color of milk. I could see the alarm in Emma Sue's eyes as she pointed one of her Colt .45s at the boy. I was up and tackling the boy before he could run. I had a hand over his mouth as I swung him to the floor.

"We can't leave any witnesses," Emma Sue was saying. "That boy can get us both hung."

I nodded, trying not to look at the fear flooding in the boy's saucer-wide eyes. I tried just as hard not to hear the pounding of his heart.

I could feel Emma Sue staring hard at me. "You don't have it in you to handle this," she said.

"I do too," I forced out. "Besides, you ain't doing any more killing."

There was a long moment where Emma Sue just stood and stared at me. "I'll wait until you do it," she finally said.

"You ain't seeing no more killing either," I said. "I'll do it. Just leave first."

She took my knife from me and wiped the blade clean. "I want to see blood on that blade," she said. "If there ain't any, I'm coming back and doing what you can't."

"I'll do it," I promised. I waited until the door closed behind her, then I dragged the boy over to a bundle of rope, cut off some pieces and tied him up.

"I don't want to kill you, boy," I whispered to him. "You understand?"

He nodded, his eyes growing even wider with terror.

"You ain't going to tell no one what you saw here, right?"

EMMA SUE

He nodded.

"You don't know what we look like. You were hit from behind. That's what happened, right?"

He nodded again. I took my hand away from his mouth. "You promise on your mother's grave?" He tried to answer me but a sob choked him off. The tears welling in his eyes started to leak down his face. "I need to hear it," I said. So low that I could barely hear him, he swore on his mother's grave. I rolled my handkerchief up and pushed it into his mouth. "I'm sorry I have to leave you like this," I told him. "But I got no choice. Now close your eyes."

After he closed his eyes I got up and wiped the blade across the open wound on the storekeeper's throat. I didn't want the boy to have to see that.

When I left the store and rode away from Main Street, Emma Sue was waiting. She made me show her the bloody knife blade. "We just can't leave any witnesses, Bo. If we do they'll catch us."

I didn't say anything. I just watched for a moment as she rode off. It was an hour later when we caught up together where we had planned.

"Bo, you did only what you had to. You did it for us."

I gave Emma Sue a hard look, hoping she couldn't see the truth in my eyes. "How much did you get?"

"Eleven hundred."

She reached over and squeezed my hand. "Maybe just one more time, Bo, and we'll have enough."

I put my free hand on top of hers, but I couldn't look at her. I couldn't let her see how I betrayed her. How I betrayed the two of us. That boy was going to talk. I knew the woman I killed in the store was his ma. I could see the resemblance in their eyes and the shape of their faces. I was kidding myself thinking that I didn't have to kill him, that he wouldn't give a full description of both of us. Now they'll be looking for a man with a small, slender woman. They'll know what both our faces look like. Our only chance now was to ride far enough away. Or hope that boy's description wasn't good enough.

Emma Sue and I had decided to go next to Abilene, which is a hard two days ride by horse. Our plan was to wait out all the news of the slaughters and then ride up to South Dakota to finish what we needed to, but I decided that I was going to talk her into riding east instead, that we had enough money to buy a small store in Boston or some other city where no one would ever hear of the goings-on in Tulsa or Chandler. The first night we camped out under the stars. It was so quiet I could barely stand it. Emma Sue noticed my unease and sidled up to me, resting her head against my chest. Her wheat-colored hair had been taken out of its bun, and now flowed halfway down her slender back.

"I know it was hard what you had to do," she said. "But you did it for us, Bo."

I stroked her hair but didn't say anything. All I felt I could do was stare at the vastness above me.

It was two days later when we arrived in Abilene and checked into the Victorian-style hotel they had downtown. Emma Sue was delighted when she saw the room. "Ever think we'd be in such a room?" she asked. Chambermaids filled up a bathtub that was right there in the room and I watched as Emma Sue took a bath, the water sudsing up from the fragrant salts that had been added to it. I don't think I ever saw Emma Sue happier, and while it made me smile, I couldn't stop worrying.

It was two days later when rumors started to spread about the slaughters that occurred in both Tulsa and Chandler. I wanted Emma Sue and me to stay hidden in our hotel room, but she just laughed off the idea.

"There's nothing to fret about, Bo. No one saw us. Now I hear the saloon has the best steaks in Kansas and that's where we're eating!"

I should've told her about the boy, but I couldn't build up the courage to do that. As we were walking back from dinner, we passed two men who turned back to stare at us. I tried not to look, but I could see them whispering and pointing at us. Emma Sue noticed it too, and I could see the consternation ruining her brow.

"What do you suppose they're whispering about?" she asked me, suspicion flashing in her all-too-blue eyes.

I didn't answer her. I just grabbed her by the elbow and hurried her along.

"You didn't kill that boy, did you?" she accused in a harsh whisper.

"Not now," I said.

EMMA SUE

When we got back to the hotel room, Emma Sue was ashen. "You didn't do it. You left that boy alive to identify us."

"That boy was too scared. He didn't know what he was seeing."

"Yes he did." Emma Sue sat on the bed. She looked so small as she clasped her hands together and tried hard not to cry. "I don't want to lose you, Bo. But I'm going to."

"You won't," I told her. "We can ride out now. If we head East, we can disappear someplace like Boston or New York."

"It's too late," she said. "They know we're here. We won't be able to outrun them."

I heard a commotion from outside. Emma Sue heard it too. I pushed the curtains aside and saw a mob outside the hotel. The two men who had been whispering and pointing at us were talking to the hotel's desk clerk, and were now running into the hotel. Emma Sue had joined my side and watched it also.

"Don't let them hang me," she pleaded. She grabbed me hard and buried her face in my chest. I could feel my shirt growing wet. "Please, Bo, not that."

I tried holding her, but she pushed away from me. "Please, Bo, if you love me as much as I love you, don't let that happen. I can't bear the thought of that, having them all stare at me dangling from a rope."

Then she lay down on the bed and waited.

I didn't want to move, but when I heard them banging on my door, I had no choice. I loved Emma Sue more than life. I couldn't let that happen to her. I couldn't stand the thought of them pawing and grabbing at her, or worse, leering at my Emma Sue as they strung her up. I did what she wanted me to do. I took one of the fine goose feathered pillows and held it over her face until she was gone. My heart was still beating, but I was as dead as she was. All that was left was to open the door and let the mob finish the chore.

When I met them standing outside the door I held out my hands to make it easy for them. One of the two men who had been whispering and staring at me and Emma Sue grabbed my right hand and started pumping it.

"Bo Wilson of Pawhuska, I knew I recognized you."

Slowly, I recognized him also. He was Tom Laraby. I recognized the other man too. Albie Henricks. I hadn't seen them since I started sheep ranching, but they both grew up where Emma Sue and I did.

Tom Laraby stuck his red face into the room and spotted Emma Sue lying on the bed. "I'm sorry," he said in a hushed whisper. "I see your wife is asleep. Still as pretty as ever. I didn't mean to disturb you two but we're forming a posse to go after some lowdown thieves who robbed the First Abilene Bank earlier."

Albie Henricks chimed in that it was the same men who did the massacres at Luke Jacobs' and the General Store in Chandler.

"That's right," Tom Laraby said. "They left a boy alive at the store in Chandler. According to him it was two men, a small one and a large one, just like the two who robbed the First Abilene. Anyway, bank's offering fifty dollars a head and when I recognized you on the street, I thought you might want to join us. Always on the lookout to help a fellow Pawhuska."

I thought how Emma Sue was at the store in Chandler. With her heavy sheepskin coat and her hat pulled down low, as fearful as the boy was he never realized she was a woman. We would've been safe. I nodded to Tom Laraby, then went back into the room and grabbed my gun and coat. When I came back to join the mob, Tom Laraby gave me an odd look. "Ain't you going to wake your wife to tell her you're going?" he asked.

I shook my head. "Better just to let her sleep," I said. If I was lucky I'd be killed on the ride. Otherwise they could hang me later when I came back. Either way it didn't much matter.

HELL HATH NO FURY

T. L. WOLF

Lucian Danvers skirted the Abo Pass heading west out of Estancia Valley where the ground had been baked hard by the July heat. So hard, it'd tried killing him twice for the sport of making a little mud with his blood. In the hazy, purple shadow of the Manzano Mountains, the valley arced up, buckling into rolling hills littered with scrawny grass and mesquite. He picked a chaparral big enough to hide in and wove his horse through it just as night was slipping in.

Honest folks didn't travel the back-trails of the New Mexico Territory—they didn't need to, so he studied the valley, looking for dust in the distance. Satisfied, he turned his attention to the horse, rubbing it down as lightning cracked overhead like a starter pistol, signaling the start of the monsoon rain that raced to the ground. He cursed the downpour for the nuisance it was, but tossed his hat down to catch some before grabbing a small shovel off the saddle to dig the horse's water trough. It was that or the alkali ponds that dotted the hollows.

It could've been the rain, maybe the clatter of the shovel fighting the ground, but it didn't matter either way—a gun cocked somewhere from behind.

"Goddamn it, I hate that sound!" Lucian said, keeping crouched where he was.

"Hold still now, Mister. I gotcha square," the voice said, sounding skittish and four, maybe six feet back in the brush. "It's wetter'n a whore's bed on nickel night out here, and I need that horse of yours."

Lucian shouted, "Every peckerwood Okie that gets a pistol in his hands suddenly has a sack full o' brass swingin' twixt his knees," and inched the shovel to his right hand while the hand of God got ready to cross-draw his Colt. "Goddamn horse thief!"

"I don't seem to have secured your fucking attention, sir," the voice yelled, closer now, mixing with the sounds of a buffalo traversing mesquite in twilight, slowly gaining ground over stick and stump until—

Lucian spun hard, releasing the shovel before he drew.

"Fu—" escaped the thief's mouth as the shovel connected.

Lucian squeezed the trigger.

The thief's head snapped back, the bullet punching through.

The rain backed off from piss to spit as they stood there. The storm's last word came from a lightning bolt that turned night to day, and Lucian took a sharp breath. "Oh, for fuck sake." He holstered and went over to the thief, slipping the pistol from a twitching hand. A name bubbled from the young lips like a prayer. It could've been a sweetheart's name, but more likely a whore's who had took the trouble to remember his. It sounded like Maryanne. The kid was between grass and hay, late teens at best. Dirt and blood mixed on his face before running down to his boiled-to-paper woolen undershirt. He danced a small jerking jig with his eyes rolled up, looking lost to the wonderment of what to do with a hole that high in his forehead.

Lucian had seen the same wounds at Five Forks, during the war, and knew what to do. "Sorry, kid, but I like that horse...a lot. It's a Indian Paint." A nudge to the back of a knee folded the kid to the ground. "Goddamned double-action Colt," Lucian grumbled. The trigger pulled heavy, making odds of accuracy worse than a game of faro.

If the boy was aware that he'd shit himself, or of Lucian, he gave no sign, mumbling on.

"You're head-shot—scrambled up there." He tapped his head to show where, immediately feeling awkward for the gesture, and knelt down, putting a hand over the nose and mouth. No whiskers. Coming as close to prayer as he dared, he said, "Can't risk another bullet, son, too loud. I'm...sorry. You rest now," and squeezed.

It didn't take long. Lip movement against his palm ceased. But he kept it there for a while, wondering how, after twenty-five years, he'd ended up doin' the same messy business as on those killin' fields when he was—

"Younger than you," he said, surprised to hear the voice he'd thought was in his head. He let go and wiped the last of the raindrops from his face before looking to the sky. *Must've been rain,* he thought, and stood.

Pistols and rifles cocked all around him, too many to count, and too dark to see. *Goddamn it, I hate that sound,* he thought.

A smoky voice said, "I'd just as soon dispatch ya to shake hands with Lucifer than look at ya. Get dem hands up!"

Lucian cursed, doing as told. That's twice the kid had distracted him. "If I knew there was a party, gentlemen, I would've brought some tater salad."

A barrel nuzzled between his shoulder blades as its owner weighed in. "Hobble yer lip, and don't so much as twitch, ya sonofabitch!"

A match cut the air with phosphorus light and sulfur, giving everyone in the environs a tiny preview of hell. Shadows danced over nine hard faces for a second before swallowing them whole, the match having moved south to hover at the tip of the boy's gory face. "Jesus," said the light bearer. He patted the body until he discovered a small book, and pulled the boy's undershirt off one shoulder, exposing a wound. "That's him, Dan."

Lucian thought he saw a pattern in the wound, tried to focus on it, but the match blew out. He put the image on his back burner. The cocksuckers that had him reaching for Glory held precedence, anyway.

Another match struck up, this one advancing on him followed close by a glint of barrel steel winking from the shadowlands between match-light and darkness. The flame revealed Lucian's slender frame, topped by a rugged, drawn face and shoulder-length black hair, all together making his age hard to guess. His eyes were what usually got him in trouble, though. Trouble with the ladies that wanted to drown in their azure depths, and trouble with men packing guns, whiskey-mad for having lost their nerve trying to stare them down.

Lucian hid the blue behind a squint and said, "Did what I had to, Mister...Dan, was it? I don't want trouble. He's a horse thief."

"Oh, I know what he is," said smoky-voiced Dan. "'Scuse me— *was*. Fuck if I know who you are, though."

Lucian worked hard not to cringe as acrid breath brushed his face. "Buster Kreb," he lied. "On my way to Albuquerque from Roswell. Just passing through."

"Well, Buster Kreb-just-passing-through-from-Roswell, did I ask you for your fuckin' life story?" Dan paused for the snickers making the rounds, tossing the match and lighting another. "Must be hidin' bull's balls in your trousers to be travelin' Apache country on your lonesome; either that or stupid. You're a piece off the trail, too. Maybe *you're* a horse thief." The flickering light didn't do Dan's face any favors. A scar, white lightning across his flattened nose, ran down to a jaw that a handful of brown teeth called home.

Lucian wanted to knock them loose, but the barrel in his back nuzzled closer, reminding him to hold his temper. "No sir, just a ranch hand looking for work. I can hold my own out here."

Dan chuckled. "Oh, I see that." He thumbed at the body, and studied Lucian a moment more. "Ranch hand, huh?"

Lucian clenched his fists, making them ready. "That's all."

The match died with a wet sputter between Dan's greasy, cigarette-yellowed fingers. He huffed, breaking the silence. "Hell, you don't seem to mind killin'. No need to go as far as Albuquerque." He turned, making his way out of the mesquite. "You want work? There's plenty for you to do right here. Baron Von Metzger's gonna need another hand, now."

More snickers sounded before the barrel left his back and the group melted back through the bush. "I'm beholden to ya," said Lucian. "What about the boy? There a...reward or anythin'?"

Laughter broke out all around him, followed by Dan's voice. "A job's your reward, and the coyotes'll take care of the funeral. Trust me—he's lucky you got to him."

Lucian grabbed his hat and shovel, grateful the darkness covered his grin. *No,* he thought. *I am. You just made my job a lot easier.*

A squat, solid figure leaned against a large porch pillar, cigar glow echoing off pallid jowls at every puff. "Well?" the figure bellowed as they rode up. The sweaty bejeweled man seemed natural-born to the luxuries visible in the windows of his monstrous two-story ranch house; it was the house that looked unnatural to the Manzano Mountain foothills, like a whore wearing too much rouge to church. An extravagant black eagle crest marked every pillar Lucian could see, alternating their gaze from left to right, pillar to pillar, across the porch's border.

"Found him, Baron," Dan said, tossing the little book on the porch. "But not before this feller did. He took care of your...little problem."

Von Metzger studied the smoke curling up before bringing his eyes on Lucian, the beady orbs poring over him, lingering. He smiled. "Did he?"

Dan nodded. "We need another hand, and he don't mind getting his dirty. I thought he could—"

Eyes still on Lucian, Von Metzger said, "I do not pay you to think, Danford. I pay you to do—what *I* say. I know exactly what needs to be done. What is your name?"

Lucian tipped his hat. "Buster Kreb, sir."

"Well, Mr. Kreb, I owe you my thanks for taking care of that nasty business. That piece of refuse...stole from me," he said, ejecting it from his mouth like sour fruit, eyes bulging. He bent, snatching the book, and was calm again. "The new U.S. Territory of New Mexico has been made safe for Christian consumption: Billy the Kid is eight years in his grave, and Geronimo has been a sideshow pet for three years running. Soon, every cocksucker with a hard-on for land will be flooding over the Santa Fe Trail." He studied Lucian for a reaction, getting none, and stood as tall as his frame would allow. "My name is Baron Marion Von Metzger. And

I intend to keep what is mine, Mr. Kreb. I want only strong, able-bodied men to make sure I do."

Lucian thought, *Betcha do, Mari...Maryanne?*—his face still straight as a cooling-board. He asked. "What'd you like me to do?"

Von Metzger flashed a smile that fell between predator and preacher. "Why, no more than what comes naturally to you, my boy. Kill anything that wanders onto, or off, my property that does not possess my express permission—beast or man. Is that a problem for you?"

The front door opened behind the Baron.

Lucian said, "No, s...ir," choking on the sure knowledge that he and his Indian Paint were good and fucked when the woman appeared.

She flowed up next to Von Metzger with grace; head poised to sniff out the slightest hint of bullshit within a five-mile radius. Covered chin to toe in black silk, auburn hair pulled into a tight, high bun, she looked every bit the lady. But Lucian knew better than anyone how deceptive looks could be. He knew the fire hiding under all that cloth, just under that soft alabaster skin of hers. Knew just how hot it could get, and ached to feel that heat again. He held his breath, and waited to see what Emily would do.

"Dearest? Do we have guests?" She swung an indifferent gaze out, resting it on Lucian.

Von Metzger followed the look to its endpoint. "No, nothing so important. Danford has brought us a new hand."

"Buster Kreb, ma'am," said Lucian, tugging the edge of his hat again.

Eyes unchanged, she returned a slight nod, no reply passing her tensed jaw.

"*Baroness* Von Metzger," he said, eyes narrowed on Lucian, then on her. "I will be in directly, dear."

She acknowledged this, returning to the house without a word.

Lucian slipped an exhale past his lips, thinking, *Damn lucky.*

Eyes drilling holes in Lucian's head, Von Metzger flicked his cigar in that direction. He said, "Mr. Kreb, I think you would be better suited to...beasts for now. See to it that he is situated, Danford," and went inside, leaving the yard to his gang and their snickers.

T. L. WOLF

Next morning, Lucian wolfed down two rocks the Mexican cook swore were biscuits, and grimaced as the coffee slid down after them.

Dan said, "Shit. Never seen a man so anxious to get coyote blood on 'is hands," setting the gang to laughing. Daylight made it plain why this pack of easy-money-misfits had taken work here, sixty-miles southeast of Albuquerque. Bandit towns swarmed around Territory cities like mosquitoes. Close enough to have a taste when they wanted, far enough away to keep from being swatted. They needed swatting.

But for once, Lucian had less time than patience, and would have to work fast. Emily was bound to do something. He could feel it. He'd just caught her off guard, that's all. Those talented hands of hers were on the plunger, charge wires running from it to the dynamite she'd shoved right up his ass. He pulled a dozen leg-traps off the bunkhouse wall. "Hour's ride back to the kid's body," he said, grabbing his saddlebags.

"Whoa," Dan said, standing up, hand on his pistol. Two upstarts followed his lead.

Lucian glared enough blue to say "fuck you" as tendrils of a grin sprouted at the corners of his mouth. "Can you think of better coyote bait?"

Dan held his gaze. "You cold-blooded..." He started chuckling. "Sonofabitch. Goddamn!" He sat down, motioning for the two to do the same. Their howls followed Lucian into the corral.

Last evening's trail was an easy find, but he kept the Paint at a trot until the house dropped below the horizon, only then letting the mare do what she wanted—what *they* wanted—lighting out across the hills as one, reaching the site in half the time.

The stink hit him a hundred yards back. "Let's see if your luck holds, Boy-O." The coyotes hadn't got to the body, but they would. He threw himself off the mare, kneeled and pulled back the torn shirt. His brow puckered at the sight of it. "Of all the fuckin'...Must've done it while Danford was chewing my ear off," he said. The wound on the boy's shoulder was gone—skinned off. He blinked, the raw patch gnawing at his recollection. He wiped the area with a piece of shirt. It was faint, but there, blistered to the meat. The boy'd been branded, but the pattern was too far gone.

He pulled a leather parfleche from one of his saddlebags, and from inside of it, a neat, folded stack of weathered papers. He scanned every one until—

"Ha-Ha!" he shouted, putting the rest back. He read it through, savoring the find before folding the newspaper clipping into his shirt pocket. "And she called me crazy for saving these things."

"Who did?" a voice called from outside the mesquite. *Her* voice.

He led his pony out, stopping short of her mare's sleek head, wondering if it was age creeping up on him or something about this area that made him deaf. "Emily, what are you doing out here?"

"You will address me as Baroness, you asshole. And you're not the only one with a fast horse." Her mare pranced in place, a twitching mass of muscle, disgusted that she'd been stopped.

He grabbed her reins, caught her leg and pulled her off the horse. "You know what I mean, goddamn it!" He held her arms down and went for her lips, the old fire driving him.

She pulled away and slapped him hard. "You bastard! You left me in Santa Fe!" Then slapped him harder, making his ears ring. "And that's for not leaving me any money!" Clenching her fist high, she kicked out into his lap. "That's for—"

He reached out and caught her cheek with the back of his hand, sending her to the ground. "That's for marrying that sick little fuckin'—" He doubled over, trying not to think of the ache in his crotch. "And kickin' me in the nuts," he croaked.

She rose and dusted herself off, cheek glowing but not swollen. "He's gonna kill you," she said through clenched teeth. "And I'm gonna enjoy it."

He said, "I never left you," just as her foot slipped in the stirrup. She stopped. "Liar!"

He was lying, but if he'd said he wanted her, she'd be out of his reach forever and halfway to the ranch before he could mount up. "Bushwhacked on an old warrant," he said, trying to catch his breath. "By the time I got back to you…well…" He tried to smile.

She shot him a derisive look and swung a leg up and over. "It's been a year! But you can't stand to see me happy, can you Lucian? He's big time. Real money. The Atchison, Topeka and

Santa Fe railroad will be laying down rails in this section of God's own private nowhere, and——"

"I know. That's why the Ring sent me." He winced. "It ain't got nothin' to do with you, Emily. Jesus H. Mahoney. Why'd ya have to kick me in the nuts?"

She reined the horse close up to him. "The Santa Fe Ring?"

From first word to last, sheriffs to governors, and whores to hooch, the Ring was the real law in the Territory. He nodded. "You're backin' the wrong horse Emily. In more ways than you know. He's quit playin' by their rules, trying to set up a new game. Probably has eyes for Albuquerque. They want him. Alive. God knows why."

Those gorgeous eyes narrowed on him, hating, maybe herself a little for loving him, but probably just him for ruining her life—again. "Goddamn you, Lucian."

"Already has darlin'."

"How much they offerin'?"

"Nothin' for a carcass. Five-thousand alive."

She said, "I want half," without blinking. "You understand? I get half!"

"Done," he said. "Give me three, four hours. Be ready."

Her mare strained at the reins like it understood, quivering, waiting for the slightest nudge. "What about the ranch hands?"

He answered with a slap on her mare's rump, firing her across the foothills, back into the wind and dust. Her talents for crawling under his skin made him wonder if he'd ever get her out.

After a slow, steady mount, he pulled the paper out of his pocket. It was two years old, from the New Orleans *Picayune*, but the statute of limitation on something like this usually lasted longer than the paper it was printed on.

It read: *Fifth Body Found! Youngest Son of Senator, Hurled Into Eternity. What madman is targeting our wealthy patron's sons...*He read on, careful of every line before *arm mutilated*, and after, hungry for more detail and finding none. It'd have to do. The article finished with: *The grieving families, combined, have offered the generous reward of $10,000 for the documented capture and/or execution of this fiend.*

"Goddamn double bulls-eye," he murmured. The Ring could take what they wanted, he'd take the rest. Maybe she'd come with him to New Orleans and they'd claim it together. No more running.

Lucian flew full-tilt into the ranch yard like the devil was chasing him, yelling, "Twenty head, maybe more! Butchered! North-ridge where the big pines are, two hours out!"

The gang tripped out from every nook and crook. Dan asked, "'Pache sign?" looking itchy to butcher and battle.

Feigning breathlessness, Lucian accounted for every hand, and nodded.

The silent promise of their bloodlust being quenched was more than the thirsty men could stand. Before Lucian's boots touched the dirt, they'd mounted up. Still breathing hard, he said, "I'll get some provisions, bullets, give my mare a chance to breathe. I'm right behind you."

Dan nodded, and they were off to chase lightning. They'd find dead cows, Lucian had seen to that. And if his luck held out, maybe a few would find the dozen leg-traps he'd set, buried in the dirt around the cows.

He tethered the mare in reach of water and hay, and eyed the house. No faces in the windows, no movement in the curtains, and no point in slinking up. Von Metzger might've heard the commotion.

On the porch, he pulled the Peacemaker, ready to deliver the news, and knocked.

Nothing.

He counted sixty Mississippis and went in.

Inside, his eyes worked hard to focus, fighting off the low light, rich adornments and carved woods that touched everything, catching him off guard. "Three whorehouses couldn't hold all this," he murmured, and shook it off. He had to stay sharp.

A search of the main floor found every door open to an empty room except the big oak set, just off the entryway. They sported carved eagles in high detail on each panel, watching him listen at them, testing their handles. They were locked.

He stepped back, took a breath and kicked the spot just below the handles. The doors gave easy and swung wide, rebounding off the walls they were fixed to with all the noise he'd hoped for. It would've been another fine entrance if there'd been anyone to see it.

Bookshelves fought with paintings for the room's wall space while a mountain of oak disguised as a desk took up the middle of the floor. By the fireplace, two leather armchairs stood guard over a small round table that was busy holding up a crystal decanter of dark amber liquid.

Where were they? Was that high-toned horse of hers in the corral when he rode up? He hadn't noticed, being so focused on getting the gang moving. Thoughts of double-cross played a familiar tune in his ear. He walked the room, cursing his pecker under his breath for getting him in trouble, for tricking him into telling her anything. He slammed his fist against the desk. *You're getting ahead of yourself, Boy-O. There's still upstairs to check.*

He harnessed the anger in a breath, trying to keep it from jumping from bad thought to worse. And in that breath, he saw it on the desk, the little black book they'd pulled from the kid. He picked it up and tried thumbing it open one-handed, gave up and holstered. "Let's see what was worth dyin' for."

Deep furrows crowned his forehead as he turned page after page. "Nothin'," he murmured. "You died for nothin'."

A soft whoosh of air sounded from behind, a blink before the burning pain in his upper arms appeared, making him drop the blank-paged book. He screamed, only able to dance where the blades led him, pointing their way into the back of his arms, pinning him face first to a wall.

"Another...Filthy...Rat-thief," Von Metzger spat. "Skewered! What shall I do with you, Rat-thief?" The blades twisted, the volume of Lucian's shrieks swelling for every hair's-breadth they moved, and then they were gone.

Dead weight hit the floor behind him, enough to bounce two paintings off the wall.

"Now I know I love you," he said, and turned.

Emily's face bloomed scarlet and she brandished the pistol at him like a club. "What do you mean *now* you know?"

Von Metzger lay motionless on the floor, a sword clutched in each pudgy fist. The bookcase next to the desk hung open like a door, exposing the hiding place beyond.

"What do you mean *now* you know," she repeated.

Von Metzger stirred.

"Emmers, I'm bleedin' and he's moving." Lucian spotted a pair of manacles on the floor of the little room behind the bookcase and went for them while she pried the swords from Von Metzger's hands.

Bending for the manacles, he spotted them, sitting on a cut-up table stained black with old blood and red with new. Next to the small eagle-shaped branding iron, the little black book looked innocent. He held his breath, opened it and counted six branded skins before shutting it, not wanting to see any more. *God help me, there's a* lot *more.*

"Lucian! He's comin' to!"

He pulled the deathroom's last three teeth and left: the book in his back pocket, the iron in hand and the manacles that he tossed to Emily.

"What's that?" she asked, eyeing the iron.

He came up to Von Metzger's stirring form and brought the iron across the plump face, making him still again.

"Never mind," said Emily.

A moment later, as Emily finished with Lucian's bandages, Von Metzger came to. He looked liquor-blind trying to focus on her. "You cunt," he slurred. "Whore. I raised you up from all the other filth, made you a baroness."

"You only married her for window dressin', ya lavender lunatic. I doubt you're even a real baron." Lucian shook his head. "Where'd you hit him, Emmers?"

Horror crawled across her face. "What?"

"I asked...you where...you hit him. Too low, it does nothing. Too high, they go silly for life. You need to hit them here," he said, and tapped the spot on the back of her head.

She pushed his hand away. "What do you mean *window* dressing?"

Lucian wasn't ready to tell her yet. Not yet. He shoved the iron in his gun-belt and turned back to Von Metzger. "Shit, your marriage wasn't legal anyway: we've been married over a ye—"

Pain radiated from the base of his skull in the exact spot he'd shown her. He fell onto Von Metzger, struggling to stay awake, to pull his boot-knife. Someone was laughing, and he realized it was Von Metzger.

"I'm sick of both of you," she screamed. "Ignoring me when I'm talkin', and talkin' to me like I'm stupid!"

Lucian watched her blurry form pace the floor.

"You shouldn't've slapped me," she added. "I warned you on our wedding night: Don't ever fucking slap me!" She took a breath, gathering herself like a yard of cloth that'd gotten away in a breeze. "I'm taking it all. Fuck the pair of ya. If either one of ya had another inch on your cock, we wouldn't be having this trouble."

That's it, Lucian thought, and plunged the knife in Von Metzger's fat inner thigh, feeling satisfaction in that fading scream as the room zeroed to black.

The smell woke him. It hung in the air like a dead man—kerosene. But he didn't smell smoke, at least not yet. "Your luck's holdin' out, Boy-O."

He tried to stand, started to fade, and grabbed the desk. Sticky wetness covered his neck, making him think twice about looking at his arms just then.

He felt the news-clipping in his shirt pocket, exhaling a breath he didn't know he'd been holding, then felt back for the little book of skins, patting nothing but denim-covered ass. He scanned the floor, panic reaching up through his gut and grabbing his heart, pulling it into his stomach. "No, no, no, no!" Yelling hurt, but it cleared a few cobwebs in trade, enough that he saw the book's outline at his feet. He sighed his relief and picked it up, pocketing it again. *Now get going before the gang gets back*, he thought. *Before she gets too far down the trail.*

Whiskey first, a little voice countered, a voice he hadn't heard in a long time. He didn't argue with it. Baby steps marked his progress to the bottle. Taking the golden liquid into his mouth felt like communion, the warmth spreading down his throat, coating his gut and clearing his head. Keeping the bottle for company, he headed outside.

She'd left his pistols, but only one was worth a damn. "Goddamn double-action," he grumbled. Both cylinders were fresh, and all he had left after the cows. Besides Von Metzger's branding iron, his gun belt was bare. It wouldn't be enough. "Bunkhouse," he reminded himself. "There're bullets there, maybe even a rifle or two."

In the entryway, he stepped over shattered kerosene lamps and picked up the box of matches sitting on the little table next to the open front door. "She was gonna torch it and lost her nerve," he said, and grinned. "She loves me."

Outside, the sun rode high, telling him it was later than he'd thought. The tight cloud of dust dirtying the horizon reiterated the sentiment. The gang was rolling in fast, maybe a mile out.

He looked at the matches. *Not a bad idea. Light the house, keep 'em busy, take my chances with the—*

The Indian Paint was gone.

"Goddammit! I mean...fuck...you...ya filthy harlot!" He took a long pull off the bottle, then tucked it under-arm and pulled a match, eyes fixed on the coming dust cloud. "Okay, alright," he shouted, and lit it, touching it to the rest, turning the matchbox into a little phosphor bomb that he tossed onto the kerosene puddle before sprinting off the porch for the bunkhouse. "But you better have my Paint when I catch you, woman! I like that horse...a lot!"

Inside the bunkhouse, he grabbed a tarnished Henry's repeater off the rack, loaded it from the ammo box on the floor and busted every window for a clear shot.

The book! He felt back and pulled it, wanting to see it—be assured it was worth dying for.

Outside, hoofbeats jumbled with shouts of confusion. Seven more voices than he'd hoped for, Danford's above all. It grated against the last raw nerve throbbing in Lucian's temples. He dropped the book—*The wrong book*, he thought. *The* blank *book, you jackass*—and picked up the bottle for another long pull.

He wondered if Emily was faring any better, if she pulled the knife from the cocksucker's leg. *If she does he'll spring a leak she can't bandage*, he thought. *Even if she doesn't, he'll bleed out from the inside, just slower.* He smiled, shouldering the Henry's, taking aim at Danford. "Either way, it's a long way to Santa Fe."

VANITY

JEREMIAH HEALY

I t was getting on toward sunset, with a full moon already rising
above the reddening horizon, when Kel McKyer reined his
walking horse to a full stop at the sign reading:

VANITY, ARIZONA
POP. 159

Kel glanced at the cluster of ramshackle town buildings maybe
a hundred yards farther east. Whoever named this place had a sense
of humor, all right. Still, Kel flicked the rawhide loop on his holster
from over the hammer of his 1874 Colt Peacemaker. No reason to
take chances on any town, especially one that was the butt of its
own joke.

VANITY

Kel dismounted and tied his horse to the hitching rail in front of "HOTEL." That was it: No other indication over the door, though both the dry goods store to the left of it and the saloon across the street had names on them, with the second's sign reading "BALDY'S." While still in the saddle, Kel had weighed a beer or a whiskey—or both—as a higher priority than a hotel bed, but he'd camped out enough nights in a row that a room in hand seemed more important than a drink.

Kel slung his saddlebags, laden with the weight of gold nuggets, over his left shoulder and climbed the three steps to the hotel's entrance. Inside, a short man with dark, wiry hair and a beard to match stood at the rear edge of the front desk, talking in a language Kel didn't understand to a young girl. She was maybe fourteen, and as pretty in an almost-woman way as the man was homely. Kel did catch her looking at him and smiling with white, even teeth before saying "Yah, Papa" at what seemed to be the end of their talk. Then the daughter smiled at Kel again and disappeared through an archway to the back. When she closed the door behind her, Kel caught a whiff of fresh biscuits and maybe venison.

The short man moved to the center of his counter. "How can I *help*?"

Kel pointed up the stairs. "Room for the night?"

"Yah, sure."

Kel tapped the saddlebag resting against his left breast. "You have a safe where I could leave this?"

"Yah," gesturing below the desk, "here *behind*."

"I need a receipt?"

"Why? I am Steinberg, owner, and I will remember you just fine."

Kel took an immediate liking to the man, but he also noticed the "why" and the "will" both came out with a "V," instead of the "W" Kel expected. "You from Germany, maybe?"

"Yah, yah," said Steinberg, grinning from ear to ear with most of his teeth, all of them yellowed. "How do you guess?"

Kel had sat with a German widow in the desert some months before, talking to her so she wouldn't die alone. "Knew somebody from there once."

Steinberg nodded. "My daughter, Sarah, and I speak the Yiddish before. Like German language, only Jewish."

Kel tried to think if he'd ever heard of a Jewish person outside the Bible stories his mother had read to him.

Steinberg swung the dusty register around so Kel could sign it, and Kel did the same with his even dustier saddlebags.

"Heavy," said the hotel owner, hefting the leather.

"They are that."

Kel finished his writing as Steinberg, squatting behind the counter, closed a solid, metal door and spun a combination dial. "What your wife's cooking smells awful good."

When the hotel owner stood back up, he swiped a sleeve across his eyes, then turned to the kitchen door. "My Ruth is buried eleven years now."

Kel decided he was glad not to have mentioned the dying widow.

Steinberg said, "My Sarah, she make the food for our guests."

"Many besides me?"

Now the hotel owner pursed his lips. "A captain of the cavalry and his men. One soldier, a poor man with big scar through his face, waits for my Sarah at our back door, help her to carry their food to the stable."

Kel had been cavalry during Mr. Lincoln's war and thought that odd. "The troopers are eating in the stable?"

Steinberg winced now, leaned forward and whispered. "They are big black fellows. 'Buffalo Soldiers,' our Sheriff Poteet call them."

Kel had heard that some units of freed slaves, led by white officers, were after Apache hostiles that had jumped a reservation nearby. "So, they sleep in the stable, too?"

"Yah, yah." Steinberg shook his head, obviously not happy with the arrangement. "Otherwise, our sheriff tell me, nobody ever eat or stay in my hotel again."

Kel thought himself and a lot of others had done major killing ten years back over that kind of thing, but, on the whole, he also thought Vanity's sheriff was probably right.

VANITY

As Kel McKyer crossed the street to the saloon, he saw a cavalry officer with blonde hair under his headgear walking with a precise stride toward a black trooper who, despite the heat, was still in his blue tunic and trousers, the squarish constellation of buttons gleaming on his chest, just like his commander's. The officer extended what from a distance looked like two bottles of whiskey to the soldier. The white man smiled as the black man took them, nodding—almost bowing—gratefully. Then an exchange of salutes, the officer turning precisely on his heel back toward Baldy's. The soldier then quick-marched around the corner of the dry goods store and disappeared.

Kel thought the man might act like a stickler for pomp, but he looks after his troops.

"And you would be, sir?"

Kel looked at the blonde officer—from the bars on his shoulders, the captain that Steinberg had mentioned. Close up now, the man's hair and mustache both were neatly trimmed. With the clean uniform, he gave off the air of a dandy.

Kel nodded to the other two men sitting with the officer at the same saloon table. One looked early forties, full enough in the stomach that he might have been a little younger. The third man was pushing fifty, a bushier mustache covering his lower lip. Kel noted a star on his shirt—probably making him Sheriff Poteet—but a shotgun instead of a revolver rested near the lawman's right side.

"McKyer's my name."

The captain grinned. "And you'd have a Christian name, too, I'll wager?"

"Kel."

Now the cavalry officer frowned. "Short for?"

"It's not. Just Kel.'"

The fat man spoke next. "Captain Crane would much like to get up a poker game, but I told him I do not play with less than four men betting."

Slight Spanish lilt on his words. Kel nodded once and slowly, more in acknowledgment of a reasonable requirement than in agreement to participate. A quick scan of the saloon showed mostly prospectors down on their luck, probably nursing warm beers.

Kel addressed the man with the badge. "Sheriff, would you be the fourth?"

"Would be, but I don't gamble." Poteet nudged his fat companion. "Oswaldo here's our mayor, so—as a politician—he's always kind of 'betting' on something." Then the lawman blinked a few times and squinted, like maybe he'd seen the newcomer before.

Kel thought about another two-bit town named "Launcelot" and the poor loser he'd had to shoot in a card game. Kel wondered if there might not be a wanted poster out on him. "Thanks anyway, gentlemen, but I think I'd rather fill my head with whiskey than suits this evening."

Crane, clearly disappointed, shook his head and turned to the mayor. "Well, Oswaldo, I guess that leaves us two short still." Then, from where exactly Kel couldn't be sure, the cavalry officer produced a deck of cards and started shuffling with just his right hand, using fingernails to tent the cards before making them dive over and under each other.

Kel thought; Well, at least once in your life you made a good decision about gambling.

At the bar, a man with a shaved head and big arms said, "What's your pleasure?"

"Whiskey?"

Baldy—he just had to be—inclined his eyebrows toward the three men at the table. "Captain there bought two bottles for his men—I wouldn't let them in here, of course."

Kel tried for dry in his reply. "Of course."

"But, I still got a few bottles left." Baldy brought one up and poured.

"Madness," Sheriff Poteet's voice rose behind Kel. "Sending black savages after red ones, then giving the blacks the same whiskey stirs up the Apaches they're supposed to be killing."

Kel turned with his drink.

Crane caused the cards to dance again in his hand. "Our orders use 'exterminate,' actually."

Kel looked at the captain, thinking he'd done a neat job of deflecting the sheriff's comment. But Kel still felt put off by the cavalry officer's choice of words. "You mean, like...bugs?"

Crane nodded. "Latest report from the Board of Indian Commissioners to President Grant. We are to 'exterminate' the Apache—Chiricahua, Rio Verde, Coyotero, no matter."

"Won't be soon enough for me," said Poteet. "I can't count how many good folk've been lost to those devils."

Kel turned back to Baldy, who asked, "You staying in the Jew's hotel?"

Real friendly town. "Is there another one?"

"No. Just going to tell you: Forget what you might've heard about them. Steinberg's a good man."

So, Baldy was at peace with religious differences, if not racial ones.

"Well," the cavalry officer's voice broke the silence as a chair scraped back. "With no good prospect of a game, I believe I'll make use of clean sheets and a soft bed. Gentlemen?"

"Same here," from the sheriff.

Kel heard more than saw the men leave, though the mirror over the bar let him know they parted ways as soon as they were through the swinging doors.

Then, from the table, "So, Mr. McKyer, come drink one with me?"

Kel shrugged. What danger could a small-town mayor be?

As he joined the fat man at the table and started to sit, Kel's new friend spoke again. "Oswaldo Gonzalez."

They shook hands.

The mayor settled some in his chair, making it creak. "And from where do you join us?"

Truth's as easy as a lie. "West. Dragon Wells."

"Ah," Gonzalez nodded. "Outside Launcelot."

Kel sipped his whiskey, thought it wise to change the subject. "You been mayor here long?"

Now Gonzalez sighed. "Long enough to witness the eyesight of our sheriff decline sorely."

Kel's turn to nod. Explained Poteet carrying a shotgun: Not much aiming needed in using it.

The mayor said, "In fact, his vision is now so gone, he has trouble reading even the wanted posters."

Kel stopped with the glass halfway to his lips, then cursed himself for probably giving something away by his reaction. "Might be he just has enough problems here."

"Possible," Gonzalez continued, "but I have had the benefit of some schooling in the law, so I take an interest in its enforcement, including checking the circulars from time to time." He paused. "I also heard from somebody in Launcelot that saw the shooting. Said a certain player did the righteous thing by just wounding the son of a bitch."

Kel mulled that. "Might we keep this between ourselves, Mr. Mayor?"

"Certainly, Mr. McKyer. Another whiskey, though? On me?"

Kel said, "Under the circumstances, I'd be much obliged if you'd let me buy us both one."

Oswaldo Gonzalez smiled and patted his stomach lightly, like the skin under his shirt was fragile. "In that case, by all means, do."

Kel and the mayor were more than halfway through their next drink when three reports cracked and echoed off the buildings outside. From the short spacing between them, Kel guessed handgun over rifle, and he was up and running while the third shot was still making its noise in the air.

Once in the moonlight, Kel didn't see anything threatening, but he nevertheless figured it might be safer to go through the hotel rather than run around the corner of the dry goods store and risk being outlined against a light-colored wall. After crossing the street and entering the hotel, Kel blew past Steinberg, who was himself already in the kitchen, running toward the back door, crying out, "Sarah, Sarah," followed by words that had the guttural ring of the Yiddish German Kel had heard him speaking with his daughter.

Once past Steinberg, Kel paused at the back door to the hotel, the stable across the alley producing black troopers, scrambling in uniforms or just undershirts and trousers, carbines in their hands.

One without a tunic stood out, a scar nearly ripping his face from northwest to southeast.

Kel thought, the soldier Steinberg said was helping his daughter with their food.

"Over here," from Kel's left.

He joined in the swell of troopers as they all approached a mixed-race sergeant—freckles on his face and burly as a blacksmith—in the opened, rear doorway of the dry goods store. He had a horse pistol out of its holster and in his right hand, the muzzle pointed down at the ground. You couldn't help but have your nose tickled by the acrid gunpowder smell hanging in the still night air.

"What happened?" said Kel.

The sergeant, still in full uniform, inclined his head behind him. "Nobody goes inside until the captain gets here."

"Let me through. Damnit, let me through!"

The troopers, maybe ten or twelve of them, separated like cattle around a moving tree for Sheriff Poteet, shotgun leveled, bulling his way forward.

"What is going on?" The mayor's voice from farther away. "Someone tell me, please?"

Poteet reached the sergeant. "Stand aside, boy."

The black man stood his ground. "The name's Wickes, sir. Sergeant Wickes, and I got my orders. Nobody—"

The lawman slapped the butt of his shotgun into the sergeant's ribs, and Wickes dropped to his knees, clutching the spot with his empty hand. Poteet stalked inside.

Kel followed, saying quietly to the sergeant, "Don't do anything foolish with that sidearm, all right?"

A pained nod as Kel passed him.

The sheriff, voice choking, said, "Oh, my dear God."

From behind him, Kel heard an anguished tone of "Sarah. My Sarah, where is she?"

Kel was looking forward and thinking, Steinberg wouldn't want to find her.

Sarah lay on some burlap feed bags as makeshift bed and pillows. Her lovely hair lay splayed over one of the bags, her eyes open and visible as two white, shining pearls in the moonlight coming through the windows of the storeroom. Sarah's left palm was open and oriented upward, the right one clenched into a fist.

And her skirt was torn, her underthings the same, down to the flesh—and blood—showing between her legs.

Kel drew even with the sheriff as this time Steinberg bolted past them and screamed at the sight of his daughter. He stumbled and sagged, finally hitting his knees and covering his daughter's privates with a flap of her skirt. Then the hotel owner yanked her shoulders to his chest, cradling Sarah like he must have back when she was still a baby. Steinberg began wailing, and Kel could see Sarah's face looked a light shade of blue, darker blue bruises around her lips and throat.

"Jesus y Maria," said Oswaldo Gonzalez from the doorway, the words coming out "Hey-soos e Mar-ree-ya," but Kel knowing what he meant.

Steinberg began to rock his daughter then, and her right hand opened. Kel caught a glint of something as it rolled lopsidedly along the floor toward his boots, like a child's top after the spin from the string has tired itself out. Kel stooped and snatched the thing before the sheriff could react—or even see it, Kel imagined. He hefted it in his own palm, then held it up to the moonlight. Heavy, like a nugget of gold, and almost one-inch round.

"A button," said Kel. "From a cavalry tunic."

Captain Crane's voice boomed from outside. "Make way, men. Make way."

Then Sergeant Wickes, from the doorway. "Captain, I tried to keep everybody out. Like you said, sir."

Sheriff Poteet turned to Kel. "Give me that button."

Kel did, and the lawman dropped it into his shirt pocket.

Now Crane's voice, close behind. "What in the world—Oh, no. No!"

Kel turned, saw even the dandy officer in just an undershirt and trousers, suspenders down, holding an obviously drunk black trooper by the armpits to keep him vertical. Kel thought it might have been the one who got the whiskey bottles from Crane earlier.

Poteet said to the captain. "Your boy here—"

"—my sergeant—"

"—tried to keep us out. Said you'd ordered that. Why?"

Crane closed his eyes and dropped his chin to his chest. "Because this happened once before."

That's when Kel McKyer realized that Steinberg was now just crying over his daughter. And that the drunken trooper had a button missing from his tunic, some tell-tale thread still attached to the cloth.

"Savages, just like I said."

Kel looked at Sheriff Poteet, sitting behind his desk in the office that fronted the three cells to the back, his shotgun lying near some papers. The drunk trooper—so far, Crane had referred to him only as "Uggie"—was lying on the bunk in the first cell, still sleeping it off. Mayor Oswaldo Gonzalez and the cavalry officer occupied two other chairs, Kel staying on his feet.

The captain shook his head. "When the earlier...attack occurred, we'd bedded down in a town also, smaller than this one, just passing through. I'd hoped then that it was only a coincidence, our being there, since there was no evidence any of my troopers were involved."

Gonzalez said, "I don't think we can say that here."

"No," Crane shaking his head and wringing his hands now, like he was trying to wash off a stubborn stain. "I told all my men: 'If anything like this should happen again, fire three shots in the air and guard the spot.'"

Kel thought Sergeant Wickes had done just about all that was possible there. "And this Uggie's button was missing when you found him?"

"Yes." The captain now slumped back in his chair. "Even in this God-forsaken country, I'm a stickler for appearances."

Kel thought, *There you go.*

"My system instills the kind of discipline any soldier needs, regardless of race. I'm certain Uggie had all the buttons on his tunic when I gave him the whiskey outside your saloon here."

That answered two questions for Kel, since he'd been pretty sure Uggie was the one who received the bottles and that he'd looked parade-ground sharp when he pivoted and marched away.

Poteet said, "I don't much like your 'soldiers' standing around outside my jail with their weapons."

Crane fixed a gaze on the lawman. "Uggie is one of their own, and I doubt there's a single trooper under my command who hasn't seen—or at least heard—of a lynching."

Then a knock that sounded kind of urgent, hammering the front door to the jail. Through the barred—and only—window in the sheriff's office, Kel caught a flicker of light some distance down the street.

Poteet closed his hand on the shotgun in front of him. "Come in."

Kel saw more lights on the street now. Irregular, and moving.

Sergeant Wickes stuck his head around the door. "Captain, there be a bunch of mens coming this way."

Crane looked at the sheriff. "Trouble?"

The sergeant said, "They's a lot of them, and the onliest one that don't have a torch or a gun, he carrying a rope."

Kel remembered the feeling from the war: the tension in the ranks just before the shooting started. Tension that enters your body like a cold ghost and sinks into your gut, making your hands shake so bad you stick them in your pockets, trying not to show the terror gripping you.

Kel was now standing outside the sheriff's front door, three steps above street level. Poteet had loaned Crane a rifle, and the mayor came up with a card-player's derringer from somewhere in that stomach area of his.

Not much good against a mob of thirty or more men, thought Kel, but at least Gonzalez's heart was in the right place.

The guy with the rope—noose already tied in it—spoke first. "We *heared* that Steinberg's little girl was holding a button off one of these...'buffalo soldiers.'"

The sheriff spoke softly, his shotgun pointed straight down beside his right foot. "Go home, John."

"The man may be a Jew, but his daughter's still white, and we can't have that in this town."

"John," said the mayor, a genuine edge of strength in his voice that Kel could admire. "All of you. Go home before you—"

"The Steinberg girl ain't going 'home' but to her grave, and we plan to deal with the bastard *what* done it."

Kel heard the click of a hammer from somewhere in the mob, then two or three more.

"Last time," said Poteet, Kel noticing the lawman's shotgun muzzle coming up a mite. "Go home. Now."

As John of the Rope started to move forward, Kel heard Steinberg's voice from the back of the mob. "Wait! Please, for me. Wait?"

The mob parted for the stricken father the way the troopers had for Sheriff Poteet behind the dry goods store. When Steinberg got to the front, Kel could see the man's eyes were red, and his face had aged ten years.

The hotel owner said, "I can come up there?"

Poteet hesitated, then nodded and shuffled aside.

Steinberg climbed the three steps before turning to face the mob. "It is my daughter dead," swiping his sleeve across his eyes, as he had earlier over his wife when Kel was registering, "so, I can talk?"

John of the Rope swung his gaze quickly among the men behind him, then back to the raised sidewalk. "We're listening, Steinberg."

The hotel owner closed his eyes once before opening them again. "When my family is in the old country still, there were men like you. They thought the right thing was for to kill Jews. We call it 'pogrom,' the mob killing us. My wife is one, when my Sarah," another swipe of his sleeve, "is just three years. We come here to America, escape pogroms. But now, my daughter is dead, and I see the same mob killing in you, men I know from this town to be good people."

Kel thought he might have just witnessed the best speech he'd ever heard.

Steinberg snorted back tears. "I want justice for my Sarah, but not..." he waved his hand now, "this."

John of the Rope seemed to back down a notch. "Sheriff, when's the next judge due by on circuit?"

"The truth? Not for a good three months. Maybe more."

In a command voice, Crane said, "My troopers and I can't stay that long, and we won't leave without our comrade."

John shook his head. "He's not leaving 'til Steinberg here gets his 'justice.'"

Mexican stand-off, thought Kel, at least for a while. Then he figured that a lot more people would be dying shortly.

"May I suggest a compromise?"

Kel thought the mayor might have spoken next, but it was the cavalry officer again. "Over drinks tonight in your saloon, I was told that Mr. Gonzalez here has some training as a lawyer."

The mayor said, "I studied some, but—"

Crane cut him off. "And Mr. McKyer, you can read and write?"

Uh-oh.

"Well," from the captain.

If it would stave off a killing ground, Kel allowed as how he could.

"And I, of course, as well. My men won't stand for a lynching, nor a jury trial with many of you before us now sitting in the box, nor leaving our comrade behind. So, my compromise is this: The mayor acts as judge, I as prosecutor, and Mr. McKyer as our comrade's defense counsel."

Some murmuring within the crowd.

John said, "And if your 'comrade's' found guilty," lifting the noose to just under his own throat, "he hangs?"

"Yes," Crane's answer both quick and firm.

John lowered the rope. "Steinberg, can you live with that?"

The hotel owner squinched his eyes shut, then opened them again, focusing on the cavalry officer. "And when happens this trial?"

"First thing in the morning," Captain Crane replied, and Kel could sense the tension go out of the air on both sides. "Dandy" or not, the man had just saved Vanity from a bloodbath.

"I won't tell you things look good," said Kel McKyer to the trooper on the bunk in the sheriff's cell, trying to sit upright by using the wall behind him as support. "Because they don't. But we're going to have a trial for your life tomorrow, and I need to know what happened."

"Sir, I don't recollect."

It came out, "Suh, I doan recollec'."

Kel pressed him. "What do you remember?"

"Nothing."

"What do you mean, nothing?"

"Sir, I mean nothing from nothing."

"Uggie, I saw you take the whiskey bottles from Captain Crane."

"That's right, sir. And he tell me, 'Uggie, you go hide one of these for your ownself.'"

Kel shook his head. "Why would he do that?"

"The captain done *done* it before, sir. One time, I saved him from this hostile about to put a knife in his back. And the captain, he never forget that."

Seemed possible to Kel, if not exactly likely. "So what did you do with each bottle, then?"

"Like the captain say, I hide one for me, outside the stable. Then I bring the other in for the rest of the boys, and they start passing that bottle around."

Not hard to picture. "And after that?"

"I tell Sergeant Wickes I got to take a piss—sorry, sir. That I was in need of the latrine."

"But instead you went for the other bottle?"

"Yessir."

"And got drunk."

"Yessir." Uggie exhaled noisily, a soured whiskey smell coming off his breath. "Yessir, that, too."

"You ever see the Steinberg girl?"

"Only when her and Dudley brung us our food."

Kel remembered the hotel owner mentioning the scarred trooper, and Kel himself even seeing him behind the dry goods store, but "defense counsel" wanted to be sure. "Dudley?"

"Yessir. The boy with the slash acrost most of his face."

Kel said, "And you never touched the girl."

"Never, sir. Never, my hand to the Lord, no. First I know of anything's be when the captain pulled my drunk rump up from the ground outside the stable here."

Kel had gone to war with a lot of men. Whites only, but some of them immigrants who could hardly speak English. And he thought he'd learned something about the difference between a soldier lying and a soldier telling the truth. Kel believed Uggie's version. "The attorney for the defense" also tried to see what could have happened.

Unfortunately, though, the situation didn't make any more sense to him than it had in the dry goods store.

"Are, uh, counsel ready to proceed?"

Captain Crane rose from behind his table in the saloon, so Kel McKyer did the same at his. Baldy had rigged a chair on the working side of the bar, allowing Mayor Oswaldo Gonzalez to sit in a judgely manner. Uggie was shackled hand and foot around the bar rail on the left. Another chair was put on the right to serve as a witness stand.

And on the bar, in front of the "judge," Sheriff Poteet had laid the tunic button he'd taken from his shirt pocket.

There weren't enough seats for all the town's adult males, women and children excluded, of course, given the kind of case it was. And at first Poteet didn't want any soldiers in the room, either. Then John of the Rope persuaded him that either the troopers would be in the room where they could be watched, or the troopers would be behind them, outside, armed and ready to shoot them in the back. So it became kind of what Kel remembered from the only two church weddings he'd ever attended. Friends of the bride on one side of the aisle, friends of the groom on the other.

And everybody armed to the teeth, just like the night before, outside the jail.

"Sergeant," said Crane as Gonzalez waved Kel to sit back down. "Would you please take the stand?"

Wickes did, his ribs still obviously hurting from the sheriff's shotgun butt the night before. In fact, the soldier actually eyed the weapon lying across Poteet's thighs as the lawman sat nearby the defendant.

Kel listened as the mayor swore the sergeant as a witness, and Crane brought out the man's full name and rank.

"Sergeant, can you describe what you did last night after we arrived in town?"

Kel heard nothing that surprised him.

"Now," said Crane, "once you had tended to the horses and found comfortable quarters for yourselves in the stable, what happened?"

"The little miss and Dudley brung us food, sir."

The cavalry officer stuck his hands in his pants pockets, strolling kind of like an actor on stage.

Kel wondered. Could Crane be scared, like you felt last night facing the mob and back in the war?

"Good food?"

"Real good, Captain. Deer meat, fresh biscuits."

"Did you see or hear anything...unusual?"

"Nossir. We thanked her kindly. And of course I wouldn't let our men drink from the whiskey bottle 'til the little miss left."

"You said 'bottle' just now. As in only one?"

"Yessir."

Crane turned to Kel. "Can we agree that I gave Uggie two bottles of whiskey?"

Kel stayed seated. "We can, account of I saw you do it."

Crane nodded and turned back to his sergeant. "But Uggie brought only one bottle of whiskey into the stable."

"Yessir."

"And the troopers shared it?"

"Yessir."

"Some more than others?"

Hesitation. "Some."

"You?"

"Nossir. I don't never touch the demon rum."

Crane smiled. "Nor whiskey?"

"No fire-water, no way."

Still in that theatrical stroll, Crane took his left hand from his pocket and waved toward the back of the room. "How about Trooper Dudley?"

Wickes hesitated again. "He drunk some."

"More than most."

The sergeant seemed pained. "Yessir."

"And then what happened?"

"Uggie say to me he have to use the latrine, sir. And Dudley, he say he want to sleep in the air, not in a horseshit—sorry, sir—a place that don't smell real good."

"And you allowed both troopers to leave the stable."

"Yessir."

"Then what happened?"

"After a time, Uggie didn't come back, so I went looking for him."

Kel pricked up his ears, sensing a chance to ask a helpful question like sensing where good water might be in open country.

Crane stopped walking. "And did you find him?"

"Nossir."

"What did you find, Sergeant?"

"I see the back door to the dry goods wasn't closed right, and I figure, maybe Uggie be in there."

"Why would he do that?"

Wickes squirmed in his chair, testing its strength the way the mayor had his own in the saloon the night before. "I don't know, sir. I just see the door be open a bit, and so I went to look."

"And...?"

The sergeant put his hand to his face, spoke through his fingers. "The little miss, sir. She was dead and...and violated, seemed to me."

Kel heard a muffled whimper from behind him. Steinberg, he guessed, given where they were in Wickes's account.

Crane stuck his left hand back in his pocket. His walk now was less stroll and more parade; in charge, strutting around like a banty rooster with his wings down.

Kel decided the man had seen too much action with hostiles to have any *courtroom* scare him.

The captain said, "What did you do then?"

"What you told us to, anything ever happen again like in that other town. I come outside and fired three shots into the air."

Now Crane moved to the bench in front of the mayor. "May I show this witness the button in question?"

"You may," said Gonzalez.

"Thank you." Crane took his right hand out of his pocket and picked up the button, then turned and moved back to Wickes, extending his hand and its contents to the sergeant. "Do you recognize this item?"

Wickes fumbled the exchange and had to fish the button from his lap. "Yessir."

"And what is it?"

"Cavalry button." Wickes held it up to his own chest. "From the front of the tunic, not the sleeve, account of it's bigger."

"Sergeant, do you know what that button is made from?"

"Brass, maybe?"

"Not exactly." The captain turned with a schoolteacher's smile to the judge-for-a-day. "It's called 'gilding metal,' and I'm told that small amounts of gold are actually bound to the buttons by a firing process." Crane turned back to the sergeant. "Have you ever held an officer's tunic button?"

"Just yours, sir. Couple months back, when you asked me to have one of the mens sew it back on to your dress uniform."

"And an officer's buttons are the same?"

"Not yours, sir. The ones you wear be heavier."

"Because?"

"I don't rightly know, sir." A third hesitation. "Maybe because they be real gold?"

"Or, at least more gold, Sergeant."

Crane pocketed both hands again, striding slower now, then turning to Kel. "Mr. McKyer, can we agree that the Steinberg girl was holding that button in her hand when you arrived in the storeroom."

Kel said, "I saw it roll out on the floor after her father went to her."

"And what did you do with this button?"

"The sheriff asked for it, and I gave it to him."

"Thank you," said Crane to the mayor, retrieving the button from Wickes and placing it back on the bar. "No further questions."

"Mr. McKyer?" Gonzalez, from his makeshift bench. "You can cross-examine the witness."

Kel thought of tests, like back in grammar school, and he had to cough to clear his throat. "Meaning what?"

"Meaning ask him questions, to help your client if you can."

Kel stood, cutting a look toward Uggie and not seeing any more hope in the black man's face than Kel had in his own heart of hearts toward defending him.

"Sergeant Wickes," said Kel playing the only card he'd been dealt, "you ever find out where Trooper Dudley was sleeping?"

"Nossir."

"How come?"

The hand to his face again. "The little miss, she...the way she was and all, I didn't want to leave the poor child alone."

"Was Dudley one of the troopers who came a-running after you fired the shots?"

"I seen him there."

"Behind the dry goods store."

"Yessir."

"What was Dudley wearing?"

Wickes seemed thrown by the question, like it was a bucking bronco. "Clothes, sir."

For the first time during the trial—maybe in all of Vanity since Sarah Steinberg's body was discovered—Kel heard laughter.

Gonzalez said, "Mr. McKyer, maybe if you re-phrased your question?"

"Right. Uh, your Honor." Kel made his brain work. "Was Trooper Dudley wearing his cavalry tunic?"

Now Wickes closed his eyes, like he was trying to see a lot of photographs all at once. "Nossir. No, he wasn't."

"But did you see where Dudley came from?"

"No. I was...I hurt some."

"From Sheriff Poteet butt-ending you with his shotgun?"

"Yessir."

"So Trooper Dudley could have—"

"Judge?" asked Crane from his table.

"Yes?"

"I think we can save ourselves some time here."

"How so?"

Crane turned. "Trooper Dudley?"

Kel watched the scarred man move slowly forward.

"Trooper," said the captain, "would you—"

Kel felt he should do something. "Judge, oughtn't we maybe have this man swear on the Bible, too?"

"Uh, yes," said Gonzalez, then to Crane, "He really should be a proper witness at the proper time, counsel."

The captain smiled, and for the first time, Kel sensed a cruel streak in the man. "Only if Dudley has to testify, I think. And I'm calling just for a short...demonstration."

Kel shook his head. "Of what?"

Crane, over his shoulder, said, "Trooper Dudley, pull down your trousers."

"Sir?"

The word came out "Shur," Kel believing because of the scarring at his mouth.

"You heard me, trooper. And it's a direct order. Pull down your trousers."

From the witness chair, the sergeant spoke, very gently. "Go ahead, Dud. It's gonna be all right."

Kel felt as embarrassed for the man as he thought Dudley did for himself. But Kel still watched.

Fighting back tears, the trooper tugged down his suspenders and dropped his drawers.

To reveal that he'd been somehow deprived of his manhood.

"Sergeant," said Crane. "Were you with Trooper Dudley when he was...injured?"

"Yessir. He be fighting real brave against the hostiles."

"And when did his wound occur?"

Wickes scratched his chin. "Three years back."

Crane turned. "Thank you, Dudley. You may pull your trousers back up."

Kel decided to change his view of the captain "taking care of his troops." Kel also realized he'd been mouse-trapped into suggesting that either soldier could have committed the crime, when clearly the scarred man could not have.

The mayor said, "Mr. McKyer, any further questions?"

"No. No, I..." Kel returned to his table and sat back down, unable to think of anything he could do.

"Captain Crane?"

"Judge, when I found Uggie, drunk, a button—that button before you—was missing from his tunic. Otherwise, the prosecution rests."

"Mr. McKyer?"

Kel took in a deep breath, let it out halfway, like he was about to bring his muzzle to bear on a man he intended to shoot.

"Judge, I'd like to have as a witness our defendant, Trooper Uggie."

Captain Crane, Kel noticed, was as quick on his feet as he'd been shuffling those cards the night before in the very same room.

"Judge, may counsel approach the bench?"

To Kel, the mayor seemed befuddled. "Uh, why...yes. Yes, of course."

The cavalry officer gestured to Kel, who was already on his feet and moving toward the bar, thinking, *If I'm rattling Crane, maybe I'm kind of getting a handle on this lawyering stuff.*

The captain said, "Your Honor, Mr. McKyer can not be serious."

Gonzalez said to Kel, "Are you?"

"Judge, I don't know what else to do."

Crane shook his head. "If you call Uggie—the defendant—to the stand, then I get to cross-examine him. Do you understand? I can ask him anything about what happened last night, and, based on the condition in which I found him outside the stable—and just steps away from the back door to the dry goods store—my job as counsel for the prosecution will be to crucify him. Don't make me do that in front of his comrades. At least so far, Uggie could be found not guilty."

Kel kept his peace until the mayor said, "Mr. McKyer?"

"Judge, I've never been in a court before, much less as the lawyer for a defendant accused of hanging offenses like rape and murder. But I've always believed that the truth will out, and to do that, Uggie needs to tell us what he knows."

VANITY

Crane looked to Kel like he was going to bust a gut. "Your Honor, the defendant once saved my life."

Kel thought, *So, Uggie was telling the truth on that one.*

"But," the cavalry officer continued, "I also owe a duty to this court, and this town's people, and—especially—to Mr. Steinberg, who fed my men and put them up for the night. Trust me, given the condition I found Uggie to be in last night, I doubt he could tell you that the sky was up and the earth was down."

Gonzalez seemed to weigh that. Solemnly.

Kel said, "Judge, it's the man's life at stake here."

The mayor seemed to reach a decision. "Very well. As I recall from my studies, any accused has the right to take the stand on his own behalf. Mr. McKyer, call your witness."

"But judge—"

"Captain Crane, this court has ruled. Now, go sit down, and wait your turn to inquire."

The cavalry officer looked as though he would bite through his lower lip, and Kel thought, Maybe you were wrong just before. Maybe the man really *does* care about his troops.

At least one who saved his own life.

Kel said, "Uggie, you're going to testify now."

The man nodded, tried to stand, but the shackles wouldn't let him.

Gonzalez said, "Stay seated," before administering the oath to him.

Kel moved away from his client, to be sure the soldier could be heard. "What do you remember about last night?"

"Nothing, sir."

"I mean, after you found that second bottle of whiskey?"

"Nothing, sir. I swear, my hand to the Lord."

A feeble attempt to raise his right one.

Kel moved toward the bench. "You ever touch the Steinberg girl?"

"Nossir, no-sir. She did a kindness to us."

Kel reached for the button in front of the mayor.

"Your Honor," Crane's chair scraping the saloon floor in a shriek like the one when he left to go to his hotel room the night before, "this is damning the accused, not 'defending' him."

Gonzalez said, "Mr. McKyer, I'm inclined to agree."

Which was when Kel picked up the button. Stared at it in his palm. Then hefted it.

"Sheriff," he said, turning, "what did you do with the button from Sarah Steinberg's hand after I gave it to you last night?"

Poteet looked to the mayor, who both shrugged and nodded. The lawman said, "I put it in my shirt pocket."

"And?" said Kel.

"And the button stayed there through 'til this morning, when I put it down in front of Oswaldo. Your Honor, I mean."

"Mr. Mayor," said McKyer, without turning toward the bench, "did you pick this button up after the sheriff set it down on the bar this morning?"

A pause. Then, "No. No, I don't believe I did."

"I don't, either." Kel turned toward Poteet and tossed the button to him.

Fumbling it at first, like Sergeant Wickes had in the witness chair, the lawman had to reach down to recover the button from the floor, then hefted it in his own palm, as Kel had.

But frowning.

Kel counsel said, "What's the matter, Sheriff?"

Now Poteet stared at the item in his palm. "It's not right."

"What's not right?'" from Kel.

"The button. It doesn't...feel right. Not heavy enough."

Kel, casual as could be, checked to be sure the rawhide loop was off the hammer of his Peacemaker. "What does that tell you, Sheriff?"

"But it has to be the same damned button! I kept it on me all night, and I've been watching it on that bar all morning."

"Except," said Kel, turning toward Crane, "when the captain here picked the button up and gave it to Sergeant Wickes, who dropped it in his lap."

The cavalry officer bridled noticeably. "This is absurd. My sergeant would never—"

Kel felt things all fall into place, like a winning draw of cards in a poker hand. "Sarah Steinberg was being attacked. She grabbed out, and her violator bruised her face and throat. The girl's right hand came away with a button from the man's tunic. But he didn't notice, not just then, probably drunk himself on lust."

Crane said, "Judge, you must—"

Kel cut him off again. "Probably not 'til he got back to his hotel room, admiring himself in the mirror over his wash basin. He saw a button was missing. And only one place it could likely be, too. In the storeroom of the dry—"

The cavalry officer said, "You, sir, are out of order."

Gonzalez wagged a finger at him. "As judge, sir, I decide that."

Kel nodded once. "So, the killer decides he has to get his button, but first hears the sergeant's three shots. The killer's desperate now, especially given the killing of that girl in the other town. So he strips off his tunic and goes looking for the alibi of sorts he set up: Uggie, the heavy drinker with his own, personal bottle of whiskey. Crane finds his soldier, passed-out drunk, and rips a button from the front of that poor man's tunic. He pockets it, then brings the trooper into the dry goods store for us to see, still drunk, with a button missing. Only our 'dandy' captain—in just his undershirt and trousers—is kind of oddly dressed for him."

"Your Honor, I demand—"

Kel over-rode Crane again. "But there's a problem: One button is a different quality, different weight even, than the other. So when he's asking Sergeant Wickes questions today, the captain picks up the button the Steinberg girl was clenching in her fist, and palms it, like the shuffling trick he did with just one hand on the playing cards last night. Crane hands the witness the button torn off Uggie's tunic the night before."

The cavalry officer raged. "Your Honor, I will not stand here and be defamed by this...this saddle tramp."

Oswaldo Gonzalez looked from Kel to Crane and back again.

Kel said, "Just ask 'counsel for the prosecution' to empty his pockets onto the table in front of him."

"I have *never* been so insulted in my—"

The mayor said, "Do it, Captain."

Kel thought Crane was going to burst. "Sergeant Wickes" said the cavalry officer, now looking to the audience, "arrest Mr. McKyer for contempt of court."

Wickes shook his head, slowly. "I rightly don't know what that is, sir."

"Sergeant, I just gave you a direct order."

"Captain, begging your pardon, but Mr. McKyer has me some confused." Wickes paused. "Maybe if you just empty out your pockets, sir, like the judge say, we—"

"Sergeant, you are relieved of your command. Trooper Dudley, place Mr. McKyer under martial arrest."

A longer pause than Wickes's before a strangled, "Nossir."

Sheriff Poteet began to level the muzzle of his shotgun. "Captain, empty your pockets. And I mean now."

Kel figured the cavalry officer would first go after the more potent weapon. Kel also figured Crane might be as quick with a gun as he'd been with cards and buttons, but the captain was even faster. He had his horse pistol out and a shot fired into Poteet before Kel could even draw.

Crane now wheeled on Kel, whose slug took the dandy in the throat, punching him back. Then a second shot, from Sergeant Wickes, up through his commander's right side. There was a moment that Kel thought he'd best add a third. But the captain seemed to forget that a handgun couldn't be held securely by only an index finger within its trigger guard, and the revolver clattered to the floor just a moment before its wielder.

Kel turned. The mayor was kneeling at Sheriff Poteet's side, joined shortly by Baldy—out of nowhere—and then Sergeant Wickes. There was no noise from the audience, Kel deafened by the three reports in an enclosed space like the saloon.

Slowly, over the ringing in his ears, Kel could hear crying. A shuddering, hacking sound he knew he'd not soon forget.

Steinberg, witnessing "justice" for his Sarah.

Kel found himself standing over the fallen lawman, who said, "Crane?"

"Dead," from Oswaldo Gonzalez. "Dead in Vanity, from his own vanity."

Poteet dipped his chin a hair, what would have to pass for a nod. Then, "Sergeant, last night...I called you and your troopers... 'savages...'."

The sheriff coughed, and Kel thought Poteet sounded like a man trying to juggle water in his windpipe.

"...and I meant it...Then I assaulted you...with the butt of my shotgun."

Wickes gnawed on his upper lip before, "I get why you hit me, sir."

"Baldy," said the sheriff, pink froth around the hole two inches from the star on his chest. Kel knew the sucking sound made it a mortal wound, and he figured the lawman knew that, too. "Whiskey."

Baldy never seemed to move away, but there was a bottle in his hand when Kel realized the barkeep was back.

Poteet looked up at Wickes. "I'd be pleased…if you'd share a…last drink with me."

The sergeant closed his eyes, then opened them again. "If you please, sir, might be I ought to go second."

Poteet nodded fully, grimaced in pain, then blinked his eyes at Baldy. After the bottle left the sheriff's lips, the dying man said, "Best damned drink I ever tasted."

Kel McKyer thought the lawman had the light of life in his eyes just long enough to see Wickes—who never touched "firewater"—take a farewell drink with him.

COWARDS DIE
MANY TIMES
ROBERT J. RANDISI

1

"Whatta we got?" Detective Sam McKeever asked the uniformed policeman as he entered the second story hotel room.

"This fella says he left the game to take a piss, and when he got back everybody was dead."

"That so?" McKeever said. He looked down at the man in question, who was sitting on a sagging sofa. Across the room five men were strewn about a poker table, two slumped over it, two on the floor by it, and one underneath. There were cards and poker chips and cash all over the place. And blood.

"Come on, I asked is that so?" McKeever said, kicking the man in the shin.

"Lay off, McKeever." The seated man raised his head and looked up at the policeman.

"Oh shit, Val?"

"That's right," Val O'Farrell said, "it's me."

"You know this joker?" the policeman asked.

"Did he identify himself to you?" McKeever asked.

"Said his name was O'Farrell," the young patrolman said. "Didn't mean nothin' to me."

"He used to be one of us," McKeever said.

"A cop?"

"A dick," McKeever said. "I said one of 'us,'" McKeever repeated, which clearly meant not one of "you." "Now he's private."

"Well," the cop said, "he's still the only one left standin' outta this group."

"Go downstairs and wait for the meat wagon," McKeever said. "I'll talk to him."

"Whatever you say."

As the cop reached the door McKeever called out, "Where's your partner?"

"Talkin' to the neighbors, to see if anybody heard anything."

"Shit," McKeever said. "Okay, go ahead." As the younger man left, McKeever said, "They're hirin' babies, and they all think they're dicks."

"I feel for you, Sam," O'Farrell said.

McKeever looked down at the private detective. Usually a natty dresser, O'Farrell was without his jacket and tie, and his white shirt looked soiled around the collar and cuffs.

"How long was this game goin' on?" he asked.

"'Bout forty hours," O'Farrell said.

"Ain't you a little long in the tooth for two-day poker games, Val?" McKeever asked.

"I'm the same age as you, you sheeny bastard."

"That's what I mean," McKeever said. "I'm too old for two-day poker games."

O'Farrell was in his forties, had left the police force in 1919 to go private. In three years he had become one of the most sought-after private detectives in New York. Tonight, however, he'd been sought after by a little guy named Kevin Allison, who had knocked on the door of the hotel room and asked to speak to him. It was while he was downstairs in the lobby talking to Kevin that he heard the shots from the second floor and rushed back up. When he entered the room and saw that everyone was dead, he'd rushed back down to the lobby, but Kevin was gone. He didn't know why

Kevin had lured him out of the room, but it had saved his life, and he wasn't ready to throw the man to the dogs—or the cops.

"I didn't see anything, Sam," O'Farrell said.

"How were you doin' in the game?" McKeever asked.

"I was winning."

"Big?"

"Not that big."

"Who were the other players?"

"Sam—"

"Val, you know Turico's gonna be here any minute," McKeever said, "and he's gonna be pissed as it is, bein' called out at midnight. The quicker you answer my questions, the quicker you get out of here."

There was very little love lost between O'Farrell and Lt. Turico. Their relationship had not been good when O'Farrell was on the force, and if anything, it had gotten worse since he left. So he needed to cooperate with McKeever and get out of there so he could go looking for Kevin Allison.

"So who were the other players?" McKeever asked, again. O'Farrell told him, and answered whatever other questions he had...

He'd just taken a hand with a full house, queens over threes, beating Tex Fitzgerald's hand of Jacks full over eights. Two full houses in a six-handed game of draw poker, and they had each drawn three cards. O'Farrell had been dealt the threes, kept 'em, and drew the three queens.

"Bad beat," Eric Monahan had said to Tex.

"Shut up," Tex had replied, bitterly. He was losing badly all night, and with good hands. O'Farrell knew how that felt. He didn't mind losing on a night when the cards weren't coming, but to lose with hands like Jacks full was brutal.

There was a knock at the door as the deal passed to Mike Pappas. The man hosting the game, Del Manning, got up and answered the door. He cracked it, spoke to someone, then turned to the table and said, "O'Farrell, it's for you."

"Deal me out," O'Farrell had said, before Pappas could deal. The Greek nodded and dealt by him.

"Come right back," the fifth man, Lenny Davis said. "You got most of my money."

"I'll be back," O'Farrell said. "Who is it?" he asked Del as they passed.

"I don't know 'im," Manning said. "He said it was important. I figured you knew him, since he knew where to find you."

"I'll be right back," he said again.

"You better," Manning said. "You got everybody's money, and you're killin' Tex."

O'Farrell didn't know Tex well. In fact, the only players at the table he knew at all were Manning and the Greek, Mike Pappas.

When he got to the door he saw Kevin Allison standing outside, nervously shifting from one foot to another. He recognized him, but they weren't friends. He wondered how the ex-pug had been able to find him.

"You looking for me?" he'd asked.

"Yeah," Allison said. "I need to talk to yuh...uh, downstairs."

O'Farrell stepped out into the hall, pulling the door closed behind him.

"What's wrong with right here?"

"Gotta be downstairs," Allison said, nervously. "It's, uh, too light up here."

"It's almost light outside."

"Please, Mr. O'Farrell," Allison pleaded.

O'Farrell stared at the man a few moments, then asked, "How did you know where I was?"

A lot was going to hinge on the man's answer, because there were only two people who knew where he was and what he was doing. Allison was going to have to come up with one of those names.

"How'd you know where I was, Allison?"

"I talked to Dorothy," he replied. "She told me."

Dorothy was a girl O'Farrell had been seeing for a few weeks. Hers was one of those names. Later, he'd find out from Dorothy how she happened to talk to Allison. At that moment he wanted to get this over with so he could get back to the game before his cards cooled off.

"All right," he said. "Let's go downstairs."

Since they were only on the second floor they took the stairs rather than the elevator. When they reached the lobby Allison took off across it like he was being chased, not running, but almost.

"Hey," O'Farrell had called, "wait up—" and that was when he heard the shots. Allison took off out the front door, leaving the detective with two options. He could chase the man, or run back upstairs and see what was going on.

He went back up and found the bodies...

He managed to get out of the hotel before Turico showed up. He hadn't said a word to McKeever about Kevin Allison. That was the only thing he'd held back. He wasn't prepared to throw the man to the wolves until he found out his whole story. He stuck to his own story about going down the hall to take a piss. He heard the shots, he said—which was about right—and came running back to find everybody dead.

Allison was an ex-pug. His fighting weight had been bantam, and he'd gone by the name "Kid Alley." There were a few places O'Farrell knew he could look for the ex-boxer, but there was also someone he knew who knew more about where the ex-pugilists hung out.

He went downstairs and around the corner from the Broadway Hotel, where he had parked his Twin Six Packard Roadster. He sat in the front seat for a few moments, going over the evening's events in his mind. While he thought, he sought to make himself more presentable, using the rear view mirror. He combed his hair with his fingers, buttoned his collar, rolled down the sleeves of his white shirt and buttoned the cuffs, then donned the jacket of his linen suit. He left his tie in the pocket of the jacket, where he'd deposited it during the ninth hour of play. He'd been forced by McKeever to leave his winnings on the table. It would have been a small price to pay for having his life spared, but after two days of playing fairly even, he had eventually gotten to the point where he was well ahead. By the time Turico got through picking the place clean he knew his winnings would be gone.

When he felt a bit more presentable he started the engine.

2

Dorothy LeMay was—for want of a better word—a songstress. O'Farrell never really thought of her as a singer because she didn't really have that great a voice. She got her jobs singing in clubs because of her great looks. Long, wavy blonde hair and a willowy but top-heavy figure got her all the jobs she wanted, as long as it was a man doing the hiring and her dress was cut low enough. The really nice thing about Dorothy was that she knew all this, and was okay with it. She had no illusions about being a great singer, she just wanted to do it for a living.

He'd met her at a night club she was singing at, invited her to have a drink with him after her set. It had been a quiet night, not too many people left in the place by the time she was done. They'd talked until somebody kicked them out of the place, and then she'd gone to his apartment with him. Ever since then they'd been seeing each other three or four times a week.

Presently, she was singing in a dive called The Martini Pit. It was only 2 a.m. by the time McKeever cut him loose and he knew he'd find her there.

He drove the Twin Six uptown, found a parking spot down the street from The Pit.

He took a little extra time again straightening himself out, and when he figured he was as good as he was going to get he left the car and entered the club.

"Good evening, Mr. O'Farrell," Cory, the red-headed hat-check girl, greeted him. She was a cute little thing, short but full-bodied, with a deep, shadowy cleavage he knew got her plenty of tips. If it hadn't been for Dorothy, O'Farrell would have taken their flirtatiousness to another level—but flirt they did.

"Hello, kid," he said, handing her his fedora. "You're looking as lovely as usual tonight."

She put his hat on a shelf, turned back and handed him his check, gave him a look he flattered himself she didn't give to many other men.

"You look a little tired," she said. "Handsome, but tired."

"Well, thanks for the first," he said, "as for the second, it's been a rough night." Two nights, actually. "Dorothy is here, I take it?"

"She sure is," Cory said. "I think she's in her dressing room, changing for her next set."

"Maybe I can catch her before she goes on, then," he said. "See you later."

With one last look at the shadow place between her breasts he presented himself to Leo, the maitre d'.

"Evenin', Mr. O," the big man said. Leo doubled as the bouncer, since Miles DeKay, the owner of The Martini Pit, was too cheap to pay the extra money to have one of each. Since O'Farrell wanted to go back to Dorothy's dressing room to see her, he was going to have to get past Leo.

"You need a table tonight?" the big man asked. "I can get you right up front."

O'Farrell was usually able to sit up front because the Pit was hardly ever more than half full. He wondered how the two owners even kept the place going.

"Thanks, Leo," he said, "but all I need is a few minutes of Dorothy's time in her dressing room. Can we work that out?"

"For you? Sure, Mr. O. Follow me."

As he followed in the big man's wake he checked out the postage-stamp-sized tables. Those that were inhabited were taken by couples ranging from their forties to their sixties. The Martini Pit was not the kind of place that appealed to the younger set. Those clubs were further downtown, or up in Harlem, like Jack Johnson's Club Deluxe (which would, three years later, become the Cotton Club).

Leo showed O'Farrell down the long, cramped hallway to Dorothy's closet-sized dressing room. She never complained about it, though, and was very happy that she had a bathroom of her own. The big man knocked on the door and said, "Mr. O'Farrell to see you, Miss LeMay."

After a moment the door opened and Dorothy graced Leo with a wide, beautiful smile.

"Thank you, Leo. Let the gentleman in, please."

"Yes, Ma'am."

Leo stepped aside and said, "There ya go, Mr. O."

"Thanks, Leo."

O'Farrell went through the door and closed it behind him. Dorothy came into his arms and said, "Kiss me quickly, before I put my lipstick on."

He kissed her and held her tightly. Every time she was in his arms he realized why he enjoyed her company. It wasn't only because she felt good and smelled good, but it was in the way that she hugged him so warmly and lovingly. He'd never received a perfunctory hug from her, a halfhearted hug. Even now, when she was minutes from going on and still had to get ready, she hugged him tightly.

She kissed him once more—soundly enough to arouse him—and then pushed him away.

"You'll have to talk to me while I finish getting ready," she said. "What brings you here? I thought you were at a poker game."

"I was," he told her, "and that's why I'm here."

She moved in and out of the room, exiting and reentering the bathroom while he explained what had happened. When he got to the part about the shooting she backed up and stared at him through the bathroom door.

"Oh my God," she said. "You could have been killed."

"Yes," he said, "but I wasn't."

"Why?"

"That's what I want to find out. Did you talk to a fella named Allison last night?" he asked. "Kevin Allison?"

"A nervous little man with a flat nose?"

"That's him. He got that nose in the ring."

"Yeah, I spoke to him. He took a chance with Big Leo, trying to get by him to see me in my dressing room. He was so insistent I told Leo to let him by."

"What did you tell Allison?"

She moved into the doorway now, bringing her hair brush with her.

"Now don't be angry with me," she said, "but I told him where you would be playing poker."

"I'm not angry," he said. "Just tell me why you told him?"

"He was very anxious to find you," she explained. "He said it was a matter of life and death. He was shaking and sweating so much that I believed him." She let her hands drop down to her sides and stared at him. "I had no idea he was talking about your life."

"He was," O'Farrell said, "and he saved it by luring me out of that room."

"Why would he do that?" she asked.

"I don't know."

"Are you friends?"

"I hardly know him."

"Then why—"

"I'm going to ask him," O'Farrell said, interrupting her, "as soon as I can find him."

"How are you gonna do that?"

"By looking. What time did he come by the club?"

"It must have been...it was between my first and second set, and I went on at ten...must have been ten-thirty, when I came off."

"He didn't come to the hotel until almost eleven," O'Farrell said, mostly to himself. "It doesn't take that long to get from the club to the hotel." The club was on twenty-third and eighth, while the hotel was on nineteenth street and Broadway. It was a walk, and not a long one.

"Maybe..." she said.

"Maybe what?"

Still brushing her hair she said, "Maybe he was scared. Maybe it took him that long to decide to actually do it."

"Maybe," he said.

"You said there were five other men in the game?" she asked, moving back into the bathroom.

"That's right."

"I wonder..." she said, and the rest was unintelligible.

"What?" he said. "What did you say?"

She backed up again so she could see him, and so he could hear her.

"I said, I wonder which one the killer wanted to kill? I mean, it couldn't have been all of them, could it?"

He stared at her for a moment, then looked away and said to himself, "That's the question, isn't it?"

He walked to his Twin Six, got into the front seat and decided to drive home. He needed to take a shower and have something to eat before he started out again. He decided he shouldn't only be asking why Kid Alley had lured him out of that room, but who in that room had someone wanted to kill so badly that they were willing to kill four other men, as well?

3

The next morning he drove down to the offices of *The New York Telegraph*, on Williams Street near Park Row, where most of the newspapers had their offices, to see his friend Bat Masterson.

He parked his Twin Six around the corner and entered the building. It was ten in the morning, and the newsroom was buzzing. He found Bat Masterson sitting at his desk, staring at his typewriter. Over the years he had made his way from lawman, gunman and gambler to columnist for the paper, and eventually to the position he now held, Vice President.

"This sonofabitchin' thing," Bat said.

"Good morning to you, too."

Bat looked up and said, "You look like crap."

"A two-day poker game and almost getting killed will do that to you," O'Farrell said.

"Well," the old west legend said, "that sounds more interesting than what I'm working on. Give."

O'Farrell "gived" the story to Bat, who listened intently and silently until the end.

"So you're lookin' for this ex-pug Kid Alley."

"And you know all the fighters in town."

"You came to the right place," Bat said, standing up. "I was just about to throw this infernal machine out the window. Let's go."

"Where?"

"I happen to know someone who knows someone..."

They tried Perry's first. It was ostensibly a drug store right next to the newspaper building, but in point of fact it was a speakeasy called The Pot of Glue frequented by the journalists and writers in the area. As luck would have it, Damon Runyon was there, sitting with the rewrite man from the *New York World* named James M. Cain.

"Do you know why the postman always rings twice?" Cain asked O'Farrell as he entered.

"No, but—"

"You will," Cain said. "You'll read it, after I've finished writing it."

Cain went past him and left, heading back to his typewriter in the *World* offices.

"What was that about?"

"Don't know," Runyon said. "He was also askin' what we knew about double indemnity. He's writing a couple of things. Some fiction. You look like hell, Val. Have some Brown Ruin, fellows."

Runyon didn't drink the stuff himself, but wasn't above pushing it.

"God, no," O'Farrell said. "I have more respect for my stomach than that."

Bat also refused.

"What brings you here, then?" Runyon asked. "And looking less than spiffy."

"We're looking for Kevin Allison," Bat said. "I thought I remembered you doin' a story on him a few years ago."

"'Kid Alley'?" Runyon asked. "What do you want with a washed up pug like him?"

"I think he saved my life tonight," O'Farrell said.

"You think?"

"I can't explain it now," O'Farrell said. "I just have to find him. Any ideas?"

"A couple of gyms, maybe," Runyon said.

"He's not fighting again, is he?"

"No," the writer said, "but he likes to hang around it."

"Any one in particular?" O'Farrell asked.

"Three or four, probably," Runyon said, and reeled them off. "But there's something else you should know."

"What?"

"I hear the Kid's running with Arnold Rothstein."

"See?" Bat said. "I knew that was the kind of thing we'd get from this kid."

"What the hell would Rothstein want with a broken down ex-pug like Allison?"

Rothstein, largely believed to be the man behind the 1919 Black Sox scandal, had of late begun running liquor into the U.S. from Great Britain. He did most of his business from a table at Lindy's, on Broadway and Forty-ninth Street.

"Rothstein is always planning and scheming," Runyon warned. "He must have something planned where he thought the kid could be of use to him. You don't want to cross him."

"Rothstein and I have already crossed swords once or twice, while I was a cop," O'Farrell said, "but thanks for the warning."

"Is there a story in this?" Runyon asked, as O'Farrell turned to leave.

"Maybe," O'Farrell said, "probably, but not one with a sports connection."

"Call me first, Val," Runyon said. "A story's a story, you know?"

"What do I look like?" Bat asked. "Chopped liver?"

"There might be enough story to go around," O'Farrell said. "I'll keep in touch. Thanks."

O'Farrell and Bat checked out a couple of the gyms suggested by Damon Runyon, but with no luck. O'Farrell thought that Kid Alley might be lying low, but why? Because he'd drawn O'Farrell out of the hotel room, thereby saving his life? Or was he more involved in the massacre of everyone else at the poker game? O'Farrell didn't even know Allison well, which confused him even more. Why would the man risk himself to get the detective out of the room?

O'Farrell replayed the scene in his head…

It was obvious now, thinking back, that Allison never had anything to tell him. As soon as they hit the lobby the ex-pug took off for the door. He knew what was going to happen upstairs. The big question was, why had he lured O'Farrell from the room?

O'Farrell decided to go home and freshen up before he continued looking for Kid Alley.

"You go on home," Bat said. "I have a few ideas about where to look. I'll be in touch."

4

O'Farrell had just stepped from his shower when someone knocked on his door. He wrapped a towel around his waist and answered it.

"Puttin' on weight, Val," Detective Sam McKeever said. "Didn't notice it when you were dressed. Must be those expensive suits."

"What's on your mind, Sam?" O'Farrell asked, backing away and letting the policeman enter.

"I tried to keep you out of it as long as I could, but it ain't possible, anymore," McKeever said. "The Lieutenant wants me to bring you in for questioning."

"By Lieutenant you mean Mike Turico?"

"You know that's who I mean."

"Do I have time to get dressed?"

"Yeah, but I'm gonna watch you," McKeever said. "I don't want you makin' me look bad by goin' out a window."

"You think I'd do that to you, Sam?"

McKeever put an unlit cigar into his mouth. "Only 'cause you've done it before."

"Not this time," O'Farrell said. "You have my word."

McKeever frowned around his cigar, then removed it and said, "Leave the door open so we can talk."

"Fine."

O'Farrell went into the bedroom and began to dress. The shower had freshened him, but his eyes still felt sticky with lack of sleep. McKeever's cigar smoke wafted in from the other room, an indication that he had finally lit the thing.

"You find out anything since this mornin'?" McKeever asked.

"No," O'Farrell said. In point of fact it had taken him most of the day simply to decide he was asking the wrong questions.

"That's too bad," the detective said. "Turico thinks you know what happened. He's gonna grill you."

"He's tried that before," O'Farrell said.

"You might wanna call a shyster before you go down," McKeever said. "I can give you the time to do that."

"That's okay," O'Farrell said. "I can handle Turico."

"Suit yerself."

When O'Farrell came out he was wearing one of his best suits.

"Oh, Val..."

"What?"

"That suit costs more than...seein' you in that is gonna drive Mike up a wall."

O'Farrell smiled and said, "That's the general idea, Sam. Come on."

McKeever escorted O'Farrell into Lieutenant Mike Turico's office. Turico remained seated behind his desk and said, "That's all, McKeever."

"But it's my case—"

"I'm not takin' your case, Sam," Turico said. "I just wanna talk with O'Farrell alone."

McKeever hesitated, then stuffed his unlit cigar into his mouth, nodded and backed out, closing the door behind him.

"You think that suit impresses me?"

"Mike," O'Farrell said, taking a seat across from the man, "To tell you the truth, I never really gave it any thought."

"The truth?" Turico laughed. "When have you ever told the truth?"

"You're my age, Mike," O'Farrell said. "You ever think about retirement?"

"No," Turico said, with a frown, "why?"

"You're getting too cynical."

"Cram it," Turico said. "Ya know, I should can your friend McKeever's ass for lettin' you walk away from the scene last night."

"Why?" O'Farrell said. "I just missed being a victim."

"You're the only one who survived the game," Turico said. "That makes you the number one suspect, in my book."

"Come on, Mike," O'Farrell said, "I was seen in the lobby when the shots were being fired."

"Yeah, but how did you know to go down to the lobby at that moment?"

"Didn't Sam tell you? I was taking a piss when—"

"Yeah, yeah, I heard. Look, O'Farrell, I actually asked you here to get your help."

O'Farrell bit back a smart remark. Antagonizing Turico since he'd left the force had become a hobby of his—mostly because it was so easy. This time, though, the Lieutenant seemed serious.

"What can I do?"

"Tell me about the other players," Turico said. "Help us figure out who the target was."

O'Farrell didn't see any harm in that.

O'Farrell gave Turico what he wanted—the names of the other players—and then went back home. As he entered the telephone rang.

"Val?"

"Bat? Where are you?"

"I'll give you the address," Bat said. "I think you better meet me here."

"What's goin' on?"

"We'll talk when you get here," Bat said. "And hurry. You wanna beat the police here."

"Bat—" he started, but the old west legend had hung up.

COWARDS DIE MANY TIMES

At one time a haven for German immigrants, Alphabet City was now inhabited by the Jews, Italians and Irish. Little more than a slum, it didn't surprise O'Farrell that Bat may have found Kid Alley living here.

He found the building he wanted on Avenue B and walked up the three flights to the apartment number Bat had given him. The door was closed so he knocked. He heard footsteps on the wooden floor and then the door swung open.

"Come on in," Bat said. "Your man is in the bedroom."

O'Farrell didn't like the way he said it, so he almost expected to find Kid Alley dead in the bedroom. What he didn't expect to find was the man's brains all over the bed sheets and wall. The ex-pug was lying face down on the bed, and you didn't have to be a doctor to know he was dead. He backed out of the room.

"Needless to say I found him like that," Bat said.

"Have you looked around?"

"Sure," Bat said. "I didn't find nothin' to tell us why he would've saved your life. But it looks like he did it at the cost of his own."

"My hero," O'Farrell said.

"What now?" Bat asked.

"If I was still a cop," O'Farrell said, "I'd start looking into the lives of all the dead poker players."

"Didn't you know 'em already?" Bat asked.

"I knew some of them," O'Farrell said, "but I didn't know everything about them."

"That sounds like a big job."

"It is," O'Farrell said. "That's why I'm going to leave it to McKeever and Turico."

"So then what are we gonna do?" Bat asked.

"We?"

Bat shrugged.

"I got some free time."

"You got any suggestions?"

"You're the detective," Bat said, "but I know what I'd do."

"I'm open to suggestions."

"Cheesecake," Bat said, "at Lindy's."

And by that he meant Arnold Rothstein.

"That is," Bat added, "if you really want to pursue this any further. Allison is dead, after all."

O'Farrell took off his hat and scratched his head.

"I owe him," he said.

"Okay, then." Bat said. "Cheesecake it is."

"You comin'?" O'Farrell asked.

"You kiddin'? I wouldn't miss it."

5

Arnold Rothstein was easy to find even in a busy Lindy's. He was the one surrounded by bodyguards. O'Farrell and Bat Masterson crossed the floor under the wary eye of those guards.

"Boss," one of them said as the two men reached them.

"Well, well," the well-dressed Arnold Rothstein said, looking up from his cheesecake, "two of New York's more famous people. Make way, boys, for Val O'Farrell and the great Bat Masterson."

O'Farrell could see the bodyguards react to Bat's name. They made their living with guns, and even a Bat Masterson in his 60's was a man to be respected.

"What brings you gents to my table?" Rothstein asked. "Have a seat, please."

O'Farrell and Bat sat—Bat, from old habits, so that he could see most of the room. O'Farrell was wondering if the old legend was heeled, and he was sure others were wondering the same.

"I understand you know an ex-fighter named Kevin Allison," O'Farrell said.

Rothstein wiped his mouth with a cloth napkin and looked up at one of his men—he was fairly young, maybe late twenties, a big guy with broad shoulders who dressed like he used his boss's tailor.

"We know this guy?"

"We use him as a runner, sometimes," one of them said.

Rothstein looked back at O'Farrell and Bat, shrugged and said, "I don't know the guy. Lenny?"

"Don't know 'im real good," Lenny said. "Like I said, he runs errands and stuff."

"This is Lenny Green," Rothstein said. "I'm groomin' him, I just don't know for what, yet."

O'Farrell looked at Green, who stared back at him with no expression.

"What's your interest in a busted-up ex-pug?" Rothstein asked.

"He's dead," Bat said.

"That's too bad," Rothstein said. "He got family? We'll send flowers."

"No family," Bat said. "From what I know of him he lived alone."

"Too bad," Rothstein said. He looked at one of his men. "Make sure we pick up the body. I'll pay for a funeral."

"I'll take care of it," Lenny Green said.

"That's big of you," O'Farrell said.

"Hey, he worked for me," Rothstein said. His brown eyes sparkled in his pale face. Others had often commented on Rothstein's "happy" eyes, his dominant feature, and O'Farrell could see that they were correct. "I take care of my own."

"You wouldn't have any idea how he was killed, would you, Mr. Rothstein?" O'Farrell asked.

O'Farrell saw that he had played it right. If he'd said, "Arnold" or "Rothstein" the man might have bristled, been reluctant to answer, but he used the more respectful "Mr." and Rothstein appreciated the deference.

"I just heard he was dead from you fellas, Mr. O'Farrell," Rothstein said. "How would I know that?"

"He was shot in the head."

"Executed," Rothstein said.

"Yes."

"Not by me or mine," Rothstein said, and O'Farrell believed him. "I don't kill my own men, even a straggler like Kevin."

His reference to the dead man as "Kevin" showed that he had, indeed, known him, and O'Farrell did not think it was an accident.

"Who would kill him, then?" Bat asked.

"A rival?" Rothstein asked.

"I don't think women were a big part of Allison's life," O'Farrell said.

"I meant a rival of mine," Rothstein said,

"And who would that be?" O'Farrell asked.

"Too many to mention, I'm afraid," Rothstein said. "I'll have to look into it myself. Or have Lenny do it. Can I help you with anything else?"

"Yes," O'Farrell said. "Do you know any of these men?" He reeled off the names of the men he'd been playing poker with. Lenny leaned down and said something in Rothstein's ear.

"I recognize the names," Rothstein admitted.

"From where?"

"The newspaper," Rothstein sad. "Seems all of those men were wiped out during a poker game a night or two ago."

"I was in that game, too."

"And you lived?"

"Only because Kevin Allison got me out of that room before the shooting started."

"Ah," Rothstein said, "now I see. Kevin saved your life, and you don't know why. So you feel you owe him, even now that he's dead."

"Maybe more because he's dead," O'Farrell said.

"You're an honorable man, Mr. O'Farrell," Rothstein said. "I always knew that about you. And I value that."

O'Farrell didn't have anything to say to that.

"So," Rothstein said, sitting back, "you came looking for my help."

"Well, first," O'Farrell said, "I wanted to satisfy myself that you did or didn't have him killed."

"And you've done that?"

"Yes."

"And what have you decided?"

"You didn't kill him."

"Why'd you decide that?"

"Well, you just told me you didn't," O'Farrell said.

"You're willing to take my word for that?"

"Sure."

"Why?"

"Because you're a man who values honor."

"But, you only have my word for that, too."

"I'm a good judge of people," O'Farrell said. "If you were lying to me I'd know it."

"You know," Rothstein said, completely disregarding the fact that he'd claimed not to know Kid Alley well, "I always thought the kid had a yellow streak in him, figured it kept him from being a winner."

"You couldn't tell by me that he had any coward in him," O'Farrell said.

"Who's that quote from?" Rothstein asked, looking at his men, who all shrugged. "You know, 'A coward dies many times...'"

More shrugs.

"Well, he only died once," O'Farrell said, standing up. He didn't bother telling Rothstein he was trying to quote Shakespeare. "That was enough."

"Look," Rothstein said, as Bat stood, "I'll keep my ear to the ground. I come up with anything I'll let you know."

"We'd appreciate it," O'Farrell said.

"Hey, old man," Rothstein said to Bat. "You still got it, huh? Got my boys shakin' in their shoes."

"I'm not shakin'," Lenny said.

Bat smiled slowly.

"I'm just an old man who sits at a desk all day."

"Yeah," Rothstein said, his happy eyes getting even happier with his smile, "right."

6

On Broadway, outside the restaurant Bat asked, "If not Rothstein, then who?"

"Who what?" O'Farrell asked. "Who killed all those poker players, or who killed Kevin Allison?"

"Allison," Bat said. "Seems to me that's the murder we have to solve. We do that, then we might be able to solve the other one, as well."

"Well, since we haven't told the police about Allison yet," O'Farrell said, "we have a head start."

"We didn't tell the police, but we told Rothstein."

"He won't talk to the police," O'Farrell said.

"He talked to us."

"That's because you're the great Bat Masterson."

"Ah," Bat said, "you mean he respects his elders?"

"Did you think he was kiddin' in there?" O'Farrell asked. "You're still Bat Masterson, Bat. Sometimes I think you forget that."

"Maybe I forget who Bat Masterson is," Bat said, "but I always know who I am."

The distinction escaped O'Farrell, and he had too many other questions in his head to pursue this one now.

"I don't believe a rival of Rothstein's would strike at him by hittin' one of his runners," O'Farrell said.

"Then Rothstein is not gonna be any help at all."

"And the kid had no family that we know of," O'Farrell said. "What about friends? Other fighters? Ex-fighters? And could he have had a girl?"

"All possibilities," Bat said. "I can check the gyms again."

O'Farrell didn't answer right away. Something had occurred to him and he was trying it on.

"Val?"

"Huh? Oh, sure, check the gyms."

"And what just occurred to you?"

"I don't know," O'Farrell replied, "just somethin' Allison said when we were in the lobby of the hotel. I'm just gonna do some checking."

"Okay," Bat said.

"You want a ride?"

"I can walk to Times Square from here," Bat said. "It'll do me some good."

It was late in the day, but still too early to find Dorothy at the club. He parked his Twin Six in front of her building on the upper east side. It was not where the swells lived, but it was a lifetime away from where Kevin Allison had died.

She answered the door swaddled in a white terrycloth robe.

"This is a nice surprise," she said, "but it would have been better earlier. I just got out of the shower."

He entered her apartment and closed the door behind her. She smelled of her bath soap.

"I'm here to talk, Dorothy."

"Oh? About what?"

Her robe was wet and was clinging to her. He tried to keep his mind on business.

"Kevin Allison?"

"Who?"

"You know," he said, "the man you sent to the hotel to get me out?"

"I sent—no, I told you, he came to me and asked where you were. Said it was an emergency."

"Yeah, you told me that," O'Farrell said, "but why did he come to you?"

"Why did he—well, I don't know." She reached up to take her wet hair off her neck, held it above her head. The movement made the robe gape, showing her breasts and nipples.

"How long have we been seeing each other, Dorothy?" he asked. "Three months?"

"I suppose—"

"You're a lot younger than I am," he said. "I've often wondered why you approached me at the club."

"You're an attractive man, Val—"

"Maybe I am," he agreed, "but not to a lot of girls your age. What are you, twenty-eight? Nine?"

"Twenty-eight."

"Almost twenty years younger than me," he said. "I was flattered—have been flattered all along, but now..."

"Now what?"

"Now I'm suspicious," he said. "You knew where that poker game was because you coaxed me into telling you." While they were in bed, he recalled.

"What are you saying?"

"I'm saying you could have set that game up to be hit," he replied.

"And I...what? Arranged to meet you three months ago so I could set this up?"

"A hit like that would have to be set up in advance," O'Farrell said. "I want to know if I'm the boob who got all those men killed."

"If I set it up why would I have you pulled out?"

"Maybe you really do like me."

Suddenly she came real close to him. The robe was half off, now.

"Baby, I do like you," she said, "you know that." Her damp breasts pressed against him.

"I think I do know that, baby." He placed his hands on her hips and gently pushed her away from him. "It just doesn't make sense to me that Kevin Allison would come to you out of nowhere, looking for me."

"So it had to be a set-up?"

"Yes."

"And you think I set it up?"

"I think you helped," he said. "What I don't know is who you helped. That's what you're gonna tell me now."

O'Farrell parked the Twin Six around the corner from his destination and walked. As he reached the Majestic Apartment Building on the corner of Seventy-second and Central Park West, he saw Bat Masterson stepping down from a streetcar across the way. He hurried across to his friend before he could cross the street.

"What are you doin' here?" he asked.

"Maybe the same thing you are," Bat said. "I got a name from Joey Pounds."

"Joey Pounds?"

"Somebody we both forgot about," Bat said. "Kid Alley's only living family—his old manager. Found him at a gym in Times Square."

"What's the name?"

Bat told him.

"Pounds said that the Kid was afraid of this guy, and didn't like him. He likes him for killin' the kid. I was just gonna rattle his cage, some."

"I got the same name from Dorothy."

"Your Dorothy?"

"As it turns out, not my Dorothy," O'Farrell said, "but I'll explain that later. Why don't we do this together?"

"I wouldn't have it any other way."

"You heeled, old man?"

"I anticipated the need," Bat said, patting his side. The way Bat's jacket was hanging O'Farrell figured he'd simply slipped the pistol into his pocket.

"Let's go."

As they started to cross the street, a horse-drawn cart impeded their progress. While they waited for it to pass, standing in the center of the street, the front door of the Majestic opened and four men came walking out. One of them was the man they were looking for, and he spotted them and immediately surmised their goal.

"Kill them!" he shouted to his companions, and drew his own gun.

The New York street erupted in a hail of lead.

Bat's old Peacemaker was out first, proving that what Arnold Rothstein had said at Lindy's was the truth—he did still have it. This was further illustrated by the fact that his first shot put one man down on the ground for good.

O'Farrell's Colt was in his hand just after Bat's. He fired two shots, one of which clipped a man's shoulder, the second a window in front of the Majestic.

Men were scrambling for cover now, including O'Farrell, but he noticed that Bat stood his ground and continued to fire, despite the fact that lead was flying all around him. He caught another man through the neck as he was trying to duck behind a roadster.

The man O'Farrell had hit in the shoulder had staggered and gone down to one knee. As he brought himself up and prepared to fire O'Farrell shot him again, this time drilling him in the chest.

Lenny Green had been firing his gun since he first shouted at his men to kill O'Farrell and Masterson. Now he was crawling along the ground, looking for cover, as O'Farrell and Bat moved out of the middle of the street to join him in front of the Majestic.

Onlookers had gathered, having first scattered to safety, and were now watching with great interest despite the fact they did not know who the participants of this New York City shoot-out were.

Lenny Green was cowering on the ground, empty gun hanging from his hand by the trigger guard.

"We're gonna have to explain this," O'Farrell said.

"They started shootin' first," Bat pointed out.

O'Farrell looked around.

"We'll need a couple of witnesses."

"You want me to pick them out?"

"You tell them who you are they'll say anythin' you want."

"You're probably right." Bat looked down at Lenny Green.

"He's not goin' anywhere."

Bat ejected the spent shells from his gun, the casings making pinging noises as they hit the sidewalk. He then loaded live rounds, holstered the weapon and went to find the witnesses. Old habits died very hard.

O'Farrell reached down and snatched the empty gun from Lenny Green's hand.

"Your boss know you set up the hit at the poker game?"

"No."

"Want me to tell him?"

"Hell, no."

"Then you'll talk to the police when they get here," O'Farrell said. "That is, unless I kill you myself. Why'd you pick on me? Send Dorothy after me?"

Green smirked and O'Farrell almost pistol whipped it off his face.

"I knew you were a regular in that game, but I never knew where the game was," Green said. "A couple of those boys needed killing."

"A couple?" O'Farrell asked. "So you killed them all?"

"If I only killed the two I wanted Rothstein would've known it was me. Or suspected. I couldn't take that chance."

"What'd you have against those two?"

Green shrugged.

"They were in my way."

Spoken like a man on the way up, O'Farrell thought, *who not only wanted to step over people, but leave them dead in his wake.*

"If it wasn't for that stupid broad sending that broken-down pug to get you out, I would have gotten away with it."

Knowing that Dorothy had sent Kid Alley to save his life was small consolation for being made a fool of. Did cuckold apply? No matter, it felt like it.

COWARDS DIE MANY TIMES

Also realizing that it was Lenny Green who either killed or had Kid Alley killed, O'Farrell tried to not shoot him in the head while he waited for the police to arrive.

Author's note

Many of the characters in this story are actual historical figures. The obvious ones are, of course, Bat Masterson, Damon Runyon, James M. Cain and Arnold Rothstein. However, Val O'Farrell is also a historical figure. Little is actually known about him save that he was a New York City policeman during the time Bat Masterson was in New York, and he left to become a private detective. What little information I do have on him came from the book Bat Masterson *by Robert DeArment. I have done other stories about his life as a private detective, and plan to do more.*

The presence of James M. Cain in this story is capricious on my part. When I started the story, Bat Masterson was not to be a factor, so it was set in 1923. In its present form it is set in 1921, only a couple of months before Bat died. Cain and Masterson would not have met, but for my poetic license, Cain spent only a short time in New York between Baltimore and Hollywood, so I had a small window to work with. Forgive me.

Below are the last words Bat Masterson typed before he died writing at his typewriter at his desk at The Morning Telegraph:

There are those who argue that everything breaks even in this old dump of a world of ours. I suppose these ginks who argue that way hold that because the rich man gets ice in the summer and the poor man gets it in the winter things are breaking even for both. Maybe so, but I'll swear I can't see it that way.

The Majestic Apartment building did and still does exist. Meyer Lansky, Lucky Luciano and Frank Costello all lived there at one time or another.

LEAD POISONING

GARY LOVISI

Blood! *Johnny Blood! Don't move!*"

I stopped walking, slowly turned around, resisting the powerful urge to draw my gun, but keeping my hand nearby should the need arise. I was sure it would arise soon. I knew that both Tommy and Red were dead now. Each had taken half a dozen slugs, lead poisoning, always fatal in that dose when a posse was lying in wait for you. I knew now they'd been lying in wait for us all along.

Somehow they *knew*—knew we were riding into town to rob the Winfield Bank & Trust. Tommy Harroway and Big Red Jenkins lay dead inside the bank. I had been waiting outside with our horses, ready to make our getaway, when everything went wrong and I found myself surrounded by angry, scowling, gun-toting town-folk.

In their lead was a sheriff by the name of Hardison—who was known as "Hard-ass" Hardison. He was a tough hard-case character. I'd heard he'd earned his name well and often.

Hardison cocked the double-barreled shotgun he was aiming at me, showing me a good close-up look at it, being as it was now pointed directly at my head. He barked, "Drop your gun, Johnny Blood. Take it out carefully and drop it to the ground *now!*"

Hardison's shotgun at such close range was an unmistakable threat and it spoke to me harder than his words ever could. I carefully disarmed, dropping my gun-belt to the ground and quickly putting my hands in the air, saying, "Don't you shoot, Sheriff. I'm unarmed and giving myself up."

"You're damned right you are, boy!" Hardison growled, still training his weapon on me while motioning one of his many armed deputies to pick up my gun and keep me covered.

I said, "You don't have to rub it in, Sheriff. I'm caught. I give up."

Hardison didn't say a word. Satisfied I was being well covered by other guns, he suddenly put down his shotgun and drew his Colt revolver.

I figured he was gonna lead me off to jail.

What he did next was so sudden and mean that I wouldn't never have expected it from no sheriff, no matter how hard a man he was. What the sheriff did next was point his revolver at me and pull the trigger. Twice. Shot me in the stomach. Point blank.

I was astonished, then doubled over in incredible pain. Gut-shot, shocked, bleeding now on the sidewalk boards, panic setting in my mind. I thought I was surely gonna die. It was awful painful, and growing more painful.

I heard Hardison shout, "Take him out to the edge of town, boys. Let him bleed to death out there with the other no-good varmints. That'll teach him to try to steal in my town."

I heard harsh laughter and then felt rough hands pick me up.

I lost consciousness soon after, to awaken I don't know how much later. Parched of throat. Shivering. I found myself lying in the hard dusty dirt of a wagon-rutted road, the hot southwestern sun beating down on my head unmercifully. I noticed that my hands were brown, cracked with dry blood. *My blood!* What the hell had happened? Where was I? I began to panic as it all came back to me.

I'd been gut-shot by Sheriff Hardison! Then dumped out here to die. I screamed and the pain welled over me in searing waves.

I held on, forcing myself to consciousness. I did all I could to keep the panic down and replace it with the only thing I had left to me then—anger. And later, I promised myself, revenge.

I cried out painfully, sorrowful at my plight, "Now why'd he have to do this to me? I had gave myself up, I had put my gun down. All fair and square. It's just pure cussed cruelness to do a man like this, shoot him down when he's unarmed and defenseless, then leave him out here with his guts all open and bloody to be pecked at by the damn buzzards."

I cried and raged and tried to fight the pain and panic. I was alone and scared more than I dared admit, and knew that I was on the way to dying.

But I guess it was them same buzzards what wanted me for a meal that saved me because they led the old Indian to me. Now he was a real old-timer, probably the oldest man I've ever seen, white, red, or black. I didn't know what tribe he was from, and he didn't tell me either. In fact, he didn't speak at all and when he did it was only in Indian lingo. I didn't unnerstand none of that talk. I don't think he unnerstood no American either. But I guess he didn't need to just then, he could plainly see how bad off I was. My time was short, so he chased away the bolder buzzards waiting for an opportunity to take a meaty peck out of me and then he administered to my wounds.

The old Indian cleaned me up, then he did some kind of patching job on me that I've never seen nor heard of before. Some special Indian medicine I reckon. The pain was terrible nonetheless. Got worse when he rubbed some kind of herb or potion deep into my wounds. Then he covered it with leaves and he sang a loud sing-song chant over me. I screamed from the pain, it was fearfully bad. Then he forced something into my mouth; some kind of herb or powder and made me swallow it. I gagged, it was a foul-tasting concoction, and I lost consciousness soon after and thankfully too, for the pain had grown truly terrible.

I slept for many days. It was the wicked fever-dream sleep.

When I came out of it, it was morning, my body stiff and warm. I found I was covered in blankets. There was a bold fire going nearby. I saw the old Indian with a pipe in his mouth, an aromatic smoke filling the air, some kind of hemp smell, sweet, and after a while it made me dizzy.

The old Indian didn't say a word, he just watched me, as I watched him. When he seemed to consider the time was right he came over to me, inspected my wounds, and in English sternly proclaimed, "You all better now. Today you rest. Grow strong. Tomorrow you leave. Go back to white man town, find man who did this to you. Do not let him get away with doing such a bad thing."

I looked at the old Indian in amazement. I didn't know he spoke English. I told him so but he ignored me and walked away. He just stared out at the horizon and began chanting that Indian lingo of his to the setting disk of the fire-red sun.

Next day, I *was* better, a *lot* better. The day after that even better, stronger. The herbs the old Indian had used on me had a miraculous healing power on my wounds. While still painful, they were not bleeding and did not smell of decay. Infection.

Later that day he gave me a holster, and there was a shooting iron in it. Not mine. I wondered where he'd gotten it. It was a good clean gun, loaded, ready for use.

"Is it yours?" I asked him.

He just harrumphed.

"Why won't you talk to me, you crazy Injun! Why won't you answer my questions?" I shouted.

He ignored me. Walked away.

I felt such powerful exasperation toward him at that point I thought I'd bust my gut open again, but he'd been of real help to me. I *was* grateful. Crazy and old though he was, I owed him a debt. But I didn't owe him my dying. I didn't know what he had up his sleeve, but I surely was not going back to that town. I was not gonna confront Sheriff Hardison. Not by a long shot.

I told the old Indian that too.

Only then did he turn and look straight at me, his hard old eyes boring down into me as he walked purposefully toward me, a grim look on his wrinkled hard face.

Well, I'd certainly gotten some kind of rise out of him. For whatever reason, he wanted me to go back after Hardison. I wondered why. Then he showed me why.

He came over to me and undid the red plaid bandana from his neck. I could see the terrible rope burns now for the first time. They were viciously wicked scars. He said, tired now, "My son, his wife, and their little ones were all hanged, killed by the white sheriff. My son stole a calf to feed his family during the winter of many snows. My son, my grandson, all dead now because of it. But the noose would not close on my old wrinkled neck, so I dangled there screaming, struggling to breathe. The sheriff and his posse laughed at the old Indian and they let me live. They rode me to a spot out of town. Then they left me to die. You understand, now?"

I nodded, nervous, staring at him like I'd never really seen him before.

"I am old, you are young and strong, and getting stronger, Johnny Blood. I saved you so you would go back and take my revenge—and your own."

He walked away. He'd probably said more words than he'd spoken in years.

I said, "Well, if that ain't one hell of a story!"

He didn't say anything, just continued walking off into the night blackness, away from our small camp.

"So what you expect me to do about it!" I hollered after him. There was no answer.

"Go back to that damn town? Bushwack Hardison!"

Quiet and darkness surrounded me.

"What the hell you want me to do?"

A far away voice spoke to me from the darkness, "Do what you want to do. Your life is your own now. But remember, a man alive in shame is a man not truly alive."

I thought about what he said and the more I thought about it, the more I knew he was right.

"Well look who's back from the grave?" Sheriff Hardison said, not scared, it was just that his interest had been piqued for once in a considerable while.

LEAD POISONING

"You gut-shot me and left me for dead," I said. My gun was out, trained on him. He didn't pay it no mind. He watched me carefully, curious. I think he was...amused.

He hadn't gone for his gun yet but I knew that he would soon enough. We were alone in a dark alley in the back of town. It was night, moonless, pitch-black, far-off flickering lamps gave only scant illumination. I saw Hardison's face, hard and intense, his eyes burning with death as I covered him with my gun.

"Just what a no-good varmint deserves," Hardison said matter-of-factly. Calm. Cold.

"No it ain't! I'd given up. I'd done put down my gun. Only then, did you shoot me. You shot an unarmed man! That ain't all, neither, you gut-shot me, you lousy bastard! Shot me just to hurt me, to make me suffer, give me a long, lingering death. You're a mean man, Sheriff."

"What you deserved. You tried to rob a bank in my town."

"But I never killed no one. I never even shot at no one..."

"So what, boy, you want me to give you another chance? You're a bad seed, Johnny Blood, I can smell your kind all over this land. You're all poison and the only antidote for the poison you spread is one of my own devising—cold, hard, lead."

"You're no better than I am. Fact is, Sheriff, you're a mite worse," I said, angry now. "I ain't never gut-shot no one. That's not a fair and proper way to kill a man."

"I gut-shot you, boy, 'cause I wanted to inflict the maximum of pain upon you. Send you down to hell in the most painful suffering way," Hardison laughed.

Then he drew his gun—but my gun was already drawn and trained on him. It was no contest. I quickly put two slugs in him. Low. In his gut. His own round went wild and missed me.

I knew that at such close range my bullets would normally have passed right through him with a clean cut, leaving two small holes, but something was wrong, something terrible had happened. My two slugs tore into Hardison's gut, churning and cutting and tearing, ripping open his abdomen, slashing his insides, and causing his soggy entrails to spew forth in a flood of bile and blood. He palsied, his eyes blown wide, his hands having dropped his gun, now desperately trying to force his squirming intestines back into his abdomen. It was a terrible image. He was in agony.

When he fell squirming to the ground I realized the truth. I checked the bullets in the gun the Old Indian had given me. Sure as shootin' they was notched with an "X" at the tip and the smell of something upon them. Garlic. I knew then why my bullets had done so much damage; they'd opened up and tore right through the Sheriff's gut like a hot knife through butter.

Hardison was dying, and soon a crowd would begin to form. People were already shouting, looking for the location the shots had come from. I stood frozen, terrified. I'd never killed a man before. Suddenly the old Indian came out of the shadows. He said, "White man justice for a white man. Now over and done. Come with me, we must not be found here."

Well, I couldn't agree more and let the old Indian lead me away. He had two horses stashed on the next street over and soon we were gone, lost in the dark of night.

We rode for a ways. Finally a dozen miles down, we split up, it was his order. He went his way; I went mine.

I never saw him again, but I often think of him.

Sometimes I hear from scouts and trackers of a legend about an old Indian medicine man who had strange powers. They say his weathered face ran with a river of tears for a son and grandson hanged by a hardcase sheriff.

I heard the legend but it never mentioned the Indian's name. I didn't know if it was true or not but it seemed likely enough to me after all I'd been through—though I don't like to talk much about it these days.

I remember howd I'd been gut-shot and how I'd gut-shot the man who had done me. Things had been set right. But I'd killed a sheriff and I was a wanted man now.

My name used to be Johnny Blood, but since then I go by the name of William Starr. I carry a gun with notched bullets, but I don't ever want to use it again. I knowed too many people who lived by the gun that died from lead poisoning.

LEAD POISONING

I travel the territory looking for the old Indian now. I felt I had unsaid things to speak of with him. I never could find him though, it was as if the river of tears had finally hit dry bottom and flowed no longer. A bad thing for me and all my questions, but perhaps a good thing for an old Indian who I was sure now had found true restfulness for once, this side of the grave. At least I hoped so. I guess it was a good thing that I had a hand in making that happen. But sometimes, I wonder.

Sometimes, when I'm sleeping alone in the arroyo, I think back when it all began. I can see Big Red Jenkins and Tommy Harroway entering the Winfield Bank & Trust. I see Sheriff "Hard-ass" Hardison and his gun-toting deputies as they close off the bank and cut down Big Jim and Tommy in a hail of lead before they knew what was happening. And then I see this face. Or think I do. It's reflected for just an instant in the glass of the bank window, I see it as I wait there with the horses, then it is gone. That's just before Hardison and his deputies were upon me. It was just for a split second, and it looked like the face of an old weathered Indian with a red plaid bandana around his neck.

Now I often think about old Indians, lead poisoning, and set-up bank jobs...

And I wonder...

THE CONVERSION OF CARNE MUERTO

JAMES REASONER

This happened in the early days of what came to be known as
the Old Company, that band of intrepid Texas Rangers led by
Captain John S. "Rip" Ford. I was the company surgeon in those
days, less than a decade after Texas had ceased to be an independent
republic and joined the Union. Those were still wild, dangerous
times, especially in the brush country along the Rio Grande, the
border between Texas and Mexico. In that time and place, a man
could die quickly, at any time, with little or no warning. Bandits
from below the border raided into Texas on a regular basis, and
bands of fierce Comanche warriors terrorized settlers on both sides
of the river. The fiercest of the war chiefs was little more than a
boy, but he was feared from the mouth of the Rio Grande to the
Big Bend. His name was Carne Muerto—Spanish for "dead meat".

But I seem to be getting ahead of myself. The first time I
saw Carne Muerto, he was not yet a war chief. Instead, he was a
wounded, frightened lad.

THE CONVERSION OF CARNE MUERTO

The running fight had lasted most of the morning. Our scout and tracker, Roque Maugricio, had located the Comanches who had raided and burned a *rancho* north of Laredo. We hit them at dawn, killing two of the Indians and putting the others to rout. I felt a moment of pity when I saw the bullet-riddled bodies sprawled on the ground—I was a healer, after all—but then I remembered what the Comanches had done to the rancher and his wife and their two little girls, and the feeling passed.

The rest of the war party fled toward the border with the Rangers in pursuit. As the Comanches scattered, so too did the Rangers, breaking up into smaller groups to continue the chase. I found myself riding with Roque and Doc Sullivan, the company's jokester but also a crack shot and one of the bravest men I ever knew. Why Doc had acquired that nickname when *I* was the company surgeon, I never knew, but it seemed to fit him.

We saw one of the fugitives racing his pony toward a clump of mesquite trees. Doc drew a bead with his rifle and brought down the pony with a single shot. The rider sailed through the air when his mount collapsed underneath him. He scrambled up and ran on into the trees, but I could tell from the way he moved that he was hurt. We closed in rapidly.

A pistol cracked from the cover of the trees, making Doc yelp as the bullet passed close by his head. Roque said, "Keep him busy," and peeled away from us, veering off so that he could circle around and come at the trees from a different direction. Doc banged away with his Colt revolver, not caring whether or not he hit anything as long as he kept the fugitive ducking for cover. After a few minutes, Roque called, "Hold your fire! I've got him!"

Doc and I hurried into the trees to find Roque standing over a young Comanche, about eighteen years of age, who had been shot through the upper right arm. He lay on the ground at the foot of a tree, glaring up at Roque, who kept a pistol trained on him.

I could tell that the wound in the youngster's arm was several hours old and knew that he had suffered it during the initial encounter earlier that morning. To ride for hours at a furious gallop while in what must have been great pain speaks volumes about the strength and determination of these people. I have long regretted that fate cast us as enemies, as there was much to admire about the Comanches. Other than their habit of inflicting the most unspeakable tortures on innocent people, of course.

But to get back to the subject at hand...Roque spoke quickly to the boy in his native tongue. Roque was half-Comanche himself, though he had turned his back on that part of his heritage and was now a valued citizen of Texas and member of the Rangers. The lad made no reply at first, but after more prodding by Roque, he finally spoke in a sullen tone.

"He says his name's Carne Muerto," Roque told Doc and me. "Claims to be the son of a chief. If it's true, we've caught ourselves a pretty good prisoner, boys."

"Can I take a look at that wound?" I asked.

"Give Doc your gun first. Don't want him grabbin' it."

I handed my revolver to Doc and knelt beside the Comanche youth. Roque had already disarmed him, so I was in no real danger, but despite that I felt a tiny shiver go through me as I saw the look of hatred in Carne Muerto's eyes. If he had not been so weak from loss of blood, I think he would have attacked me with his bare hands.

The wound in his arm had bled quite a bit, but I could tell that he was in little real danger from it. The bullet had gone straight through the fleshy part of his arm and missed the bone. I fetched my bag from my horse and cleaned and bound up the wound. Barring corruption, I thought the injury would heal cleanly.

Then, since Carne Muerto's pony was dead, we put him on my horse and I rode double with him as we headed back to rendezvous with Captain Ford and the rest of the company.

By the middle of the day the Rangers had regrouped and we were on our way to our temporary headquarters, an abandoned *rancho* near Laredo. Though several more Comanches had been killed during the skirmishes that morning, the young man taken by Roque Maugricio, Doc Sullivan, and myself was the only prisoner. Captain Ford, a tall, lean man with a close-cropped white beard and piercing eyes, was pleased when he discovered the identity of Carne Muerto.

"If he's really a chief's son, we might be able to trade him for some white captives," the captain suggested. There was a fairly steady traffic in such exchanges in those days. "We'll take him to Fort McIntosh."

After a brief stop at the *rancho*, we rode on to the fort at Laredo. The adobe buildings of Fort McIntosh, arrayed around a central parade ground, were on the very banks of the river itself. The American flag flapped lazily in the hot breeze as the Rangers rode in.

As we dismounted in front of the post's headquarters building, I saw a man and a woman standing in the shade on the porch. While there were women in that part of the country, they were rare enough so that any female drew attention, especially one as attractive as this lady. Her hair, which was pulled back into a severe bun, was the color of burnished copper. Her complexion was very fair, the sort that burns easily in the sun of the border country. She was about twenty-five years old, I judged, a mature woman who still retained a bit of her youth.

The man who stood with her was an army officer, a lieutenant about the same age, with a dark mustache that curled up on the ends. I didn't know him and thought that he must be newly arrived at the fort. As I watched, he slipped an arm around the woman's waist in a possessive gesture. She was his wife, I told myself. Officers were usually allowed to bring their families with them wherever they were posted, even to frontier forts such as this one, but I wasn't sure it was always a good idea.

The prisoner drew a great deal of interest and not a few rude comments. One burly sergeant wanted to know why we hadn't just shot the young heathen instead of taking him alive. The woman on the porch heard that and seemed disturbed by it. She spoke to her husband, who shook his head as he replied quietly to whatever she had asked.

Captain Ford, Roque, and I took Carne Muerto inside, and we were shown immediately into the office of the colonel who commanded the post. The man grinned and said, "What's that you've got there, Rip, a mountain lion cub?"

"Says his name is Carne Muerto and claims he's the son of old Gato." The captain had questioned the prisoner at length, with Roque translating, but he hadn't gotten much more out of Carne Muerto than we had discovered originally.

"Dead Meat, eh?" the colonel said. "Fitting name for one of those savages."

"I thought we might get word to Gato and see if he'd be interested in working a trade. I don't know if he's got any white captives right now, but those bands of Comanch' nearly always do."

The commanding officer nodded in agreement with Ford's suggestion. "Want me to have him locked up in the guardhouse until we decide what to do with him?"

"I thought that might be best—" Captain Ford began, but he stopped as someone came into the office behind us.

"Colonel, you can't lock that prisoner up," a woman's voice said. "It would be inhumane. Why, he's nothing but a boy, and he's hurt!"

I looked around and saw the young woman with copper-colored hair, followed closely by the lieutenant, who looked worried and upset. He said quickly, "Begging the colonel's pardon, we don't mean to intrude—"

"Then don't, Lieutenant Patrick," the colonel said, not bothering to conceal his irritation at this interruption.

Still trying to fix things, the lieutenant said, "It's just that Julia is new to the frontier and doesn't understand—"

"I understand perfectly well, Bartholomew," she said. "I understand that this poor young man needs help, and it's my Christian duty to give it to him."

Captain Ford said, "Ma'am, I believe in the Lord, too, but I'm not sure He'd want you getting mixed up in this."

Julia Patrick turned on him. "Are you in charge of those so-called Rangers?"

"Yes, ma'am. Captain John S. Ford, at your service."

"Did you shoot this young man?"

"Well, I don't rightly know if it was my bullet put that hole in his arm or not," Ford said. "There was quite a bit of lead flying around at the time."

"Has he been tortured?"

Captain Ford frowned. "No, ma'am, not by us. Fact of the matter is, it was our company surgeon here who patched him up and kept him from bleeding to death."

That didn't do much to mollify Mrs. Patrick. She sniffed and said, "After it was you and your men who brutally wounded him."

"Lieutenant..." the colonel said in a warning tone.

"Yes, sir." Lieutenant Patrick gripped his wife's arm. "Come along, dear—"

She pulled away from him. "Colonel, I demand that this prisoner be turned over to me for safekeeping until arrangements can be made to return him to his people."

That took us all by surprise. I'm afraid we stared at her. The colonel finally said, "That's impossible. He has to be locked up."

"You didn't hear what the men outside said, Colonel," she argued. "They hate the Indians, and I'm afraid that if this young man is put in the guardhouse, something terrible will happen to him."

That was possible, I supposed. The soldiers who had fought the Comanches before had good reason to hate them, and if some fatal "accident," shall we say, were to befall Carne Muerto, I knew the Army would not investigate too vigorously.

Captain Ford rubbed at his bearded jaw in thought and said after a moment, "The lady may have a point there. We don't want anything bad happening to the boy until we find out whether or not we can make use of him."

That brought another sniff of disapproval from Julia Patrick, but she didn't say anything else.

"But he's a savage!" the colonel said, as if that should have been blindingly obvious to everyone. "We can't turn him over to a...a woman!"

An idea occurred to me. "What if he was guarded at all times?" I said.

"I can't spare any men for that!"

It seemed to me that if the colonel could spare men to stand watch over the guardhouse, he could have assigned a trooper to keep an eye on Carne Muerto. But rather than make that argument, I said, "I can stay and watch him."

Captain Ford frowned. "I don't want to lose my company surgeon."

"Yes, but we're not going out on patrol again immediately," I pointed out. "I assume you're going to send Roque to see if a trade can be made..."

The captain nodded. "That was my plan."

"So the company may not be leaving the *rancho* until he gets back. And if I may remind you, Captain, while I'm a doctor, I am also a Texas Ranger."

Ford chuckled. "True enough, old friend." He looked at the post commander. "What do you think, Colonel?"

"Well, I don't like it very much, to be honest...but what do you say, Lieutenant Patrick? You're the one who'd have two guests in your house."

The lieutenant looked at the colonel, at the three of us Rangers, and at the prisoner. But in the end he looked at his wife, and that meant the decision was a foregone conclusion.

"I suppose it would be all right," he said.

That was how Carne Muerto came to stay with the lieutenant and his lady...and how the course of more than one life was set.

"Don't trust the son of a bitch for a second," Roque told me before he rode out to seek Gato, Carne Muerto's father. "He don't want you to know it, but he speaks a little English and Spanish. He knows what's going on. And if he gets a chance, he'll cut your throat."

"You're not telling me anything I don't already know, amigo," I assured Roque.

I have to admit, however, that I was surprised by what happened over the next few days. The colonel insisted that Carne Muerto be handcuffed, and not even Julia Patrick could argue him out of that. But other than that precaution, and the fact that I was always with him, the Comanche youth stayed in the small house where Lieutenant and Mrs. Patrick lived much as any guest might stay there. Mrs. Patrick insisted that he wear white man's clothes and take his meals at the table with us, and although he was sullen at first, within a couple of days Carne Muerto seemed at ease in his new surroundings. I tended to his arm, which was healing nicely just as I expected, and Mrs. Patrick tended to what she saw as his spiritual needs.

She began reading the Bible to him the first day he was there.

THE CONVERSION OF CARNE MUERTO

Although as a physician I am a man of science, I find no great conflict between scientific tenets and the Word of God. Still, I saw little point in trying to impart the Lord's teachings to a heathen. Carne Muerto, though, seemed interested. He lost his sullen attitude and no longer bothered to conceal the fact that he understood and could speak a little English. I sat on the porch of the lieutenant's cabin with them for long hours, smoking my pipe as Mrs. Patrick read from the Scriptures and talked to Carne Muerto about his immortal soul.

By the time a week had passed without Roque having returned from his scouting mission, Carne Muerto was asking Mrs. Patrick what he would have to do in order to be saved from the fires of Hell.

"Simply accept the Lord as your savior, my young friend," she said to him as a beatific smile shone on her face. She refused to call him by his name, feeling that it was too savage.

Carne Muerto tapped his chest with a fist. "God here," he said. "Jesus here."

"Praise the Lord!" Mrs. Patrick said. She reached over and hugged him—something which I'm vaguely embarrassed to admit bothered me. "You've accepted Christ into your heart. Do you know what this means?"

He shook his head.

"It means that all your sins are forgiven and that when you die, you will ascend to glory, to be with Our Heavenly Father and all the hosts of angels. And you will live forever."

Carne Muerto smiled. I had to admit that the expression made him look younger and not nearly as savage and frightening as he had that first day we brought him to the fort. I asked myself if I truly believed that he had converted to Christianity. While I was skeptical by nature, I had to admit that I had no real reason to doubt him. After all, missionaries had been coming to Texas and converting the heathens for a couple of hundred years. In fact, some of the first white men to explore this rugged land had been Spanish priests.

And wasn't it often said that the Lord works in mysterious ways?

Now, you may ask where Lieutenant Patrick was during all this, and how he felt about his wife ministering to the young captive. For the first four or five days of Carne Muerto's sojourn with the couple, the lieutenant was there, and he wasn't too happy about the way things were going. Although I certainly wasn't trying to eavesdrop, several times I heard him engaging his wife in quiet but heartfelt arguments about the subject of how much time she was spending with Carne Muerto. Needless to say, the lieutenant did not emerge victorious from any of these arguments.

Following that, he was sent out on a routine patrol with a troop of cavalry, so he wasn't at the fort when Carne Muerto's conversion took place.

That evening I checked the dressing on the boy's wounded arm. The holes left by the bullet had closed up nicely and were almost healed. I'm sure the muscles of his arm were still stiff and sore, but I saw no need to replace the bandage. "You'll be all right now," I told him.

He nodded. "Carne Muerto all right. Carne Muerto saved. Good as white man."

Mrs. Patrick heard what he said and beamed approvingly. "Of course you're as good as any white man," she told him. "God doesn't care about the color of your skin."

I truly believe that she was right about that. Of course, she was wrong about many other things.

At night Carne Muerto slept on a pallet on the floor. Before he lay down I always moved one of the handcuffs to a leg of the wood-burning stove, which was too heavy for one man to budge, so that he couldn't get away. I slept on a divan across the room, out of his reach.

I take all the blame for what happened next. At first I had been extremely cautious with the lad, but as the days passed and he became cooperative and almost friendly, I fear I relaxed my vigilance slightly. So it took me by surprise when I unlocked the cuff of Carne Muerto's right wrist and he hit me with it, striking with his left arm so that the loose cuff slashed across my face with stunning viciousness.

THE CONVERSION OF CARNE MUERTO

I was knocked to my knees by the blow. Carne Muerto kicked me in the chest, driving me backward onto the floor. Like a wild animal he pounced upon me. His hands went to my neck and closed about it. The fingers dug cruelly into my flesh. I couldn't breathe, and I feared he was going to crush my throat. I fumbled for the holstered revolver on my hip.

Before I could draw the weapon, Julia Patrick stepped into the room. She had been to the privy out back before retiring for the evening and was already in her nightdress and robe. When she saw Carne Muerto kneeling on top of me, trying to strangle me, she cried out, but her hands were over her mouth and muffled the sound.

"No!" she said as she hurried forward. "My friend, please, I beg you! Stop what you're doing!"

He took one hand away from my throat, but only to ball it into a fist and smash it into my face, stunning me even more. I lay there half-conscious as he sprang up and turned toward Mrs. Patrick.

"Carne Muerto saved!" he said. "Sins all forgiven!"

"Yes, yes, but…you can't just kill that poor man." She caught hold of his arms and leaned close to him, speaking urgently. "You have to repent of your sins. That means you have to turn away from them and sin no more—"

If I had been able to draw my gun at that moment, I would have seen to it that Carne Muerto sinned no more. But I was still too stunned, my muscles unable or unwilling to do my bidding. All I could do was watch as Carne Muerto grabbed Julia Patrick, jerked her against him, and kissed her with the lustful intensity of a full-grown man. As she struggled, he dug a hand in her hair and tore loose the pins that held it in a bun. The coppery masses tumbled down as he forced her to the divan.

I rolled onto my side and tried to get up, but then consciousness slipped away from me. I slumped to the floor and passed out.

When I came back to my senses, the first thing I heard was muffled sobbing. I pushed myself onto my hands and knees and crawled across the room to the divan, where Mrs. Patrick lay with her nightclothes in tatters. One didn't have to be trained as a physician to see that she had been assaulted in a most savage and brutal manner. But she was alive and so was I, and in all honesty both of those things surprised me. I would have expected Carne Muerto to slit our throats before he escaped.

He was gone, of course. He had slipped off the post entirely, it was soon discovered.

But before I raised the alarm, I did my best to ascertain if Mrs. Patrick was seriously injured. Her eyes were wide and staring. I said, "Mrs. Patrick! Can you hear me? Mrs. Patrick!"

She began to mumble something. I had to lean close to her to make out the words. "Forgiven," she said. "Forgiven...he said all his sins were forgiven..."

She had no injuries other than bruises and scrapes. At least that was the case as far as physical injuries were concerned. The look in her eyes told me that the wounds to her spirit and her mind went much deeper.

I left her lying there on the divan, staggered onto the front porch of the little cabin, drew my pistol at last, and fired three shots in the air. That drew plenty of attention.

The colonel immediately sent a rider to the *rancho* where the Rangers were gathered. Since I had determined that Mrs. Patrick was not in need of medical attention, she was turned over to the care of the colonel's lady and the other officers' wives on the post. I waited in the colonel's office, miserable, until Rip Ford strode in.

"I'm sorry, Captain—" I began as I started to my feet.

Ford waved me back into the chair. "It's not your fault, old friend. I should have left Doc or one of the other men here with you. I've never doubted your courage, but you're maybe a mite too trusting."

"Never again," I said with a bitter taste in my mouth. "I'll never trust anyone again."

The captain had no patience for self-recrimination, so he ignored me and turned to the commander. "We'll get on the trail right away, of course. Might still be able to catch him. Maugricio's not back yet, but several other men in the company are good trackers."

This time I came to my feet. "I'm going with you."

Captain Ford glanced at me and said, "You're hurt."

I raised a hand to the bloody gash left on my forehead by the blow from the handcuff. "I don't care. This is nothing."

"Suit yourself." Ford turned back to the colonel. "What about Lieutenant Patrick?"

"His patrol is due back in tomorrow morning. I'm sure he'll want to come after you."

"More than likely. Don't let him."

The colonel frowned. "I can order him to stay put, but I may have to put him in the guardhouse to keep him from deserting."

"Then do it," Ford said. "I don't need a man crazy with anger getting in the way out there."

The colonel shrugged and nodded. "All right. You're riding out tonight?"

"The sooner the better," Captain Ford said.

We didn't catch Carne Muerto—not that night. And not on any of the other occasions we did battle with his war parties over the next few years as his reputation grew. Not until some time later were we able to put an end at last to his depredations.

Meanwhile, Mrs. Patrick seemed to recover from her ordeal, but three months after the incident, her husband came home to find that she had hanged herself from a beam in their home. Her Bible was open on the table beside her, but the window was open and a border breeze was riffling the thin paper of the pages, so if she had meant for her final message to be a Bible verse, there was no way of knowing which one it was.

Lieutenant Patrick remained in the army but requested a transfer to another post, a request that was, of course, granted. He was killed three years later, leading a charge against the Apaches in Arizona Territory...a charge that some said was foolhardy, even suicidal.

As for myself, I went on to have many adventures with Captain Ford and the Old Company, but after that I never carried a gun again and took no part in the battles that the company fought. My contribution was limited to patching up their wounds when the shooting stopped.

The captain and I never talked much about what had happened. I viewed the incident as a fundamental failure on my part. But once as we rode across a lonely stretch of border country, Ford said to me, "You know, I honestly think that no two people ever see the world just alike. They may think they do, but they don't. Take Carne Muerto. I reckon he took what that poor woman told him to mean that if he became a Christian, he could do whatever he wanted to, no matter how bad, and the Lord would still forgive him for it. He took it as *permission* to sin, rather than a prohibition against it."

"You might be right, Captain. When he was talking to Mrs. Patrick, he seemed sincere enough."

Ford nodded. "When you get right down to it, that's why none of this can end well, old friend." He waved a hand to indicate our surroundings, but I knew he meant something larger than that. He was talking about the whole clash between our culture and that of Carne Muerto. "We look at the same things, but what we see is different. Worlds apart, amigo. Worlds apart."

I knew he spoke the truth, but at the same time this was one of the few occasions in his life when Rip Ford, truly a far-seeing man, was too short-sighted. Yes, there were vast differences between our people and those who opposed us, but in the end that gulf would be bridged as it always is.

For in the end, no matter who we are or where we come from or what our beliefs, we wind up the same…carne muerto.

LAST SONG OF ANTIETAM

PATRICK J. LAMBE

Out of the seven of us, my twin sister Liz and I are the only ones who remember the covered wagon trip out here from Philadelphia, and the consternation of my parents when their lame horse finally stumbled in the dust for the last time. The trail guide avoided my father's eyes as he handed down two sacks of grain and a slab of bacon from the supply wagon. My parents stared at the rest of the covered wagons as they continued westward, a look of concern and pity on the faces regarding us from under the canvas covers as the settlers left us there.

Lizzie and I were old enough to gauge the seriousness of our situation, but my mother wouldn't put up with our crying. She picked up the babies and set the rest of us to singing gospel songs as my father strained against the yoke, inching the wagon forward.

My mother claimed he'd returned from his sojourn with the Union Army a changed man. She said only part of him shuffled back from Antietam, but I don't agree with her. I figure it was at this time, staining the harness meant for a horse with his sweat, when my father lost all his appetite for the simple pleasures of the world.

LAST SONG OF ANTIETAM

After days of struggle, we came upon a crick with a supply of fertile soil, and my father smiled for the last time in his life.

We built a lean-to against the side of the wagon and snuggled up to each other nightly against the cold after work was done for the day. The entire family fashioned the sod we cut out of the earth into something that looked like a house. Father set my brothers and me to hauling rocks from the riverbank, which we piled on the side of the house until we had a respectable fireplace.

A toothless prospector sold us an equally toothless mule that fit into the yoke almost as awkwardly as my father. I was getting big enough to help with the heavy labor and we turned the earth over with a rusted plow we'd hauled halfway across the burned-out country.

The work was unending and hard on a body, and there wasn't much joy to it. We passed the days singing as we toiled. Father never joined us in song, and he would occasionally slap one of us when the music assailed his hearing.

The first harvest grew straight and true and we sold it off at auction. We used the money to buy up some livestock and a horse and some luxuries for the house. Our efforts had finally paid off, and we lived in a proper Christian homestead.

Other families settled into the area, but we were generally too busy working on the farm and my father's company too sullen for much socializing. Eventually there were enough people to form a congregation. We'd been living here a few years by this time, and, although it was against the old man's wishes, my mother prevailed upon him to let the family help build a church out of crooked pine trees cut from a stand in a bend in the river.

The work was unending but it wasn't as bad when my mother was still alive. She allotted us time to sing and to learn our figures and ciphers. And she made sure we attended the church we'd helped build every Sunday. My brothers and sisters would sing gospel songs for the congregation. I generally abstained from the festivities, content to sit in a pew next to my father the few times my mother dragged him to church as my family regaled our neighbors with their warbling.

But the birth of little Caleb was too much for her, and she died without ever holding him in her arms.

Lizzie swaddled the younger ones in their Sunday clothes the week after the funeral, but my father made her stop. It was the middle of harvest time and he said there was too much work to be done at the farm, especially since the family was one short now. My sister changed everyone back into their work clothes and set about her chores.

This state of affairs continued for three weeks, until well after the harvest was in. On the fourth Sabbath, my father found the wagon, children, Sunday clothes and horse gone when he set out before dawn to feed the livestock.

We toiled side by side that Sunday, harder than I've ever worked before or since. Digging a fence post, my father broke a shovel handle. He paused, staring at the shattered implement in his hand, the blood from where the wood had splintered his limb running down the shaft into the earth.

"I want to show you something, boy," he said. He led me up to the house and placed the blood-stained handle on the mantle in the living room, next to the Bible. Then he pulled a small wooden box from under his bed. Wrapped in papers and leather was a long-barreled pistol. "I killed three rebels at Antietam with this," he said as he loaded shells into the chambers, one at a time. "They weren't even men yet, just scared boys. I wasn't much more than a boy myself, just a little older than you are today. I haven't fired it since."

He placed a number of shells in his overall pockets and set out to the field, me following behind him. He placed some of the old jars my mother used to preserve food on a tree stump, and he proceeded to teach me how to shoot. Soon the field stank of gunpowder and preservative. After we were done, my father showed me how to clean and oil the gun.

"Killing those boys was an awful thing, but it had to be done. Sometimes a killing can't be avoided." He paused with the rag as the sounds of my siblings returning in the wagon came upon us. "I showed you how to use this gun today in the hopes that you'll never have to. Now get back to your chores."

He wrapped the gun and returned to the farmhouse. He sent the children out to help me in the field, all except Lizzie. He beat her with the broken shovel handle until her cries were loud enough that I had to stuff the ears of the younger ones with rags so they could concentrate on their fieldwork.

But Lizzie would not be swayed, and the next Sunday, as my father slept out in the barn with the horses to make sure she wouldn't be able to harness them up, she simply walked the young ones near five miles to church, little Caleb residing in the crook of her arm.

My father, resigned by my sister's determination, relented. And every Sunday she would take the young ones to sing Gospel. The whole lot of them sorely anticipated this day. But the old man rarely spoke to her again, excepting for conversation that had to do with the running of the farm or the care of the little ones.

After the harvest my father allowed me to accompany my siblings to Church on Sundays. He would never come himself though, not even on Christmas morning.

With Lizzie's encouragement, I joined in and drew great pleasure singing with my brothers and sisters. It was my only respite from unrelenting labor next to my father at the farm.

The congregation appreciated our singing, and folks started coming from neighboring towns just to hear us. People baked us cakes and slipped us small amounts of change after the services. We made sure the food was all gone by the time we got home and we hid the money in Lizzie's bedspread in fear of what our father would do to us if he found out. One spinster made a suit for Jacob, the second youngest boy, when she saw the tatters of his Sunday best. The clothes had served each of the boys before him and were in a sad state by the time he'd grown into them.

This we couldn't hide from the old man. He beat poor Jacob near to unconsciousness and forbid us from taking handouts when he saw him wearing the new clothing. He made Lizzie and me burn the finery in the fireplace.

He never forbade me from going to Church, but I stopped during the harvest season. We had a bad year, and I felt I owed it to him and the young ones to help out as much as I could at the farm.

One Sunday the wagon returned, filled with singing. This was a great anomaly because my siblings were usually all sung out by the time they got back from Church. Lizzie positively glowed as she helped the young ones get ready for supper. She smiled more doing her Sunday chores that afternoon than the sum of our whole family had during the previous year.

After supper, I helped her haul the kitchenware out to the well for cleaning, and she told me about a new circuit preacher who had come out to see her and the young ones perform. She angled her head toward the house, to make sure our father wasn't in spying range, and she took out a silver dollar piece she'd squirreled away in her clothing. "The preacher gave this to me, and said there was more if we'd come sing for his traveling show. He'll be here through to next week, then back in two months expecting an answer."

Knowing what a row it would cause with my father if he found out, we didn't say anything to him that week. I accompanied them to Church the following Sunday and found that the image I'd assigned to the preacher was nothing like the real man. He was young, with a head of blond hair slicked back with pomade. He shook my hand and ruffled young Jacob's hair as he told me how much he admired our version of "Jubilee of the Apocalypse." He said he reckoned it was the best he'd ever heard. The second I saw Lizzie averting her eyes and turning red when he talked to us, I knew she was in love with him.

We discussed our prospects with the older of the siblings, and they were inclined to accompany the preacher, especially when Lizzie explained to them that singing would earn more than back-breaking farm work would ever provide. She told them it would be better to end the day with their vocal boxes being the only muscles that ached.

She worked up her courage for a week, and I waited outside the farmhouse, with the young ones gathered around me, when Lizzie talked to our father about it. It was the first and last time any of us ever raised our voice to the old man, and only the providence of God helped poor Lizzie live through the experience. I took the young ones to Church for the two weeks it took for her to heal up, telling the concerned congregation she'd fallen off a horse.

They were at Church when my father put his hand to the brim of his hat and squinted at something far off that caused him to pause in his work. I looked in the direction that had caught his attention, and saw a curious cloud form at the horizon. It was unlike any I had ever seen, dark and clinging low to the ground. It moved toward our homestead, plunging the parched grass underneath it into shadows.

My father swatted a large bug from his neck, watching as the cloud approached. He dipped a ladle into the water bucket, took a sip and handed it to me. "Have you ever seen anything like it?" he asked.

The bug's brother alighted on me, and I caught it in my hand unoccupied by the ladle. "Reminds me of something out of the

Bible," I said. Opening my hand I examined the bug. It looked like a large grasshopper, but it wasn't. It was a locust, the first of millions that comprised the swarm descending on our crops.

I waited until I could see the bones poking through young Caleb's skin before I asked my father about the preacher's proposition. Lizzie made a thin stew out of a couple of rabbits I'd caught. I brought the stew in a bowl out to the fence line the old man was repairing by torchlight. He'd started the mending during the day, but switched to doing it at night because he couldn't abide the vultures staring at his labor from the railing.

I couldn't see much use in fixing a fence when all that was left of the cattle the fence was meant to keep in was the whites of their bones.

He looked up from the wire and accepted the bowl in his work-scarred hands. The locusts had aged him ten years during the few hours it had taken them to eat through our crops. The fissures in his face had deepened and his eyes looked hollow out in the firelight.

"We'll be needing a new rope for the well," I said. The locusts had eaten halfway through the hemp, and the frayed cord had finally given out earlier in the day.

"We'll get one made of chain this time." He sipped hungrily from the bowl.

"The preacher offered us cash money to sing."

He stopped slurping and spilled out what was left of the stew onto the ground, threw the bowl after it. "Singin's not an honorable way to earn a living boy, and I can't spare any hands on the farm excepting Sundays."

"We could sell the farm, the Preacher says..."

"I don't want you listening to that Preacher outside of his sermons."

"He just wants to help out the people in the community."

"I don't like the looks of that Preacher. Something's not right about him."

"We could start out slow. Travel around after the crops are planted and be back in time for the harvest." I picked up the bowl from the ground.

"You're getting a little too big to hit, but if you continue with this line of conversation, I'll be sorely tested." He took off his hat and wiped his brow with his sleeve, then he cracked his knuckles, one by one, eyeballing me the whole time.

"You're getting a little too old to hit." I put the bowl on the top of the fence post, turned and walked back to the house.

The empty bowl was still there in the morning, a buzzard straddled over it.

I took the wagon into town to pick up what little amount of seed we could afford and I stopped in at the Church after making our purchases. I found the Preacher in his office. A young boy was with him, going through a picture book. The Preacher took the book from the boy's hands and placed it in a drawer in his desk, then he sent the boy on his way.

"I'm sorry, but we won't be able to go on circuit with you." I played with the brim of my hat with my hands.

The Preacher took a bottle and two glasses out of the bottom drawer, poured us each a shot of rye.

"Liz told me about the trouble out on the farm."

I took the glass and drank the liquor down. "Liz shouldn't be telling the like of you our family business."

"No reason to get angry. I'm just trying to figure out why you're all so loyal to your father."

"He's had a hard life since my mother died. He's trying to do his best by us."

"You're practically a grown man now. You don't have to listen to every word your father says."

"That's not the same message I'm hearing from your sermons."

"I saw the bruises around your sister's eyes. Someone has to stand up for her."

"She seems to be smitten with you. Why don't you stand up for her?"

"You just told me to stay out of your family's business."

"And I hope I don't have to tell you again."

"It's a shame to starve when salvation's so close at hand. Something's got to be done about your old man before he kills one of you. If you're not man enough yet to look after your family, I'll see to it that the Sheriff pays your farmhouse a visit." He corked up the bottle and put it back in his desk drawer.

I put on my hat and stalked toward the street.

"I hope to see you on Sunday," the Preacher said to my back. "Your siblings sound better when you're singing with them."

My father and I were storing what was left of our hay supplies in the rafters of the barn. I'd work the pulley to hoist the bale up, and the old man would direct the bundle with a rope around it from the floor, then I'd tie it off to a beam and we'd both climb up and muscle the straw into the rafters.

I tell myself it was the hunger that weakened my arm that day when the largest of the bales tumbled down onto my father when he was positioned directly under it. The county sheriff who came out afterwards agreed with me when he saw the malnourished condition of the young ones and the bruises that adorned my sister's face, refusing to heal.

We sold the farm for a pittance, and what was left of the family took off with the preacher, singing and earning money. Things were great at first; with plenty to eat and some spare change in our pockets, we embarked on our new life with enthusiasm that I'd thought our father had beaten out of us.

Caleb and Jacob were happy for the first few weeks. The preacher took careful pains to educate them, buying them books and taking the time to see to their education. They became sullen and withdrawn after a spell, taking on a weathered look that reminded me of my father every time I laid eyes on them. I thought their sudden state as orphans had a lot to do with it, but I soon found out that this wasn't the only contributing factor to their unhappiness.

My sister paused by a store in Butte when we were passing through, admiring the wedding dresses adorning the window, but it was not to come to pass.

She came to my room late one night; her healed up face filled with tears. She told me what the preacher was doing to the younger ones when he thought we weren't around, when he was supposed to be teaching them their catechisms.

So now I'm sitting in the little ones' room while Lizzie takes them to the stagecoach to San Francisco. I have my father's gun cradled in my lap, and I'm waiting on the Preacher. I'd broken into his room when he was saying his sermon and I saw the kinds of picture books he'd been showing to the kids. The one good lesson my father taught me has stayed with me: sometimes a killing has to get done.

I don't know what's gonna happen after the gun sings out for only the second time since Antietam. There's talk about work for able-bodied men building the transcontinental railroad, and I suppose Lizzie could get work singing in a saloon. She's grown into a real beauty and men stand in line to talk to her after Church services. I'm sure they'd pay good money to hear her sing and play the piano.

The only thing I do know for sure, I'll never sing again.

THROUGH THE GOLDEN GATE

TERENCE BUTLER

Dirty Tommy stood in the shadows and waited. Soon enough he watched a drunk stagger from The Boar's Head and fall when he missed the step from the boardwalk into the muddy street.

"Let me help you, sir," he said, springing to the man's side. He pulled the man up and slipped an arm around his waist. Then he steered the drunk into the black darkness of an alleyway between two deadfalls and went to work.

He pushed the man's head against the wooden wall and held it there with one hand while he got out his sap. He removed the man's new hat and set it gently on the rim of a rain barrel, located his target behind the ear and sent him into unconsciousness with one heavy blow.

Running his hands over the body, Tommy found the wallet in the inside coat pocket. He put it in his own coat pocket and removed the watch from the vest and the wedding ring from the finger.

He had to be quick so none of the others would see him. There wasn't any two of them who would hesitate to rob him of the proceeds of his labors. Police were not a concern; there weren't any of nights in the Barbary Coast.

The pockets were empty except for a penknife and a few coins, and those went into Tommy's trousers.

Tommy stood and pulled out the wallet and tore it open.

"Shit!" he whispered.

The wallet was empty too. The whores and the dive keepers had beaten him to the money.

"Well, alright, give me them fucking boots," he muttered as he squatted and removed the man's almost new boots.

Standing over the sprawling drunk, a bitter sneer twisted Dirty Tommy's face. He spat and delivered a savage kick to the unprotected face. The man moaned and tried to pull himself into a ball.

"You should've kept some of your money, you sorry bastard," Tommy said. He turned away and slunk to the opening of the alley, looking both ways before stepping into the mud and horseshit of the street. He'd call it a night now and sell his goods in Portsmouth Square in the morning.

Hurrying along the wooden sidewalk, headed for home with the booty, Tommy roughly calculated the value of the items he'd stolen.

"It ain't near what I should get," he thought, "But if Lilyanne fucked a few sailors and didn't drink all her profits, we're another day closer to navigating out the Gate for good."

He cursed himself again for associating with Lilyanne. Her drunken ways made her as much a liability as a help. But all the whores were drunk, and he'd known her for so long he felt partnered with her. Besides, she was the one who'd showed him the cubbyhole where he lived beneath the El Dorado. Dirty Tommy was a thief and a coward but he wasn't stupid. He knew better than to get drunk like most of these boys did every night. He had a place to hide with only one way in and out and some gunny sacks to lie on, and though it was cold and damp he didn't have to sleep exposed in a doorway or pay for a flea-infested cot. He could save his hard-earned money and some of hers too.

He turned onto Pacific and moved west, up the hill. The street was lit only by the light coming from the saloons and whorehouses, and the sounds of piano music and wild laughter and breaking glass floated on the chill night air. At the El Dorado he waited a bit, making sure no one would see him dart around behind, and then he was on his knees, and pushing his precious goods in front, crawling into his hole under the roughly framed building.

Soon he would fall into a restless sleep and dream of Peru, where he could live in his own shack on the beach and pick exotic fruits from the trees.

She was waiting for him at noon in Portsmouth Square. Her hangdog demeanor and inability to look him in the eye told him that she probably didn't have much for him.

"Well, let me have it. What's your excuse this time?"

"I don't have no excuse! That goddamn Shanghai Kelly has took all the sailors off the streets and no one can afford pussy ever since the last fire burnt the docks! You know Big Louise expects us to pay for our crib even if we don't get the mark to go up the stairs. And besides, what have you got? A hat and some stinking boots?"

He stared at her, trying to control his anger. If they'd been somewhere more private he'd slap her silly. But he needed her money to get where he wanted to be, so he took a breath and looked around at the teeming crowd gathered in the Square.

Disgust filled his belly like a coiled snake. Drunks and dopers lay sprawled in their own filth. Foreigners of every stripe gesticulated and shouted in their ugly tongues, trying for a leg up, an advantage. It was beginning to seem like there were more foreigners than Americans in San Francisco now. He almost couldn't remember the excitement he'd felt when he'd arrived, but now he felt he'd do anything to get out.

He sat down on the rough bench next to her, elbows on his knees, his gaze directed at the cobbles beneath his feet.

"We got to get some money. We got to get out of here, Lilyanne."

She put her hand on his arm, gripping it tightly through his coat, her body tense with sudden excitement.

"I got an idea, Tommy, and I want you to just listen to it."

THROUGH THE GOLDEN GATE BRIDGE

He turned and looked at the wreck of her face, her yellowed and puffy eyes.

It wouldn't be long and she'd be forced to walk the streets for whatever she could get.

Her urgency was real. She wanted out too.

He nodded and she went on.

"There's this old miner that hit it big back in '49 and then sold his claim to a New York outfit for a lot of money. He lives up in Downieville and comes in about four times a year for the night life. He don't want no pussy; too old I guess. But he pays the same for you to just sit and drink with him. He likes me Tommy! Says I remind him of the girl he left in Iowa when he come out to the goldfields. He's too smart to flash a roll, but I know he must have a heap of cash on him!"

She tightened her grip again and lowered her voice, pleading with Tommy to consider her idea.

"We could sidetrack him somewhere when he first gets to town, and get his whole roll. I could tell him a story, tell him I want him to take me on a boat ride, and you could be waiting for us at the dock. We could be gone to South America clean as a whistle!"

Tommy remained hunched over and staring at the ground. But he began to feel something akin to hope as he thought over her idea. It was time to be bold, to take advantage of a rare opportunity. As hard as they had worked to get ahead, he and Lilyanne deserved a chance like this.

He leapt to his feet, bursting with newfound energy.

"Goddamn it Lily, let's do it!"

"He's due in any day," she said, smiling up at her man.

Tommy sat at a window table in the Old Ship and nursed a beer while he watched the El Dorado, Lilyanne's brothel, across the street. He wasn't making any hay by rolling drunks but he felt alright. He'd have plenty of money once they picked old Covington clean. He was just a little nervous about being in this particular saloon.

The clientele where he sat watching were a true slice of the Barbary Coast pie and chilling to listen to. They were Shanghai Kelly's crew of runners, a gang of murderers that provided shipmasters with drugged and victimized sailors to man their vessels, and he shuddered as he listened to their stories of stealing men the way others did horses. Tommy knew he'd end up aboard some hell-ship bound for the far reaches of the world if he fell in with them.

One of them, a bruiser with a nose smeared all over his face, approached his table with a false-looking smile and stuck out a paw.

"Nick-O they call me, brother, and what about you?"

Tommy tried to appear confident as he grasped the huge mitt and shook.

"Shanks. Tommy Shanks," he said in a loud voice, smiling an equally phony smile.

"Would you like to join us at the bar? There's plenty of room."

Tommy glanced at the space the men had conveniently made for him at the bar and saw the tell-tale crack of the trapdoor in the floor that would deliver a victim addled by a mickey to a skiff waiting below.

"Well, I do appreciate your offer, but I'm waiting for my partner to arrive from Sacramento and I'm keeping an eye peeled for him." And then, man to man, "His first stop is always the El Dorado, you know."

"Partner, eh? And what sort of business might the two of you be engaged in?"

"Goods and services, sir, and it's a hard way to go, but starting to look up."

The smile left the battered face and a growling curse issued from the thug's mouth.

"Horse shit, I say. You're a burglar most likely and so's your partner."

Tommy shrugged and continued to smile.

Nick-O stared hard at Tommy for a moment, then dismissed him with a wave and returned to the bar.

The men whispered among themselves about him and eyed him suspiciously after that, but with the courtesy of thieves to one of their kind, they let him sip his beer in peace.

He used the time of waiting to plan what he and Lilyanne would do. There wasn't much to it actually, just get the old man into a boat and row him out on the Bay and take his money. They'd have to leave him there, Tommy supposed, and he'd never killed anyone before. The thought of it made him queasy and he started to feel guilty even before he'd done it. But he knew he'd have to get over that and he suspected that once he had the money in his pocket he'd feel differently. What he'd do about Lilyanne would have to wait. For now, he had a borrowed boat tied up at Battery Point, a large fisherman's knife stowed under the seat, his brass knuckles and his blackjack in his pockets and his determination to the fore. He concentrated on the El Dorado and thought about how it was going to be truly the source of his fortune.

On his third evening in the Old Ship, Dirty Tommy was suddenly startled to see Lilyanne appear at the door of the El Dorado and look across the busy street in his direction, wave, and go back inside. That was their signal. She had the old man in hand and was ready to set their game in motion.

Tommy stood and drained his beer mug and hurried to the door, tossing a grin at the runners who jeered him as he went.

"We'll be seeing you," he heard Nick-O roar when the swinging doors squealed closed behind him.

As he held himself back from sprinting to the waterfront, all of Tommy's thoughts were on the task at hand. There was still light in the sky and the afternoon wind had died, leaving the bay glassy and undulating with a slow roll and a soft splash on the pilings. He'd outfitted the borrowed double-ender with a small sign that read "Water Taxi" and pulled it up on the beach where it would be easy to board. He just had to sit calmly and appear to be waiting for a customer. He walked through the sand to the boat, sat down on the gunwale and rolled a smoke. He stared back at the end of Pacific Street. His stomach was roiling and he wished he'd taken time to empty his bowels now that he was stuck here waiting. Tommy had never been good at waiting.

Then he saw them making their way across the sand to his boat. He could tell by the sound of Lilyanne's laughter that she was drunk as usual and he silently cursed her, vowing to kill her if she ruined this by doing something stupid. He looked at Covington and was surprised to see that he was a big man and moved with grace through the clinging sand. He was helping Lilyanne to walk and didn't appear to be as drunk as she.

Tommy was big too and strong from years spent farming, but fighting was never something he enjoyed. He hoped this man was going to scare easily and not present any problems. She had said that he was old, and now that they were close, he could see that Covington was around sixty years of age and yes, he was definitely drunk, but Tommy knew the man would not be a pushover.

And then Lilyanne was speaking to him, calling across the few feet of space that remained between the two of them and Tommy.

"We want to ride around to North Beach and see the city lights! Can you take us?"

"Of course, Ma'am and Sir. Welcome aboard."

Out on the Bay with Lilyanne in the bow and the old man facing her, the two continued to drink from a bottle that she produced from her purse. They laughed and sang sailor's songs as Tommy rowed northward, imperceptibly pointing the boat further from shore. Occasionally he would ship his oars and turn to gauge the condition of his prey. Once the old man turned to offer Tommy a drink and Tommy thought that he seemed quite a bit drunker. Perhaps the salt air was affecting him. Darkness had fallen over the hills behind Alameda and the sun was a red smudge on the horizon beyond the Golden Gate. It was almost time now. He turned and looked at Lilyanne, tilting his chin to let her know that he was almost ready. She looked drunk but she also looked scared.

Abruptly, Covington announced that he had to piss. The boat was moving up and then down as Tommy steered it athwart the waves and when the old man stood and began to unbutton his pants he pitched forward into Lilyanne's lap. Tommy had turned to caution him and maybe to begin his assault, but then he was amazed to see her deftly pick Covington's breast pocket and secret the man's bankroll into her low-cut dress. Tommy exulted. Now all he had to do was kill him and push him into the Bay. Tommy drew the curving knife from under the seat.

Lilyanne saw Tommy watching and she threw back her head and laughed a wild laugh and began to struggle with the weight of the drunken old man, trying to stand and move away so that Tommy could do his job.

"I got it Tommy!" she shouted, "Get him now!"

Tommy's joy turned to dismay at the same time as Covington's reaction to what he had felt her do and what he had heard her say made the old man check his pocket and turn towards Tommy. This time he didn't offer a drink. He held a Derringer in his fist.

"You sons of bitches! You dirty bastards! I'll kill the both of you!"

He pushed himself up and jerked Lilyanne to her feet. She was crying now and trying to get away. Covington ripped her dress down the front and the bankroll popped out and fell into the bilge water in the bottom of the boat.

The three of them stood for a few seconds staring at it. The waves slapped against the side of the boat and it wallowed as it turned abreast of the tide.

Then they were all moving. Tommy and the old man dove for the bankroll, each with a weapon in his hand. The two men met before either could grasp the treasure and began a struggle to kill each other, Covington trying to bring his pistol to bear and Tommy attempting to plunge the blade into Covington's gut.

Lilyanne at first tried to hit the old man with an oar but she swung wildly and it slipped from her grip and went into the Bay. She then moved about the grappling men until she could see a chance to reach in and snatch the bankroll, and then she did it, and jumped up on the bow seat, her breasts exposed and her hair undone, holding the money high and screaming at Tommy.

"Kill him Tommy! Kill him!"

The old man twisted his pistol hand in Tommy's grip and turned it just enough to point it at her and then he shot her. She went over the side with the money still in her hand.

Tommy stuck the knife into Covington's back and left it there as he dove into the water and swam to Lilyanne. The tide was carrying her away and he had to swim hard to get to her. He had seen her floating face down before he dove and so he knew that she was probably dead, but he hoped that somehow she still held the money. Just before he got to her she slipped under the surface and was gone. He dove a few times trying to find her but the water was cold and it was full dark now and he knew he had to get back to the boat.

A thin moon cast enough light for him to make out the boat drifting toward him on the tide. He could see Covington's still form slumped over the gunwale, the knife protruding from his back. He paddled and side-stroked his way to the boat, trying to conserve his strength to pull himself over the side into safety. When he finally reached the boat he was exhausted and had to cling to the side until he regained a little strength. Then he pulled himself up and lay panting in the bottom for a while. He thought of what had taken place and what there still was to do. He had to summon the strength to get Covington's body overboard and then he had to row to shore and walk back to his burrow in the Barbary Coast and begin over without his partner, Lilyanne.

When he began to think about her and what she'd done tonight though, he grew angry and started cursing her memory. If only she'd have kept her drunken whore's mouth shut, they could have kept to their plan and all would now be as they'd hoped for.

The anger gave him a burst of energy and he wobbled to his feet and considered Covington, who lay dead as a mackerel, his arms trailing over the side.

Tommy decided to go through the dead man's pockets even though it gave him the shakes to do it. He had to make sure there wasn't any more money to be had. He took a deep breath and did it, producing a few gold coins and a nugget on a chain. A gift for Lillyanne, perhaps? A cold-blooded chuckle escaped his throat.

He started to pull the knife from Covington's back but when he tried to grasp it his hand went weak and pulled away from it as if it were bad luck. He shivered and knew it was not just from being cold and wet.

Then all at once, he grabbed the old man's feet, one in each hand, and lifted and shoved him into the cold waters of the Bay.

"Maybe you and Lilyanne will find each other down there and kiss and make up!" he shouted as he watched the bubbles rise and then stop.

Exhausted again he slumped on to the seat and looked around. It was time to determine where he was and to start making for shore. He was shocked to see that he was almost through the Gate and out to The Heads where several ships lay at anchor waiting for an incoming tide to enter the Bay or for crews to be brought out to them. The tide he was on must have been running faster than he'd realized. He was now a few miles from the city and his nearest landfall would be at the Presidio. He'd better start rowing or be taken out to sea by the tide. He turned to get the oars and with a start realized he only had one. Then he remembered seeing Lilyanne swinging one around wildly and realized that she had probably lost it overboard.

"Goddamn you, you stupid whore! What else can you do to me tonight?" Tommy wailed, despair beginning to creep into his soul. He'd have to try and use the one oar to steer close to the anchored ships and hail them for rescue. He began to paddle as if he were in a canoe, first one side, and then the other. It was brutally difficult work as the beam of the boat was much wider than any canoe and he had to stay on his knees to move from side to side. Making it even more difficult was the increasing speed of the tide as it rushed through the relatively narrow opening of the Golden Gate and the fact that he had to navigate across its flow to where the ships were.

There was new strength in his desperation now and soon he could see that he was making progress toward the ships. He started to shout, hoping someone would be above decks and hear him. He could see lights on the decks so maybe they were working on gear or rigging.

"Halloo the ships! Man overboard!" he shouted, willing his voice to rise above the rush of tidewater and wind.

"Aaahoooy the ships! Man in the waaterrr!"

He drifted past one ship and then another, still shouting, his voice growing hoarse and his throat burning with the effort. There were more ships but they were further apart now, and his paddling was not doing any good in getting him closer. Someone had to hear, and soon.

There was part of him that was praying. He hadn't prayed for many years and had often expressed his contempt for those that do, but now he needed more help than just what men could provide.

"God, please help me now," Dirty Tommy prayed. "Please help a sinner and I promise I'll change. I'll stop robbing and drinking and whoring and I'll stop saying bad things about Lilyanne. I apologize for hitting her and cursing her and I'll never hurt another woman."

And that's when he heard the voice calling to him and saw the skiff approaching with a light in the bow. He stood and listened for their call and he answered back until they drew up alongside in the darkness and tossed him a line. He made it fast and then he fell down in the bottom of the boat and started to cry.

And he kept on crying when a man with a familiar voice brought the light close and held it up so he could see who had rescued him. Tommy could see a broken grin in a ruined face peering at him from behind the flickering light.

"Well, hello there, brother!" Nick-O said. "Are you ready to ship out now?"

ABOUT THE AUTHORS

Trey R. Barker's newest books are *The Cancer Chronicles*, which are his blog entries during a year of chemo for malignant cancer, and *Remembrance and Regrets*, which is a collection of dark crime stories. He's the author of
more than 120 other short stories, a play, the novel *2000 Miles to Open Road*, and a previous collection of supernatural stories based on old blues songs, *Where the Southern Cross the Dog*. A Texas native, he now lives in northern Illinois with is wife, LuAnn, and their three Canine-Americans. After a plethora of jobs during his life, he's settled into wearing a badge for the Bureau County Sheriff's Office.

Desmond Barry is the author of three novels. His first, *The Chivalry of Crime*, won a Western Writers of America Spur Award and the Medicine Pipe Bearer Award. His shorter prose has been anthologized in *Sea Stories*, *Wales Half Welsh*, and *London Noir;* and has appeared in *The New Yorker* and *Granta* magazine among others.

Jon L. Breen, author of eight novels and over a hundred short stories, has won two Edgar Awards in the biographical-critical category. His most recent books are the comic courtroom novel *Probable Claus* (Five Star) and *A Shot Rang Out: Selected Mystery Criticism* (Surinam Turtle/Ramble House).

Ken Bruen hails from Galway in the west of Ireland, where he currently lives with his wife and daughter. His past includes twenty-five years as an English teacher in Africa, Japan, south-east Asia and South America, a PhD. In metaphysics and some of the most acclaimed novels of our time. Recent novels include *Once Were Cops, Sanctuary,* and *Cross*.

Terence Butler lives in Central California and is a relatively new writer, coming to it later in life. He's had some non-fiction pieces published, and a story in "Hardboiled," and spends a lot of time reading his favorites, Peter Rabe, Elliott Chaze, John D. MacDonald and Lawrence Block, in the hope that their magic will rub off.

Jan Christensen has had one mystery novel published along with over fifty short stories, mostly mysteries. Many of her stories are online, two have been nominated for Derringer Awards, and a few are in anthologies and older print magazines. You can find out more at: www.janchristensen.com

Bill Crider is the author of more than fifty published novels and numerous short stories under his own and other names. His short fiction has been nominated for the Anthony, Derringer and Edgar awards (winning the first two). His latest novel is *Murder in Four Parts* (St. Martin's). You can find his homepage at www.billcrider.com, or take a look at his peculiar blog at http://billcrider.blogspot.com.

ABOUT THE AUTHORS

Ed Gorman was born in Minneapolis, Minnesota, and he currently lives in Iowa with his wife Carol, who is also a writer. He's been a full-time fiction writer for almost a quarter century, working in suspense (his favorite genre) and Westerns, with a handful of horror short stories and novels. His fiction reflects his primary influences—Richard Matheson, Robert Bloch and Cornell Woolrich—and among his best-known books are *The Autumn Dead* (mystery), *Cage of Night* (horror) and *Wolf Moon* (Western). He also collaborated with Dean Koontz on *City of Night*, the second novel in Koontz's modern Frankenstein series. His work has been awarded the International Horror Guild Award, the Anthony Award, the Shamus Award and the Spur Award. He has also published six collections of his short fiction, and has contributed to a wide variety of publications, including *The New York Times*, *Redbook*, *Penthouse*, *Ellery Queen*, *The Magazine of Fantasy & Science Fiction*, *Poetry Today* and *Interzone*.

Jeremiah Healy, a former Sheriff's Officer and Military Police Lieutenant, is a graduate of Rutgers College and the Harvard Law School. Healy is also the creator of the John Francis Cuddy private-investigator series and (under the pseudonym "Terry Devane") the Mairead O'Clare legal-thriller series, both set primarily in Boston. Healy has written eighteen novels and over sixty short stories, sixteen of which works have won or been nominated for the Shamus Award. He served as the President of the International Association of Crime Writers ("IACW") from 2000-2004, and he was the International Guest of Honour at the 34th World Mystery Convention in Toronto during October, 2004. Last year, Healy concluded his term as a member of the Mystery Writers of America's National Board of Directors.

Steve Hockensmith is the author of the "Holmes on the Range" Western mysteries starring cowboy detectives "Big Red" and "Old Red" Amlingmeyer. The first book in the series was a finalist for the Edgar, Shamus, Anthony, and Dilys Awards, and the second, *On the Wrong Track*, features a prominent role for legendary Pinkerton operative Burl Lockhart. In 2010, Hockensmith branched out into horror-comedy with the New York Times best-seller *Pride and Prejudice and Zombies: Dawn of the Dreadfuls*. He can be found on the web at www.stevehockensmith.com.

Pat Lambe says, "The first time I heard my native state called New Joisey was by some guy who didn't know the difference between the Dome at Rahway and the Dome of the Rock. I tried to explain it to him, but realized I didn't know the difference myself. The ten people who can handle their r's in the state call it New Jersey. I've lived here most of my life; busted my hump as a restaurant worker, lumber yard dog, truck driver, dispatcher, college scam artist, construction drone, etc. I'm currently working as a telephone technician while writing crime stories."

Bentley Little was born in Arizona a month after his mother attended the world premiere of *Psycho*. His best friend in grammar school was Stephen Hillenburg, who went on to create the Nickelodeon cartoon *Spongebob Squarepants*. Bentley received his BA in Communications and MA in English and Comparative Literature at California State University Fullerton, the alma mater of James Cameron and Kevin Costner. A brilliant student who graduated at the top of his class, he was nearly expelled in his junior year following a rancorous closed-door confrontation with college administrators. The reasons are unknown as his records remain permanently sealed. His Master's thesis was the novel *The Revelation*, which was later published and won the Bram Stoker Award in 1991. Since then, he has written ten more novels and his work has been translated into seven different languages. Several of his novels have been optioned for film. Published reports that for several years Bentley worked in a series of carnivals and strip clubs throughout the Southwest or that he founded a radical environmental group to perform acts of eco-terrorism can neither be confirmed nor denied.

Gary Lovisi is a MWA Edgar-nominated author and the editor of *Hardboiled* magazine, which was just presented with the Western

Writers of America, Spur Award, for publishing the best short story of 2010. Lovisi's latest books are *Dames Dolls & Delinquents* (Krause Books, 2009), *West Texas War & Other Western Stories* (Ramble House, 2008) and *Ultra-Boiled,* hard crime stories (Ramble House 2010). He is the publisher of Gryphon Books and you can contact him via his website at: www.GryphonBooks.com.

Norman Partridge's fiction includes horror, suspense, and the fantastic—"sometimes all in one story" says his friend Joe Lansdale. Partridge's novel *Dark Harvest* was chosen by *Publishers Weekly* as one of the 100 Best Books of 2006, and two short story collections were published in 2010—*Lesser Demons* from Subterranean Press, and *Johnny Halloween* from Cemetery Dance. Other work includes the Jack Baddalach mysteries *Saguaro Riptide* and *The Ten-Ounce Siesta*, plus *The Crow: Wicked Prayer*, which was adapted for film. Partridge's compact, thrill-a-minute style has been praised by Stephen King and Peter Straub, and his work has received multiple Bram Stoker awards. He can be found on the web at www. NormanPartridge.com and americanfrankenstein.blogspot.com.

Jerry Raine is the author of five crime novels, including *Frankie Bosser Comes Home, Slaphead Chameleon,* and *Some Like it Cold.* He is currently working on his sixth. He lives in London, England, where he plays guitar and writes songs, and occasionally performs.

Robert J. Randisi has been called by *Booklist* "...the last of the pulp writers." He has published in the western, mystery, horror, science fiction and men's adventure genres. All told, he is the author of over 540 books, 50+ short stories, 1 screenplay and the editor of 30 anthologies. He has also edited a Writer's Digest book, *Writing The Private Eye Novel,* and for 7 years was the mystery reviewer for the *Orlando Sentinel.* In 1982 he founded the Private Eye Writers of America, and created the Shamus Award. In 1985 he co-founded *Mystery Scene Magazine* and the short-lived American Mystery Award; a couple of years later he was co-founder of the American Crime Writer's League. In 1993 he was awarded a Life Achievement Award at the Southwest Mystery Convention. In

2009 he received the Life Achievement Award from the Private Eye Writers of America. He has had a book published every month since January of 1982.

His Rat Pack novel, *Everybody Kills Somebody Sometime,* featuring Dean Martin, Frank Sinatra and other members of the infamous Pack, was published in October 2006 and received a starred review from Booklist. It has also been optioned for an independent film, for which he has written the screenplay. His most recent novel in the Rat Pack series was *You're Nobody Til Somebody Kills You* (SMP 2009). The next will be *I'm a Fool to Kill You* (Severn House, 2011).

Randisi was born and raised in Brooklyn, N.Y., and from 1973 through 1981 he was a civilian employee of the New York City Police Department, working out of the 67th Precinct in Brooklyn. After 41 years in N.Y, he now resides in Clarksville, Mo., an Artisan community of 500 people located right on the Mississippi. He lives and works with writer Marthayn Pelegrimas in a small house on three acres, with a deck that overlooks the Mississippi.

A lifelong Texan, **James Reasoner** has been a professional writer for more than thirty years. In that time, he has authored several hundred novels and short stories in numerous genres. Writing under his own name and various pseudonyms, his novels have garnered praise from *Publishers Weekly*, *Booklist*, and the *Los Angeles Times*, as well as appearing on the *New York Times* and *USA Today* bestseller lists. He lives in a small town in Texas with his wife, award-winning fellow author Livia J. Washburn.

Jim Sallis has published multiple collections of poems, stories and criticism, the definitive biography of Chester Himes, a translation of Raymond Queneau's novel Saint Glinglin, and by last count thirteen novels, including the six-novel Lew Griffin series, the three Turner novels comprising *What You Have Left*, and *Drive*, currently in production as a major film. His latest novel, *The Killer Is Dying*, is due in May of 2011. An editor of *New Worlds* "back when dinosaurs ruled the earth" and longtime columnist for the *Boston Globe*, Jim continues to contribute a quarterly books column to

ABOUT THE AUTHORS

The Magazine of Fantasy & Science Fiction. He was the recipient of the Lifetime Achievement Award at the 2007 Bouchercon.

Harry Shannon has been an actor, an Emmy-nominated songwriter, a recording artist, a music publisher, VP Music at Carolco Pictures and a Music Supervisor on Basic Instinct and Universal Soldier. His novels include *Night of the Beast, Night of the Werewolf, Daemon, Dead and Gone* (a Lionsgate movie), and *The Pressure of Darkness*, as well as the Mick Callahan suspense novels *Memorial Day, Eye of the Burning Man*, and *One of the Wicked*. His collection *A Host of Shadows* is from Dark Region Press, as is his new novella "PAIN." Shannon has won the Tombstone Award, the Black Quill, and has been nominated for the Stoker. Contact him at www.harryshannon. com or via Facebook.

Terry Tanner was born in Cactus Flat, Arizona. He worked as a movie projectionist, radio announcer, defense plant guard, meter reader, lumber mill laborer and hard rock miner before joining the army. He returned to college after a three-year enlistment and graduated from Arizona State University in 1965. He served two years as a Patrolman on the Phoenix Police Department, three years in the US Border Patrol and thirty years with Customs before retiring as a Senior Inspector in 2001. His work has recently appeared in *Hardboiled* and his police memoir, *Fishers of Men*, is currently seeking a publisher. Mr. Tanner is widowed, lives alone in Tucson, and has four adult daughters and two grandchildren.

T. L. Wolf still has the picture of his first horse-ride—sitting straight-backed on an old Appaloosa, a firm grasp on the saddle-horn but little else, his cowboy hat perched at an angle much too cocky for a five year-old. His mother should've seen it coming. Moments after the photo, he spurred the horse with a piercing, "HYAH!" The ride lasted four minutes ending with an ungraceful dismount, a cracked head, a lost horse, and one panic-stricken mother. They never did find that horse. He's since moved to Los

Angeles, where cracked heads are the norm. "Hell Hath No Fury" was his first published story.

Dave Zeltserman lives in the Boston area with his wife, Judy, and his short crime fiction has been published in many venues. His third novel, *Small Crimes*, was named by NPR as one of the 5 best crime and mystery novels of 2008. His novel, *Pariah*, was named by the *Washington Post* as one of the best books of 2009. *Killer*, the 3rd book in his 'man out of prison' noir trilogy was published in the US this May. His next book, The Caretaker of Lorne Field, will be out this August, which *Publisher's Weekly* in a starred review calls "a superb mix of humor and horror." His upcoming novel, *Outsourced*, is currently in development by Impact Pictures and Constantin Film.